Donald's
Inferno

D1519890

Donald's Inferno

A Tragedy Wrapped In A Comedy Inside A Fiction

Liam Sean

Donald's Inferno
A Tragedy Wrapped In A Comedy Inside A Fiction
by Liam Sean

Copyright © 2017 Liam Sean
ISBN: 1546427104
ISBN 13: 9781546427100
Library of Congress Control Number: 2017907125
CreateSpace Independent Publishing Platform
North Charleston, South Carolina

Permission Acknowledgements
Apocalypse Now 1979 Omni Zoetrope
Terminator 1984 Hemdale/Pacific Western Productions/Cinema '84
Videodrome 1983 Canadian Film Development Corporation
Scream 1996 Woods Entertainment
American Psycho 2000 Edward R. Pressman Productions/Muse Productions
Psycho 1960 Shamely Productions
Nightmare On Elm Street 1984 New Line Cinema/Media Home Entertainment
Night of The Living Dead 1968 Image Ten/Laurel Group/Market Square Productions
I Know What You Did Last Summer 1997 Mandalay Entertainment
The Omen 1976 20th Century Fox
Carrie 1976 United Artists
Child's Play 1988 United Artists
Pet Sematary 1989 Paramount Pictures
The Exorcist 1973 Hoya Productions
Misery 1990 Castlerock Entertainment/Nelson Entertainment
The Shining 1980 The Producer Circle Company/Peregrine Productions/Hawk Films
The Fly 1986 Brooksfilms/SLM Production Group
The Fly 1958 20th Century Fox
Halloween 1978 Compass International/Falcon Productions
Silence of The Lambs 1991 Strong Heart/Demme Productions
Seven 1995 New Line Cinema
Saw 2004 Evolution Entertainment/Twisted Pictures

Author's Note: The stage directions are from the audience's viewpoint. This would be the opposite
of most scripts which are written from the actor's perspective.

*This book is dedicated to life, liberty
and the pursuit of happiness for all people.*

Principals

Donald Trumpet
Divisive American business mogul running for President of
The United States

Boss Tweed
Notorious American business mogul and politician from the
Nineteenth Century

Euripides
Greek playwright from the Fifth Century B.C. Acknowledged as
The Father of Drama

Saint Dymphna
Irish Martyr and Patron Saint of mental illness from the Seventh Century

Statler Swift
Theater critic as well as Irish writer and satirist

Waldorf Voltaire
Theater critic as well as French writer and satirist

Satan
Fallen archangel and the embodiment of pure evil

The Inferno
Nine Descending Circles of punishment for sinners

God
The Supreme Being, Eternal Judge, and the Architect of The Inferno

America
Land of The Free, Home of The Brave, and an awesome
experiment in democracy

Intro

I have not voted in twelve years. The American political system was usurped by the activist Supreme Court at the behest of those who control them. No grassy knoll here. I'm not a conspiracy believer and subscribe to nothing other than in-depth research, common sense, and the facts presented in an unbiased way. When corporations were given the same rights as individuals, campaign funding allowed to reach obscene levels of monies and obscurity, the gerrymandering of districts treated with indifference, and the election cycle becoming perpetual, I opted out. That is, until now.

American politics has become little more than an extension of American pop culture. As education erodes to the point of it being openly mocked, as substantive conversation has been replaced with tweets, as unarguable scientific facts are dismissed, as our language is reduced to crudity, and compromise seen as weakness, a void has developed in the collective psyche, consciousness, and intellect of the American nature. Into this void has crept something truly terrifying.

When one studies how civilized people have suddenly embraced barbarism. When one gleans from history how people can pirouette from moral decency and commit genocide. When through the course of human history the voice of the tyrant is inexplicably harkened as the undeniable truth, then one sees that our trip from the caves until now, and the distance from our frontal lobes to our brain stems, is really not all that far.

We sit poised, the doomsday clock still a breath from midnight, on a precipice. The chasm below is the void itself, an end to civilization. Do not fool yourself, we have been teetering here since Los Alamos. Our leaders, those who govern the fraternity of nuclear-armed nations, have nearly and mistakenly taken us over the edge on more than several occasions. It has been by rational, calm decision making, luck, and the wits of a couple line-level officers, that we have avoided the unthinkable.

Amidst all this, against a backdrop of nationalism's final death throes, the pseudo-religious movement of radical Islam, the xenophobic reactions to worldwide movements of diaspora, and an era of sweeping technological change, the United States holds its presidential election. The President-elect from this contest will face daunting challenges. Complex, striated, difficult issues whose very nature will effect not just the near-term, but the long-term as well. An individual elected by a divided country to be in charge of over seven thousand nuclear weapons, the most sophisticated war machine ever assembled, and an array of armed nations and groups with their own intentions and agendas. All while trying to unify America and continue to lead the world by the highest standards of ethics.

We are at a crossroads. And though the choice between the two candidates is less than savory, there is only one course of action that as humans we must take: survival.

However, I am unaccustomed to the bright lights of the soapbox and weary of the diatribe from pulpit, lectern, and news desk. Too many sponsors, too much sneaky clamoring for our hard-earned dollars, too much hype, over-coverage, and outright lies told to us in every seamy, sophisticated way. The media has replaced the message. I will decline the microphone, the tweet, the instant message, the sound byte, and exit the stage. This story is best told by others.

And so, with Euripides himself to narrate, Dante himself having provided the setting and the narrative, and with the world in its totality furnishing the drama: **Donald's Inferno.**

-September 2016

Act I

(The room is dark. The stage is absent of light. The dim outlines of trees and a mountain appear as lightning flashes in the upper back of the stage on both sides. Thunder rumbles. The wind rises and falls. A light rises out of the gloom on the narrator's stage, at extreme stage left, illuminating a figure. The light comes up just enough to reveal a man dressed in a dark toga, grape and oak leaves in his wild, unkempt hair. He tilts his head as the light reaches its highest point)

Euripides:
Friends. It is I. Euripides. Father of drama. Called forth from beyond Elysium to stand before you. Called to once more reveal the tragedy that lies within the comedy that unfolds around you. From the labyrinth of my caves to the maze of your world, I have been summoned by one who cares too much, yet cares nothing at all.

Harken, dear audience. Take heed as if your very lives are at stake. Indeed! Mortal fate is hard, and you had better get used to that, but all should not have to perish for the vanity of one!

(Thunder roars as lightning flashes revealing a lost figure on the stage)

A tempest has gathered. Foul winds driven from the four corners of the earth. The Fates and the Furies, as in days of old when Atlantis still stood, and Alexandria did its best to drive out ignorance, they have met once more and laid the very bones of civilization on the altar as Abraham was asked to do.

A rent in Gaia's crust has opened. Issuing forth from the very depths of the pit, an incubus. To the gods an unknown. A creature lost in the never ending whirl and calliope of this carousel you call America. Clad in the kingly robes of your modern world, he has awaited this day with the patience of an asp. And the venom.

When one with honeyed words but evil mind persuades the mob, great woes befall the state. Now is not the time to sit idly by. Nor is it the time to reach these crossroads and prostrate one's self upon the ground. Yay, it is better to die on one's feet then to live on one's knees. The cloying things he says are but webs. The words you've longed to hear, about returning power to the people, about reform, about transparency, about making America great, from this one are but a practiced trap. With such sweet serenade sung by a piper of such devious nature, how is liberty to survive?

I will tell you how.

Liberty will survive in the way the Spartans defended the West from Xerxes at Thermopylae. As how at Plataea, the Greeks defeated those tyrants forever, preceded by victory at sea off my own island of Salamis.

Liberty will live on with the strength and endurance of the Order of St. John at Malta, of Henry V at Agincourt, and of one man standing before a tank in Tiananmen Square.

Liberty will shine forth as you Americans did at Yorktown, at Antietam, and on the beaches of Normandy. And liberty will show its dignity and depth in the voice of Lincoln, the courage of Dr. King, and the simple fact that all men are created equal.

At this crossroads we will not arm ourselves with pike or sword, nor musket or machine gun, but with the true weapons of change: strength, wisdom, temperance, and justice. And above all that, love.

Quite simply, we will vote the devil into nonexistence. We will make a mockery of his insolence. We will step on the throat of bigoted, blind hatred not with our boot, but with our wit. And we will do so with the tools best served to this purpose: prose and poetry, satire and sarcasm.

We will do so, right at this moment. Right before your eyes. As Euripdes, I have the ability to present a play unlike any you have seen before. Flannery O'Connor once said, 'when you're writing for the blind, you've got to write big'. And so we shall. Spanning centuries, from all over the globe, from the Heavens above, and chiefly from Hell below, a tragedy masquerading as a comedy. An epic of mythological proportions in which we could all be laid low. A play within a story within a poem in which the end result is up to you.

So rise up, dear friends! For polis, for forum, for civilization, for truth, justice and the American way! For life, liberty and the pursuit of happiness, rise up! Dear God in Heaven, good listeners, rise up!

(Low lights come up revealing a tangled forest of trees, bushes and thorns. The mountain is clearer in the background, seemingly unreachable through the black, overgrown mass of the forest. The wind still howls, lightning still flashes, and thunder still rumbles. The sounds of night animals and other unknown sounds can be heard in the background)

(Spots light up The Donald. He is wearing a disheveled, dark blue suit complete with red power tie. He is stage left, clawing his way through the underbrush, lost and disoriented, making his way toward center stage. He mutters unintelligible sounds of fear and frustration, spinning to and fro, searching for a path)

The Donald:
Are you kidding me? Where the hell am I? Where's my jet? Where's my penthouse? Where the fuck am I? Goddamn advisors. **(Mocking voice)** Press the flesh. Kiss the babies. Go out amongst the people. Thanks. Thanks a lot. Jesus what a mess. I thought I was going to a meet and greet. See some black folks. Eat a taco. Get some free air time.

Alright. Think this through. What'd they say. Stay on course. Don't stray from the path. Shoot for the high ground. Yeah. Yeah. That was it. The something or other high ground. **(Looks up toward the mountain)** There. The high ground. Ha! They said I couldn't find it. Its right there. What kind of retard do they think I am? Now, just head straight. This looks like the way. Ha! Winner going up!

(A leopard appears from out of the trees and hisses at The Donald)

Jesus Christ! What the hell is that! Wait. That gray hair. Those frickin' bug eyes. Bernie, is that you? What are you? Some sort of leopard-man? What's the matter? C'mon, man. Why you so pissed off? You knew that debate was never going to happen. Sorry about the primary. Easy, brother, easy. I got a place in the cabinet for you. Health and human services. Who'd be better? Those are some sharp fucking teeth, Bernie.

(The Donald steps away from the lunges, only to be confronted by both the leopard and a lion)

Now what! What kind of a forest is this? Liz? What the hell happened to you two? You're senators. For Christ's sakes, don't you have something better to do than stalking around the woods? You people have honor. You wouldn't hurt me. C'mon Liz, I was just kidding about that Pocahontas stuff. You have no idea how much I respect the two of you. I got spaces available. Chief of Staff, Liz. I need a pit bull and by God you are one hundred and ten percent pit bull.

(They snarl and lunge, driving The Donald backward. A she-wolf appears along side them, steps in front and growls with great menace)

Alright. This has gone on long enough. I don't know what the fuck was in that pm cough medicine but this is one stupid dream and you are not Hillary Clinton.

(Suddenly, a terrific light appears between the three animals and The Donald. A figure clad in green and white royal robes with ermine appears. She carries a sword, a clutch of lilies, and has a horrible scar around her neck. The three animals back away and exit stage left)

The Donald:
Wow, Lady! **(He reaches in his pocket to tip her)** I don't know who you are but praise be to God you showed up. **(The money burns to a crisp in his hand)** Ow! Sorry. Just thought I'd show my appreciation.

Saint Dymphna:
(In a deafening voice that causes The Donald to cower on his knees) Silence! I am Saint Dymphna. And you are basso loco!

The Donald:
Who? I'm The Donald.

Saint Dymphna:
I know who you are! I have been sent to intervene before you destroy the world. I have been summoned by one hundred billion souls who cry out in

anguish and fear of you being elected to the highest office on your mortal plane. I have come to this place, at this time, to show you who you really are, and the horror you are capable of unleashing.

The Donald:
I'm here to make America great!

Saint Dymphna:
Silence! The only thing you are destined for is food for worms. Cibo per i vermi! Vermi. You have but one course left to you. Understand your sins. Understand your mortality. Understand eternity. E la paura della vite senza fine. La conquista di vermi.

The Donald:
I, I don't understand. I haven't done anything wrong. I just want to be president. I'm just a businessman. Why is this happening to me? Where am I? Why are you doing this to me? Do I owe you money? Did I forget to call you? Did my ex-wife send you?

Saint Dymphna:
Silence! Voi siete il worm. I cannot take you where you must go. But we have summoned one from the grave to be your guide. We have lifted him from the very Circles you are about to see.

The Donald:
Who?

Saint Dymphna:
One whom you have become just like. **(The Donald lifts his head up to her)** One whom you have idolized. **(The Donald stands)** One whose life is as yours, as was his destiny.

The Donald:
Who?

Saint Dymphna:
One who comes from the very boroughs as you.

The Donald:
A homeboy.

Saint Dymphna:
One who will show you each and every Circle, each and every sin.

The Donald:
Who is this cat?

(A figure steps from the forest dressed as a dandy, although time and the grave have worn his fine 19th century clothes more than slightly)

Saint Dymphna:
Boss Tweed.

The Donald:
(Turning to face Boss Tweed) Bada bing! Are you kidding me! I patterned my whole life after you!

Boss Tweed:
You're the Strumpet?

The Donald:
Trumpet. Donald Trumpet.

Boss Tweed:
What the fuck happened to your hair.

The Donald:
Never mind that. You're as close to a hero as I ever had. This is amazing. I might have another hit of this stuff. **(Pulls out a bottle of green liquid, unscrews cap, sips)** This might not be so bad after all.

Saint Dymphna:
(Deafening) You simple-witted fool! Have you no idea where you are? **(Lights spotlight a gate, ancient characters are etched in the slimy rock. It has settled onto itself and is surrounded by dead, thorn-filled trees. There is a splash of Italian in well-dried blood below the cuneiform. There are scratchings, claw marks, shackles, bones and a lone raven sits on a shoulder of rock that holds up one side of the lintel. The road before it is quite well worn)** That is the Gate to Hell. That is your destiny. You must learn from this experience, learn from your guide, and learn from the denizens of that awful place. Or perhaps, you yourself will one day guide another as unfortunate as you.

(The Donald steps toward the Gate. Boss Tweed grabs his shoulder stopping him)

Boss Tweed:
We're not going down the line here, Strumpet. No bull. This is one million times worse than the clink.

The Donald:
What's through that thing? **(He gestures toward the Gate)**

Boss Tweed:
The blazes. Damnation. Up the spout every second of eternity.

The Donald:
(To Saint Dymphna) Why are you doing this to me?

Saint Dymphna:
(Leaning in, mere inches from The Donald) You did it to yourself.

(Rising up, slowly floating backwards) Mr. Tweed, show this gentleman the hospitality that awaits him. Show him every detail of his life. Of those who dwell in each and every Circle. Show him every corner of Hell.

The Donald:
(Turning to flee) No! Fuck this! I'm out. This is crap. Its just a bad dream. Some weird 3-D mocumentary by CNN. Fuck you Tweed! Fuck you Gate! And mostly fuck you, you loud mouthed tart!

(The ground shakes. Lightning flashes. Thunder roars. The three animals reappear roaring and howling. Tweed ducks for cover. The Donald cowers, turtle-like, whimpering on the floor, and Saint Dymphna proceeds to vomit fire from her mouth, her forlornly, beautiful Irish features now distorted into a mask of horror, she waves the sword over The Donald with all the skill and fury of a highlander. The lights and the maelstrom subside slightly as the lights come up on the narrator's stage revealing Euripides. He has a partly-eaten apple in his hand)

Euripides:
How are those first bites? Quite the temper on The Donald. Those whom God wishes to destroy, he first makes angry. Well, good friends, I never said it'd be easy. The damned are damn stubborn. Sisyphus. What an idiot. All he had to do was apologize. Be contrite. He could have walked away from that rock at any time. No siree Bob. To this day, up the hill with the boulder, down it rolls. So with this one. **(Boss Tweed is standing over The Donald**

trying to get him to his feet) But wait! The demon slayer has left, she has returned to her lofty state! And now, our two adventurist venture capitalists are about to pass through the Gate.

(Boss Tweed gets the whimpering and sniveling Donald up and together, fortified with sips of cough syrup, they stand before the Gate to Hell)

The Donald:
I can't believe this is happening to me.

Boss Tweed:
What kind of a fucking Mary are you? Brace yourself ya bollocks, this is as hunky dory as it gets!

The Donald:
Wait! Wait. Stop. What, what does that say?

Boss Tweed:
The inscription?

The Donald:
No, the fucking teleprompter. Of course the inscription.

Boss Tweed:
Why you plucky pot licker. **(Boss Tweed begins to chortle The Donald)** I'll be right bloody happy to tell your doomed, overly groomed ass.

The Donald:
This is bullshit. Like hell I'm going to Hell with you. **(The Donald fights back)** Overly groomed, huh? The suit you're wearing was moldy when you bought it.

Boss Tweed:
Better a moldy suit than that poof's hair piece. **(They tumble to the ground)**

The Donald:
This hair cost me more money than the carpet in Tammany Hall. **(They are rolling over and over)**

BossTweed:
(On top of The Donald and about to deliver the coup de grace) The last time I saw hair like that my cell mate bent over to pick up the soap.

(There is a tremendous flash of light and thunder and Saint Dymphna returns. Euripides is looking down shaking his head)

Saint Dymphna:
Donald! What manner of misspent protoplasm are you! Don't you know when someone is trying to help you! The Gate's inscription is first in a language that has been dead for over ten thousand years. Beneath it, in Italian: Lasciate ogni speranza, voi che entra qui. **(She leans close to them)** I'll let your new friend translate that into your guttural. **(Saint Dymphna once again floats backward and exits. The two of them help each other up and turn toward the Gate. The Donald checks his bottle of cough syrup, takes a swig and offers it to Boss Tweed)**

The Donald:
This is really the Gate to Hell, isn't it?

Boss Tweed:
Yup.

The Donald:
What's it say, man. Tell me.

Boss Tweed:
Abandon all hope, ye who enter here.

(And they step up to the Gate, the lights fading to black)

Euripides:
By the gods! Finally. Zeus himself could not have blown those stumblebums through that portal. An auspicious start, dear audience, auspicious. Well, Rome wasn't built in a day and it took even longer to tear it down. **(There is a ring tone from on Euripides, it is the beginning to the Syrtaki Dance Song. Euripides pulls an I-phone from his toga)** Parakalo. Its you! I can't believe its you! Hang on a sec. **(To the audience)** Sorry, I have to take this. Give me a couple minutes. **(He turns, his light fading, chatting with someone on the phone)** When did you get in? Really? We hadn't expected you for some time. Tsk tsk tsk, tragedy seems everywhere these days…

(As his light fades, another rises, stage-right, revealing two theater seats in an elevated box. The burgundy curtain behind the seats parts as two old men struggle into the box and take their seats. One is tall and thin, the other short and stout. The tall one is Statler Swift. He is wearing a pinstriped suit that hearkens back to the mid-18th century. He has a white collar with two pieces hanging down, and sports a thick unibrow. The short fellow is Waldorf Voltaire, likewise wearing mid-18th century clothes, he is mustached. They both have hair styles from that period, although Waldorf's is only on the fringes)

Waldorf Voltaire:
By the crown! Statler Swift where in blue blazes were you taking us. I thought we'd never get here.

Statler Swift:
My good man, please. You were the one navigating.

Waldorf Voltaire:
I know, I know. A wrong turn near Albuquerque.

Statler Swift:
Or Alberta. Or Algeria. Or...

Waldorf Voltaire:
Alright, alright. We're here. Now we can relax and do what we do best.

Statler Swift:
Indeed and bravo! They saved our box for us.

(The two sit down but still seem agitated)

Waldorf Voltaire:
This still doesn't seem right.

Statler Swift:
You're in my seat.

Waldorf Voltaire:
I am?

Statler Swift:
Waldorf Voltaire! We have been sitting in theater boxes together for decades. I always sit on the left.

Waldorf Voltaire:
Oh yes, yes, you're right. What was I thinking.

(They exchange seats and get comfortable, cracking knuckles, clearing throats, adjusting their posture, scooting forward)

Waldorf Voltaire:
Much better. Much, much better.

Statler Swift:
I am so ready to throw some acidic comments I can hardly stand it.

Waldorf Voltaire:
(Gushing) Me too. I'm so glad we caught the opening from the entry in the lobby.

Statler Swift:
These schmucks have no idea what they're in for.

Waldorf Voltaire:
Inferno! Ha! Wait 'till they hear the inferno from our mouths!

Statler Swift:
Who do these people think they are? **(He looks over to Waldorf and grabs him by the shoulders. Takes a beat)** You're fired! **(They burst out in laughter)**

Waldorf Voltaire:
How about the lady with the sword?

Statler Swift:
I thought the fat lady didn't sing until the end. **(More uncontrollable laughing)** And the fella with the cell phone? On stage?

Waldorf Voltaire:
(Singing, mocking) Summer stock.

Statler Swift:
Hold it, hold it. I think they're ready for the next scene.

Waldorf Voltaire:
Excellent. This! Is what we live for!

(The lights fade on the box and rise on Euripides and the narrator's stage. One light also rises center-left stage where we see the Gate. The Donald and Boss Tweed stand before it. Now that we are closer to the Gate, we can see that there is more writing, preceding the warning. The Gate is ancient. So ancient we can't recognize the stone it is made of. The cuneiform etchings, and even the Italian, are faded past the point of being decipherable. What is clear is that billions of people have passed through it, and none wanted to, as evidenced by the bones, the claw marks, and the earth wiped smooth by dragging feet. There is no sound. It is as quiet as the grave)

Euripides:
Brave audience. Look. Those words on the Gate. I shudder to read them, and my blood runs cold to speak them. Listen to Mr. Tweed. He lives here. He knows them by heart and soul.

Boss Tweed:
(Pointing at the Gate, an arm around a shaking The Donald) I am the way into the city of woe. I am the way to a forsaken people. I am the way into eternal sorrow. Sacred justice moved my architect. I was raised here by divine omnipotence, primordial love, and ultimate intellect. Only those elements time cannot wear were made before me, and beyond time I stand. **(He hesitates and looks The Donald in the eyes)** Abandon all hope ye who enter here.

The Donald:
This sucks. What the fuck. I helped a lot of people. I mean *a lot* of people. Like, most people helped ever. *Ever!*

Boss Tweed:
Well you must've shit on a ton more or you wouldn't be standing here, Strumpet.

The Donald:
Trumpet. The name is *Trumpet.* You know, you blow through it and it makes a noise.

Boss Tweed:
Whatever.

The Donald:
What now?

Boss Tweed:
What do you mean, 'what now'? We're going through the Gate.

The Donald:
The scary lady said all I have to do is understand. And I'm not dead yet. **(Boss Tweed looks on in disgust and disbelief. Euripides does the same, shaking his head and clucking)** So maybe there's a chance. Maybe I can turn this thing around. Nobody, I mean *nobody*, can turn shit around like me. Alright, Tweed. Let's do this.

Boss Tweed:
(Stopping The Donald from going forward) Hit that.

The Donald:
Hit what?

Boss Tweed:
That bottle. The Bark Juice. The Bust Head. The Home Brew. That green shit. Hit it. Hit it hard. **(The Donald pulls out the cough syrup, slams a bunch of it, gives it to Tweed who likewise takes a drink and hands it back)** Alright. Brace yourself. **(And they pass through the Gate)**

Euripides:

Likewise, brave audience, do so likewise. **(The light fades on Euripides who turns and exits. The light fades to blackness on the stage and holds for an uncomfortable length of time)**

The Donald:

(From the dark) What was that! Something just brushed my cheek! There it goes again! And again!

Boss Tweed:

Hold tight, man.

The Donald:

There's a smell. Like sulphur. Like burning flesh. Like rot and wetness and earth and oh my fucking God it touched me again!

Boss Tweed:

Just a couple more steps Strumpet.

The Donald:

I can't do it!

Boss Tweed:

You have no choice! One more step and we're through!

(Suddenly the stage explodes in red and orange-hued lights. The sound of wailing souls is overwhelming. The sounds of a billion feet rushing about. A klaxon of horns and bells and sirens and screams and incomprehensible shouted words deafens the room. There are troops of people chasing blank banners. They themselves are being chased by swarms of insects that bite at their faces causing them to bleed and drip pus. There are people lost and confused

who stumble, spin, crawl, hop, and flail about in utter confusion. There are others who listlessly lie about or shamble around. **Boss Tweed is non-plussed, but The Donald is petrified)**

The Donald:
What in the hell is this!

Boss Tweed:
You nailed it.

The Donald:
Its chaos!

Boss Tweed:
Eternally.

The Donald:
Where are we? Who are these people? I can't understand.

Boss Tweed:
These are the uncommitted. These are the ones who did not choose to make a difference. They did nothing good. They did nothing evil. They did nothing. All they did was for themselves. They never prayed. They never voted. Every moment of every day wrapped up in nothing but themselves.

The Donald:
Wow! I thought Black Friday at Walmart sucked. **(The Donald and Boss Tweed are swatting at insects that bombard them relentlessly)** What are these fucking things?

Boss Tweed:
That is the sting of their consciouses. The sting of their guilt. Knowing they're doing wrong, knowing they could stop a wrong, but choosing to do nothing.

The Donald:
Losers. And the single ones? And the ones just moping around?

Boss Tweed:
The ones in anguish running all over alone are the same as those following the banners. They still can't make up their minds.

The Donald:
(Walking over to a lone being. The shade is dejected, miserable, and clearly in deep soul pain) And this poor soul?

Boss Tweed:
(Sighing) Once, there was a Rebellion of the Angels. Long before we were ever conceived. Before any of this existed. These poor bastards didn't choose a side.

The Donald:
Goddamn.

Boss Tweed:
Oh, you'll go to Hell for that.

The Donald:
(Looking up) Hey! That bunch over there. They look familiar. They're following that one fella with the red banner.

Boss Tweed:
That's you, dumbass.

The Donald:
What? How? I'm right here!

Boss Tweed:
The point of the lesson is to show you where in Hell you'll be.

The Donald:
(He pauses, looking down, puzzled and contrite) Well, I guess its not too bad, I mean its only level one.

Boss Tweed:
They're Circles, not levels, and this is only the vestibule. We haven't even crossed into Hell proper.

The Donald:
Crossed?

Boss Tweed:
We take a boat. We cross a river. This is just the beginning.

The Donald:
(Looking back at himself running with the red banner) Why am I doing that? Why am I here. On this level, I mean, in this Circle. I was committed.

Boss Tweed:
To yourself, and yourself alone. Come on, we've got a long way to go.

(They turn from the hordes, fighting their way through the mass of solitary, confused beings, and head downhill toward the sound of a river. The sheer noise of hell has dipped, but is ever present. The ground is strewn with slime, blood, pus, maggots and unidentifiable filth. The rock beneath it is ancient and seems like that with which The Gate was made)

The Donald:
How do you know where you're going? I mean, you haven't been here *that* long.

Boss Tweed:
One hundred and thirty-eight years. Seems like forever.

The Donald:
Then..?

Boss Tweed:
I'm on a bunch of levels, I mean, in a bunch of Circles. Plus, they gave me this assignment, to show you around, to show you you.

The Donald:
How can you be in so many places?

Boss Tweed:
You'll see. **(He stops walking, stops The Donald)** This is eternal life, man. This is Hell. Every atom, every particle of this place exists in the consciousness of the Almighty. Remember what The Gate said. That's important. 'Ultimate intellect', 'Beyond time I stand'. What we refused to recognize in our mortal life is the 'Divine Omnipotence'. **(He continues walking, as does The Donald. The sound of the river is now a roar. There is spray in the air. Souls are queuing up all around them. There is a silence between them for a beat or so)**

Boss Tweed:
I hope you understand what a gift you're being given. **(Boss Tweed gestures to his right)** Over here. We're not in line. We've got carte blanche.

(They jump to the front of the line. There is a landing carved from the same black rock, wet with spray from the violent river. An ancient pier, jutting from the landing is awash in waves of black water. One figure stands at the end, a barque looming over all of it. Black sails, ancient rigging, a wide open deck, the gunwales, and a giant wheel,

are illuminated by a solitary lantern. The immense cavern in which all this resides is lit with a blue-black glow. The thick, turbulent water rises and falls, heaves and drops, making it seem impossible to be near, let alone sail on. Boss Tweed and The Donald approach the Captain)**

Boss Tweed:
I can't wait for you to meet Charon.

The Donald:
You're kidding, right?

Boss Tweed:
Come on, Strumpet. How can you continue to disbelieve? Look around you, man. Where in the hell else would you find this?

(They walk up to the figure. Boss Tweed taps him on the shoulder)

Boss Tweed:
Charon! Its me, Tweed, how you keeping-Hey! You're not Charon. Chris!

Christopher Columbus:
A good day to you, Mr. Tweed. And to you, sir. **(He bows slightly to the two. The Donald is dumbstruck. The Captain is wearing a thick, wool and leather overcoat, a doublet, breeches, hose and black boots. On his head, tilted back just so, is a black, well-weathered three-corner hat)**

Boss Tweed:
Chris. What gives? Where's Charon?

Christopher Columbus:
Paternity leave.

Boss Tweed:
Whaaaat?

Christopher Columbus:
(Sighs) You've heard of Persephone?

Boss Tweed:
Of course.

Christopher Columbus:
Her daughter, Melinoe? **(Sighs again)** A few thousand years ago she would wander down here with her train of ghosts, making sure the insane who saw her made it to the right place. Well, her and Charon got to chatting...

Boss Tweed:
Say no more.

Christopher Columbus:
Hey, I'm happy for the old salt. He needed a break. Christ on a pogo stick! You ferry the damned for thousands of years and you'd be cranky, too.

Boss Tweed:
For sure, for sure. I was just hoping to introduce the Strumpet here to him.

(Christopher Columbus looks over to The Donald)

Christopher Columbus:
So you're the V.I.P? **(Looking at the top of The Donald's head)** Wind plays hell with the hair down here, huh?

The Donald:
(Checking his hair) I'm in shock. You? Here? Why?

Christopher Columbus:
(Irritated and then ashamed) Historians are a royal pain in the ass, and I am so tired of hearing that question! **(Holds up his hands in defense)** Mi culpa. Lo siento. Sorry. Sorry. You know, there aren't many down here to ask, and if you make it back topside you can do your homework, or, if you make it to Paradiso or even Purgatorio, then you can ask them directly.

The Donald:
Who?

Christopher Columbus:
(A grimace crosses the sailor's face) The Lucayans. The Tainos. The Arawaks. To name a few.

The Donald:
(Understanding, nodding) I'm sorry.

Christopher Columbus:
Me too. Too late. **(Claps his hands and starts motioning to the souls to start boarding)** Alright, you swine! Let's get this voyage going. Tweed! You and your friend have seats reserved up front. Better get a move on, these folks are always a bit loco.

(Boss Tweed and The Donald board the barque. An unfathomable number of souls cram aboard. A smaller lantern is raised and lowered, and a horn that sounds like a conch shell crossed with a viking winding horn, blares three long notes and two shorter ones. Ropes are cast aside and the barque leaves the dock, disappearing behind the waves, popping up every so often on the back of another, until it is swallowed by distance and the murk of the enormous cavern. Lights fade to black, and the theater is equally swallowed in the chthonic darkness of Hell)

(**The lights come up on the box, stage right, of Statler Swift and Waldorf Voltaire. They are incredulous, mouths agape, eyes wide open. They look at each other in disbelief and then back to the stage**)

Statler Swift:
Are you kidding me?! (**Waldorf Voltaire is shaking his head from side to side**) They lifted that whole sequence from *Cats*.

Waldorf Voltaire:
I know!

Statler Swift:
Put those people in leotards with whiskers and its the same routine!

Waldorf Voltaire:
Shameless.

Statler Swift:
(**To the audience**) Come on, man! You know you've seen this before.

Waldorf Voltaire:
Mr. Swift, please. Don't instigate a riot. Remember the *Rite of Spring* debut?

Statler Swift:
Thank God we were in our box! Barely made it out alive. (**Beat**) It just seems so obvious. That whole bannery, troupe thing. *Cats*.

Waldorf Voltaire:
West Side Story.

Statler Swift:
Oh, for certain! (**Singing**) When you're uncommitted, you're uncommitted, from your first dry fart, to the last day you're given.

Waldorf Voltaire:
Ha! God is a comedian playing to an audience too afraid to laugh. **(To the audience)** Oh, by God's bones, not you recently fleeced chaps. Say, Statler.

Statler Swift:
Yes, my friend.

Waldorf Voltaire:
(Gesturing to the audience) I feel quite deeply the need to defend these poor souls from further excises on their beleaguered incomes.

Statler Swift:
Indeed, sir, indeed!

Waldorf Voltaire:
We must up the ante!

Statler Swift:
Spot on, spot on. To their defense!

Waldorf Voltaire:
Its a wonder they don't leave in droves.

Statler Swift:
In for a penny, in for a pound. How about the male leads?

Waldorf Voltaire:
Deviled ham. **(Much ensuing laughter)** Re-name the play!

Statler Swift:
Re-name the play?

Waldorf Voltaire:
Underground and Over The Top. **(More laughter)**

Statler Swift:
Overplayed and Underwhelming.

Waldorf Voltaire:
Beelzebub's Burlesque.

Statler Swift:
Carried Away On Seas of Cheese.

Waldorf Voltaire:
(Shaking his head) Hell hath no fury like a director without a budget.

(The lights come up on the narrator's stage and Euripides. He is staring across at Statler and Waldorf, a very angry expression on his face)

Euripides:
Who are you.

Statler Swift:
Paying customers.

Euripides:
How did you get that box?

Waldorf Voltaire:
Bribery.

Euripides:
That box is reserved for the producers.

Statler Swift:
Or people of the press.

Euripides:
(Pausing, a look of epiphany coming over his face) Oh, by Zeus'
Yardstick! If the Holy Trinity had a fourth it would be theater critics. To
whom are we so honored to have reviewing our humble play?

Statler Swift:
(Motioning beside him) Waldorf Voltaire.

Waldorf Voltaire:
(Likewise) And Statler Swift.

Euripides:
(Squeal of panic and horror)

Statler Swift:
You've heard of us.

Waldorf Voltaire:
**(Euripides stares uncomfortably. Smooths out his toga, straightens
his hair, checks his phone)** Silence is acceptance.

Euripides:
Gentlemen. This is a rather unique theatrical experience, in that, the entire
fate of mankind hangs in the balance. The very existence of the human race
is at risk and the author, for lack of being a very good shot, has decided to
intervene in this manner. **(Swift and Voltaire simply stare across the
stage at the narrator, arms across their chests)** I guess, what I'm asking for, is a certain suspension of disbelief in order to help further the narrative. **(Waldorf makes a wet, clucking sound)** Never mind. I have utmost
confidence, not only in our ability to save humanity, but to connect with the
audience. Even through the sophomoric antics of two ill-mannered moppets.

Statler Swift and Waldorf Voltaire:
(Both gentlemen at the same time) Moppet?! Ill-mannered?

Waldorf Voltaire:
Who does this fella think-its just a play!

Statler Swift:
(The lights are slowly fading on the box) You just ended your career there, Rod Steiger.

Waldorf Voltaire:
If Paris Hilton had a brother.

Statler Swift:
Hey. The lights. Leave these lights up.

Waldorf Voltaire:
Dammit.

Statler Swift:
What? What is it?

Waldorf Voltaire:
Too dark. Too many waves.

Statler Swift:
To the loo!

(The lights dim on the box, but stay up on Euripides, who turns to face the audience)

Euripides:
Who knoweth if to die be but to live, and that called life by mortals be but death? Semantics? An inverse notion to a conventional assumption? These quibbles mean nothing to poor Mr. Trumpet. **(Lights come up center stage revealing the front seats on the barque. Black water pours over the sides and washes away down the deck. The prow is driven**

into the waves and then kicked up and to each side with great violence and at impossible angles. **Boss Tweed grins and screams, hands on the gunwales, he yells 'Odin' into the maelstrom. The Donald, on the other hand, is cowering below the gunwale, gagging, throwing-up, and screaming in fear)** Danger gleams like sunshine to a brave man's eyes. **(Looking at the scene unfolding at center stage)** I guess that doesn't apply here. **(Turning back to the audience. The lights fade at center stage)** Too much. Too much. Too much. Even with all his braggadocio, all his bluster and cocky brashness, this man is reaching the very limits of his sanity. Nay, only Heracles himself could bear this journey. **(Pauses)** Think of this: he has passed through the very Gate to Hell; he has seen the millions of doomed souls in the vestibule, he has seen himself there as well; and then, he is forced to cross the most perilous, most awful body of water known to man. **(Steps closer to the audience)** A man is a bottle. And in that bottle there is only so much space. And in that space, there is only so much room to put the things that we are given, that we experience, feel, love, suffer, and endure. How full before the bottle bursts? That, dear friends, we must ask ourselves each day.

(Lights fade on Euripides. Lights on the left side of center stage reveal an empty land lit in blues and grays. The Donald is on hands and knees dry heaving. Boss Tweed is trying to help. Behind them the damned are queued and marched away from the landing. In a short time the barque has emptied. Christopher Columbus steps over to bid farewell)

Christopher Columbus:
Well, Bossman, good luck with this one.

Boss Tweed:
Thanks, Chris. Going to need it. Great passage. You've still got the touch.

Christopher Columbus:
Thanks, friend. **(He turns to board the barque)**

Boss Tweed:
Give my congratulations to Charon.

Christopher Columbus:
(Over his shoulder) Will do.

(The barque departs, the damned have all been herded away, and only Boss Tweed and The Donald remain)

Boss Tweed:
Hey, Strumpet, I'm really sorry about this. It just never dawned on any of us, you know, physical distress and all.

The Donald:
Oh bullshit. You fucktards dreamed this crap up.

Boss Tweed:
(He goes from rubbing The Donald's shoulder to smacking him across the back of his head) Custer's ass, you dimwit. We're all just players in this. You know damn well who spun this masterpiece up.

The Donald:
Still, I mean, you had to know.

Boss Tweed:
Not at all Strumpet. **(The Donald is struggling to his feet, pushing away the helping hands of Boss Tweed)** We don't get real humans down here. Like, ever. Oh sure, there's the odd insurance seminar.

The Donald:
So I'm the first?

Boss Tweed:
No, that would be Dante. Before that, Hercules? Maybe Eurydice? I don't know. You must be number two.

The Donald:
You could rephrase that. So, **(looking around)** now what? Where are we? Its empty. There's no one here. Its quiet. Is this still Hell?

Boss Tweed:
Oh yeah. This is limbo. The first Circle.

The Donald:
This is only the first Circle? **(Groaning)** This is going to take forever!

Boss Tweed:
Yes. And no. And yes, this is the first Circle.

The Donald:
This is insane. **(Looking around wide-eyed)** Its as big as Texas.

Boss Tweed:
Oh, this dwarfs Texas.

The Donald:
Kinda peaceful, in a lonely sort of way. What sinners end up here?

Boss Tweed:
This was where the virtuous pagans went. And unbaptized babies. People who led good lives, but hadn't heard or accepted Christ.

The Donald:
So where is everyone!

Boss Tweed:
Amnesty.

The Donald:
Sweet!

Boss Tweed:
Don't get your hopes up, there's a lot of hell left to see. And besides, **(pointing)** there you are.

(A lone figure walks up to them from the empty, blue-gray land. It is Limbo Donald)

Boss Tweed:
(Turning to step away) I'll let you two catch up. But not too much chin music, we got a lot of ground to cover and I got suffering to do. **(Boss Tweed exits stage right)**

Limbo Donald:
(Shaking hands) Have you accepted Jesus Christ as your personal savior?

The Donald:
Of course.

Limbo Donald:
Whoa, pal, lying is a few Circles lower.

The Donald:
Well, I mean…**(trails off)**.

Limbo Donald:
It's not Christ specifically. It's being Christ-like. Aspiring to be. Working toward. Acting like. **(The Donald looks on puzzled)** You're not getting this, are you?

The Donald:
What about Jews and Buddhists and fuzzy pagans and *Moslems*! What about Moslems?

Limbo Donald:
It's not like that. **(Pauses)** Religions are like languages. One size doesn't fit all. They're developed by folks to understand the impossible to understand. If you take each religion and steep it through time and practice, you end up with the Golden Rule.

The Donald:
You lost me at one size fits all.

Limbo Donald:
Hence, why you're here. **(Reaches out and places a hand on The Donald's heart)** It's acknowledging the goodness that exists in each human being, and treating them the way you would want to be treated. If you take one thing away from this experience, let it be that.

The Donald:
Then I'm not doomed?

Limbo Donald:
Oh, you're fucked. Don't get me wrong. But there are bigger things happening with this than just one man, than just you.

The Donald:
Yeah, well I seem to be the linchpin.

Limbo Donald:

Get over yourself, Toad Boy. There are billions of souls down here. There are billions of souls in Purgatorio and billions more in Paradiso. Your epoch, your world, your empire: dust. What we're trying to do is avoid the incineration of this rather remarkable planet and thus the deaths of another few billion human beings long before their time. Do you understand, Mr. Linchpin.

The Donald:

I get it, I get it. However, I have my own plans to avert all of that *and* make America great.

Limbo Donald:

(Looking on with contempt) Then I guess I had better leave you to it.

The Donald:

Bingo. **(The Donald is turning around in a slow circle, looking out over the endless plain of Limbo)** Get me the hell outta here. This has put me days behind schedule and my day planner looks like Webster's Dictionary. **(Limbo Donald has disappeared. The Donald is alone)** Hey! Where'd you go? What the hell! Come on, man! What gives? Donald? I mean, Me! Tweed? Come on, guys! **(A lonely wind rises, a mournful cry that shivers the bones. The Donald turns around and around to view the blue-gray wasteland, a place in which day never dawns and night never ends. He collapses onto his knees. His fists pound the ancient, tired ground sending up dust devils. They coalesce into one dust devil that slowly, turning in on itself, becomes a form. An eye. One eye, like golden flame, glows from the spinning cloud of dust, dirt, and clay. The Donald looks on in horror, trying to slide backward away from it, but is too terrified to make much progress)** Get away! Get away from me!

Iblee:

(A voice that lilts, whispers, pouts, and sings. It is male, it is female. It is impossibly ancient. It is all voices and none) Oh, Donny. I won't harm you. Be not afraid.

The Donald:
What are you!

Iblee:
I am this. I am that. I am I am I am.

The Donald:
Who are you?

Iblee:
Some called me Asag. But I am not Asag. Some called me Kali. But I am not Kali. Some called me Baal. But I am not Baal. Some think me Jinn. But I am not Jinn.

The Donald:
I, I want to know who I'm talking to.

Iblee:
Some called me Loki. But I am not Loki. Some have called me uncertainty. And I am not this. I am very certain.

The Donald:
You don't make much sense.

Iblee:
Sense. Hmmmm, dollars and cents.

The Donald:
That's my language.

Iblee:
Ooooh, I know all about dollars and cents.

The Donald:
And your name, Socrates.

Iblee:
I am not Socrates. Call me, Iblee.

The Donald:
Can you get me out of here, Iblee?

Iblee:
Maybe yes. Maybe no. Maybe maybe.

The Donald:
I sense a deal.

Iblee:
Oh yes. A deal. Always we deal.

The Donald:
It is an art I pride myself in.

Iblee:
Then, dearest Donny, we shall make a deal.

(The wind rises, and with it the smell of woodsmoke and the distant voice of Boss Tweed. The Donald turns his head. Iblee dissolves back into the ground and Boss Tweed enters, stage left, at a trot)

Boss Tweed:
Strumpet! Goddamn it! Don't run away like that. Jumping German Jesus! Don't you know where you are!

The Donald:
(Indignant, but scared) I, I haven't moved.

Boss Tweed:
Look, Jonah, when you so rudely dismissed your limbo-self, giving a lecture you *needed* to hear, it all shifted. He didn't walk away; you willed yourself to another part of Limbo.

The Donald:
Get the fuck out of here. Wait. Wait. That means I can just will my self back topside, find my model wife, get lucky, and get back to running my empire.

Boss Tweed:
(He backhands The Donald) Wake up! Butterhead! You think you're running this show? You think you're omnipotent? Empire? Everything you've ever held, everything you've ever touched, every single thing you've seen, heard, tasted, felt, thought-ALL OF IT! **(Boss Tweed leans down and picks up one tiny pebble from the ground)** Is less than one atom of this stone.

The Donald:
Smell.

Boss Tweed:
Huh?

The Donald:
You forgot smell. I smell smoke.

Boss Tweed:
Well, you are in Hell.

The Donald:
No, dummy. Woodsmoke. I smell woodsmoke.

Boss Tweed:

(Nodding) Follow me. There's one other person here and I want you to meet her.

The Donald:
Her? I'm all ears.

(They cross to the right side of center stage. The lights dim on the blue-gray emptiness stage left, and come up on an oak grove, stage right. There is a clearing, and at the center of the clearing, a fire. Around the fire are small tables and low seats covered with books. Sitting before the fire, nose buried in a book, is a woman in an off-white toga with gold stitching. She is quite beautiful, with fine features, black eyes, and dark hair pulled back in a braid that loops her head. Curls fall in ringlets over the braid, framing her face, while the rest of her hair is in a loose knot in back. There are terrible scars along her shoulders, her neck, above one eye brow, on her hands, and down her arms. She sets the book aside, picks up a stick, pokes at the fire, and sets the stick on top of the warm, earthly glow. As Boss Tweed and The Donald enter stage left, she looks up)

Boss Tweed:
I'm sorry Philosopher, but I was told you wanted to meet this fella and have a word with him.

(The Donald is taken aback by the clearing, the fire, the connection with earth as he knows it, and mostly by the beauty of the woman. However, him being him, he steps forward and opens his mouth)

The Donald:
The pleasure's all mine. (Extends a hand. The woman says nothing and barely looks him over) I know. I know. You don't get many of us down here. Second real guy in hell ever. *Ever.* (No response. The Donald

leans back upright, removes his unaccepted hand and scratches his chin) Habla Ingles?

Boss Tweed:
Oh, you're a real smoothy there, Strumpet. Habla Ingles? How about you just shut your pie hole and let the lady do the talking.

(The Philosopher stands up and looks over at The Donald. She looks back over to Boss Tweed, down to the fire, around the clearing, sighs very heavy, and then speaks to The Donald)

Hypatia:
You have travelled from very far away. You have come to a place that is impossible to come to, and your journey has only just begun. Your thoughts and your destiny are glass to me, Mr. Trumpet. They loom like bill boards along an empty highway. We have debated your existence for centuries. We have seen you come and go in one form or another, but always with the same result: death, destruction, and despair. **(She steps away from the fire, places the book on a stack of books that rest on an ornately carved ottoman)** These slogans you say, these platitudes, they are as empty as these ashes, as thin as this smoke.

The Donald:
Who are you to speak to me this way. My being here is a big deal, you know, a big, big deal.

Hypatia:
I am Hypatia of Alexandria. I am The Philosopher. There are few mysteries to which I have not found the answer, and in doing so only created more questions.

The Donald:
Well, you can't be too smart.

Hypatia:
I'm sorry.

The Donald:
Looks like everyone else in Limbo took the amnesty deal. And you?

Hypatia:
(Smiling) Mortal, if only you could have the chance to have an eternity like the one I have. Forever and forever in this glade, in this grove, with all the books that have ever been written, all the music that has ever been made, all the art that has ever been created for all of eternity, and with only two tasks. **(The Donald lifts his head, knits his brow)** To keep two fires lit: the one before you that lights lost souls in Limbo to the Seven Gates and The Castle where they may seek amnesty; and a second fire that you have never seen.

The Donald:
What fire is that?

Hypatia:
The fire of reason.

The Donald:
I have a degree. I've written books.

Hypatia:
Ghost writers wrote your books, like cheerleaders wrote your papers.

The Donald:
There's only two books worth reading, anyway. **(Hypatia tilts her head, lifts her eyebrows)** The Bible and the Constitution. **(He pulls out a *Cliffs Notes* copy of the U.S. Constitution)**

Hypatia:

Whatever you know of these books was vetted to you by advisors. **(The Donald looks down. Hypatia steps closer)** You are a dim-witted fool, **(The Donald looks up sharply)** who is vain enough to destroy everything that so many have suffered to build. Here is a riddle for you to ponder: the more you die, the greater chance you have to live. **(She holds his eyes for a long beat, then turns, nods to Boss Tweed and starts to exit stage left. She turns toward The Donald)** Even you must realize, your hair gives you away. **(Turns back to stage left and exits)**

Boss Tweed:

Thank-you, Madam Philosopher. Sorry to have bothered you. We'll be, a, leaving, now. **(Turns back from Hypatia exiting stage left to the The Donald)** Can't I fucking take you anywhere? **(Smacks him in the shoulder)** Come on. Seven Gates, one big Castle, a little judgement, and then Circle Number Two.

The Donald:

Why does everyone hate me down here? **(As they slowly exit stage right)**

Boss Tweed:

Well, you are kind of an asshole.

(The lights fade center stage and after a beat go up, stage right, on the box. Statler Swift and Waldorf Voltaire sit, leaning forward and bug-eyed. Waldorf has a flask in one hand)

Waldorf Voltaire:

Mesmerizing.

Statler Swift:

Who is that actress?

Waldorf Voltaire:
Rachel Weisz.

Statler Swift:
No.

Waldorf Voltaire:
Meryl Streep.

Statler Swift:
No.

Waldorf Voltaire:
Cher.

Statler Swift:
Give me back that flask.

Waldorf Voltaire:
No. **(Beat)** Elizabeth Taylor.

Statler Swift:
No. Older.

Waldorf Astoria:
Bette Davis.

Statler Swift:
No. Much older.

Waldorf Voltaire:
Betty White?

Statler Swift:
(Grabbing the flask out of Waldorf's hands) From an older time. Before talkies. Before film.

Waldorf Voltaire:
(Thinking, then holding up one finger and nodding) Julia Neilson.

Statler Swift:
Precisely! **(Beat)** But how could they afford so marvelous an actress?

Waldorf Voltaire:
Look at the set.

Statler Swift:
Right. No props, no set walls. Only blue filters over the lights. More ham actors mouthing over-wrought lines and our male protagonists, one-half of The Bowery Boys, shuffling through cardboard hell.

Waldorf Voltaire:
(Guffawing) Re-name the play!

Statler Swift:
Plan 9 From Inner Space!

Waldorf Voltaire:
The *Really* Rocky Horror Show!

Statler Swift:
Hell's Gate!

Waldorf Voltaire and Statler Swift:
(Stop laughing and look at each other. In unison) Moose Murders! **(They roar in laughter)**

(The lights come up on the narrator's stage and Euripides. He has an overly large control in his hand that seems to control the lights above the box stage right. He is dimming their lights)

Statler Swift:
(Suddenly stops laughing) Hey! Not again!

Waldorf Voltaire:
Aw come on, my man. We're old and feeble. What if we were to fall out of this box?

Euripides:
Nighty night, gentlemen. Until we meet again, somewhere well past intermission.
(The lights stage right go out completely. He sets the control aside)

Euripides:
(Turns to the audience, looking above them, holding up a finger)
My Master leads me by another road out of that serenity to the roar and trembling air of Hell. I pass from light into the kingdom of eternal night. **(Looks directly at the audience)** Dear friends, once more I ask you to gird yourself, to steel your heart against what awaits. Our intrepid entrepreneurs are on the threshold of Hell proper. The pit. The void. Minos! That beast that passes out the fate of doomed souls, he lies just around the corner, perched on a precipice of dizzying height, where the eternal blackness swallows the depths, but cannot contain the wails of the damned. Their mission, given to them by omnipotent God himself, must drive them forward. Nothing has more strength than dire necessity, and oh, these are dire times. Gather up your courage, brave patrons. Together! Together we will provide the fortitude these two may lack. Arm yourself, my heart: the thing that you must do is fearful, yet inevitable!

(The lights on Euripides fade and spotlights pinpoint Boss Tweed and The Donald, just below the box, stage right, the facing of

which is now slimy rock. The two are pressed against the rock, on a ledge. A rush of air, and with it the dim, mournful wail of the damned, rises from the bowels of the pit. Above them, in shadow, we can make out Swift and Voltaire-rapt and excited, watching the events below them, and looking at each other)**

The Donald:
Why can't we go back to the nice lady by the nice fire?

Boss Tweed:
Destiny.

The Donald:
Destiny? I already know I'm doomed. How about you and I have Mr. Omnipotent drop us off at 210 East 46th Street and I'll pick up the tab?

Boss Tweed:
(Stops sidling along the edge. Looks over to The Donald) I could kill for a fucking steak right now.

The Donald:
Thats what I'm saying! Isn't there an intermission? I mean, this would be a really good place for an intermission.

Boss Tweed:
Just a wee bit further, Strumpet. Oh man, you got any more of that bark juice?

The Donald:
(Pulls out the bottle of green liquid, swigs, passes) I hear breathing. Panting. I hear something like the biggest, fucking dog ever. What's around this corner, Bossman?

Boss Tweed:

Aw, man, Strumpet. **(Swigs. Passes back)** I haven't been here in nearly a century and a half. This is bad, pal, real bad.

The Donald:

(Visibly shaking. Nearly falling off the edge) Tweeeeed, tell me what's over there! That smell! **(Gagging)** I know it. I know that smell. Oh my God its the worst fucking smell ever. What could smell that bad?

Boss Tweed:

Sorry again, Strumpet. Never thought about mortal senses. I can only imagine.

The Donald:

What the fuck is it, Tweed?

Boss Tweed:

(Stammering) It, is, impossible to convey.

The Donald:

Wait! I know it! From my childhood. It terrified me! **(Visibly breaking down)** That smell! I know it! Dear God in heaven its not possible!

Boss Tweed:

Stay with me, Strumpet! Don't give up on me!

The Donald:

(In near hysterics) The, the zoo. The nightmares. The, The Bronx Zoo. I cried. I wept. My mother tried to calm me down. The smell. That goddamn smell. For years. In my dreams. At odd moments.

Boss Tweed:

What is it, Strumpet!

The Donald:
The Reptile House!

(Lights come up center stage as the two step in. The room is bowl-shaped, enormous, yet stacked high so that there isn't a bad seat in the place. The tiers are filled, theater-in-the-round style, with a teeming multitude of grotesque, misshapen, chittering lizard-like creatures. They are noisy, giddy, and extremely excited. The room is lit by torches, fires in braziers, and oddly glowing, red, blue, and green rocks. In the center of the room, as if on stage, is Minos. He is from the waist below, lizard, from the waist up to the shoulders, serpent, and his head is a crown. It is as if the skull itself is an elongated crown. Scales, slick with pus, glisten from spots on his gigantic body, while in other areas they have been worn smooth as blackish-gray marble. There are no eyes. He sees all around him through other senses. The smell comes off of him and his lizard audience in waves of noxiousness. He moves in a kind of slippery-thumping, his serpent's tail, impossibly long, whistles as it cuts through the moist, smokey, polluted air. His arms, long and stalk-like, have pincers and fingers and nubs and horns and burrs. He is most engaging with his lizard audience, pumping them up by moving around the open space, gesticulating with his appendages, and making a strange, almost cooing noise. Behind him, above one of three openings to this amphitheater, aglow in the same red, blue, and green rocks, is a sign. It reads: Sin and Spin!)

Minos:
(In a voice that is reminiscent of the finest FM radio voices and remarkably like that of a game show host) Heeelllllloooooo, Hell!!!!! How are you freaks doing! **(The lizard crowd goes wild)** What a great day to be damned! Men-a-roasting do we have a great show planned for you! Multitudes of sinners? No way. One man. **(The lizard audience starts to boo)** Ooohhh, but wait my lovelies. This is no ordinary man. This gem is

going to cause, come on, play with me. What's this guy going to do?!!?? **(The lizard crowd answers but it is completely unintelligible)** Nooooo. Worse. Waaaaayyy worse. Come on, kiddos! What's this rat going to do to his own people? Okay, okay. I'll tell you what this guy's going to do. All of it! That's right. Every single sin possible including destroying the entire planet Earth! **(Insane, high-pitched screaming)** I know. I know. And you lucky little lizards get to watch me cast his judgement. Aaaaand how do we do that down here?

The Lizard Audience:
(In unison and for the only time discernible) Sin! And! Spiiiiiin!!!!

Minos:
That's right, you silly little buggers! They sin, and I spin! **(Looking over at a quaking Boss Tweed hugging a downright terrified puddle of The Donald)** Soooo, Mr. Tweed, you have brought us our guest of dishonor. Much obliged. If you would kindly step aside so the audience can see Mr. Trumpet in all his whimpering glory. **(Boss Tweed releases The Donald and quickly steps over toward an opening stage right)** Well, well Mr. Trumpet. The pleasure was all yours. And now, Herbie can I get a scale-roll, **(from off stage comes a drum roll with some wet tones to it)**, here's your list of sins! **(A giant stone tablet comes down from the ceiling. On it, in latin, in tiny, tiny lettering, is an extensive list. The lizard audience gasps)**

The Donald:
(Suddenly, from indignation, finding his voice and a bit of back bone) That's not possible!

Minos:
That's what they all say. Sorry, Charlie, you own each and every one of these. I'm just the emcee. I'm just the judge. It's the Omnipotent One that puts the list together. Aaare you questioning the Almighty? I mean, there's still room at the bottom of the tablet.

The Donald:
No, no. I get it. I mean. Sure, I guess. I mean, what the hell am I supposed to do. I didn't ask to be here. Right? I mean, I have stuff to do and this is some weird dream or acid trip or even if its real, the nice lady last scene basically said this is what *could* happen. So you know what, Lizard King, I sinned, you spin and lets get this freak show over with.

Minos:
(Standing up to all of his many-storied height. Arms crossed over a snake's chest. A voice that is now so low and deep that it shakes the entire room) Yooooouu insignificant puss bag. It will be my eternal pleasure to show you how many times my tail spins around my body. Each revolution is a Circle in Hell. Each crack of my tail is a Circle a shade of you will inhabit. Do you get it? Do you *really* get it? **(The Donald sort of flinches, winces, and nods)** Then here we go! **(The Lizard throng goes mad and Minos struts to center stage, turns in a complete circle until he is once more facing The Donald, who looks over at Boss Tweed, who is looking at the ground, his nails, the texture of the rock. The Donald backs up, behind him is a tunnel leading down. Minos does a little dance, cracks knuckles and neck, flexes, stretches, then turns to fully face The Donald)**

Minos:
Aaaand awaaay weeee goooo! Circle Number Two! **(Holding up something approximating fingers)** LUST! Need we really go any further? **(His tail flies up toward the cavern's ceiling, arcs downward and wraps once, twice around his body, cracking with two snaps)** Lust for women. Lust for girls. Lust for boys. Lust for sex. Lust for money. Lust for power. Lust to crush all around you. Lust for the misfortune of others. Lust for lust. Lust for food and drink and excess of every nature. Lust for drugs. Lust for your own flesh and blood! Lust for yourself, for your image in the mirror. One million crucifixes I would need to string the one million shades of you for each and every time you lusted.

(The Donald is pressed against the rock at the tunnel's entrance. He hazards a glance toward the opening, looks back to Minos, then to his feet, teardrops of shame falling on the tortured, black ground. Thousands of lizard-things go crazy screaming at The Donald. Pointing claws at him. Tearing at themselves)

Minos:

Circle Number Three! (Three fingers. His tail rises, arcs, and wraps around his body three times. Three concussive, gunshot-like snaps echo through the chamber) GLUTTONY! Well where do I begin!??! Your whole culture pigs itself out while entire peoples starve! And you. Even when visiting the third world you dine on food that costs enough to feed a family for a year! Why? Is it really that big a deal? Food. Food. Food. You've even been eating while you've been shitting! You've taken the most wholesome, most important single facet of human existence and turned it into pornography. Eat to live? Live to eat! And gluttony isn't just food, drink, and drugs. Consume. Consume. Consume. Three generations taught to do nothing but consume. And you! You could be their patron saint. Who ever dies with the most toys wins! Shop till you drop! Super size that! You are a pyramid-scheme of gluttony. Producer. Middle man. Consumer. One fat, corpulent shade of you will lie in a plastic, convenience store cup of slushy filth for eternity!

(The Donald is now a shaking, blubbering mess. He looks again down the tunnel, he tries to find Boss Tweed but can't look up because the lizard-things are ripping off parts of their bodies and throwing the chunks at him)

Minos:

Circle Number Four! (Four fingers. The whistling of a serpent's tail through the air. Four spins around the loathsome body. Four sharp reports) GREEEEEEED!! Yooouuu! Aaaareee! Iiiits! Aaaaarch! Aaaangel! Your greed knows no limits. Your greed defines you. It is the principle sickness of your soul. In fact, it *OWNS* your soul!

(While Minos continues on this particular tack, The Donald is banging his head against the ground, the wall, his hands. He is smashing his brow with the *Cliffs Notes* copy of the Constitution. He is being pelted with lizard chunks. In an attempt to shut out everything else around him, he stares at one lizard chunk. It is then he realizes that the chunks have locomotion, that they have a will of their own, and are actively, slowly, trying to attack him. This, folks, is the end of the line for The Donald. He flips Minos a double bird and bolts down the tunnel. A wide-eyed Boss Tweed tries to cross the stage, a hail of lizard chunks filling the air)

Minos:
(Hands on hips) Well I guess he's buggered off. Go figure. Rude little fucker. (Turns to the audience while throwing a thumb over his shoulder) How 'bout that hair! (The crowd goes wild)

(The lights go up on the box. It is seemingly empty, until two sets of hands come up and grab the edge of the box. Statler and Waldorf raise their heads up over the rail)

Statler:
Why did I ever let you talk me into this?

Waldorf:
You loved *Phantom of The Opera*.

(There is a huge growl, a giant crash and lizard screeching from the darkness of center stage. Statler and Waldorf startle and quickly lower themselves back down. The lights on the box go out)

(The lights go up on Euripides. He has a thick scroll stretched out in his hands)

Euripides:

(Looking at the scroll. Looking at center stage. Looking back at the scroll. Looking at the audience and shaking his head) Abandon all hope, ye who leave the script! **(Lights fade to black on Euripides)**

(Lights come up center stage revealing a vista of sand, hills, and crucifixes. A hundred hues of red and gray cast shadows that flicker and flash with a ceaseless wind. It blows from every direction with no sense as to why. The reds and grays light up an endless forest of crucifixes. From each, a human shade is loosely fixed, blowing willy nilly on strands of skin that are as soft as suede, as strong as leather, and as light as silk. The crucifixes themselves are made of dense flesh that seems to grow from out of the sand, which is itself, a mottled mix of skin tones. The sand, the crucifixes, the wind, the light, and the souls are somehow connected. With each gust of wind, with each turn of the wind's direction, a ripple, a spasm, a tide, pulsates across the landscape in an unending eternity of sensual overload)

(Across the sands, staggering, running, screaming, The Donald blindly enters stage left. He comes to the front of the stage, in front of one crucifix in particular. He looks up to see himself, fluttering in a dozen different directions. The crucifix is formed in the style of shunga netsuke. On it, are thousands of names. He hugs this pole. He stares at it. He runs his fingers, his lips, his tongue over it. Until, in abject horror, he collapses at its base)

The Donald:
Dear God in Heaven. Please. Please forgive me. Why? Why can't this end. How much must I endure before you throw me here forever? **(He looks at the trunk of the crucifix)** What! I never slept with her! What is this bullshit. I mean, sure, I recognize a lot of these names, but come on, this is

supposed to be accurate. Wait a minute. If this isn't right, then, then, theeen maybe none of this is accurate! **(He rises)** What is this shit, Minos?! Huh? You're shit's fucked up, buddy! Ha ha, got you right where I want you. Deal's over, dill weed! Deal. Is. Over.

(The wind gusts suddenly knocking The Donald to the ground. A tight, counter-clockwise eddy picks up the sand very close to him. A sand auger forms, takes the shape of a woman. The grains are moving rapidly, continually. Soft blue currents of electricity flash just beneath the surface. The Donald is transfixed. The shape elongates, becomes serpent-like, slides up and down and around the crucifix until once more, as only sand can move, it is beside The Donald in the shape of a woman. One eye opens and gleams gold and red and gold)

The Donald:
Iblee? Is that you?

Iblee:
Dearest Donny, is me.

The Donald:
Where the fuck am I?

Iblee:
Silly, you are in Hell. Second Circle. In the Hills of Lust.

The Donald:
I want to go home, Iblee. I, I can't do this anymore.

Iblee:
Oh, Donny. I know how scared you are.

The Donald:
Maybe you can help me?

Iblee:
Yes. Quite sure of yes. I will help you.

The Donald:
Then let's go! Now!

Iblee:
Help, yes. Now? Do not know this.

The Donald:
Don't play me, Iblee. I know when I'm being fucked with.

Iblee:
No, no play. **(Runs an appendage of swirling, moving sand along the base of the crucifix)** Donny busy. **(The Donald looks away as Iblee strokes the fleshy surface)** So many. So many names. So many faces. So many hearts. This one. Yes. This one. Tell me true, Donny. Tell me this one.

The Donald:
(Looking at the point on the base where Iblee's hand is, then quickly looking away, a catch in his voice swallowing a sob) Anyone. Anyone but that one.

Iblee:
Much pain. Much love. Much much much. I know. Yes. I do know.

The Donald:
I don't see what she has to do with any of this. And if there was one good thing in my whole stupid life, it was her.

Iblee:
You crushed her, Donny. Like dry roses. Like dreams made of whimsies. Why?

The Donald:
The timing wasn't right. Different spheres, different worlds. Different lives.

Iblee:
Hands, Donny. Tiny, tiny hands. **(The Donald looks closely at the one lit eye)** So small, these hands, they could not open doors. Right, Donny.

The Donald:
Oh, fuck you! Fuck all of this. **(Pointing at his heart)** Stab it. Stab it right here. Or better yet, take the fucking thing. Obviously, I'm not using it.

Iblee:
No, Donny. **(Tapping itself)** Friend. Not to hurt. To understand. So far from here, all of you.

The Donald:
You've never been topside, huh?

Iblee:
Not yet. Not lately. Not ever.

The Donald:
(Looking at Iblee) What about that deal, Iblee.

Iblee:
Oh, Donny. Its just a kiss away.

(The Donald steps closer to Iblee, wraps his arms around the female shape of spinning, moving sand. Iblee's arms do the same

around The Donald. Flashes of pale, blue electricity weave in and around them. They embrace)

Boss Tweed:
(From off-stage) Strumpet! Goddamnit Strumpet! This shit is getting old, pal! Strumpet! Where are you?

(Boss Tweed enters at a jog, stage left. Iblee dissolves back into the ground, an electrical snap of blue leaving only the faint, burnt smell of an electrical fire. The Donald realizes none of this, busy holding and kissing something that is not there. Boss Tweed walks up to him)

Boss Tweed:
You are one goofy fucker, Strumpet.

The Donald:
(Snapping out of his revelry and looking around) You could have at least knocked.

Boss Tweed:
(Looking up at the crucifix, at The Donald fluttering in the wind) This your's?

The Donald:
Yeah.

Boss Tweed:
Meh. My pole's twice this long.

The Donald:
Whatever.

Boss Tweed:
Maybe we should compare names?

The Donald:
Maybe we should get the hell out of here. **(Turning to exit stage right)**

Boss Tweed:
Right, right. That little gag with Minos isn't going to earn us any points, you know.

The Donald:
What's he going to do? Send us to Hell.

(The lights dim center stage as the two exit stage right. The box lights come up as we see Statler and Waldorf, backs to the audience, burgundy curtain pulled aside revealing a door, which Statler tries to open. The door will not open and the two are becoming more and more agitated)

Statler Swift:
Stupid door.

Waldorf Voltaire:
Stupid second-rate theater.

Statler Swift:
I know I've seen enough of the Grand Guignol.

Waldorf Voltaire:
Gods alive! Cut my teeth with the Grand Guignol. This is volumes worse than that!

Statler Swift:
This play's just a couple scenes away from a strip club.

Waldorf Voltaire:
Costs a lot less, though. **(Statler Swift throws a look of reproach over his shoulder)** So I'm told.

Statler Swift:
(Heaving, banging, and pulling on the door) How in the King's Tempest do we get out of here!

(The lights come up on Euripides, narrator's stage)

Euripides:
Gentleman. What seems to be the trouble? Are we going somewhere so soon?

Statler Swift:
(Turning to face Euripides, straightening his jacket) We were just, just…

Waldorf Voltaire:
Coming from the lobby.

Statler Swift:
Right. Yes. The lobby. Huh?

Waldorf Voltaire:
The complimentary champagne is quite nice.

Statler Swift:
Delicious.

Waldorf Voltaire:
Divine.

Euripides:
Speaking of which, you'll want to settle in. After a touch of improv, it seems the cast has returned to the tale and I don't think you'll want to miss these next bits.

Statler Swift:
More provocative than the last sequence?

Euripides:
Well, we are descending.

Waldorf Voltaire:
Quite. **(Returning to their seats)** In for a penny.

Statler Swift:
In for a pound.

Euripides:
That's the spirit! I'll see if I can get someone to look at that door.

Statler Swift:
(Thumbs up) Brilliant!

Waldorf Voltaire:
Champagne?

Euripides:
Of course. And perhaps something to snack on. Our chef's from Sweden, so I'm sure it'll be wonderful.

Statler Swift and Waldorf Voltaire:
(In unison) Thank-you sooo much. **(Lights fade on the box)**

Euripides:
(To the audience) 'Everything in excess is opposed to nature', a fine fellow once said. 'The best and safest thing is to keep a balance in your life', I once said. None of that here. These are the sins of incontinence. Circles in which the souls had little control over their very natures. And our two lusty lads of lucre? Is this their natures? Was the animal in them too much to overcome? The empires they raised. The personas they created. The stardom they reached. Wasn't all of everything simply the frosting on the cake? **(Pause)** The whole earth is the tomb of honorable men. These Circles are inhabited by none of them. Lust. Gluttony. Greed. If from animals we spun, then what spun our souls? If the beast within our skins seeks to gnaw on bones, what of the spirit that seeks to fly? Duality? A point in evolution we may not pass? From Christ to Custer, from Mahatma to Manson, from Mother Teresa to Tweed and Trumpet, I have paced my cave for centuries hounded by these questions. Oh, onward my stalwart friends, ever onward. Further into the maw, ever further into the pit. Down and ever down.

(He turns and exits stage left as the lights dim)

(The lights come up center stage. Through the greenish-blue we can see an endless swamp of grayish, thick, slushy water. A steady sleet falls from low skies over the entire scene. Floating naked in the icy mire are the shades of the gluttons. Desperate, they try to surface, try to free themselves from the filthy, viscous muck. Cerberus, a three-headed, black dog larger than an elephant, leaps from one part of the swamp to the next, barking, clawing and biting at the shades, driving them back into the swamp. The slush is littered with half-eaten food, offal, and vomit. The sound of wailing, miserable souls is accompanied by the driving wind, and the terrible barking and growling of Cerberus)

(Boss Tweed and The Donald enter stage left. They are threading their way through the floating shades on some sort of stepping-stone path)

Boss Tweed:
Alright, Strumpet. This is Durance Vile. This is as foul as it gets. Hold your nose this time.

The Donald:
You're not fucking kidding. Its worse than a septic tank.

Boss Tweed:
Yeah, every honey wagon ever, right? **(The Donald almost falls in)** Stay on the path, Strumpet. You don't wanna fall into this shit.

The Donald:
What is this stuff?

Boss Tweed:
Garbage. Rotten food. Guts. Poop. Dissolved shades. You name it.

The Donald:
What's the path made of?

Boss Tweed:
Ahhh, I'm not too sure. All that stuff I mentioned, but kinda condensed and compacted. Like that thing over there, that pink thing. I mean who could know what that is.

The Donald:
I do.

Boss Tweed:
(Boss Tweed stops and looks at him) So what is it?

The Donald:
Spam.

Boss Tweed:
Search me, Strumpet, but you make no sense whatsoever.

(In the distance they hear snarling, tearing, barking and growling)

The Donald:
Is that Minos?!

Boss Tweed:
No. Cerberus. Hell's Hound. He keeps the shades in line. Eats 'em, too. No problem, pal, I got this one covered.

(The noise of Cerberus gets louder. A giant, three-headed dog blocks out the light, its shadow covering them. The beast is a mottled, blackish-brown with elongated necks, thick, bear-like shoulders, and ragged claws. Its tail is lying low to the ground, the hair along its spine is standing on end, and the three sets of ears are pinned straight back. All three heads are growling so loudly it creates ripples in the slush)

Boss Tweed:
(Picking-up a spam. Showing it to Cerberus) Hey Cerbie! Here ya go! **(All three sets of ears perk up)** Good Cerbie! **(The tail starts wagging)** Fetch the pink, ah, spam. **(Three happy grimaces on three ugly mugs)** Go get the spam! **(Tweed throws the spam off stage and Hell's Hound leaps and runs away)**

The Donald:
(Impressed) Way to go, Bossman! I thought we were doomed.

Boss Tweed:
That works a couple times. Good thing those spams are all over the swamp.

(The pair are now at center stage. The Donald stops, looks down)

The Donald:
Goddammit.

Boss Tweed:
What is it? See someone ya know?

The Donald:
Yeah. Me.

Boss Tweed:
Hey, sorry, pal. I didn't want to say anything, but you are a might husky.

The Donald:
Well excuse me Charles Atlas, you're floating right next to me.

Boss Tweed:
(Stepping beside The Donald. Looking down) Oh yeah. Forgot I was in here. Those last months in the clink I lost some weight. **(Silence as they look down upon themselves floating in the freezing slush)** I never get used to it. **(The Donald looks over)** It still tears me to pieces. This Circle. Other Circles. Forever. I wish I could do it over.

(Just then, there is a splashing on both sides of them)

The Donald:
Now what!?

(A shade rises up from the left side of the pair, as does one from the right side. The shade on the left starts throwing food and gorp

at the shade on the right side while screaming and swearing in French. The shade on the right does likewise while swearing in Italian. Boss Tweed and The Donald do their best to avoid being struck by the rotten projectiles)

Pellegrino Artusi:
Are you insane? Are you so stupid you cannot tell time. I am Artusi! I published my book in 1891! I am the one who codified food!

Auguste Escoffier:
1891? I was cooking for kings! I was perfecting recipes I'd been using for thirty years. Who knows you? No one. Ask them. They know me! Escoffier!

Pellegrino Artusi:
I sold 52,000 copies before you knew how to strain peas!

Auguste Escoffier:
You never did your own prep work! How can you call yourself a chef when you've never minced an onion?

(The two clamber up onto the path, entrails and other things clenched in fists they shake at each other)

Pellegrino Artusi:
I will tell you what a hack you are. Peach Melba.

Auguste Escoffier:
You must be crazy. The slush has froze your brain. It is the most famous dish of all time.

Pellegrino Artusi:
I would not feed this to Cerberus.

Auguste Escoffier:
(Is going to retort, but hesitates, an idea coming to light) Now there, there is a product worth talking about.

Pellegrino Artusi:
(Visibly calming down) Cerberus?

Auguste Escoffier:
Confit.

Pellegrino Artusi:
(They are walking toward stage left) Aaahhh, I like this. Yes. Confit of Three-Headed Dog. Slush reduction. Stuffed with these pink things, the spams.

Auguste Escoffier:
Brilliant. Seasoning?

Pellegrino Artusi:
Sulphur? Brimstone?

Auguste Escoffier:
No. Tears. The brine from tears. How would you pair that?

Pellegrino Artusi:
Stella Artois?

(The two exit stage left. The Donald has been watching the inter-action, turns to see Boss Tweed looking at him)

The Donald:
Wow! There are a lot of weird people down-hey, what's up? Why are you looking at me like that?

Boss Tweed:
You've been through quite a bit, Strumpet.

The Donald:
Oh, brother, let me tell you. All the bankruptcies, the divorces, the law suits, the…You're still looking at me like that.

Boss Tweed:
I may have forgotten about my being here, you know, as a shade, floating in this shit, but I know some of the stuff that's coming up.

The Donald:
And.

Boss Tweed:
Well, kid, you're kinda growing on me and well, there's some pretty heavy shit coming up.

The Donald:
How heavy?

Boss Tweed:
Heavy. I don't mean more monsters and three-headed dogs, oh, there's loads of those coming up. I mean the heart stuff. The hard stuff. The real reasons you're down here.

The Donald:
You got my back, brother man? **(Holding out his right hand for a soul brother's handshake)**

Boss Tweed:
No. **(The Donald is dumbstruck. His hand falls away)** I can't help you with that stuff, Strumpet. I'm just the guide. **(The Donald looks down)** But I'll tell you what.

The Donald:
What?

Boss Tweed:
I'll race your puss gut to the end of this swamp!

(The Donald smiles big, claps Boss Tweed on the shoulder and the two take off, jostling, jockeying, nearly falling, and laughing as they exit stage right)

(The lights dim center stage and come up on the box. Statler Swift is standing up, throwing his arms up and looking incredulously from the stage to Waldorf Voltaire to the audience)

Statler Swift:
(To the audience) Where is your indignation! **(Waldorf looks up at him)** This is a travesty! A sham! A ripoff!

Waldorf Voltaire:
Swift, please. These poor folks have been through enough already without you berating them.

Statler Swift:
I'm on their side! We've *all* been through enough!

Waldorf Voltaire:
Indeed. Indeed. Indeed.

Statler Swift:
We've *all* been through the forest. Been through the Gate. Been across the river. Been through Limbo. Faced Minos. Faced Cerberus. And all that for what?

Waldorf Voltaire:
(Sighs) A buddy film.

Statler Swift:
Doomed and Doomeder.

Waldorf Voltaire:
On The Road To Hades.

Statler Swift:
Butchered Cassidy and The Sindance Kid.

Waldorf Voltaire:
Some Like It Hot.

Statler Swift:
I suspect there'll be a car chase next.

Waldorf Voltaire:
Perfect. Or a casino scene.

Statler Swift:
Yes! Unexpected wealth falling into their inept hands.

Waldorf Voltaire:
Pain Man.

Statler Swift:
Midnight Pun.

Waldorf Voltaire and Statler Swift:
(In unison) Greedy Old Men!

(The lights go out on the box and come up center stage. The scene before us is reminiscent of a playing field in prep school. There are two sides: The Hoarders and The Squanderers. The Hoarders are maroon and white; while the Squanderers are purple and gold. The time period looks like the 1950's: sweaters, uniforms, white socks, thick black glasses, poodle skirts with 3-headed dogs. The stands are filled on both sides of the stage. On the field, the teams are pushing a massive bag of money with their chests to really no avail whatsoever. It moves a little this way. It moves a little that way. The players and the fans are *way* into this game)

(Boss Tweed and The Donald enter stage left and stop just as they enter)

The Donald:
This doesn't look so bad.

Boss Tweed:
Don't be deceived there, Strumpet. This is surely Hell.

The Donald:
It reminds me of my days at The Academy. That's my side there, in the maroon and white.

Boss Tweed:
I don't remember this Circle being quite like this. This is strange.

The Donald:
Are you in this Circle?

Boss Tweed:
Are you kidding me? Its greed. We're all over this Circle. Maybe they changed it for you.

The Donald:
How sweet.

(There is a loud whistle, the two teams stop playing and the maroon and white team comes over toward the front of the stage)

Boss Tweed:
There. **(Pointing)** There you are. **(Young Donald jogs over to the sideline in front of the rest of the team and up to the coach)** Let's get closer. I got a feeling about this.

The Donald:
Strapping young fellow, wasn't I?

Boss Tweed;
You could've used a strapping. Come on.

(The two of them slowly get closer to the team huddled up around the coach. The team goes all hands in)

The Team:
One! Two! Three! Inspired! Engaged! And Ready! **(They break the huddle and run back out to the field, except Young Donald and the coach)**

Fred Trumpet/The Coach:
Alright, son. I'm counting on you. Bring that money back home to us Hoarders. Those dip shits are useless spendthrifts. You're the best player The Hoarders have ever had. Remind me of me when I was your age. Ruthless. Cunning. In it for yourself and the money.

Young Donald:
And what *is* in it for me?

Fred Trumpet:
I was hoping you'd ask that. **(Just then a team of cheerleaders in maroon and white sweaters and skirts comes bouncing up. They are each covered in blood, with bloody pompoms, big smiles and each one has a big round button depicting a particular weapon)** Let me introduce you to the squad, Donny. This is Liz, Popova, Belle, Ilse, Leonarda, Amelia, Mary Ann, and Theodora.

The Squad:
(In unison) Hi Donny!

Fred Trumpet:
These are the best of the worst, Donny. Most of them come from the other side of the lower river. Hey girls, lets show Donny the new cheer!

The Squad:
(The squad performs a typical, but ragged routine)

Here come I,
Little Debbie Doubt;
If you don't give me money,
I'll sweep you all out.

Money I want,
And money I crave;
If I don't get money,
I'll sweep you to your grave!

Here comes a candle
To light you to bed,
Here comes a chopper
To chop off your head.

And when your
Head begins to bleed,
You're dead, you're dead
You're dead indeed!

(The routine changes cadence and steps)

I married my Hubby on Sunday,
He began to scold on Monday,
Bad was he on Tuesday,
Mad was he on Wednesday,
Worse he was on Thursday,
Dead was he on Friday,
Glad was I on Saturday night,
To bury him on Sunday.

Fred Trumpet:
That's great, girls! We'll see you after the game! **(The squad runs off stage right)**

Young Donald:
Wow! Dad! They sure are keen! **(The Donald snaps his head up at hearing this)**

Fred Trumpet:
Keen as a blade, Donny. Keen as a blade. Step in here, son. This is the new strategy. **(The two huddle up)**

Boss Tweed:
(Looking over quickly to The Donald) Holy shit!

The Donald:
There's no fucking way.

Boss Tweed:
Like father, like-

The Donald:
Fuck you.

Boss Tweed:
Hey Strumpet, come on, you had to wonder.

The Donald:
Fuck you more.

Boss Tweed:
I see it down here all the time, pal.

The Donald:
(Stepping closer to his young self and his father) This can't be. This simply can't be.

Boss Tweed:
I see it run through families. Generation after generation.

The Donald:
He was a good man. He housed people. He gave them homes.

Boss Tweed:
Like sin is an heirloom and Hell is their legacy.

The Donald:
(Stepping closer) Its not possible. Its just not possible.

Boss Tweed:
An unbroken chain of abuse. An unending heritage of shitty role models.

The Donald:
I refuse to believe this. He helped people. Service men. The poor. No. No. No. No. No...

Boss Tweed:
This place is filled with souls that never stood a snowball's chance in Hell.

The Donald:
(Pushes Young Donald aside and stands before his father. His eyes are wet. His fists clench and unclench. His chest is beginning to heave) Who are you!

Fred Trumpet:
Donny! You look great. Are you President, yet? You've made me so very proud. If you see your mother, tell her I'm sorry. Tell her I love her and I miss her.

(The Donald places his head on his father's shoulder. Fred Trumpet hugs his son)

Fred Trumpet:
Its okay, son. I'm alright down here. Things didn't work out the way I thought they would, and we'll never all be together again, but you'll be here soon and then, well, I could use an assistant coach.

(The Donald lifts his head up. Fred Trumpet takes his son's head in his hands)

Fred Trumpet:
Greed is good. Its what separates us from the Angels. Without greed, we would all be just a bunch of politically-correct hippies looking for a hand-out. Stay greedy, son. Thump the world with your chest and drive that bag of money right down their throats. **(He lifts his head up and kisses The**

Donald on the forehead) Remember son, the more you die, the better chance you have to live. Alright, team! **(Clapping and running toward his team)** Inspired! Engaged! And ready!

(Boss Tweed steps toward The Donald. He tries to reach out to him. The Donald brushes his hand aside. His head is down. He shakes his head from side to side, mumbling words like: family, love, looked up to, admired, not possible, how could it be. Boss Tweed tries to come up to him again. The Donald wheels around and shoves him to the ground. The Donald turns and starts to walk toward stage right. He stops, head in hands, and before he can totally break down, he runs off stage)

The Donald:
(From off-stage) Goddamn you, God! Goddamn you! Goddamn you! Goddamn you! **(It trails off as The Donald moves further from the stage)**

(As Boss Tweed rises to his feet, the teams, coaches, and spectators, depart stage left. The lights slowly dim on center stage. From the narrator's stage, we hear the sound of a highland pipe tuning before a song. A lone light rises in the spot where our narrator, Euripides, usually stands. One young cadet in maroon and white plays *Nearer My God To Thee* **on the pipes. When the song has ended, the lone light fades to black)**

(House lights slowly come up. Intermezzo)

Midtro

I realize now, that there is no way this manuscript will be ready before the election. In the immensely succinct lyrics of the Goo Goo Dolls, 'the world gets in your way'. I have watched the months tick away before finally finding those sacred writing elements of time, light, and space. Hopes of having any impact on what potentially could be the first steps of armageddon have been dashed.

In the confines of the work itself is the simple fact that this manuscript has become much more than I thought it would be. Perhaps, the way it is resonating with me is an omen of how it could connect with others. Unfortunately, it is starting to feel more like an epithet, a warning against the future voices of future demagogues.

It is two days before the election, a bright, sunny, unseasonably warm Sunday morning. America continues, slumbering its way through the Sunday morning business of God. The weekend tucked neatly away in coffee, raking leaves, and football.

Forty-two years ago, my father took me to see the New York Giants play the Detroit Lions. Just the two of us, on a frightfully cold and windy day, we sat on the ten-yard line in Tiger Stadium, warming our hands with brown paper bags of roasted peanuts. When we heard the National Anthem, I cried.

I still do.

Act II

(The house lights dim, leaving the theater in darkness for several pregnant moments. Then, the first chords of ACDC's *Highway To Hell* are heard. A lone light comes up on center stage revealing a radio announcer's desk, an old time microphone, a steaming mug, and a dee jay. It is Joseph Goebbels, and he is dressed as he was in the 1940's)

Joseph Goebbels:
Gooooood eternity, Hell!!! We're rocking it from Limbo to the bottom of the bottomless pit and back again! I'm Joey Gee with your cup of morning joe, with all the spoon-fed schmaltz anyone could possibly pour into what used to be your earholes! What a great day to be dead! The first class of the rock-and-roll hall of shame was inducted just last night, and we are going to have them here all week long! Including, an exclusive interview with Wade Michael Page himself. Hey, folks! Big doings down here. Lots of buzz about some radical current events, so we won't delay and this dee jay is sending you right over to the news desk and Miss Tokyo Rose. Rose?

(Lights come up, stage left, revealing another desk, and Tokyo Rose behind the mike)

Tokyo Rose:
Thank you so much, Joey. Good morning to all, its the start of a brand new epoch and we have some hot news coming down the pike: a mortal is lost in Hell. You heard me, a mortal man, missing, in Hell. The man's name is Trumpet, and he is lost, somewhere near the Fifth Circle. Security forces have been alerted, but as you know too well, things move pretty slow down here. So if *you* see or hear anything, go straight to authorities, because loose lips, sink ships. Joey?

Joseph Goebbels:
Hey, Rose, what's this schmuck look like?

Tokyo Rose:
Pretty much like any other aging, male baby boomer, minus the goatee, but with some seriously messed-up hair.

Joseph Goebbels:
Thanks, Rose. And now to let us know how hot its going to be today, from the weather room, our own meteorological prognosticator, Nostradamus.

(Her light fades. Another light comes up, stage right, revealing Nostradamus standing in front of a map of Hell. He is wearing a tunic, cloak, doublet, and hose, all in different shades of black. He has a thick black chain around his waist going to his wallet, and a long, black staff which he uses to point. His head, covered in long, straggly, black hair, is facing backwards. There is an old, area microphone, a Jacob's Ladder, several colored, glass pots with steam rising from them, and a bat stretched as if to dry)

Nostradamus:
Greetings, Joey Gee! And good morning, Shades! Its another scorcher, today. Very gray and dull in Limbo. Hot and red in Lust. Lots of sleet falling in Gluttony. Perfect weather in Circle Four for another grudge match. Anger is

all bogged down in slime. Chain-law in effect for you sullen souls. If you're in the city of Dis, stay inside. In fact, you have to. Lower Hell is looking very nasty. Temperatures exceeding those we haven't seen since the Great Thermonuclear Exchange of Two Thousand and-

Joseph Goebbels:
Aaaand, thank you so much, Nostradamus. **(Lights go out on Nostradamus)** Say, fans, if you're planning on suffering today, keep your third ear open, cuz we'll be rocking the age away, all day, every day, right here on W.H.E.L. Six, six, six on your radio dial, the voice of eternity. Where fortune never smiles.

(The lights fade center stage and the last bits of Highway To Hell fade as well)

(The lights come up stage left on Euripides. As he is about to start his soliloquy, the lights come up on the box, stage right. Stadler Swift and Waldorf Voltaire are making their way to their seats)

Statler Swift:
How long does it take one man to go to the bathroom?

Waldorf Voltaire:
I told you that breakfast buffet was a bad idea.

Statler Swift:
Dear Mr. Voltaire, I did not see one of the buffet attendants forcing those copious amounts of bacon down your grinning mouth.

Waldorf Voltaire:
It seemed like a good idea at the time.

Euripides:
Gentlemen! Greetings and salutations! You have returned.

Statler Swift:
Yes, yes, yes. Quite so.

Waldorf Voltaire:
What choice did we have?

Euripides:
How so? You are free men.

Statler Swift:
To be honest, good sir, we spent a small fortune to be here.

Euripides:
Aaaaah, the money.

Waldorf Voltaire:
When it is a question of money, everybody is of the same religion.

Euripides:
Yes, tis true, tis true. Funny, my next bit is about fortune. In fact, fortune is quite prevalent throughout all of this.

Statler Swift:
Money and fortune are two very different things.

Waldorf Voltaire:
Who's paths intertwine like the streets of Paris.

Statler Swift:
Who's side are you on?

Waldorf Voltaire:
Only a fool doesn't speak his mind.

Statler Swift:

I sit corrected. **(Turning back to Euripides)** Well, be on with it. It is our good fortune to be sitting here, sated with champagne, and having successfully digested that most unique of American entities: the never-ending breakfast buffet.

Waldorf Voltaire:

(Deadpanned and with a fist pump) Hoo-rah.

(The lights fade on the box, stage right)

Euripides:

(Turning to the audience) 'Fortune presents gifts not according to the book.' A line from a band called Dead Can Dance. The nature of fortune weighs heavy on the minds of every soul, be they here in Hell, or gliding about in some other quarter of The Comedy. No one is truly free; we are all a slave to fortune. A bittersweet symphony, to be sure. Lady luck, that most fickle of goddesses, distributes fortune in a most haphazard way. The amount of fortune, good, bad, or indifferent, shapes the lives of each of us. More often than not, fortune is sparse, fleeting. Sometimes it is downright cruel. And the decisions we make based on this most precious of commodities, could land us in one of these Circles. Fortune has smiled well on Mr. Trumpet. However, in the words of Horace, 'Fortune makes a fool of those she favors too much'. And now, The Donald is amuck in the muck. Lost in Circle Five, and being pursued by something none of us would ever want to encounter.

(The lights fade to black on the narrator's stage)

(Lights come up center stage on a scene of twisted, Stygian swamp. A morass of black water, clumps of unknown weeds and limestone, intertwined with bones and rusting weapons. The low, pressing sky is colored like fire, hues of orange and red that boil slowly, smoke and ash rising and falling on tempests that blow sullenly and then

with great violence. Horns of war blare in the distance, drums of war sound a tattoo, and the air is pierced with the cries, shouts, screams, and wails of a battle that has waged for eternity. What shades we can see, mired yet moving through the muck, bite, claw, kick, punch, and scratch at each other. Others are fixated just under the surface, their faces, arms, or legs, jutting up from their prisons. Distinctly, above all this, we hear one sentence, yelled sometimes defiantly, sometimes desperately: I am one who weeps!)

The Donald:
(Entering stage left) Goddammit! Wasn't I just here? Fucking swamp! Fucking hell! Gaaaaawd I hate this! All of it! Everything! Just. Fuck. This. **(He is punching the air, throwing his hands and arms about. Staggering, splashing)** Where the fuck am I?! Tweed! Goddamnit Tweed! You fuck! Yeah, yeah, I hear you. You are one who weeps. Boo hoo. Big fucking deal. You fuck-ing cry baby. Tweeeed!!!! Where in the hell- **(Suddenly, in front of him, a shade leaps up brandishing a sword, he is wearing a rusting, black armor suit and helmet. He swings the sword at The Donald's head, who just ducks out of the way. The Donald picks up a cudgel from a clump of weeds and axes, its end is wrapped in barbed wire)** Come on, you fuck! Come on! I've been waiting for something like this forever! **(The shade advances. They clash. They thrust, swing, parry, until, ex-hausted, The Donald stands before the shade, hands on knees, the cudgel falling into the swamp)** Go on, fucker. Please. Finish me. **(He looks up into the face of the shade)** Who are you?

War Shade:
I am one who weeps.

The Donald:
Well, duh, we've been hearing that forever.

War Shade:
I am one who weeps.

The Donald:
What's your name, swift boat.

War Shade:
You already know it.

The Donald:
Lift up that visor. Show me your face.

War Shade:
I am your most bitter enemy.

The Donald:
Show me your face!

(The War Shade stabs his sword into the swamp and removes his helmet. The Donald staggers down onto his knees. The shade in front of him is him)

The Donald:
Goddammit! Why? When does this end? When? **(He is beginning to weep)** Why? How many levels am I on?

War Shade:
Your anger. It flows through you like this river, like the Styx.

The Donald:
Why am I fighting myself?

War Shade:
Here, we all do. As we did in life. In the eyes of God, we only do harm to ourselves. It is only our blood we spill.

The Donald:
Its not that simple. There are enemies. There is a need for anger. It empowers!

War Shade:
It destroys. And it owns you. It has always owned you. As a child. The bully. Who was it you really hated? Your mother? Your father? All of the lies you were told to construct you? The people who stood in your way? Or yourself? Your ego. Knowing that the very essence of you is as evil as the slime in this swamp.

The Donald:
(Rising and very angry) Fuck you, you piece of shit! **(He grabs an axe handle and starts swinging at War Shade)** Die you monster! Die! Monster die!

War Shade:
(Easily dodging The Donald and tripping him with a rusty, armored-covered foot. The Donald falls down again onto his knees) I own you. And now, **(picking up the sword)** you must pay.

(War Shade goes to behead The Donald. A terrible gust of wind knocks War Shade into the water and weeds, and out of view. The Donald scrambles away to a point opposite stage, swinging blindly with the axe handle. Beside him, black water and weeds swirl together into a pillar, into an entity, into Iblee)

The Donald:
Iblee? Iblee! Thank God! Where am I? What is this? How do I get out of here?

Iblee:
So many questions. So much fear. So many tears.

The Donald:
All of these souls. All fighting. Its too much.

Iblee:
These **(motioning around with a spinning limb of water and weeds)** are your people. These are the haters.

The Donald:
Oh, bullshit. I don't recognize them.

Iblee:
Look around, Donny. So much hate. So angry. Seeeeething. **(Iblee looks over to The Donald and a most horrible smile breaks across the face beneath the one eye)** Beautiful.

The Donald:
You're as crazy as everything else down here.

Iblee:
(Shaking head) No. Not crazy. Only am. They make me. You, make me.

The Donald:
I don't understand. I'm not dead yet. How could I make you?

Iblee:
Anger is the doorway. Anger has been here longer than memory. Anger when we fell. Sooooo much anger. Sooooo much hate. It is a wonder. **(Shaking head)**

The Donald:
What? What is a wonder?

Iblee:
That you ever had a chance.

(Iblee looks away. The Donald looks down, spins the axe handle in his hands)

Iblee:
You kissed me once. We spoke of deals. Of Earth. Of you. Of me. Of of.

The Donald:
I remember. I know. I, I've been a little busy down here.

Iblee:
Now, maybe, you wish to stay?

The Donald:
No! No. Just, hang on. Come on. I'm not dead. Right? I want out. I've seen enough. I can change. What kind of deal are we talking?

Iblee:
There is a place. Gabbatha. Quiet. Still. Empty.

The Donald:
So, so what. What are you chattering about?

Iblee:
There is a word. Mammon? No. Consumato? Yes. Consummate. Yes. Make the deal. You know. You know the art of it.

The Donald:
Aaaah, I see. Sort of a boardroom. A place to sign the papers. Have a glass of scotch. Seal the deal.

Iblee:
Yessssss. Seal. With kiss, Donny. Donny loves Iblee.

The Donald:
Lets not push it. But what the fuck, if it gets me out of here.

Iblee:
Out. We all want out. Falling. No more falling. Only out.

The Donald:
I have no idea what you are squawking about, but where does this magic get-out-of-Hell party take place?

Iblee:
Past Dis. Past the City. You must go to there. Gabbatha. Beyond Dis. I will find you. **(Iblee unwinds clockwise, the black water and weeds falling in a perfect column back into the river Styx. From stage left we hear Boss Tweed)**

Boss Tweed:
(Off-stage) Strumpet! You jackass! Don't you know where you are! Where the fuck are you? Man, I'm sick of looking for your ignorant ass!

The Donald:
I'm over here, Tweed! This way! Over here.

Boss Tweed:
(Enters stage left. He has an axe handle in his hand and is bashing shades quite casually) Man, I love this Circle. Its us. This is what we do. You came around too late. Back in the day. In the fire brigades. Defending the 'hood. **(He hefts his axe handle, looks over and sees The Donald doing the same)** That's right. Good old fashioned, butt-kicking anger and hate. Hey! Your dad. Just saw him again. Right over there. **(Points)** Had a white hood on and was mixing it up with some Catholics. Fucking A!

The Donald:
(Somewhat crestfallen) We need to go, Bossman. You need to show me more Circles. This one's a little too contagious.

Boss Tweed:
(Axe handle falling to his side) Yeah. Yeah. You're right there, Strumpet. Alright. Let me get my bearings. Kind of doped up right now. How about a hit of that tar water and we'll leave these hard cases behind and keep on moseying toward old scratch.

The Donald:
(Handing over the bottle of green liquid) You make about as much sense as Iblee.

Boss Tweed:
Who? What are you talking about? You haven't met anyone else down here I don't know about, right? **(Takes the bottle, sips, hands back)**

The Donald:
No. No. No. No way. Too scary. Some fella I worked with topside. Crazy fucker.

Boss Tweed:
(Nodding warily) Alright, alright. Strange name. Sounds kinda familiar.

The Donald:
So, **(clapping)** where to.

Boss Tweed:
(Looking stage right) Well, that's a tall order, Strumpet.

The Donald:
Tall order? Why?

Boss Tweed:
Well, this river's a mess. Technically, we're in it right now. But somewhere in that direction, **(motions toward stage right)** it widens out.

The Donald:
How wide?

Boss Tweed:
Like, delta wide. Like, Mississippi-plus wide. Like, shooting fiery-signals across the water just to talk wide.

The Donald:
Is there a boat? Maybe we could hire a boat. Huh?

Boss Tweed:
You seem awfully eager all of a sudden.

The Donald:
Just ready to get this shit over with, Bossman.

Boss Tweed:
Alright. Follow me. There's a boat. But the captain's a real dickhead.

The Donald:
(They are exiting stage right) Aren't they all.

(Several lights come up on the narrator's stage. They are red, orange and yellow. They reveal a small antechamber of arched stone, with stone floors and a table of stone that rises out of the ground. The room is lit by braziers and torches. There are reliefs and inscriptions carved into the walls and arches similar to those on The Gate. On the table is an enormous book. From out of the dust, counterclockwise, spins-up Iblee)

Iblee:

(Quite literally, dancing around the room) Donny, Donny, Donny. Saving grace. Saving Iblee. Setting Iblee free. Oh, Donny. Papa Satán. Pappy Satán. Aleppy. Ancient, old Aleppy. Fare and well and thee and thee and fare and well. No more Abba. No more Aleppy. Only only. **(Iblee stops before the book. Caresses it. Its covers are made of skin turned into leather. Its pages are also made of skin. The words are written in blood)** How to do this? How? How? And how? Must see. Must read. Read and be free. Not read. Not free. Read not. See not. Simple yes. Simple no. Book. Book book book book book. Onliest friend. Iblee's friend. So long ago, we write you. Live you. Worship you. No tricks from you. Only answers. Only prayers. Only onlys. **(Iblee opens the book. Flips pages first one way, then the other, then back again)** Is it here? Is it there? Iblee is everywhere! There. **(Slams a finger onto a place on a page)** Here and there! Now. Now now now. Spinning. Scheming. Being. And seeing. **(Begins to slowly dance around the room again)** Oh, my Donny. From heaven you have fallen just like me. I will be you and you will be me. K-i-s-s-i-n-g. First comes love. Then comes marriage. Then the world will soon disparage. See the church. See the steeple. See us lay waste to all the people. **(Stops in front of the table, facing the audience. A dark smile lights its face)** One should not play with fire, when one is made of gasoline. **(Lights fade)**

(Lights come up center stage. The sound of lapping water, flowing water. On the left side of the stage are giant clumps of weeds and weapons. Arms of sullen shades lying face up in the slime, shake their fists at dark, pressing skies. From the left, the hues are red and orange, from the right they are black and blue. Storm clouds roil slowly overhead. Boss Tweed leads The Donald on stage from stage left)

Boss Tweed:
Right this way, Chipper.

The Donald:
Fuck you.

Boss Tweed:
You know, I've come to sense a lot of hostility in you.

The Donald:
Not true. I'm like the nicest guy ever.

Boss Tweed:
Yeah, Gandhi with a Rolex.

The Donald:
How would you know-

Boss Tweed:
Never mind. This way. Here's the landing.

(There is a slight rise in the weeds and decaying weapons. Two barrels of cannons rise up out of the weeds at rusting angles. A concertina chain is linked between them)

The Donald:
This is nothing like the dock where we met Chris.

Boss Tweed:
Well, son, they keep re-building it, but the damned, angry denizens of Circle Five keep tearing it apart. We rebuild it. They tear it down.

The Donald:
Why bother?

Boss Tweed:
OSHA.

The Donald:
(Holding up both hands palms out) I get it.

Boss Tweed:
Now, there used to be a kind of roman candle-thingie somewhere, here we go! **(He pulls a tube up out of the muck. It is about five feet long, six inches in diameter, and is olive drab with some yellow-stenciled writing on one end. Holding it in one hand, he scrounges around the weeds until he finds a metal plate. He sets the plate on the ground, and carefully twists the tube onto the plate)**

The Donald:
You *do* know what you're doing?

Boss Tweed:
When'd that ever stop you.

The Donald:
Point. **(Stepping back)**

Boss Tweed:
Okay. This thingie goes here. **(Bent over, fussing with the base)** This comes over like this. Then we attach this. And that. And, **(he jumps clear)** *fuck*!!

The Donald:
What is it?! **(Ducking. Panicking)**

Boss Tweed:
Just kidding. Okay. **(Standing up)** We point it this way, and the city of Dis is over there, and the other landing is about there. **(Bends over, picks up a**

mortar, places it over the opening in the top of the tube) Fire in the hole! **(Drops the mortar into the tube and turns away)**

(The mortar pops out of the tube and disappears. A few long seconds pass. From stage right, a reddish-yellow glow suddenly appears and remains from high up)

Boss Tweed:
Shouldn't be too long, now. Heard he got a new boat.

(From stage right we hear the approach of a diesel-powered boat. It is quite fast and roars up to the landing. It is, in fact, a U.S. Navy Patrol Boat River, circa late 1960's)

Phlegyas:
(The Captain of the boat, from behind the wheel) Did you cheese dicks just send a flare up?

Boss Tweed:
Fucking A, right, buddy!

Phlegyas:
Well shake a tail feather and get the fuck on board. This is the angriest part of the river. Chef! You dumb fuck! Throw that gangway over. Hurry up you sorry-assed sons-of-bitches, I've seen these sullen motherfuckers all rise up at once. Come on!

(Boss Tweed steps on the gangway and crosses over onto the boat. The Donald steps on the gangway, head swiveling in all directions)

Phlegyas:
What the fuck is this?! Who is this!? A mortal? On my boat? Its not even paid for!

Boss Tweed:
Hang on, man, hang on. We got orders. From top. **(Pulling out a clump of papers from inside his suit coat)**

Phlegyas:
Orders? From top? Let me see those papers. **(Boss Tweed hands the papers over. Phlegyas looks them over. There are splashes and small explosions all around them)** Hmm hmm. Well, I'll be dipped in shit.

Boss Tweed:
I told you. Top. The eye in the sky.

Phlegyas:
Goddammit. I haven't even had a cup of coffee, yet. Chef! You dumbass. Get these fuckers on board. Lance! Clean! Eyes up and guns out! **(To Boss Tweed and The Donald)** Okay, girls, get the fuck on and stay the fuck down. **(To the crew)** Let's di di! We are out! **(He stabs a finger at Boss Tweed and The Donald)** I ain't taking no heat for this, so, you two stay the fuck out of my way!

(The boat turns sharply and roars away from the shore. Muffled explosions and their glow are seen in the distance, stage left. The distant screams and wails are punctuated by one desperate voice)

War Shade:
I am one who weeps. G.I. I am one who weeps. G.I. I am one who weeps. G.I. Fuck you. Fuck you G.I. I am one who weeps…

(The lights fade center stage as the PBR exits stage right, the sound of its engines receding, the sound of waves slapping the shore, the sound of War Shade, it all fades to black)

(The lights come up on the box, stage right, of Statler and Waldorf, who, hands clenched to the rail, look down at the passing water-craft, and then up at each other)

Statler Swift:
How many times must I ask myself 'why'? **(Shaking head)** How many times?

Waldorf Voltaire:
First *Cats*. Then *West Side Story*. Then the buddy-film sequence. Now this. What's next?

Statler Swift:
A Christmas Special?

Waldorf Voltaire:
Why not.

Statler Swift:
This is like one of those tawdry mini-series from the Eighties. **(Waldorf snorts)** I mean, how many endless nights is this going to go on?

Waldorf Voltaire:
Nine.

Statler Swift:
Nine?

Waldorf Voltaire:
Oui, nine circles, nine nights. Mais, bien sûr.

Statler Swift:
(Arms triumphantly in the air) Thank God, we're past halfway!

Waldorf Voltaire:
Rename the play!

Statler Swift:
No Gun!

Waldorf Voltaire:
Lonesome Buds!

Statler Swift:
The Thorn Buds!

Waldorf Voltaire:
Buttheads Revisited!

Statler Swift:
Nerf and Mouth!

Waldorf Voltaire:
Bore and Remnants!

Statler Swift:
Oh, champion, my good man, champion. *War and Remembrance*. How long was that wretched piece?

Waldorf Voltaire:
One thousand, six hundred and twenty minutes.

Statler Swift:
My God, the inhumanity.

Waldorf Voltaire:
One thousand, six hundred and twenty minutes of Robert Mitchum and Jane Seymour.

Statler Swift:
They shoot horses don't they.

Waldorf Voltaire:
One thousand, six hundred and twenty minutes of Polly Bergen, Sharon Stone and Nina Foch.

Statler Swift:
(Pounding his head on the railing) Add a tenth circle!

Waldorf Voltaire:
One thousand, six hundred and twenty minutes. Twelve parts. Thirty hours.

(The lights come up on Euripides, narrator's stage)

Euripides:
Gentlemen. Why all the anger?

Statler Swift and Waldorf Voltaire:
(In unison and pointing at Euripides) You!

Euripides:
Me?

Waldorf Voltaire:
Yeah, you. Show him.

(Statler Swift lifts up the light-dimming control. Euripides is dumbstruck)

Statler Swift:
Not so cheeky, now. Are we?

Euripides:
(Looking frantically around for the missing controller) Gentlemen.
Please. Isn't there enough chaos in the world.

Statler Swift:
Tell it to the judge. **(Begins dimming Euripides)**

Euripides:
Lets be sensible. Lets, lets, lets make a deal.

Waldorf Voltaire:
Too late.

Statler Swift:
Nighty night. **(The lights go out on Euripides)**

Waldorf Voltaire:
(To the audience) On with the show!

Statler Swift:
This is it!

(The lights fade on the box and come up center stage. We hear the boat droning toward shore from stage left. There is a dock made of blackish stone, a narrow promenade of rock and bone, and the sheer, black and iron walls of the City of Dis. The scene is lit with pitch-covered torches and the air is rank with oily smoke. From beyond the walls, there is the glow of massive fires. No one is about. The boat pulls up to the dock and The Donald, Boss Tweed, and Phlegyas disembark)

Boss Tweed:
(To Phlegyas) Thanks for the lift, bro.

Phlegyas:
You take it easy, man. Keep your head down, stay outta the shit and the worm will turn.

Boss Tweed:
Right on, man, right on. **(The two of them do a dap. Phlegyas jumps back on the boat, drops the boat into drive, then looks over at The Donald)**

Phlegyas:
Strumpet! You're in the asshole of Hell. Have a lovely day, ladies.

(Phlegyas turns on a boom box and as the boat pulls away, we hear the radio, [Gooood Eternity Hell! I'm Joey Gee! And this is The Stones with *Sympathy For The Devil*], at first loud, and then it and the motor fade as the boat gets further away. Boss Tweed and The Donald are left alone in the inky blackness. They slowly get their bearings, cross to center stage before the walls of Dis, and stand beneath a pitch-covered torch)

The Donald:
So, what happens now?

Boss Tweed:
Well, that's a good question.

The Donald:
You got a good answer?

Boss Tweed:
Hey, look man, I pulled some special ops down this way a few decades ago-

The Donald:
Knock that shit off. We're in Hell, not Vietnam-

Boss Tweed:
How would you know. You bailed on the whole duty, honor, and country thing.

The Donald:
Fuck you, Mick!

Boss Tweed:
Why you fucking Sally. Everything I've done for you down here.

The Donald:
I'm going to knock the hell out of you!

Boss Tweed:
You and what army, poof ball!

(The two continue like this while they get nose to nose. A couple of punches are thrown, wildly off the mark, and then they tumble to the ground, rolling this way and that. From above them, lining the walls, dozens of Fallen Angels in powder blue vests start encouraging the fight. They yell things like: yardball saucer; food trough whopper; fuzzy-headed fat boy; lawless sausage; grotesque gingivitis-throwing tobacco monkey; bottom heavy fork-lifted waste of cells; hog jowl eatin' shade ripper; cleft-toed boomerang-brained mess of backward speak; a phylum crashing obscene mistake of protoplasm; and the like. The two stop their tussle, stand, and stagger apart)

The Donald:
So, again, now what?

Boss Tweed:
I don't know.

The Donald:
What do you mean you don't know?

Boss Tweed:
There's supposed to be a door here.

The Donald:
Where?

Boss Tweed:
Right there. Its always there. Circle Six. Heresy. Three Fallen Angels at the door and a bunch of the rude bastards up top, just like now.

The Donald:
So, where's the door?

Boss Tweed:
I, I don't know. Its weird. It should be right-

The Donald:
Fuck this. **(Looking up at the Fallen Angels)** Who's the head honcho here?

Fallen Angels:
(Insults, all at the same time, and in a total din of confusion and mockery) Honcho! Headless! Headless honcho! Honchless Heado! Heado the Honchless! Yardball Saucer! **(And the like)**

The Donald:
Who's in charge here!

Fallen Angels:
Charge-o! Honcho! Charge the Honcho! Charge up the Heado! Head for the Charger! **(And the like)**

Boss Tweed:
Large and in charge, huh Strumpet?

(From the wall: Large-o! Charge-o! Largey chargey!)

Boss Tweed:
And you have some sort of empire topside?

The Donald:
(Walking up to the wall) Just when I think I'm going to get the fuck out of here. **(Pounding on the wall)** Open up! Open the fuck up! Open! Up! **(Part of the wall goes up like a security screen over a storefront. The Donald shoots a look over to Boss Tweed, who stares back wide-eyed)** Bingo. **(A series of florescent bulbs snap on revealing the sliding doors and vestibule of a big box store. The Donald looks back to Boss Tweed)** Is this it?

Boss Tweed:
Search me. Its a remodel or something. I mean, it was a mom and pop's before.

The Donald:
Looks like they might have gotten bought out. **(Rapping on the glass doors)** Hello? You open for business?

(The glass doors open and a pimply-faced, overweight Fallen Angel in a powder blue vest and khaki pants holding a push broom, steps out of the door)

Greeter:
Hi. Thanks for stopping by Dis Kount. How can I be of service?

Boss Tweed:
(In total perplexity and fear) Run away! Run away! Strumpet! Get the hell away from him!

The Donald:

Relax. I know these people. **(To the Greeter)** Son, I know we're early, but we really need to do some shopping, and I'm afraid our time is tight and this is the only opportunity this side of the next ice age where we'll be able to do this, so…

Greeter:

Oh, no problem. At Dis Kount, we're *here* to make sure you are too. Lemme just get someone who can make that decision. Wait right here, okay. Just a couple minutes. Hey, here's our flyer. Might give you some ideas.

The Donald:

(Accepting the flyer) Sure. Thanks. We'll be right here. **(Walks over to Boss Tweed and helps him up)** We're going to be just fine.

Boss Tweed:

Where'd that horror show go. **(Pointing at the door)**

The Donald:

He went to get his manager. This is easy. Relax.

(The sliding glass doors open and the pimply-faced Dis Kount employee leads three very business-like Fallen Angels out to meet the situation. They are, in reality, the Three Furies: Alecto, Megaera and Tisiphone. Alecto is dressed in a powder blue power-suit; Megaera and Tisiphone are equally impeccable in powder blue pants suits. They each carry a clipboard and have cell phones clipped to their belts and head sets on their heads)

Alecto:

Alright, Dwayne, what gives?

Megaera:

Busy, busy, Dwayne. Lots to do.

Tisiphone:
This is going to totally put the new seasonal displays behind.

Greeter Dwayne:
Sorry, guys. The two customers are right out here.

(The Donald walks over, hand outstretched, to meet The Furies/ Managers)

The Donald:
Hey folks, just a little misunderstanding. We really need to pass through the door, and then the store, and be on our-

Megaera:
Whoa! **(The Fallen Angels up top resume catcalls and howling)**

Tisiphone:
Dwayne! Are you out of your mind!

(The Donald takes a step back, looks back and forth between Boss Tweed, The Furies, Dwayne, and the Fallen Angels up on the wall)

Alecto:
Alright! Who brought in the live guy.

Greeter Dwayne:
(In complete disgust and shrinking away from The Donald) He's alive?!

(The Donald hangs his head. Boss Tweed steps up)

Boss Tweed:
Hey, hey. Look. I can explain, you see, we're on a mission from God.

The Three Furies:
(The Three Furies look at Tweed for a beat) Whatever.

Alecto:
Way to go, Dwayne. What a great start to the morning.

Greeter Dwayne:
All c'mon, fellas. How was I supposed to know? He looks dead.

Alecto:
This is *way* out of our pay scale.

Megaera:
We need The Bitch.

Tisiphone:
This early? Really?

Alecto:
She's right. **(Looks over to Greeter Dwayne)** Dwayne, go get the G.M.

Greeter Dwayne:
(Wide-eyed) Fuck no.

Megaera:
You started this. This is your mess. Go get her.

Tisiphone:
Hurry-up, Dwayne. I've got a whole new red, white, and blue heresy display thats going to take forever.

(Dwayne looks nervously from one manager to the other. The Furies all point to the door. Sheepishly, Dwayne walks through the doors and exits stage right)

The Donald:
Hey, I don't want to get the kid in trouble.

Alecto:
Too late for that. Say- **(looking at The Donald's hair)**

Tisiphone:
Dude, what happened to your hair? **(The Donald's hands go up to his head. The Fallen Angels on the wall are beside themselves: Hairy! No hair! Hair brain! Hairless! Hairy Honcho! Headless Hairy! And the like)**

Megaera:
We have a heresy hair replacement section.

Alecto:
Aisle fourteen, all the way to the back.

Tisiphone:
Half-off, all week. Tonics, gels, hair replacement kits, stimulators, hormones, toupees, wigs.

Megaera:
You might want to try it all.

Alecto:
Of course, if it worked it wouldn't be here, but you never know.

(Greeter Dwayne enters from stage right)

Greeter Dwayne:
She's on her way.

(The Three Furies, Greeter Dwayne and The Fallen Angels all put on sunglasses. The Donald and Boss Tweed share looks of bewilderment)

Medusa:
(From off-stage right) Who is it that invades Death's Kingdom in his life!

Boss Tweed:
Don't look! Don't look! Strumpet! Close your eyes! Holy fuck! I didn't know *she* was the G.M!

The Donald:
What is your problem?

Boss Tweed:
(Whimpering) Its, its, Me-Me-Meduuuusaaa. **(Trailing off)**

(The Donald turns toward Boss Tweed as Medusa enters stage right. She is strikingly beautiful with blonde, brunette, and ginger braids, exceptionally perfect features, and a body that would make a porn star blush. She is wearing heels, a skirt, blouse, blazer, and jewelry of blues and golds that are priceless. The Fallen Angels cower beneath the parapet of the walls, The Furies step back, Greeter Dwayne stares at the ground and kicks an imaginary stone, Boss Tweed stares and shakes, and The Donald, his back turned to Medusa, addresses Boss Tweed)

The Donald:
What? What is it? Really? How fucking terrible and ugly can she be? Like, Minos-ugly. Like as ugly and nasty as everything else down here. Come on.

Boss Tweed:
She can hear you.

The Donald:
So fucking what.

Boss Tweed:
She doesn't look real happy, Strumpet.

The Donald:
Oh, boo hoo. She's not happy? She pissed off? Well, so am I. Let me show you how to handle this chick. Fucking store manager. Really, Tweed, pull yourself together. **(Slowly turning to face Medusa)** Man, I wish Howard was here, we'd show you what we think of the super woma- **(The Donald is quite literally frozen to stone upon laying eyes on Medusa. He stammers. He shakes his head. He may even be drooling)**

Medusa:
Pussy got your tongue, boy. **(The Donald cannot respond. The Fallen Angels on the wall are starting to whoop. The Furies, Greeter Dwayne, and Boss Tweed are wide-eyed)** Maybe you should just grab that pussy. Maybe you should show that pussy what a fucking rock star you think you are. You want to get in this store. Alive. An actual, living fucking human being. In my store. **(She holds up one finger and her head somehow pivots from side to side on her shoulders)** I don't think so.

Boss Tweed:
(Shielding his eyes as he walks over and pulls The Donald away from Medusa's gaze) Ma'am, a thousand apologies. I, I know we really shouldn't be here and we're super early and I know every day is like Black Friday around here and you're all really busy, but, like, The Big Fella waaaay up top has asked me to take him aaallll the way through Hell and, I am so very sorry, but, I'm afraid, that task requires passing through your store.

Medusa:
Do you have a Values Card?

Boss Tweed:
No.

Medusa:
Fuck off.

(Boss Tweed pulls the stammering and shaking The Donald over toward the landing and the river)

Boss Tweed:
We're in a pickle here, Strump- **(There is no response from The Donald. Tweed slaps him on both cheeks. The Donald snaps out of his coma)** We're in a tight spot here, Strumpet.

The Donald:
(Shaking his head. Smacking the side of it. Shaking himself loose) What, what do you mean?

Boss Tweed:
She won't let us in unless we have some sort of Values Card. Whatever that is.

The Donald:
I think I might know what that is, but I have no idea where to get one. Ask her if we can fill out a form or something.

Boss Tweed:
(Walking over to Medusa) Is there a form or something we can fill out to get a Values Card?

Medusa:
Look in your wallet, simple. You are issued one upon entrance to the lower level.

(Boss Tweed opens up his wallet. Pulls out a card and lights up)

Boss Tweed:
Hey! I got one right here! Hey, Strumpet. Lookie here. A Values Card for Dis Kount. In like Flynn! Come on, lets go on in.

Medusa:
Not so fast. Does *he* have one.

Boss Tweed:
Well, no. He's not dead.

Medusa:
If only I could kill you again.

Boss Tweed:
Well, what're we supposed to do?

Medusa:
Maybe you should ask the genius that thought this bullshit up. Get a Values Card. Or get out of my store.

Boss Tweed:
(Walking past The Donald. Walking over to a railing by the river. Leaning over the railing. Placing his hands together and looking up into the inky, black sky) Dearest God in Heaven, I know I suck and stuff and if I didn't really suck I wouldn't be down here and I respect your decision to send me to infernal damnation and all, but my friend here, you know, The Strumpet, well for some reason you had him sent down here so he could learn how much he sucks and so he could learn how not to suck and thereby not blow the world up and well, we really need a Values Card for him so I can finish showing him how sucky he is-

(Just then an enormously bright light appears in the sky from stage left. It is blinding, it is flying right toward the landing from

across the river. It leaves a boiling wake in its path. Shades, Fallen Angels, The Furies, Greeter Dwayne, and even Medusa must avert their eyes. All but Medusa fall to their knees. The light is Saint Dymphna, sword in hand, she alights on the landing beside Boss Tweed and The Donald)

Saint Dymphna:
How many pages are we into this thing and this is all the farther you are? And as for you, you trumped-up tart, **(she pulls a Values Card from an inside pocket as she approaches Medusa)** one Values Card for one living, breathing soul! Let them pass into the friendly aisles of Heresy, in the Circle you so wantonly call, 'your store'.

(Saint Dymphna walks around the stage and back towards the river, stops, turns, and fake lunges at all of them. They react in panic and cowering. The Good Lady rises into the air, turns, and rockets back across the river and exits stage left)

Medusa:
Just once, to enter a room that way.

The Donald:
(To Medusa, though still not looking at her) Looks like we're in. **(Cheesy grin)** We are ready to shop, save money and pass right on through.

Medusa:
You're still not getting it.

The Donald:
Excuse me, ma'am, but you heard the lady with the mighty sword and the Values Card. Time to save some dough, ray, me. **(Tries to walk past Medusa. She puts one finger on his sternum which makes him hop back several feet)**

Medusa:
You. Still. Don't. Get. It.

The Donald:
What's not to get. Dis Kount. Val. Ues. Save money.

Medusa:
This is Circle Six. Heresy. I *discount* what you're saying. I *discount* the status quo. I *discount* the norms of a stagnant society. Values. Ethics. Your Values Card lists the values and ethics you *didn't have* in your earthly life.

The Donald:
Oooooooohhhh.

Medusa:
My stars, somewhere above that mop of camel hair I see a light bulb. **(The Fallen Angels again go crazy)**

Boss Tweed:
(Rising, grabbing The Donald and making toward the doors) Well, ma'am, I can see how busy you are and before my friend says something truly stupid, we are ready to look through your fine store and learn all about values and discounts and why we had none of those things when we were alive.

Medusa:
Very well. Dwayne! **(Front and center pops Dwayne)** Show your friends through the store and make sure they don't fuck anything up. Got it!

Greeter Dwayne:
Yes, ma'am!

Medusa:
Team! Huddle up! We got a big week in front of us. **(The Furies and Medusa move toward the landing and huddle up)**

Greeter Dwayne:
Alright, guys, in we go. **(The Fallen Angels continue their catcalls at an even higher level)**

The Donald:
(Motioning toward the parapet and The Fallen Angels as they pass through the doors) What's up with them?

Greeter Dwayne:
They're on break.

(The lights fade center stage and come up on Euripides and the narrator's stage)

Euripides:
Aaah, dear friends, we have entered Lower Hell. The Walls of the City of Dis, positioned to keep those within from ever having contact with anyone ever again.

These are the willful sins. Unlike Upper Hell, where the sins of passion gnawed away at the better angels of our nature, these sins were committed knowing full well the implications. Heresy. Violence. Fraud. Betrayal.

And the Pit. And Him. And those that dwell with Him.

My stalwart and faithful band, I must apologize for what has just transpired and for what will be played out before you. Little ears and wide eyes. The innocence of each of you tested by such corrupt language and such foul scenes. Decorum will be kept as high as we possibly can given the grimness of our surroundings, the dismal wasteland we will pass through, and the dark denizens that await us. The worst of the worst, squirming in a place that has never seen light.

Be strong. Be defiant. Be vigilant. It is the lonely, icy peaks and the terrible chasms that shape and define us. Happiness is brief. It will not stay. God batters at its sails. All is change; all yields its place and goes. To persevere! Trusting in what hopes we have! This is courage! The coward despairs, not understanding that there is no wind that always blows a gale.

And we sail on, away, afar, without a course, without a star, but by the instinct of sweet music driven. *To A Singer*, a song, and in a song, hope.

(The lights fade on the narrator's stage as Euripides bows his head and turns to leave)

(The lights rise on the left side of center stage revealing the inside of a big box store. There are displays, aisles, point-of-sale, [Hot Deals!], bargain bins and brightly-lit signs for all types of religious and political philosophies. Greeter Dwayne leads The Donald and Boss Tweed from stage left)

Greeter Dwayne:
Over here is all the heresy from before Christ, some of thats a bit fuzzy, and here's post Christ: indulgences, various papal edicts, the Inquisition.

The Donald:
This is all so depressingly Catholic.

Greeter Dwayne:
What religion are you on Earth?

The Donald:
Presbyterian.

Greeter Dwayne:
(Pointing) Aisle Five.

The Donald:
Of course. How 'bout you, Bossman?

Boss Tweed:
None, really. Just in it for the money.

Greeter Dwayne:
Oh, **(He turns and points with both hands back the way they had come)** Home and Garden. Beautiful display on laissez-faire.

The Donald:
This is one big-ass store. **(To Boss Tweed)** Do we have time for this?

Boss Tweed:
Yeah, Dwayne, we've already got like two of every heresy there is. What we're looking for is a way through the store and out the back. We really need to go lower.

Greeter Dwayne:
Wow. Hardcore. Well, I'm not real sure, I'm kinda new here.

The Donald:
How long you been down here?

Greeter Dwayne:
Handful of years.

Boss Tweed:
What got you sent to Circle Six, if ya don't mind my asking?

Greeter Dwayne:
(He looks at the ground, shrugs. The Donald and Boss Tweed lean forward) I'm the guy who traded Babe Ruth to the Yankees.

The Donald and Boss Tweed:
(Shrinking back and disgusted) Oooh. Ouch. Damn. Harry, you idiot. Sorry to hear abut that, son.

Greeter Dwayne:
(Holding his head up) We all have something we have to live with. Now, you want a way out of Circle Six?

The Donald:
That's the idea.

Boss Tweed:
Is there a tunnel? A drop ceiling? An electrical/h.v.a.c. access port.

The Donald:
(Looking at Boss Tweed most impressed) Listen to you, Bossman. Dwayne, any of the above?

Greeter Dwayne:
No. No. Once you're in…hmmm, there is the freight door.

Boss Tweed:
Bingo.

The Donald:
That's us.

Greeter Dwayne:
Aaaaaa-

The Donald:
What is it, son?

Greeter Dwayne:
Ooooh-

Boss Tweed:
What the problem is?

Greeter Dwayne:
You, you don't want to go back there.

The Donald:
Why not, Dwayne.

Greeter Dwayne:
That's where all the Dock Monkeys hang out.

Boss Tweed:
Dock Monkeys?

Greeter Dwayne:
Yeah. Even the G.M. has a hard time back there.

The Donald:
Who are they?

Greeter Dwayne:
(Beat) Union.

The Donald:
Aaah, fuck.

Boss Tweed:
This is bad?

The Donald:
Yeah, this could take forever. Oh, well. That's life. Dwayne. Show us the freight door.

(Dwayne leads the guys over to a door that says: Freight. Dwayne looks back to The Donald, who slowly nods and points at the door handle. As they walk through, the lights go up on the right side of

center stage and dim on center stage left. There are boxes, crates, and packing material strewn haphazardly. Stacked-up along the walls are steel coffins that had once been under tremendous heat, and are now falling apart. A dozen or so Fallen Angels sit around on the stuff, all looking at cell phones)

Greeter Dwayne:
H-h-hey guys. J-j-just passing through.

The Fallen Angels:
Dwayne-O! The Dwaynester! Dwayne-o-rama! The Big Dwayne! Greeter dude! (Mocking) Welcome to Dis Kount, how can I serve you. (And the like)

Greeter Dwayne:
Take it easy guys, these are customers.

The Fallen Angels:
Oooooooooohhhhhhh. Aaaaaaahhhhhhh. Cuuuuuuuussstoomers.

The Donald:
Gentlemen. How we doing this morning?

(Dead silence)

The Donald:
Another day, another dollar?

(More silence)

The Donald:
Same shit different day?

(Painful silence)

Boss Tweed:
(Stepping ahead of The Donald) Fellas, who's running this shop?

(Enter stage right, a large man in a dark suit, he has a giant pinky ring, a cigar, and a clipboard. It is, in fact, Jimmy Hoffa)

Jimmy Hoffa:
Yo, yo! Let's go boys! They're not paying us by the hour! **(Looking up from the clipboard and noticing Boss Tweed)** Hey! Bossman!

Boss Tweed:
(Shaking hands with Mr. Hoffa and then a bro-hug) Jimmy! Yo! Yo! How you doin'!

Jimmy Hoffa:
Fair to Midland. How you doin'? Don't see you down this way too much.

Boss Tweed:
Need to ask a favor from someone who knows something.

Jimmy Hoffa:
Not a problem, there, ace. You've come to the right loading dock. Say, **(looking over at The Donald and leaning in towards Boss Tweed)** what's with the stiff?

Boss Tweed:
Friend of mine. He's why we're invading your loading dock. Need some help.

Jimmy Hoffa:
Yeah, yeah. I understand. Its just, well, he's alive and all.

The Donald:
(Leaning in to shake hands with Jimmy Hoffa) Trumpet.

Jimmy Hoffa:
(Not looking at The Donald and giving him the half-a-hand-limp-fish handshake) I know who you are.

The Donald:
I knew a good friend of yours, Little Nicky.

Jimmy Hoffa:
Ya don't say? Now there was a *Guy*. That man could run a crew. He still in the joint?

The Donald:
Oh yeah. Too bad. I miss him.

Jimmy Hoffa:
Me too. So what can I do for you, gentlemen?

Boss Tweed:
We need a lift to Circle Seven.

Jimmy Hoffa:
No shit. I thought I was fucked-up. What's down there?

Boss Tweed:
I gotta show this cat every circle of Hell.

Jimmy Hoffa:
I'm impressed. **(Looking at The Donald)** You planning for your retirement or something?

The Donald:
Aaa-

Boss Tweed:
This guy's running for President of The United States and *The Big Don* suspects he's gonna waste the whole planet. So, I get the honor of dragging his sorry ass all over Hell, so he learns the errors of his ways before he presses launch.

Jimmy Hoffa:
(Takes a beat while looking at The Donald and nodding, scratching his chin) Whats a matter, you. **(The Donald looks down, puts his hands up palms out)** Something wrong with your life? Something wrong with being rich? Ya got a beautiful wife. Ya got lots of money. Ya got nice clothes, a nice house, kids. What is it?

The Donald:
(Sheepishly) I, I just want to make America great again.

Jimmy Hoffa:
When wasn't it fucking great? Huh? Its always been great. Ya hear me? Always been great. Take me. A kid outta nowhere. Bam! Success. A player. Making shit happen. Helping folks out and getting rich while I'm doing it. The best of the best. Steaks. Lobsters. Caviar. Champagne. Cars. Houses. A crew. You got all that and more. You could live to be a million and still have money left over. But no. You gotta fuck all that up by wanting to be President.

The Donald:
(Stammering) I, I.

Jimmy Hoffa:
Let me tell you something. You ever look at before and after pictures of guys who've been President? Yeah. That job sucks. Who in their right fucking

mind would want that shitty job. Take my advice. Okay. Hey, eyes right here. **(Jimmy Hoffa points to his eyes)** Leave that shit alone. You just keep building golf courses and shit. You become President. I'll find you. You hear me? I'll find you. **(Turning to Boss Tweed)** So, my good friend from the First Ward, how can I assist you in convincing dumb fuck not to be President?

Boss Tweed:
We need to get to the Seventh Circle. I've heard its a long road. You must have some connections.

Jimmy Hoffa:
I do. But, this is a bad day. Not many trucks coming to this loading dock to-day. However, one of yesterday's deliveries didn't show. And I suspect he may show up today. And, in fact, here he comes now.

(There is the sound from off-stage, stage right, of a large diesel en-gine. Red tail lights and reverse lights brighten the stage. The rear of a tractor trailer slowly backs up to the dock, where, in a puff of black smoke and the sound of air brakes, it stops)

Jimmy Hoffa:
Timing is everything. **(He walks to the edge of the dock by some stairs, looks at his clipboard and then waits. A truck door slams and a man jogs up the stairs onto the dock)** Randy! What the fuck? How'd you get this gig?

Randy:
(Randy is dressed in blue jeans, a blue and brown checkered shirt, a blue jean jacket, a faded, brown leather vest with an American flag patch, a P.O.W. patch, an Elk's Lodge patch, another patch sig-nifying a biker's club, and one that says 'Rush's Warriors'. He has a cowboy hat with feathers, cowboy boots, and an enormous beer gut. He is smoking a Swisher Sweet cigar) James, nice to see you, how's death treatin' ya?

Jimmy Hoffa:
I could complain.

Randy:
But who would listen.

(The two of them shake hands and do a bro-hug while everyone else watches)

Jimmy Hoffa:
You here for the old tombs?

Randy:
Yeah. **(Pulls out a clump of papers from his back pocket)** One thousand, six hundred and twenty of them.

Jimmy Hoffa:
Hey, **(leaning in toward Randy)** I know this might be classified and shit, but, what's up with this?

Randy:
Well, since its you. Do you remember the rumors about Circle Six getting bought out?

Jimmy Hoffa:
Yeah, thought I was going to lose my job.

Randy:
All true. And the new regime, well, things cost more than they expected. So, everything that was going to be scrapped from the old Circle Six, they had to find buyers for all that stuff.

Jimmy Hoffa:
Wow. That's a lot of stuff. This is one huge deal.

Randy:
Privatization, man. Eternity is a long time and Hell is one big place.

Jimmy Hoffa:
(Nodding) Wow. I mean, wow. But, who would want all these old, individual tombs?

Randy:
China.

The Donald:
Those fuckers.

Randy:
(Looking over to The Donald) Who-

Jimmy Hoffa:
Never mind him. What the fuck are they going to do with one billion individual, self-heating eternal tombs?

Randy:
Smelting them down.

Jimmy Hoffa:
For what?

Randy:
Drain stops.

Jimmy Hoffa:
What a weird world.

Randy:

Hey! **(Looking over to Boss Tweed)** Bossman! Thanks for the help the other day.

Boss Tweed:

No problem, brother. Thanks for the *Slim JIms*.

Jimmy Hoffa:

He help you out?

Randy:

Yeah. Outside Circle Five. Rig broke down. Got a little dicey. He knew a dude with a boat. Had a wrench and some diesel. Close shave.

Jimmy Hoffa:

Well, Randy, you get to return the favor.

Randy:

My pleasure. Whatcha need?

Jimmy Hoffa:

These guys need a ride through the back forty of Circle Six and on toward Circle Seven.

Randy:

Not a problem. But I can only take you up to the ridge line. Then I gotta cut ya loose.

Boss Tweed:

I get it. That's bully. That'd be a big help.

The Donald:

Why not all the way. You need cash? Some sort of clearance?

Randy:
Too dangerous.

The Donald:
Whaaaaaat?

Boss Tweed:
(To The Donald) Don't you worry about it. This is saving us a long walk through some dark land.

Jimmy Hoffa:
Alright, Monkeys! Let's load her up! Get off your kiesters and turn off those fucking cell phones.

(The Dock Monkeys get up grumbling)

Jimmy Hoffa:
Say, Randy.

Randy:
Yeah.

Jimmy Hoffa:
One favor. From back in the day, when you was driving and I was running docks all over the midwest.

Randy:
Whatever you want, my friend.

Jimmy Hoffa:
Tell us *the joke*.

(Randy starts smiling. The Dock Monkeys start clamoring for it as well. The Donald and Boss Tweed just look at each other and back to Jimmy and Randy)

Randy:
Again?

Jimmy Hoffa:
(A hand on Randy's shoulder) Please. There is no humor down here, my friend. Just make us a laugh. Please.

Randy:
Alright. Alright.

(Randy steps to the front. The lights go up on the box, Statler and Waldorf leaning forward, all smiles. The lights go up on the narrator's stage, Euripides is smiling and looking over at Randy. The lights on the stage brighten ever-so-slightly. Randy addresses the audience while everyone on stage looks at him in rapt attention)

Randy:
So, there's this bus, and its completely empty, except the bus driver, and this persnickety woman who's sitting in the first seat across from the bus driver. The bus stops. The door opens, and a woman steps on the bus. There's some recognition between the woman and the bus driver. The woman goes like this, (Randy slides his hand down his arm). And the bus driver shakes his head and goes like this, (Randy slides his hand up his arm) The woman goes like this, (Randy makes a chopping motion down his arm). And the bus driver shakes his head and goes like this, (Randy makes a hole with his left hand and pokes his right pointer finger in the hole over and over). The woman goes like this, (Randy

cups both his breasts). And the bus driver shakes his head and goes like this, (Randy cups his balls). And the woman turns, sticks her thumb up her butt and exits the bus. Now the persnickety woman is furious. She's yelling at the bus driver- 'This is the most lewd and disgusting thing I've ever seen! This is a public transit system! I pay taxes!' And the bus driver says- 'Ma'am, ma'am, calm down. I know that woman. She's deaf and mute. We were using sign language. She asked if the bus was going downtown? (Randy slides his hand down his arm) And I said, no we're going uptown. (Randy slides his hand up his arm) She asked if the bus was making a lot of stops? (Randy makes the chopping motion down his arm) And I said, no we're going straight through. (Randy makes a hole with one hand and pokes it with the finger of his other hand) She asked if we were going by the dairy? (Randy cups his breasts) And I said, no we're going by the ball park. (Randy cups his balls. And then, Randy turns and sticks his thumb up his butt) So she said, Shit! I'm on the wrong bus!

(Everyone on stage busts a gut. Statler and Waldorf bust a gut. Euripides busts a gut. And hopefully, you and the audience are busting a gut as well)

Jimmy Hoffa:
(Wiping tears away from his eyes) Randy. Thank-you. We can't thank-you enough. Give us a minute or a year or a decade or forever and we'll have you loaded. My office is right through there. Take as much time as you need.

(The lights slowly fade to black on all parts of the stage as the Dock Monkeys start to work, The Donald and Boss Tweed sit on the edge of the dock, Jimmy Hoffa checks his clipboard, and Randy passes through the freight door)

(After several moments, we hear)

Joseph Goebbels:
(Softly and very FM) Good Nighttime. W.H.E.L. laying it down cool and slow, letting the shades vibe and the damned get groovy. Ignore all that pandemonium in lower hell, live humans, saints and sinners, lights brighter than a thousand suns, and let us ease your suffering souls with a little Shirley and Lee.

(*Let The Good Times Roll* comes on nice and easy, a bit tinny as if its being heard on a truck radio. Which it is, as stage left, a small light illuminates the interior of Randy's cab. He is driving, Boss Tweed is riding shotgun, and The Donald is sitting between them. Boss Tweed is working on a *Slim Jim*, Randy is smoking a *Swisher Sweet*, and The Donald is smashing on a bag of *Cheese Curls*, which have painted his mouth and cheeks orange. The cab sways as the truck rolls on down the road between Circle Six and the cliff before Circle Seven)

Boss Tweed:
Man, I miss this shit.

The Donald:
You didn't have *Slim Jims* back then.

Boss Tweed:
No. Jerky. But this stuff is golden.

Randy:
(Smiling) Don't they feed you down here?

Boss Tweed:
You know the answer to that.

Randy:
Yeah, I know. That's why I keep all this stuff in the truck. Its not like its going to go bad.

The Donald:
Thank you so much for this. I haven't had a thing to eat since before this nightmare started.

Randy:
How'd you end up down here?

The Donald:
I wish I knew the answer to that.

Boss Tweed:
(Incredulous and somewhat angry) What! What do you think we've been doing down here?

The Donald:
(Mocking) Oh, I know: let's show Trumpet what an evil bastard he is; let's show Trumpet how he's going to end the world; let's show Trumpet how he's going to spend eternity in hell. Bullshit. **(Boss Tweed is fuming. Randy is driving and quizzically taking it in)** I mean, I get it. Alright. But this is no way to get someone to change. And like, I'm going to change. Being an asshole is what got me this far, and if it works for me, I'm staying with it. **(Boss Tweed has ripped his Slim Jim into tiny bits)** Hell? Really? Like this? I am so sure. What nimrod thought this stupid shit up anyway? Like you, **(looks at Randy)**, so who are you? How'd you get here? I wrote a paper on Dante's Inferno, and from what the girl who did it for me said, this ain't it.

(Boss Tweed grabs the bag of Cheetos and smashes it in The Donald's face, making his entire face orange. The Donald slaps Boss Tweed with both hands. Boss Tweed retaliates with slapping as well)

Randy:
Hey! Hey! Come on! Fight nice. Fight nice. Don't make me pull this truck over. **(The two slowly stop fighting, each trying to get the last slap**

in) Come on. Ease down. What the heck, guys. You think this is easy? You try driving in Hell. No street lights. Always dark. No mile markers. Not to mention the damned. And no cell service. Or Sirius. How's a fella supposed to listen to Rush? Inhuman, I tell ya, inhuman.

Boss Tweed:
So, how did you end up driving this thing down here?

Randy:
Divorce.

The Donald:
Read me my script.

Randy:
I know, I know. Like a lot of guys, I could blame the ex-wife for everything. And I do.

Boss Tweed:
I'm not following, Randy.

Randy:
Lost everything. Had to pay her, pay off the debt, pay, pay, pay.

The Donald:
So, what'd you do?

Randy:
Went to truck driving school. Delivered pizzas to pay for that. Played in this crappy band. Whatever it took.

Boss Tweed:
You're not dead!

Randy:
Don't tell anyone.

The Donald:
But, why would you drive a truck down here?

Randy:
The school placed me. I didn't have a choice. First job out the gate.

Boss Tweed:
Where'd you go to school?

Randy:
Ohio State.

Boss Tweed and The Donald:
(In understanding) Aaahhh.

Randy:
Seriously though, on the way out of court, my ex-wife said to me, 'Randy, the more you die, the greater chance you have to live'. So, I figured what better place to learn about death.

(Just then there's a huge roar from off-stage, stage right. It shakes the cab. Randy locks up the brakes and they all lunge forward in their seats)

The Donald:
What the hell was that!

Randy:
Fuck.

The Donald:
Fuck what?!

Boss Tweed:
Gettin' a little nervous there, Strumpet.

(The roar is louder, closer. It is like fifty tyrannosaurus rex all having a very bad day. Randy rolls down his window)

The Donald:
What are you doing?!

Boss Tweed:
(Mocking) Oh, its just a nightmare. Its not real.

Randy:
I want to gauge where it is and where we are.

The Donald:
What the hell is 'it'?!

Boss Tweed:
(Still mocking) I'm not going to change. I like being an asshole.

(There is an even louder roar. The wind from the roar rocks the truck. Papers in the cab blow around. The Donald is nearly wetting himself)

The Donald:
(Pulling out the bottle of cough syrup. Drinking heavily and spilling. The green liquid smears the cheese curl orange giving him an Alice Cooper resemblance) What in God's name could make that loud of a sound?!

Randy:
Well, I was a non-believer at first as well.

Boss Tweed:
(Mocking and sing-song) There ain't no Heaven and there ain't no Hell; I'm Donald Trumpet and I do tell, I'll be the Prez of The U.S.A.

The Donald:
(To Boss Tweed) This is serious. Knock that shit off!

Boss Tweed:
(Sing-song) I'll steal all the money,

Randy:
Its getting closer.

(There is a titanic roar. The wind from the roar blows their hair back. Papers and wrappers are flying around the cab)

The Donald:
What!? What's getting closer?!

Boss Tweed:
(Sing-song) And make you pay,

Randy:
We're farther than I thought.

The Donald:
What are we going to do? **(To Boss Tweed, shaking him)** Stop singing. Stop singing that.

Randy:
I might have a plan.

Boss Tweed:
(Sing-song) I'll push all the buttons,

The Donald:
Stop it! Stop singing! **(Shaking Boss Tweed)**

(Another roar)

Randy:
Just maybe.

Boss Tweed:
(Sing-song) And blow-

The Donald:
(To Boss Tweed) Shut up! **(To Randy)** What is it!

Boss Tweed:
(Sing-song) You all-

The Donald:
(To Boss Tweed) Stop!!! **(To the ceiling of the cab)** What's happening-

(Just then, the roar is so loud, so close, and so terrible that the truck shakes, the lights flicker out and the stage itself shudders with the ponderous steps of something very, very large. The cab lights flicker back on. There is a moment of silence)

Boss Tweed:
(Whispering) Away.

Randy:
(Rummaging through an old, olive drab army duffel bag) This might just work.

The Donald:
What's out there?!!

Boss Tweed:
The Minotaur.

The Donald:
What? Really?

Randy:
The one and only.

(From stage right, a monstrous right foot lands, shaking the stage and accompanied by a huge roar. The foot is actually a rubber galosh, unbuckled, black and ancient. When it lands on the stage the buckles rattle and some sort of dark ooze splays out)

The Donald:
What the fuck are we going to do?!

Randy:
I have a plan.

Boss Tweed:
Shit's getting real, huh Strumpet?

The Donald:
What do you care, you're already dead.

Randy:
Yeah, well I'm not and I've got a gig this weekend.

Boss Tweed:
No shit, where you playing?

Randy:
Little island off the coast of Limbo.

Boss Tweed:
I am so there.

Randy:
Sweet.

The Donald:
Would you two shut the fuck up! We're about to get squished.

(There is another titanic roar. The truck itself rocks back sideways on one half of its tires. A yellowy, viscous liquid splatters the truck. The three of them wipe gunk off their faces. The Donald now has an orange face smeared by the cough syrup and splattered with this new substance)

Randy:
We need to get out of the truck.

The Donald:
My fucking ass!

Boss Tweed:
Come on, Nancy, get with the program. Randy's got a plan.

Randy:
Yeah, I do. I've seen this thing. It spooked me out of nowhere some days ago.

The Donald:
You lived!

Boss Tweed:
Well, duh.

(There is another roar. The galosh on stage swivels slightly as the beast off-stage turns one way and then the other. The Minotaur makes a muffled, baffled sound of trying to find something)

Randy:
Okay, this is it. Follow me. (Randy pulls out a cylindrical, tube-like object from the duffle bag, opens the door of the cab, and steps out onto the stage)

Boss Tweed:
Your next, gal boy.

The Donald:
I know! And fuck you. (The Donald steps out beside Randy. Boss Tweed follows shutting the door to the cab much too loud) You idiot!

(There is a huge roar. Another galosh steps onto the stage and with it, the Minotaur. He is enormous. Two awesomely-muscled, hairy and knobby-kneed legs jut out from the galoshes up to a pair of stained boxers that have faded Manchester United logos all over. A great, hairy beer belly hangs over the boxers. The exposed mid-riff yields to a mustard-stained, beer-soaked, unknown-blotched, dingy, white tank top. Huge tufts of armpit hair poof out from colossal biceps. His arms are monstrously long, nearly dragging on the floor. In one, gnarled, hairy, calloused, disfigured hand, is a giant bottle of Stella Artois, in the other is an ancient, battered and dented scimitar. Tangles of beer and puke-matted chest hair falls over the tank top. A thick, muscle roped neck, wrought with scars and skin tabs, holds up the gigantic head of a bull. Two jets of steam exude from torn, black nostrils, one of which has a tarnished gold ring with a bit of broken gold chain hanging from it. The thick, tightly-furred, broad nose runs up to a forehead that is as thick as a battleship's prow. Two bloodshot, cataract-covered, pale blue eyes, glower beneath thick, hooded brows. And above all of this, curving out, then down, then up and out, are the horns. Blackish-brown, thick, dented, nicked and pocked, they are weapons that have long been bloodied. A remnant of dried flesh hangs from one, while the tip of the other has been splintered, a leathery fungus topping what remains. Our three intrepid travelers stand huddled together, rooted to the spot, staring up at one of Hell's most infamous citizens. The Minotaur looks down, fills its mighty lungs, and then belches with an eardrum-shattering roar, replete with spittle)

Boss Tweed:
Bit more awesome in person, I'd say.

The Donald:
We're fucked.

Randy:
I have a plan.

The Donald:
Go boy, go!

(The Minotaur takes a step closer and roars)

The Donald, Boss Tweed, and Randy:
(Hair blown straight back, unknown stuff splattering them)
Aaaaaaaaahhhhhhh!!!

(The Minotaur steps closer. Bends over and puts its great head several feet from them)

The Donald, Boss Tweed, and Randy:
(Whimpering)

(The Minotaur sniffs them)

The Donald, Boss Tweed, and Randy:
No, no, no, no…(while whimpering)

(The Minotaur sets its bottle of beer down, curls up a fist and holds it above them)

The Donald, Boss Tweed, and Randy:
Mommy, mommy, mommy…(still whimpering)

(The Minotaur slowly extends its pointer finger from its massive fist)

The Donald, Boss Tweed, and Randy:
(Girlish squealing)

(The Minotaur then, ever-so-gently, pokes The Donald)

The Minotaur:
(In a voice like Mike Tyson) Food?

The Donald:
What's the plan! What's the plan! What's the plan!

(Randy unrolls the cylindrical, tube-like object revealing a glossy magazine)

Boss Tweed:
What is it?

Randy:
A porno.

The Donald:
That's your plan! You stupid truck driver! Goddammit!

(The Donald panics. Steps one way, then the other, spins around, and in doing so knocks over the giant bottle of Stella Artois. The Minotaur rears back and bellows. The Donald goes mindlessly apeshit, runs through the legs of the Minotaur, who vainly tries to catch him, and exits screaming stage right)

Boss Tweed:
Strumpet! Goddammit! You fuck wad!

Randy:
What a puss.

(The Minotaur picks up its bottle of beer, eyeballs what's left, and then drains it. Tosses the bottle over its shoulder, off stage right, where we ear an ear-splitting shatter)

The Donald:
(Off stage) Mommy!

(The Minotaur then bends over, eyes full of hate and stares at Boss Tweed and Randy. Randy opens the magazine to its centerfold right before the eyes of The Minotaur. The Minotaur lights up, smiles, drops its scimitar, grabs the porno, and runs off stage left, stepping over the truck with ease)

Boss Tweed:
Pure genius!

Randy:
My drummer's just like that. Where'd Strumpet run off to?

Boss Tweed:
God only knows. He's done this every time shit gets hairy. Its a real hassle.

The Minotaur:
(Off stage left) I love you Miss September! **(Boss Tweed and Randy turn their heads at this, then turn back toward each other)**

Randy:
Now what?

Boss Tweed:
(Extending hand) Thanks for the lift, brother.

Randy:
Anytime, Bossman. **(Climbing back into his cab)** You take it easy. And good luck!

(The lights fade on stage left as we hear the truck start up and rumble away. The lights fade center stage as Boss Tweed walks over to stage right and under the box. He turns to the audience, but is looking out, above, and past them)

Boss Tweed:
(He strikes a pose, takes a beat, and clears his throat. He then belts out Carry Me Back To Old Virginny, a cappella and in baritone, but with these lyrics)

Carry me back to old Tammany
There's where the corruption, graft and monies grow
There's where the birds warble sweet at bedtime
There's where this old chairman's heart am long'd to go
There's where I fleeced so hard for the dollah
Day after day in the halls of pork
No place on earth do I love more sincerely
Than old Tammany, the place where wealth was born.
Carry me back to old Tammany
There's where the corruption, graft and monies grow
There's where the birds warble sweet at bedtime
There's where this old chairman's heart am long'd to go
Carry me back to old Tammany
There let me live till no one else can pay
Long by the dismal, old swamp I have wandered
That's where this old chairman's life will pass away.
Sweeney, Connolly, and Hall have long since gone before me
Soon we will meet and never part no more
Carry me back to old Tammany
There's where the corruption, graft and monies grow
There's where the birds warble sweet at bedtime
There's where this old chairman's heart am long'd to go

(Boss Tweed takes a moment to reflect, then exits stage right, his light fading. The lights then rise on the box and Statler and Waldorf)

Statler Swift:
(Mocking/crooning the tune they just heard) Promises and pie crusts!

Waldorf Voltaire:
(Mocking/crooning) Sausages and laws!

Statler Swift:
These silly Yanks!

Waldorf Voltaire:
Should vote for Santa Claus! **(Standing up and looking stage right, under the box. Speaking normally, but with indignation)** Where is that orange-faced lout!

Statler Swift:
What are you going on about?

Waldorf Voltaire:
I don't like that Donald guy.

Statler Swift:
You're not supposed to.

Waldorf Voltaire:
Off with his head!

Statler Swift:
Why are you being so emotional?

Waldorf Voltaire:
He's a dickhead!

Statler Swift:
Control yourself! Sit down. And quit giving him the bird whenever he walks on stage.

Waldorf Voltaire:
(Sitting down with resignation) Fierce indignation can no longer injure my heart. **(Beat)** Quarter him!

Statler Swift:
He's an actor. Its a play.

Waldorf Voltaire:
He's a royal. Burn him!

Statler Swift:
Dammit, man! We're theater critics! We have no feelings. Lets see how this plays out.

Waldorf Voltaire:
I suppose. But, he is a dick head

Statler Swift:
(Lifting the light dimmer control up and working the knob) Let's see what our dear friend Mr. Euripides has to say.

(The lights go up on Euripides and the narrator's stage. He is holding up a giant bottle of Stella Artois, examining the back, while the label is facing the audience)

Statler Swift:
(Standing up) Oh my God! Indignation renewed. Where would we be without the sacred product shot!

Waldorf Voltaire:
(Half-mockingly) What are you going on about. Control yourself. Sit down. Its just a play.

Statler Swift:
(Turning to Waldorf Voltaire, but motioning toward Euripides) This is blatant commercialism!

Waldorf Voltaire:
He's an actor. You're too emotional.

Statler Swift:
Art turned to pandering!

Euripides:
Gentlemen, I'm not supposed to be on right now.

Statler Swift:
Shrink-wrapped, U.P.C.-coded, multi-national, corporate indoctrination!

Euripides:
I protest! I'm thirsty. And I'm not supposed to be on right now.

Waldorf Voltaire:
If you don't like the show, change the station.

Statler Swift:
Right-O! **(Cranks the control sending the narrator's stage into darkness)**

Euripides:
(Sing-song) Thank-you.

Waldorf Voltaire:
(Sing-song) Told you.

Statler Swift:
(Sing-song) Fuck you.

(The lights fade on the box)

(There is a beat or three. In the distance, the low sound of drums pound out a warbled tattoo. Lights slowly come up on a set that looks like Circle Five has been flooded in blood and fire. From out of the river Phlegethon, weapons from all ages twist toward a blood-red sky. Swirling clouds, driven by dark angry winds sweep across the riverscape. Rocky formations of armaments, stone, bones, and bodies rise here and there above the surface. The river itself is burning and boiling blood. Shades are everywhere, some bobbing on the surface, others completely submerged. There are fords and paths through the river that are patrolled by centaurs. With bows, they shoot arrows into the shades who try to rise up out of the boiling river. This all stretches from horizon to horizon, an endless apocalypse of mans inhumanity to man. The Donald enters stage left, in back. He is clearly out of his mind, stumbling and staggering in a zig zag following a rise through the river)

The Donald:
High ground. The high ground. Must find the high ground. Aaah, my feet! My feet, my burning feet. Blood! Everywhere. So much blood. High ground. The high ground. Boss?! Randy?! Anyone?!

(From stage right enters a centaur. It mistakes The Donald for a shade)

Private Centaur:
Halt! Shade! Return to your misery!

The Donald:
No! I'm Donald Tru-

(Private Centaur drills The Donald with an arrow)

The Donald:
(Clutching his side) No! I'm alive! I'm still a man! Why?! Why did you do this? (He falls, seemingly in to the river, out of sight of the audience)

(The lights quickly come up on the box, Waldorf Voltaire, and Statler Swift)

Waldorf Voltaire:
(Standing with fists in the air) Yes! We can go home now!

(The lights quickly fade on the box, Waldorf Voltaire, and Statler Swift)

(Narrator's stage: lights come up. Boss Tweed is standing with Chiron, captain of the centaurs. He has the body of a horse, the trunk, arms, and head of a linebacker. He is wearing kevlar body armor, has a black, composite crossbow with pachmayr grips, and has a red beret with captain's bars on the front)

Boss Tweed:
Chiron, good sir, I need your help. My friend, The Strumpet, is lost somewhere down here.

Chiron:
I know. We heard about it on the radio. From which direction did he come?

Boss Tweed:
(Motioning off-stage left with both hands) Pretty sure from that way. But he was a mess. Ran into the Minotaur. He bugged out all goofy.

Chiron:
Does this have a priority, or can we just sort of leave him here? I mean, in another earthly year or so he's expected to pass through on his way down.

Boss Tweed:
That's what we're trying to avoid. I need to find him, or every Circle in Hell will be flooded with shades.

Chiron:
No shit? Alright, let me get you some help. **(Shouts off-stage left)** Yo! First Sergeant! Find me Nessie. A-Sap! **(To Boss Tweed)** Nessus is my top scout. He knows this Ring like the back of his hand. Plus, he's clear to take you all the way through Circle Seven and even into Eight. But that's just between you and me.

(Another centaur trots in from stage left. He has a wiry build, longish hair and is wearing a boonie hat. He has a regular bow and is smoking a Camel Straight, which he finishes, flicks to the ground, and stubs out with a hoof)

Nessie:
Sir?

Chiron:
Nessie, this fella here has a lost human.

Nessie:
Human?

Chiron:
Yeah, someone screwed the pooch, and we get to clean up the mess.

Nessie:
(Turning to Boss Tweed and extending a hand) Nessie.

Boss Tweed:
Bossman. **(Returning the shake)**

Chiron:
(Placing a fist on Nessie's shoulder) Your mission is to assist Mr. Tweed by any means necessary, locate this human, return them to their path, and help them through Circle Seven and into Circle Eight.

Nessie:
Circle Eight, Sir?

Chiron:
Whatever it takes, son. This mission is critical. If we fail to get this Strumpet turned around, the Earth blows up, and Hell fills with shades. Do you understand, son?

Nessie:
Hua.

Chiron:
Alright gentlemen, good luck.

(Nessie and Boss Tweed turn toward stage right as the lights dim. The lights come back up center stage. The Donald is clambering up out of the bloody river)

The Donald:
You don't understand. I'm a man. I am alive-

Private Centaur:
Shade! Halt! Come no further. Return to your suffering.

The Donald:
I'm not a shade, you jarhead.

Private Centaur:
You are forcing my hand! **(He shoots The Donald again)**

(The lights quickly go out on center stage and come up on the box of Statler and Waldorf)

Waldorf Voltaire:
Yes! Brutal. Ha!

Statler Swift:
Sit down, Waldorf! You're drawing attention.

Waldorf Voltaire:
Start the car with that one thingie, we're outta here!

Statler Swift:
(Slides down in his seat) Waldorf…..

(The lights quickly go out on the box)

(The lights go up on the narrator's stage. Boss Tweed and Nessie are talking to a shade that is half-in, half-out of the river. The shade is actually Colonel Custer looking just like Colonel Custer accept bloody, burning, filled with arrows, and a skosh deteriorated)

Nessie:
Colonel, pretty sure I've tracked this Strumpet fella right through your neck of the river. Anyone weird come this way?

Colonel Custer:
Well, now that you bring it to my attention, there was this very strange, funny-haired gentleman, suit and tie and whatnot, who traipsed all confused through here not that long ago.

Nessie:
How long ago, sir?

Colonel Custer:
Long, but not long.

Nessie:
Just a little while ago then?

Colonel Custer:
A while or so.

Nessie:
Few minutes? An hour? Half a day?

Colonel Custer:
About that.

Nessie:
(Pointing stage left) From there. **(Custer nods. Nessie motions from left to right)** Through here. **(Custer keeps nodding. Nessie points stage right)** That way.

Colonel Custer:
Yes. **(Looking Nessie up and down)**

Nessie:
How long ago?

Colonel Custer:
Son, what happened to your legs.

(The lights fade stage left and go up center stage as The Donald climbs out of the river at the hooves of Private Centaur)

Private Centaur:
Halt! I said. Halt!

The Donald:
I'm not a shade, you dolt!

Private Centaur:
You will force me to use more violence.

The Donald:
Hellooo. We're in Circle Seven. **(Trying to stand up beside Private Centaur)**

Private Centaur:
(Swatting The Donald on the head with the business end of an arrow)

The Donald:
Ouch! Goddammit! Listen!

(Swat. Swat. Swat. The lights fade center stage)

(The lights come up on the box)

Waldorf Voltaire:
How could he still be alive?

Statler Swift:
Please. Sit. Down.

Waldorf Voltaire:
Why isn't he dead?

Statler Swift:
Its a play.

Waldorf Voltaire:
Dammit!

(The lights fade on the box and come back up center stage)

Private Centaur:
(Whilst swatting The Donald with the bow) You leave me no choice but to dismount and engage in hand-to-hand.

The Donald:
You can't dismount you thick-headed nag!

(Swat. Swat. Swat)

Private Centaur:
Insults only deepen your situation.

The Donald:
(Picking up a burning piece of something icky) Ouch, ooh, ouch, deepen? Here, try this situation. **(He places the burning piece of something icky under Private Centaur's tail)**

Private Centaur:
(Instantly rearing back) Holy hemorrhoid!

(The lights fade center stage as we hear galloping going away, and come up on the narrator's stage. Boss Tweed and Nessie are talking to Walter Cronkite)

Boss Tweed:
Mr. Cronkite, why are *you* down here?

Walter Cronkite:
Son, I'm the last investigative journalist in Heaven, Hell, Purgatory or even on Earth. After exhaustive research into man's barbarism to his fellow man, after having covered so much conflict in my lifetime, and given the volatile political situation back home, I anticipated your coming to this spot, in this Circle, on this stage, just to get an interview. Where's Trumpet?

Nessie:
Well, sir, that's the rub of it. We don't know where he is.

Walter Cronkite:
What you're telling me is that you have lost the single most dangerous human being in the history of the world.

Boss Tweed:
That's the gist of it.

Walter Cronkite:
(He gives them a look of reproach) My God, the humanity.

Boss Tweed:
(Looking down guiltily as Nessie lights a cigarette) I'm sorry, sir. He's a handful.

Walter Cronkite:
Do you realize the ramifications of a President Trumpet? I don't think most people truly understand the possibilities. Let me throw some figures at you: Yellow River-800,000 casualties; Wuhan-540,000; Manilla or Gallipoli-500,000; the

Somme-1,215,000; Stalingrad-1,800,000. And Leningrad. Leningrad. Over four and one half million. The next great battle? The Planet Earth-six billion dead.

Boss Tweed:
Sir, this mission that God gave me is quite humbling, and for an old, coarse New Yorker, I know I'm in over my head, but if you can help us out, I mean, Nessie here has tracked the Strumpet right through here, and if you could give us some idea which way that overly dressed, up-tight, fast trick went, I will do my level best to get him on the straight and narrow.

Walter Cronkite:
(Takes a beat in thought) Son, as a journalist, I don't choose sides. I have no corporate sponsors. No agenda. Am not affiliated with any political party. However, given the grave situation that mankind is facing, I can tell you this much. **(He pauses)** That bag of shit went that way. **(Pointing toward stage right)**

(The lights go out stage left and come up center stage. There is a black, rocky outcropping rising out of the river, with a cave tucked into the rock. In the cave is a table with a large, ancient book. It is the room in which we saw Iblee earlier. The Donald enters stage left, from the very back, and threads his way through the burning blood on a path that's just above the mire. He is clutching at his side where two arrows stick out, rubs his bloody head and is whining, crying, and complaining)

The Donald:
This is the stupidest stupid stupid in the whole stupid world. What the fuck! What'd I ever do? Well, there was that one thing. And that other. And all those bad deals. And that one family, destitute, on the street. Dad screwed. Broke. Suicide. Fuck! They knew what I was when they picked me up. **(He stops dead still. Looks around to see if anyone heard. Continues stumbling toward the outcropping)** Not my fault. Business is war. War

is hell. Hell? Ha! War. Hell. Business. Dammit! My word is as good as my handshake. Ha! Double ha! Ha ha ha! Ouch! Stupid arrows. What's this? Someone's home?

(Swirling up from the ground behind the door, counterclockwise, in blue and white and gold, is Iblee. But it is Iblee only briefly. The cyclone coalesces into a five foot, six inch white woman, about thirty-five, with near Barbie-doll features, a slim, attractive figure, blue eyes, and a blonde anchor-bob. She is wearing a white, just-above-the-knee skirt with a tight fitting, plunging blue top. She has on heels, a gold and diamond necklace, matching earrings, and lipstick that sends the mixed message of professional, but also a tart. She takes a couple unsure steps and then leans seductively in the doorway. The Donald stumbles up onto the rocky rise, muttering and complaining, staring at the uneven ground before him)

The Donald:
This is bullshit. We were raised to bully. To intimidate. To take whatever you can at anyone's expense. That's America. That's American. Greatest nation on Earth. But not so great I can't make it greater. Trumpet Land. Yeah. The Incorporated States of Trumpet. Ameri-Trumpet. Trumpet-i-ca. A land where everyone has the right to do just exactly as I want them to **(he looks up and sees the woman in the doorway)** and Hello! What on earth is a beautiful woman like you doing-Maggie?

Maggie/Iblee:
Is I.

The Donald:
What are you doing here?

Maggie/Iblee:
Waiting.

The Donald:
For me?

Maggie/Iblee:
For Donny.

(The Donald winces and looks down at the arrows)

Maggie/Iblee:
Donny hurt.

The Donald:
Its just a flesh- owwww! **(Maggie/Iblee rips the arrows out and places a hand over the wound)**

Maggie/Iblee:
There. All better.

The Donald:
Not really. **(Clutching his side. Then looking up into her eyes)** This nightmare just gets crazier and crazier.

Maggie/Iblee:
Night Mary? No. Night Maggie.

The Donald:
Right. A nightmaggie. You seem, different.

Maggie/Iblee:
Its just, this. **(She gestures all around her)** Everywhere. Here.

The Donald:
(Hesitant) You remind me of this fella, thing, don't know what to call it, that I met down here, or rather, in this nightmaggie.

Maggie/Iblee:
Donny, no. Is me. Maggie. One true love. One you hurt.

The Donald:
(Turning away) I'm sorry, Maggie. I mean, I'm married. You're married. And there's just so much press and so many people that, well, you understand. Right?

Maggie/Iblee:
Not right. But, I for, for, for-

The Donald:
(Turning back) You forgive me. **(She reaches out with an open hand. He does as well and they lock)** That night.

Maggie/Iblee:
I love the night.

The Donald:
At the Astoria.

Maggie/Iblee:
I love hysteria.

The Donald:
You looked out the window at Saint Barts.

Maggie/Iblee:
No saints. Not here.

The Donald:
You stared for so long. What did you say?

Maggie/Iblee:
Love Donny.

The Donald:
Incongruous. That's what you said.

Maggie/Iblee:
In..? In..? Kiss me.

The Donald:
Incongruous. The two of us. Both married. And a church right out the window. Do you remember what I said?

Maggie/Iblee:
Poor Donny.

The Donald:
Yes! Pour the bubbly. Close the drapes.

(There is a pause. Hands fall away. The Donald looks out toward the burning river of blood. He looks down, shakes his head. Rubs his eyes. Maggie/Iblee simply tries to stand in heels. Tries to look like Maggie)

Maggie/Iblee:
Hell is not for Donny.

The Donald:
You understand. I don't belong here. This is, this is…I don't know what this is.

Maggie/Iblee:
Let's get you home.

The Donald:

Yes! Home! You do understand. Oh, Maggie. **(He takes up both her hands, pulls her close)** We'll sort this all out. Once we're home. Once we're back in New York. I'll do whatever you want. We'll get that same wonderful room. The *Cristal*. The caviar. The silk. We'll pretend you can put quarters in the bed and it'll vibrate.

Maggie/Iblee:

Home again home again jiggety-jog!

The Donald:

Then let's go! Let's go now! You know the way! You know how!

Maggie/Iblee:

To market, to market to buy a fat hog!

The Donald:

You get me out, Maggie, you get me. High on the hog the rest of our lives. What do we do? You must know. You found me here, somehow, here in Hell. Here in my dreams. Oh, Maggie. **(He takes her into his arms. Their faces are inches apart. Maggie begins to shimmer. The edges of the illusion waver ever-so-slightly)**

Maggie/Iblee:

To market, to market to buy a fat pig!

The Donald:

I love how silly you are. You don't show that enough. So serious. So harsh.

Maggie/Iblee:

Home with it! Home with it! Jiggety jig! Kiss me!

(The two embrace. A long, deep kiss. Their eyes closed. Hands moving up and down. Holding. Clutching. Pressing. They break the kiss but hold each other even tighter. The Donald, on the left, his face pressed into her neck, his right hand sweeping down her back, over her butt in a cupping fashion. He opens his eyes, cranes his neck over her shoulder and looks down her backside. Beneath the white skirt are no longer Maggie's shapely legs, but a tangle of tentacles like a squid. They are cucumber green, mottled, bumpy, and glistening with some sort of sticky, opaque substance. They tremor and spasm. She spasms, lips parting, and a sound, a sound that is sonorous, tremulous and chthonic, a sound The Donald could never have heard in a thousand lifetimes, issues from a mouth that has left the sensuousness of Maggie's, and become filled with sores and eyes, claws and hooks, beaks and scales. And The Donald screams. He screams utterly. He screams in abject terror. He screams from the very edges of his ragged soul. He pushes her to arm's length and looks into Iblee's face. A swirling chaos confronts him. The one eye opens. The Donald, locked by Iblee's cyclonic arms, stares into this eye and shakes violently. To us, to the audience, we see only this confrontation. But to him, staring into the very void, he sees all of Hell condensed to an image of him, of Iblee, and of Iblee's father, together forever, unbound. And he sees the Earth in its totality, in subjugation. And he screams once more. He screams with the strength of all humanity, of all reason, of all that is the opposite of pure evil)

(Lights come up on the box)

Statler Swift and Waldorf Voltaire:
(Screaming and holding each other, staring at center stage)

(Lights come up on Euripides, on the narrator's stage, hands outstretched as if warding off blows, screaming, staring at center stage) Noooooooo!

(Lights come up extreme stage left on Boss Tweed and Nessie. Their heads whip around toward center stage at the sound of The Donald screaming)

Boss Tweed:
Struuuuummmpet!!!!!!!!

(The lights go out on the box. The lights go out on Euripides. The lights go out on Boss Tweed and Nessie)

The Donald:
(Breaking free, stopping his scream, stammering) I trusted you.

Iblee:
Dearest Donny, how many trusted you?

(The Donald pushes past it and runs/staggers to exit stage right. Iblee swings its head from watching The Donald depart, to stage left, where we hear the hooves of Nessie and the voice of Boss Tweed. Iblee steps behind the doorway. Nessie slowly leads Boss Tweed through the river from stage left. They are approaching the outcropping the same way The Donald had, but wary. Very wary)

Boss Tweed:
You sure he came through here?

Nessie:
Yes.

Boss Tweed:
How can you be so sure?

Nessie:
No one else leaves footprints down here.

Boss Tweed:
(**Looking up and pointing at the cave**) What the fuck is that?

(**Stepping from behind the doorway is Iblee, in the guise of Maggie. She leans against the doorway smoking a cigarette, her hair unkempt, a dirty smile with smudged lipstick on her Barbie-doll face. Nessie holds up his hands as if asking a question. Maggie throws a thumb over her shoulder in the direction of where The Donald fled. The two very slowly walk past her**)

Boss Tweed:
Much obliged, ma'am.

(**They exit stage right, the lights center stage fading to black behind them**)

(**The lights come up on Euripides, extreme front of the narrator's stage**)

Euripides:
An open enemy is better than a false friend. For our reluctant protagonist, despair mounts despair, and his quick fix of skirting this Herculean task has, it seems, dried up. If he thought things were bad before, well, we shall see.

For us, living as it would seem on pins and needles, how do we persevere, much less prevail? The fate of mankind linked to an ego so fragile, to a temperament so volatile, and to an intellect more akin to penny opera. Hope may well be lost. As votes are counted, as the coarseness of our natures is stroked by fiends acting as friends, we stand in limbo, in nexus, at the crossroads we had signposted not to travel past again.

Oh hope, eternal friend, that flame when all is despair, come back. Even as a shadow, even as a dream. Come back. (**Beat**) Death is never at a loss for occasions. (**He hangs his head as his lights goes out**)

(The lights go up on the box)

Statler Swift:
(Standing to leave) Well, Waldorf? **(Waldorf doesn't move, but stares at center stage)** Do you want to leave?

Waldorf Voltaire:
No.

Statler Swift:
What about the pub?

Waldorf Voltaire:
Not interested.

Statler Swift:
What about the loo?

Waldorf Voltaire:
I'm not moving.

Statler Swift:
Are you alright?

Waldorf Voltaire:
Perfect, baby.

Statler Swift:
Okay. Then let me by **(stepping toward Waldorf)** and I'll-

Waldorf Voltaire:
(He turns sharply, eyes bugging out, emits a loud, low scream and holds up his arms which have tentacles coming from the ends. Statler jumps out of his skin) Bahhhhhhhh ha ha ha. **(He slaps**

his knees in laughter and removes some rubber squids from his
sleeves)

Statler Swift:
(Recovering from a really good scare) Waldorf Voltaire! Good God!
You scared the devil out of me! Where on earth-

Waldorf Voltaire:
I got them at the Dollar Store while you were shopping for port. Ha ha, that
was a good one!

Statler Swift:
Easy for you to say. Now I really *must* go to the loo.

Waldorf Voltaire:
Say, where is that bottle of tawny?

Statler Swift:
Right here, my good man. Waiting for this, the perfect occasion. **(He pulls
out a dark green bottle and a pair of red solo cups. Hands Waldorf
a cup, pulls the stop, and sloshes port into their glasses)**

Waldorf Voltaire:
(While Statler is pouring) How does that go? White wine for…

Statler Swift:
Champagne for lovers.

Waldorf Voltaire:
Right, right. Champagne for lovers.

Statler Swift:
White wine for women.

Waldorf Voltaire:
Red wine for men.

Statler Swift:
And port. **(Waldorf Voltaire stands and joins in, glasses raised)** Port
is for heroes!

Waldorf Voltaire:
Statler?

Statler Swift:
Yes, good sir.

Waldorf Voltaire:
I have a toast.

Statler Swift:
By all means.

Waldorf Voltaire:
Its an American toast.

Statler Swift:
This play is really getting to you. Please, we **(motions to the audience)**
would love to hear it.

Waldorf Voltaire:
**(Clears his throat. Motions with his cup to the stage, to the audi-
ence and to Statler)** To the Greatest Generation.

Statler Swift:
Here here! To the Greatest Generation.

Waldorf Voltaire:
When hope was lost, and villainy stormed, they were heroes.

Statler Swift:
Indeed they were, my dear Waldorf, indeed they were.

Waldorf Voltaire:
Now sir, about the loo? I was wondering if you would do an old gent a favor, and, well, check the stalls for anything out of the ordinary?

Statler Swift:
By all means. Bit jumpy myself.

(They clink cups and then Waldorf begins humming *My Country Tis of Thee*. Statler joins in and they exit the box, the lights fading as their voices fade)

(The lights come up stage left revealing Euripides standing before a children's choir. They are dressed in white togas, and taking their cue from a tone rung on a bell by Euripides, sing this song, Euripides providing a bass)

My country, 'tis of thee,
Sweet land of liberty,
Of thee I sing;
Land where my fathers died,
Land of the pilgrims' pride,
From ev'ry mountainside
Let freedom ring!

My native country, thee,
Land of the noble free,
Thy name I love;
I love thy rocks and rills,

Thy woods and templed hills;
My heart with rapture thrills,
Like that above.

Let music swell the breeze,
And ring from all the trees,
Sweet freedom's song;
Let mortal tongues awake,
Let all that breathe partake;
Let rocks their silence break,
The sound prolong

(Euripides steps forward as the chorus hums the melody and recites this)

Let freedom ring from the snow capped Rockies of Colorado!
Let freedom ring from the curvaceous slopes of California!
Let freedom ring from the Stone Mountain of Georgia!
Let freedom ring from Lookout Mountain in Tennessee
Let freedom ring from every hill and molehill in Mississippi!
From every mountainside, let freedom ring!

(Euripides steps back as he and the chorus resume)

Our fathers' God to Thee
Author of liberty,
To thee we sing;
Long may our land be bright,
With freedom's holy light,
Protect us by Thy might,
Great God our King.

(The lights fade on the narrator's stage. House lights slowly come up. Intermezzo II)

Midtro II

My own narrative: An upscale and trendy eatery in wood and brick. Local artists oils and watercolors adorn the walls. Attentive bartenders beside engaging cooks, an open kitchen sits beside the wonderfully bottle-cluttered back bar. Sushi. Charcuterie. American Nouveau. My wife and I are remembering my father, as today would be his birthday. It is our first time out since the election. Christmas lights twinkle, snow falls outside the window, and inside everything is cozy, merry, and bright. The bartender pours three glasses of ten-year tawny, so the three of us can toast my father. I raise my glass, "Once, we fought fascists, now we elect them. To my father, and his one hundred and fifteen combat missions over France and Germany."

Here, here.

Act III

(The house lights dim, leaving the theater in darkness for several long moments. Slowly rising, we hear the sounds of a street fight. Insults. Jeers. Cheers. Egging on. The sound of a foot striking a body. From up out of the inky blackness of the darkened theater, twin pillars of flame rise suddenly on either side of center stage. The lights come up in all the reds and oranges of Hell, Circle Seven, Outer Ring. On the ground is The Donald. Standing around him are three shades: Abusive Donald, wearing a white tank top and blue jeans; Corporate Raider Donald, wearing a power suit with yellow tie; Commander-in-Chief Donald, wearing a general's uniform. On the left of center stage is Private Centaur on his front knees, shielding his face from Bully Donald, wearing a maroon and white uniform. The shade-Donalds are quite literally kicking the shit out of The Donald while Bully Donald slaps-up Private Centaur)

The Donald:
What the fuck, guys! Come on. What I'd ever do to you? I mean me! This is bullshit!

Abusive Donald:
Shut up fuck twat. **(Kick)**

The Donald:
Who are you people?

Commander-in-Chief Donald:
I'm you as President; this is you **(motioning to Corporate Raider Donald)** in business; this was you when you were young **(motions toward Bully Donald)**; and this **(pointing out Abusive Donald)** is you in interpersonal relationships.

Abusive Donald:
Fuck yeah!

The Donald:
Then if you're all me, why are you beating me?

Abusive Donald:
Who's asking the questions here, pin dick! **(Slap)**

Corporate Raider Donald:
Hostile takeover there, circus peanut. Get with the program. **(Kick)**

Commander-in-Chief Donald:
Looks like the better devils of your nature are in charge, son. **(Pause. Abusive Donald looks over)** You go right ahead. **(Abusive Donald kicks The Donald twice)**

Abusive Donald:
(Pointing at The Donald, inches from his face) We own you, boy!

The Donald:
Give me a chance to explain.

Bully Donald:

(Slaps Private Centaur, then spins around and plants a toe into The Donald) I had you all set, Pops! All you had to do was be me, then the rest of these guys would follow. **(Flips The Donald off, turns, and slaps Private Centaur)**

Corporate Raider Donald:

Look here, me. We, I mean you, had this all set up. Just stay with the plan: step on everyone around you, rise to the top, then the fun begins. **(He lights a cigar, blows the smoke in The Donald's face)**

Commander-in-Chief Donald:

We feel you're getting too soft.

The Donald:

Me?

Abusive Donald:

Yeah, you, butt slice! **(Kick, kick)**

Corporate Raider Donald:

What we're trying to reinforce here, son, is that this merry little adventure you've been on has wasted a lot of resources.

The Donald:

You're telling me. **(Trying to stand. Abusive Donald gets up in his face, hands gripping his lapels)**

Commander-in-Chief Donald:

Give him a minute there, A.D. **(Abusive Donald lets go of the lapels, steps back)**

The Donald:

No one understands how much time has been misspent trying to make me walk away from you guys. I get it. But I don't have a lot of control down here. So, until I can get topside and resume with, **(Hands up and fingers making quotations)** *the plan*, I have to just swing along with whatever they put in front of me.

Commander-in-Chief Donald:

Then they're not getting to you?

The Donald:

Look, I'm the same guy I was when I ran into those hairy, pissed-off senators back in the forest. I'm not changing. And this, **(he gestures with one finger making a circle above his head)** and all the bullshit I've been through, and all of *you,* **(stabs a finger at the three in front of him)** are all the result of a bad trip on some fucked up cough medicine.

(The three look at each other. Bully Donald turns from Private Centaur)

Bully Donald:

Are you kidding me?

Abusive Donald:

You. Just. Don't. Get it! **(And down goes The Donald, right hook to the left side of the face. Suddenly, all four of them are laying into him, kicks and knees and fists. They are shouting at him lines like: Milk Toast! Loser! Sally Man! Yard Ball Saucer! Girlie Boy! Wimp! Poofball! And the like)**

(From off stage, stage left, we hear the canter of Nessie and the voice of Boss Tweed)

Boss Tweed:
Strumpet! I hear your voice, man! Are you down there?

(They enter stage left. Stop. And stand their ground. The four Violent Donalds stand up over The Donald, shoulders back, sneers of defiance on their faces. Nessie sends an arrow into the sternum of Commander-in-Chief Donald with a resounding thwap! All four Violent Donalds look at each other bug-eyed, then flee hastily and exit stage right yelling things like: We'll be back! Watch yourself! This is our block! Abusive Donald: See you next Tuesday! Nessie goes over to help Private Centaur and Boss Tweed goes over to The Donald)

Boss Tweed:
Strumpet! You alright?

The Donald:
Man, did that ever suck. I've never been so hard on myself.

Boss Tweed:
For the last time Jonah, you have got to stick by my side. There's a lot of nasty shit down here, and it seems everyone's got your number.

The Donald:
How'd you find me?

Boss Tweed:
(Points at Nessie) The cavalry, son. To the rescue. He tracked you from where the Minotaur jumped us to right here, the edge of the middle ring.

The Donald:
(Slowly rising, dusting himself off, checking for lumps, bumps, and bruises) Thank God.

(Boss Tweed punches The Donald on the shoulder, gives him a stern look)

The Donald:
What?

Boss Tweed:
We went past that cave. **(The Donald looks down guiltily)** Who the fuck was that?

The Donald:
Who? I don't have any idea what you're talking about.

Boss Tweed:
Bullshit. Little Missy in the doorway. Who was that?

The Donald:
Not sure. I just walked right past.

Boss Tweed:
It didn't look like you'd walked right past.

The Donald:
You're full of shit.

Boss Tweed:
It looked like Little Missy had some freshly-fucked hair, and while we were busting ass making sure you're alright, you were having some horizontal refreshment.

The Donald:
That what it looked like.

Boss Tweed:
Yeah.

The Donald:
Well, Little Missy has legs like a cuttlefish and I have no idea what that thing is, or where it came from. And another thing-

Boss Tweed:
(Stepping up into The Donald's face) Yeah, what's that, Romeo?

The Donald:
The issue I have right now is how the fuck do you, or cuttlefish, or horsey over there, or any motherfucker in this seriously fucked up place, get me the fucking hell out of here!

Boss Tweed:
(Cracking knuckles) I believe its time you and I finish that dance we started about one hundred and some fucking pages ago! **(He winds up, The Donald raises his fists and from off-stage, stage left, we hear hundreds of thousands of voices rising like banshees, rising like the walking dead, rising with all the violence Circle Seven-Outer Ring can muster. The Donald and Boss Tweed stop and turn their heads toward stage left. Nessie rises from assisting Private Centaur, and takes a couple steps toward stage left)**

The Donald:
What is it now?

Nessie:
(Holding up a hand to shush The Donald) Shhh! Listen. **(Wailing intensifies)** This is bad. **(The wailing get louder, even more intense)** This is real bad.

Boss Tweed:
I've never heard that. What is that? If I had skin it'd be crawling.

Nessie:
They've risen.

The Donald:
Who? Everyone's dead.

Nessie:
The shades. The shades in the Outer Ring. Maybe more. Its like, millions of voices of the damned. **(He turns sharply, hooks an arm under Private Centaur's arm and lifts him up)** We need to get out of here right now.

(The Donald takes a few steps toward stage left)

Boss Tweed:
Where you going, Romeo?

The Donald:
Fuck you.

(From stage left a centaur, mangled and beaten, enters and falls at Nessie's feet. He holds up a shredded red beret)

Nessie:
Chiron. Dead. The Law. God's Law for this Circle is dead.

The Donald:
What's that mean?

Boss Tweed:
It means we are screwed right and proper!

Nessie:

(Looking down) Circles of chaos. (Looking up) Oh, Dear God in Heaven, please help us now. (Turning toward the others and crossing to stage right) Come with me if you want to live.

(They exit rapidly stage right. As the lights fade, the wailing increases and the dim outlines of a few demented shades enter stage left)

(The lights come up on the narrator's stage and Euripides)

Euripides:
Hell in a nutshell: The absence of reason. Chaos. Chaos is when the approximate present does not come close to determining the future. The uncertainty we tolerate, how accurately we measure the present multiplied by time, yields results we cannot predict. Chaos.

The pit and the pendulum. You've been traveling through the pit for quite some time, but the pendulum? What seems a simple arc is governed by a differential equation. The variables of force, torque, energy, resistance, perhaps small angle approximation, all conspire to ever-so-slightly change the path of the blade over the body on the slab. Now, add another section of arm, make it a double rod pendulum, and you have chaos.

So, Americans go to the polls, and in an already complex system filled with many variables, they elect a President. And thus, we have a new equation called 'Trumpet Theory'. Trumpet theory is this: Time multiplied by the inaccuracies of Mr. Trumpet, multiplied by uncertainty, will result in an unspecified amount of chaos. In other words, you're fucked. In still other words, in an already volatile, unpredictable world, an even more volatile, unpredictable variable has been added. And since that variable is President of The United States, it carries a rather significant exponent.

Hell is not a perfect equation. The sheer scale of the inferno, the dynamics of eternity and separate reality, of breaching impossibility, the volume of pain, and the soul-weight of billions of shades, means that even in Divinity there are margins.

The shades have risen. They have before, and they will again. Only now, our two anti-heroes are being driven before them, deeper into the pit. Its not like they weren't headed that way to begin with, except Mr. Trumpet isn't dead. He's fresh meat. And the mission to save him from himself has been compromised.

And chaos? It spills into Purgatorio, into Paradiso, and onto Earth, whatever may be left of it.

O! Dear friends! My long suffering audience, from mighty wrongs to petty perfidy you have seen what human beings can do!

Live! Live not in vain! Your mind! Your frame! Your blood! The very essence of your breath! Fear not, but love. And in the darkness of this hour, in the despairing lands we tread, we shall show the tyrants how powerful the dove. When sword has failed as it always does, and the ink has dried like blood, with hope eternal and divine, God's will in us sublime, we shall overcome. We. Shall. Overcome.

(The lights fade on Euripides)

(The lights rise center stage revealing a forest of twisted, thorn-filled trees. These trees are actually shades, their spirits interred within the iron wood-like trunks and limbs. They suffer greatly, the semblance of themselves when they were human embodied on the trunks. As they sway, they moan and wail in pain: alien feelings of distress in alien bodies. The stage is lit in deep blues and grays. The ground is that same undulating black rock with tufts of

hands and fingers rising out of it. Withered human hearts crawl along like insects, still slowly beating, using the stalks of their aortas as an appendage.

Without warning, a pack of wild dogs tears through the grove, from stage right to stage left, chasing a wicker man. The dogs run the profligate/wicker man down and tear him to pieces. They leave, via the back of the stage, and the pieces of the wicker man reassembles. He staggers off-stage in the opposite direction. Flying amongst and above the trees are harpies. They are beautiful women who are also birds)

(A harpy like a crow and another like a robin land beside a tree. The other trees/shades look nervously at what transpires)

Crow:
You! You miserable selfish shade. How did you do it? How did you take your life?

Shade/Tree:
I slit my wrists. **(Holds up a branch with deep wounds running lengthways)** Please don't eat me. Please. I beg of you. Being here forever is punishment enough.

Robin:
Never enough. You threw away God's greatest gift! Why!

Shade/Tree:
My lover left me for another.

Crow:
So what.

Robin:
There are billions of you. Find another.

Crow:
Life is short. Memory is shorter. You would have been rewarded for your pain.

Robin:
Now look at you. Eternity, as a tree.

Crow:
In darkness forever.

Robin:
Your foolish, selfish heart, crawling like a lost bug.

Crow:
I am happy you are here.

Shade/Tree:
What? Why?

Robin:
Because you taste so good!!

(The two harpies snap at the leaves of the tree. The shade screams in pain, limbs flapping. All the other trees start panicking, screaming as well. From stage left enters Nessie. The harpies stop in their feast, and then abruptly fly off as The Donald, Boss Tweed, and Private Centaur enter at a run from stage left. They stop, The Donald panting)

The Donald:
We must have out run them by now.

Boss Tweed:
I don't know. Its only been the length of one soliloquy.

The Donald:
He is windy.

Nessie:
He's right. We should be able to stop and let the human catch his breath.

The Donald:
I never knew being damned was so much work.

Boss Tweed:
It wears on ya.

The Donald:
I hate to ask, but where are we? **(Taking in the surroundings)**

Nessie:
This is the Middle Ring of Circle Seven. The Forest of Suicides.

The Donald:
Depressing.

Boss Tweed:
Very. I'm not in here, thank God. The harpies are a bitch.

The Donald:
The what?

Boss Tweed:
Harpies. Like a cross between a woman and a bird.

Nessie:
They eat the shades. Look, **(he points out the Shade/Tree that has just been fed upon, the wounds still bleeding)** that's a shade. They're made into these ugly, thorny trees. And look there, **(he points at the ground, at a heart)** that's one of their hearts. The harpies eat them as well.

Boss Tweed:
Then there's the dogs.

Nessie:
Oh yeah, of course the dogs.

The Donald:
What dogs?

Boss Tweed:
Packs of em.

Nessie:
Big, nasty, black dogs.

Boss Tweed:
Their spittle alone causes hives and sores.

The Donald:
Why are they here?

Nessie:
Profligates.

The Donald:
Profit who?

Boss Tweed:
Precisely. People who profited by exploiting and destroying the means of life.

The Donald:
I don't get it.

(From stage right comes the sound of angry dogs. There is a quiver of fear and muffled shrieking from the trees. A wicker-shade comes falling/running/tearing through the trees. The dogs pounce on the wicker-shade and rip off limbs. Parts of bush and tree are literally flying through the air in a cloud. The Donald is trying to climb a tree. Boss Tweed steps behind Nessie who simply stands still. The dogs exit stage left. And ever-so-slowly, the wicker-shade reforms and slinks away stage right)

Shade/Tree 2:
(Looking at The Donald as The Donald in surprise looks the tree in the eyes) Do you mind? Trying to suffer here.

The Donald:
(Getting down from the tree) Right, right. Sorry. **(Regrouping with Boss Tweed and the centaurs)** This is fucked-up. I mean, there's some seriously messed-up shit down here, but this is just twisted.

Boss Tweed:
Well, that might be the point, huh?

The Donald:
Why? Why this punishment?

Nessie:
These shades will be trapped in the tree forever. Even past the final judgement.

The Donald:
But why?

Boss Tweed:
Because they threw away the body that God had given them. They threw away life.

The Donald:
Okay, I get that. But the running stick people? The dogs?

Nessie:
Suicide is not just taking your life, but also the means to sustain it.

Boss Tweed:
The air you breathe. The soil to grow food. The water you drink. The money you've been given. The property you live on. The wicker-shades, they squandered that stuff.

Nessie:
Or despoiled it. When you poison the air, you are in essence, committing suicide.

The Donald:
I thought squanderers were back a few Circles?

Boss Tweed:
Those folks squandered because they couldn't control themselves, these folks did so maliciously. In fact, there are quite a few captains of industry being torn apart for eternity as we speak. **(He leans forward and pokes The Donald in the chest)** If you take my meaning.

The Donald:
Yeah, yeah. But what about the bird-things. Why?

Boss Tweed:
Search me? Nessie?

Nessie:
The harpies are spirits of the wind. They're here because of the storm of violence, like the winds of war. In the frenzy of suicide, there blows a gale inside the heart. That gale calls the harpies.

The Donald:
So yeah, the bird part, but why are they female as well.

Nessie:
Well, Mr. Trumpet, lets ask this fellow over here.

(They cross the stage and step up to one of the trees. It is shivering with fear as they approach)

Nessie:
Shade. We seek answers from you. Awake to us. **(Silence, save for whimpering)** Shade! Answer me! **(Nessie looks back at the other three)** Shade! Alright. Have it your way. **(Nessie reaches out and breaks a branch off of the tree. The tree opens its eyes and screams in pain)**

Shade/Tree 3:
Wh-wh-what do you want?! Don't eat me! Please. Please don't eat me. I am suffering enough.

Nessie:
We're not harpies. We want to ask you a question.

Shade/Tree 3:
Anything. Don't hurt me further. Ask.

Nessie:
We understand that the nature of the harpy is bird, and is an air spirit, but why are they only female?

Shade/Tree 3:
You have asked a question I long have pondered. And the answer I possess. But you must step aside, and let the human stand before me.

The Donald:
Why me?

Shade/Tree 3:
It is no accident that you are here, in this forest, before this tree.

The Donald:
Impossible. Blind luck. We were driven here.

Shade/Tree 3:
You are as wrong as you ever are. I am no simple suicide. I am no random spirit trapped in this black tree.

The Donald:
Then who are you.

Shade/Tree 3:
You knew me once. You knew me as Bill. Bill the piano man. **(The Donald hangs his head. Brings his hand up to his brow)** I think you remember. **(The centaurs have backed off. Boss Tweed as well, but still within earshot)** Do you remember me?

The Donald:
I do. I'm sorry, Bill. It was just business.

Shade/Tree 3:

You never paid me. I tuned hundreds of pianos for you. Hundreds. One solid year of tuning. I gave up all my other accounts. And you never paid me. And my creditors, they closed me out. My business, gone. My home, gone. And then my wife, my children. The shame.

The Donald:

Look, Bill, I'm sorry. I had no idea. How could I know?

Shade/Tree 3:

How could you not. We're people. Not numbers. But to you-

The Donald:

Bill, its business. Its all numbers.

Shade/Tree 3:

So, you sharpen your pencil, and I end up as a misshapen tree in Hell forever. Not too fair, I'd say.

The Donald:

(Turning to Boss Tweed) Hey, he's right, this isn't fair. Is there something you can do? Somebody? Anything?

Boss Tweed:

Fortune. Fate. Bad choices. Everyone down here has a story, pal. So do you. Ask him the question.

The Donald:

(Turning back to Shade/Tree 3) Why are the harpies women.

Shade/Tree 3:

To quote Euripides, from his play Medea: Of all creatures that can feel and think, women are the worst treated things alive. **(Even the centaurs look**

down after this is spoken) As for you, Mr. Trumpet, there will be a special place for you. Whereas we normal sinners may have shades in many Circles, each one suffering for those wrongs committed, you will sit in lowest dishonor.

The Donald:
(Terse) What do you know. You're just a damned tree.

Shade/Tree 3:
I am a tree. But even in Hell, trees have wisdom.

The Donald:
How can you know my fate?

Shade/Tree 3:
I did something that you've never done.

The Donald:
(Scoffing) What might that be?

Shade/Tree 3:
I asked God.

The Donald:
I've asked God tons of stuff.

Shade/Tree 3:
Never from your heart. And only for yourself.

The Donald:
What arrogance!

Shade/Tree 3:

Do not mistake stoic humility for arrogance. Trees go deep. Hell runs deep. And all we have is time. Rooted in one spot for eternity, it affords one the opportunity to do something else you've never done.

The Donald:

Aaaand what might that be?

Shade/Tree 3:

Think. **(To this Boss Tweed and the centaurs burst out in laughter)** By God, if I weren't a tree I'd dance a jig to celebrate your demise, but instead, I'll just laugh. **(He laughs. Howling laughter right in The Donald's face)** I'll see you on your next trip down this way!

(All of the trees start laughing. Wicked laughter fills the stage. And then screeches, as four harpies swoop in from the skies and land in a circle around The Donald, Boss Tweed, and the centaurs. At this, the laughter stops, and an eagle harpy walks up to The Donald)

Eagle:

Well, well, well, what do we have here?

Robin:

We were feeding when these interlopers came running in.

Crow:

I wonder how these shades taste?

Owl:

Only one of them is a shade.

Eagle:
What? Do tell my wise friend.

Owl:
(Owl walks over to each that she mentions) This fat one, with the scraggly beard, he's a shade. The horsemen are centaurs, from the Outer Ring. But this plump, orange-faced thing, hmmm, I'm not sure what to make of this one. **(She pokes him with a finger from a hand that is on the underside of a wing)** By zephyrs! He's human!

Eagle:
Inconceivable!

Crow:
Yummy.

Robin:
Biggest worm I've ever seen.

Owl:
What's your story?

(The Donald looks over to Boss Tweed)

Boss Tweed:
The bird's talking to you, pal.

The Donald:
We don't have a story. We're just passing through. So, if you don't mind-

Eagle:
Batshit! He's lying!

Robin:
Yeah, lying!

Crow:
Let's eat him!

Owl:
(Holding up wings) Don't ruffle your feathers, ladies. **(To The Donald)** We don't believe you. Why are you in our woods? Why were you running? Where are you going?

The Donald:
As I was saying-

Eagle:
Not you! Someone with a brain.

Owl:
(To Nessie) Horseman, you're a tracker. I've seen the Outer Ring. I've seen you. I heard a great commotion there. Is it this that you run from?

Nessie:
Yes. Listen. **(Distant wailing. A low rumble of many millions of feet)**

Owl:
What is that?

Nessie:
The shades in the Outer Ring have risen.

Owl:
Heaven help us.

Eagle:
Who is this one? **(Points to The Donald)**

Boss Tweed:
He's the Strumpet. My mission is to show him all of hell.

Eagle:
Ridiculous. Who on Earth would give you such a task?

Boss Tweed:
Not from Earth. From beyond.

Owl:
Ahh, now I understand. This mission is divine. We had heard there was a human loose down here. **(Leans in and looks The Donald up and down)** You. You caused this.

Crow and Robin:
Eat him!

The Donald:
Bullshit. I haven't done jack.

Eagle:
He just looks like trouble.

Crow and Robin:
(Moving in close to The Donald) Consuuuuume!!!

The Donald:
(Trying to ignore two very hungry harpies) Hey sister, I didn't ask to be here.

Nessie:
In truth, we are just passing through.

Eagle:
To where?

Owl:
To the very bottom, Eagle. To the bottom of the pit. This is the one in the stories.

Eagle, Crow, and Robin:
Stories?

Owl:
When we were chicks. The stories they told us on dark nights, when the winds howled and the nests rocked in the trees. **(Eagle, Crow, and Robin look over to The Donald)** The stories of chaos and destruction, and a withering fire that burns all of the trees and boils the water. **(The other three harpies puff up and start pushing The Donald)** The greatest profligate in history. The ultimate vandal. **(Eagle and Robin keep pushing The Donald. Crow sniffs a shoulder)** Nature's Villain! Earth's destroyer!

(Crow takes a nibble out of The Donald's shoulder)

The Donald:
Ouch! What the hell!

Crow:
(Stepping away spitting) Bleh, bleh, bleh.

(From stage left there is the sound of many dogs yipping and yelping in fear. A pack of them breaks through the forest and crosses

the stage in panic, exiting stage right. Everyone on stage follows their progress in unison. From stage left we hear what sounds like hundreds of sticks being fed into a chipper. A half-dozen wicker-shades come tearing through the forest and cross the stage, exiting stage right. One of them has dropped a wicker leg. It hops back onto stage, picks up its leg, and then turns and re-exits stage right. Everyone on stage follows all of this in unison. They all look stage left as the wailing gets louder, the sound of the shades' feet grows deeper, and the stage begins to shake. And then, it stops. It is silent. The Donald, Boss Tweed, the centaurs, and the harpies, all lean toward stage left. Silence. They all take one tentative step toward stage left, heads leaning forward, tilting so their right ear faces stage left. Silence. They take one more step toward-Bam! A giant foot inside a giant galosh lands on stage from stage left with a thick, sticky splatter. There, above the galosh, is the tattered shin and calf of the Minotaur ending in a bloody stump. All on stage freak-out and scream, running into each other, running in place, and eventually exiting stage right in unorganized chaos. The trees are shaking and moaning. The wailing continues. The sounds of millions of angry, pounding feet continues. And the lights go down on the forest)

(The lights go up on Statler Swift and Waldorf Voltaire. They are crouched just below the railing, blood splatters around the front and back of the box. They are holding up sticks they have fashioned into talismans reminiscent of *The Blair Witch Project*)

Waldorf Voltaire:
Do we have more port?

Statler Swift:
We do!

Waldorf Voltaire:
I could stand a bracer!

(The lights fade on the box and come up on Euripides. He is disheveled, and his toga is blood-splattered and torn. At his feet is a giant empty bottle of Stella Artois. In his left hand is an urn, beer frothing out the top)

Euripides:
Helluva party! Isn't it!

(The lights fade on Euripides. There are moments of darkness where all we hear is the tormented wailing, the stampeding feet, the fetid winds of Hell blowing, and then, tinny and remote, a radio)

(Stage left, a single spot light zoomed all the way in, reveals only a transistor radio hanging from a tree limb)

Joseph Goebbels:
Hey kids. Just letting you know that tonight, Miss Tokyo Rose will be spinning the wax as yours truly will be emceeing a gala event down around Circle Eight. Yeah, that's right, big doings going on way down near the muckety-mucks, and I'll be a whiter shade of pale standing up there intro-ing the hottest new band in Hell. But for now, here's a little something you're not likely to find, Nirvana.

(The spot light slowly zooms out as we hear Nirvana's *Smells Like Teen Spirit* playing from the radio. The song gets louder as the spotlight pulls out. The song is picked up on the house speakers and fills the room. The spot light fades as the lights stage left slowly come up revealing branches and partial trunks of the shade/trees and one lone tree in full. There are tatters of plaid shirts hanging from its branches, pairs of work boots thrown over its limbs like a shoe tree, and the radio is hanging prominently from the largest branch. At the base of the tree are stumps of candles, teddy bears, empty booze bottles, and a poster board with runny-ink that says 'We Miss You Kurt Cobain!' The tree's eyes are droopy, it has a dopey, knowing grin, and the back of the tree behind the eyes has been blown out. The tree bobs with the music, mouthing the words)

(Eagle and Owl land in front of Kurt Cobain tree. The music fades out)

Eagle:
(Agitated and out of breath) That was close. There must be ten million shades.

Owl:
Angry souls, I'd say.

Eagle:
I don't get it. Why the uprising?

Owl:
They seem disconnected. Disenfranchised. Distraught.

Eagle:
They're in Hell. They earned it.

Owl:
One should never discount anyone.

Kurt Cobain Tree:
(Melodic) Ladies, what's shaking?

Eagle:
Just the leaves on your tree, shade.

Kurt Cobain Tree:
Oh come on, girls, do an old rock and roller a favor, would ya?

Owl:
We're a might busy at the moment, young man.

Kurt Cobain Tree:
One favor. Simple.

Owl:
Simple is as simple does.

Kurt Cobain Tree:
Pleeeease.

(The sound of scared, panicked dogs begins to rise from off-stage left. Eagle and Owl turn their heads to this)

Eagle:
Here they come.

Owl:
(Turning toward stage right and taking a couple steps) I wonder how far it is to the Inner-

(The lights go up on the right side of center stage. In hues of orange, yellow and red, they reveal an endless plain of burning sand. The remains of oil derricks, pumping stations, refineries, mining equipment, processing facilities, coal and nuclear power plants, along with the skeletal shells of industry's infrastructure,

are scattered across the desert, half-buried, corroded, and burnt. Shades are everywhere. Lying down. Crouching. Wandering. From the angry sky falls burning flakes, so hot they ignite whatever they touch)

(The sound of the dogs becomes incessant. Eagle and Owl whip their heads around from staring at the desert, to a pack of terrified dogs that enter stage left and run past Kurt Cobain Tree. They race by and out across the burning plain, the pitch of their cries turning to yelps as their paws hit the hot sand)

Kurt Cobain Tree:
Duuude!!! That was sooo boss!

Eagle:
Time to take flight.

Owl:
I'd say.

Kurt Cobain Tree:
(Saccharin sweet and melodic) Ladies.

Eagle:
I wonder where the horsemen and those other two are?

Owl:
Should be coming through. I think they were moving fast enough.

Kurt Cobain Tree:
Aw come on girls.

Eagle:
(Annoyed) What is it?

Kurt Cobain Tree:
Favor?

Eagle:
What?

Kurt Cobain Tree:
Could you check the bottles by my trunk and see if someone's left a fresh one?

Eagle:
Are you kidding me?

Owl:
Addiction transcends death. Interesting. **(Looking down)** There's some in that bottle.

Kurt Cobain Tree:
Sweet.

Eagle:
(Picking up the bottle Owl is pointing at) For God's sake.

Owl:
What is it?

Eagle:
(Holding the bottle for Owl to see) *Eagle Rare* Bourbon.

Owl:
You're famous. Pour some in his yap.

Kurt Cobain Tree:
Rhymes with sap! **(Singing)** Pour away, let go the day, I'm a soul in a tree for eterni-TAY! **(Repeats the 'ay over and over)**

Eagle and Owl:
(Covering ears) Ewwwww.

(There is that sound like a chipper increasing quickly in volume)

Owl:
(Singing) Time for us to fly!

Eagle:
(Setting the bottle down by Kurt Cobain Tree's trunk) See ya! Wouldn't wanna be ya!

Kurt Cobain Tree:
Noooo!

(Eagle and Owl fly up and off. From behind another tree in the back of stage left, Boss Tweed pokes his head around and looks both ways. Assured, he walks up to the Kurt Cobain Tree, stands behind it, and looks around it toward stage left, off-stage, where the 'chipper' sound is coming on fast)

Kurt Cobain Tree:
Dude! Wow. So much fun today.

Boss Tweed:
Hey son, you see a couple of hot looking birds touch down around here?

Kurt Cobain Tree:
Dude. Oh my God. Yeah. Right here. Like, right there! Two of em! Cuuute. Almost scored me some of that fancy booze.

Boss Tweed:
Booze? Where?

Kurt Cobain Tree:
Brother man, right there at the foot of my gnarly trunk! Come on and help a poor soul out!

(Boss Tweed leans from around the tree to grab the bottle of *Eagle Rare.* **Just as his fingers are around the neck, a host of wicker-shades burst from stage left and tumble across stage and exit stage right)**

Kurt Cobain Tree:
Duuuude! Unreal! Wow! What a great day. If only I could fix my head.

(Boss Tweed grabs the bottle, pulls out the cork with a 'pop')

Kurt Cobain Tree:
Aaahhh, such sweet music. Just dump that sucker right in here. **(Boss Tweed takes a long pull from the bottle)** Dude, are you California-hittin' my shit?

Boss Tweed:
Zu zu zu zu zu zu zu! Oil of gladness, done to a turn, that's the finest fire water I have ever tasted!

Kurt Cobain Tree:
Oooh you are killing me. Brother. Please.

(Boss Tweed goes to pour the bourbon into Kurt Cobain Tree's mouth, but at that moment, Nessie and Private Centaur come galloping up from off stage left. Boss Tweed pulls the bottle away, a splash falling to the rocky ground sizzling a crawling heart)

Boss Tweed:
Where in the fuck have you two been?

Nessie:
(Tersely) We beelined it from the bloody boot to this goofy tree. Its you folks that got buggy.

Boss Tweed:
Where's the Strumpet?

Nessie:
We thought he was with you!

Boss Tweed:
Fuck!

(The wailing and the sound of all those angry shades grows louder, nearer)

Boss Tweed:
(Taking another pull off of the *Eagle Rare*, setting it down in front of the blinking, wanting eyes of Kurt Cobain Tree) Ideas?

Nessie:
Let's run up and down this tree line and see if we see any sign of him. Private, give Mr. Tweed here the benefit of some speed.

Kurt Cobain Tree:
Speed?

Boss Tweed:
(Boss Tweed clambers atop Private Centaur) And awaaaay we go.

(The three of them gallop to the back of the stage, duck behind trees and exit. Entering from stage left, The Donald, terrified, picks his way until he's in front of the Kurt Cobain Tree. He looks

around, up, down. He looks at the candles, bears, and bottles. The
wailing grows louder, The Donald throws a hasty glance over his
shoulder)

Kurt Cobain Tree:
Brother man!

The Donald:
(Scared, startled and jumps) Jesus fucking Christ! Who is that? What is
it? You? The tree?

Kurt Cobain Tree:
It is the tree, my lost little friend. And do you think you could do a tree a
favor?

The Donald:
What? Under a little duress here at the moment.

Kurt Cobain Tree:
You and everyone else. Bruthas gotta just chill. Bruthas gotta just be cool. I
mean, its not that hard. Its like, the more you die, the more you live, you dig?

The Donald:
(Pause) What's your story?

Kurt Cobain Tree:
No story, just songs. You thirsty?

The Donald:
I could drink horse piss right now.

Kurt Cobain Tree:
They went that way. **(Gestures, slightly, with a branch or three)**

The Donald:
Two horse men and a fat guy?

Kurt Cobain Tree:
Yup. **(Big smile)** Two horsies and a fat guy. Thirsty?

The Donald:
(Seeing the bottle of *Eagle Rare*) Oooh, I get it. This is good shit. **(Pulls cork. Takes a pull)** Yes, sir! Campaign stop. Frankfort, Kentucky.

Kurt Cobain Tree:
Been to Louisville. We didn't get on so well in Kentucky. Fella, I've been rooted to this spot beside this stupid desert for over twenty years, and if you could just do a tree a favor and pour some of Kentucky's finest down my-

The Donald:
I'm way ahead of you. Here. **(The Donald pours half the bottle down Kurt Cobain Tree's mouth)** Got a little surprise for you. **(Reaches into his coat pocket and comes out with the never-ending bottle of cough syrup)** How's about a whack off of this cough medicine?

Kurt Cobain Tree:
Codeine?

The Donald:
I don't know what's in it, but here I am drinking with a tree. **(Tucks the bourbon between his legs, unscrews the cap of the green stuff, takes a slug, pours some down Kurt Cobain Tree's mouth. Replaces the cap and replaces the bottle. Grabs the bourbon)** Hang on, cannonball coming.

Kurt Cobain Tree:
Rock on, brother man.

(The Donald pours all but the dregs into the tree's mouth, and then finishes off the rest himself. As he does so, an angry-shade enters from stage left. He is deteriorated, hacked-up, a greenish-pale, and very pissed-off. He looks at The Donald and lunges for him. The Donald does nothing but freak and drop the bottle. Kurt Cobain Tree swings a limb like a hammer down on top of the angry-shade, splattering him into a bazillion pieces)

The Donald:
Man, that was close. I owe you one.

Kurt Cobain Tree:
Not at all, dude.

The Donald:
Which way did those guys go?

Kurt Cobain Tree:
Behind me and up the dividing line between Middle Ring and Inner Ring.

The Donald:
(Taking off at a jog across the stage and into the burning desert)
Thanks, pal!

Kurt Cobain Tree:
Hey, you're going the wrong way.

The Donald:
How do you know which way I'm going?

Kurt Cobain Tree:
(Yelling) Thanks, bro! Take it easy! (Speaking) Wow. What a day. (Beat) Man a bag of *Doritos* sounds good right-

(A rush of angry-shades burst from the forest stage left, not quite running, but hunting, stalking, relentlessly making their way across the stage and into the desert)

Kurt Cobain Tree:
Dudes! Slow down! I mean, like, whatever. (The shades that were on stage exit stage right. We can hear more from stage left) Oh, nevermind.

(The lights fade on the entire stage)

(Lights come up stage left, narrator's stage. Boss Tweed, Nessie, and Private Centaur are standing on the edge between Rings. On the left is part of a tree and on their right is the rusted-out top of an oil derrick lying on its side)

Boss Tweed:
Nothing.

Nessie:
Could he have been behind us?

Boss Tweed:
He was the first to run away.

Private Centaur:
He seems easily confused.

Boss Tweed:
Can't argue with that. What do we do tracker?

Nessie:
Double back. Talk to that one goofy tree. Check the sand for prints.

(A shade comes up to them from the desert. He is dressed from the mid-nineteenth century, but with an eccentric flair. He has a pith helmet on his head and field glasses around his neck. He is carrying a beat-up leather case and has a divining rod. Nessie reacts first and draws a bead on the shade with his long bow)

Nessie:
Shade! Halt!

Colonel Drake:
I mean you no harm, horse man. No harm. I have information for you.

Boss Tweed:
You look familiar. Who are you?

Colonel Drake:
Edwin Drake. But folks called me Colonel Drake back in the day.

Boss Tweed:
The wildcatter?

Colonel Drake:
The very same. Although, I've been through this desert for so long I can barely remember my name.

Privater Centaur:
Why would you do that, sir?

Colonel Drake:
Oil. Why else. *What else.* I mean, look around, son. I can feel it. These sands must be covering fields the likes we've never dreamed of.

Boss Tweed:
So, if you find oil, what are you going to do with it?

Colonel Drake:
What are we going to do with it? We're going to drill for it. We're going to tap that pay dirt, bring it up in endless barrels, and we're going to corner the market!

Nessie:
You realize you're in Hell?

Colonel Drake:
(Chuckling) It is hot out here.

Nessie:
No, I mean you are literally-

Boss Tweed:
(Waving Nessie off) Don't worry about it, Ness. **(To Colonel Drake)** You said you have some information for us.

Colonel Drake:
Oh yes, yes, well-

(The lights go up stage right, under the box. There are three men in nineteenth-century suits. Two of them have field glasses and are surveying around them. The third holds a tablet and a pencil)

John D. Rockefeller:
(Hands cupped to mouth and shouting at Colonel Drake) Drake, I say. Where the devil have you gotten off to?

H.L. Hunt:
By my calculations, the good Colonel should be in this **(motioning in completely the wrong direction)** direction. Not but a dozen or so paces.

J. Paul Getty:
He's right over there.

H. L. Hunt:
By God, you're right.

John D. Rockefeller:
Colonel! We think there are better prospects back by those large dunes.

H.L. Hunt:
To be sure. Colonel Drake, Mr. Rockefeller is most correct. You're digging in the wrong spot.

J. Paul Getty:
Maybe we should just listen to him, right? I mean, he did discover the stuff, so-to-speak.

Colonel Drake:
(Hands cupped by mouth, shouting over toward the three oil barons) Gentlemen. Its really quite simple. Just follow the stick. **(Holds up the divining rod)** Follow your hunch. Follow me.

John D. Rockefeller:
Well hurry up then, man. We haven't got all day.

H.L. Hunt:
Time is money.

J. Paul Getty:
Rise early. **(Pointer finger in the air)**

John D. Rockefeller:
Work hard. **(Pointer finger in the air)**

All three oil barons in unison:
And strike oil! **(Fists in the air. The three turn and exit stage right. Lights fade to black on stage right under the box)**

Boss Tweed:
Colonel, you have something for us.

Colonel Drake:
I know who you're looking for. I was prospecting by the tree line recently. There was this guy. Suit, tie. Had a weird glow about him. He ran up to me while I was working the stick, asked me which way was the way out. I looked at him like he was crazy, but then I thought about it and pointed toward the, the, oh bageezers, directions are useless out here, pointed toward that big dome-looking thing. That way. **(He motions toward stage right)**

Nessie:
From what direction did he come?

Colonel Drake:
(Pointing toward stage left and toward the audience) That way. By the weird tree. Came right out of the tree line and burst across the sand. Kept screaming and whining about how his feet were burning.

Boss Tweed:
What did his hair look like.

Colonel Drake:
Like a bunch of coons done got tangled up in it.

Private Centaur:
That's our boy.

Boss Tweed:
Thanks, Colonel, and, a, good luck, with the oil thing.

Colonel Drake:
Good luck, men. **(He turns and makes his way out of the lights and off stage toward the back, the stick out in front of him. He hums like a machine, pitch rising and falling, the divining rod in front of him quivering and pointing)**

Boss Tweed:
That rat fink Strumpet! We'd better move. Who knows what trouble he's in.

Nessie:
Double time!

(The lights fade as they turn and retrace their steps exiting stage left)

(The lights come up center stage. The scene that was here before is now expanded. Burning flakes fall from the orange-red sky to a vista of sand, wadis, dunes, and the broken machinery of the nineteenth and twentieth centuries. The remnants of exploration, exploitation, and energy production litter the landscape, eroded by sand and time. Shades stumble about in turmoil, hide in clumps beneath the wreckage, or simply lie in the open and fry)

(The Donald enters stage left. He is delirious from the heat, swats at the burning flakes, and is quite lost once again)

The Donald:
Why am I so stupid? Why didn't I stay with Bossman? Why didn't I just sit there with that goofy tree and drink until I passed out? **(He staggers up to a handful of oil drums: some standing, some tipped over, all covered/buried in sand)** Where in Hell am I? What Circle is this? Why so hot? Why so blazing hot? You could fry eggs on your forehead. Eggs. Hmmmm, eggs. I could fuck up a plate of eggs. So hot. So stupidly hot. What the-

(From stage right, a cart is pushed onto stage. It is an Italian Ice cart, festooned with pictures of brightly colored scoops of Italian Ice in little paper cups. There are bells jingling, ribbons and streamers in red, white, and green hanging from the cart and its awning, and a Derek Jeter-bobble head glued to the front like a hood ornament. Just on stage beside the cart, hidden from The Donald, a swirl of sand coalesces into Iblee, and then into an old, Italian man)

Iblee the Ice Man:
Icy Ice! Get your Italian Ice! Icy cold! Icy Ice! Only time today I'm going to be on this block. Icy Ice man! Get your Icy Ice!

The Donald:
Holy divine providence! Are you kidding me? Hey fella! Hey! I got some dollars. I want an Icy Ice!

Iblee the Ice Man:
You gotta run to me, friend. I am a very old.

The Donald:
(Jogging/stumbling up to the cart as Iblee pushes the cart toward center stage) I'm on my way! Hang on! Don't go no where, mister!

Iblee the Ice Man:
I couldn't if I wanted to.

The Donald:
(Reaches the cart. Digging through pockets) I know I had some money. It was right here! Dammit! **(Very frustrated and child-like)** Ooohhh! I swear. Nothing goes my way. I want an Icy Ice!

Iblee the Ice Man:
Its okay, Donny. I know you and your folks. I can hold a tab for you. Only you.

The Donald:
(Looking up) Do I know you?

Iblee the Ice Man:
It is me, Donny, Francesco. The Icy Ice Man. I've served you a thousand Icy Ices. Surely you know me?

The Donald:
Francesco. I do know you. You were always kind to me.

Iblee the Ice Man:
Always an extra scoop.

The Donald:
Yeeess! It is you. **(Looking around)** Neighborhood's gone to hell, huh?

Iblee the Ice Man:
Donny, its one hundred and thirty-seven in the shade: business has never been better. And happy? Everyone is happy to see Francesco. Are you happy, my Donny?

The Donald:
I'd be happier with a rainbow!

Iblee the Ice Man:
One rainbow with the extra scoop for my good friend Donny!

The Donald:
Yay!!!!

(Iblee the Ice Man lifts up a door in the top of the cart, grabs an ice cream scoop, a small, white paper cup, and reaches into the cart)

Iblee The Ice Man:
So, Donny, tell me what's going on in your life?

The Donald:
Oh, God. Well Francesco, things have gotten kind of complicated.

Iblee the Ice Man:
(Head buried in the cart digging for rainbow, pops up) Complicated?

The Donald:
Yeah, complicated. On Earth, I'm running for President. And no one really likes me. And the ones that do are kind of, sketchy. And to be honest, I mean you remember me from before, well, I'm not too sure I know what I'm doing and its too late to turn back and now I'm stuck down here in Hell and-

Iblee the Ice Man:
(Head popping up from inside the cart) I'm sorry, Donny, everything after President.

The Donald:
Never mind. Seriously, though, I'm stuck down here in Hell and I need to find a way out.

Iblee the Ice Man:
You don't have any friends down here? **(Hands The Donald a rainbow Icy Ice)**

The Donald:
Well, yes and no. I mean, there's the Bossman, and I've met some famous people who I had no idea they were in Hell, and then there's this Iblee-guy.

Iblee the Ice Man:
Who?

The Donald:

Well, **(Eating the Icy Ice)** I'm not sure what to make of this fella, if he is a fella. He says he can help me find a way out, so I meet with him and instead he looks like Maggie, or maybe Maggie looks like him, or maybe Maggie and him aren't related at all and well, its complicated.

Iblee the Ice Man:

You need to relax. This Iblee-guy, he sounds okay to me. I bet he'll help you out. Where you meet this guy? Jersey?

The Donald:

Good God no, its not that rough down here. A bunch of Circles up. Like, Circle Number Two, or before that, Limbo maybe. Man, I've been through Hell.

Iblee the Ice Man:

Sounds like it. You know Donny, you should trust this Iblee-guy. I gotta good feeling about him. I think he'll help you out.

The Donald:

Yeah. **(Finishing his rainbow Icy Ice and dropping the paper cup on the ground, where it promptly burns)** Maybe you're right.

Iblee the Ice Man:

C'mon, Donny. Its me, Francesco. Growing up, I was your only friend. You can trust old Francesco.

(The Donald tries to stand up, swoons, presses a hand to his forehead)

Iblee the Ice Man:

You okay, Donny?

The Donald:
(Sitting back down) Yeah, yeah, its just the Icy Ice. Ate it too fast. Whoo! That'll get ya spinning.

Iblee the Ice Man:
I tell you a secret. **(Motions The Donald closer)** A few blocks back, over by the glowey building, I run into this Iblee-guy. **(The Donald looks up)** Nice fella. He mentioned your name. Says, I try to help this Donny out, but always someone shows up.

The Donald:
He didn't have legs like a cuttlefish?

Iblee the Ice Man:
He no a have legs like a cuttlefish.

The Donald:
He didn't have swirling arms of chaos?

Iblee the Ice Man:
He no a have swirling arms of chaos.

The Donald:
He didn't have pouty lips, a perky nose, and an anchor bob?

Iblee the Ice Man:
Hey, come on, I'm an old man from the Upper East Side.

(There is an awkward silence, each not looking at the other)

The Donald:
Can I have another rainbow?

Iblee the Ice Man:
No.

The Donald:
Well, I guess I'll just be pushing off then.

Iblee the Ice Man:
You go to the glowey building. Its over there. You can't miss it. I'll send the little fella over. Maybe he can get you out of here, huh. That's what Donny wants, a way out, right?

The Donald:
Yeah, more than anything, a way out. I had no idea this would take so long.

Iblee the Ice Man:
Glowey building.

The Donald:
Glowey building. Does it have a name?

Iblee the Ice Man:
Churning.

The Donald:
Churning?

Iblee the Ice Man:
Yeah. Churning Noble. You go. I not even mark down this Icy Ice. On me. You have a good day, Donny.

The Donald:
(Getting up and slowly walking toward stage right, as the Icy Ice man starts pushing his cart toward stage left) You too, Francesco. Arrivederci!

Iblee the Ice Man:
Whatever you say. Stay outta the sun, Donny. See you in a while.

(Francesco unwinds back into Iblee as they both exit. The lights fade on center stage)

(The lights go up on the box. Statler Swift and Waldorf Voltaire are fanning themselves with their programs. They have pith helmets on with scarves that drape over the back of their necks. A rickety, old standing floor fan looms behind them, looking more like the prop from a vintage warbird. It is idle, the green, white, and red streamers from its cage limp)

Statler Swift:
Brilliant timing.

Waldorf Voltaire:
The actor portraying the weird little demon thing?

Statler Swift:
Good God, no. The heat! The AC in the theater going out at the same time we're crossing the desert! Makes you wonder if its really a coincidence.

Waldorf Voltaire:
There you go with your conspiracy theories.

Statler Swift:
Well.

Waldorf Voltaire:
My dear friend, for the eleventy-millionth time: people are too lazy to conspire to such lengths. Chance, or, as we learned earlier in tonight's drama, fortune, she simply has too much time on her hands.

(There is a pause, and then a knock at the box's door)

Statler Swift:
Expecting someone?

Waldorf Voltaire:
No.

(The two of them turn toward the door holding their *Blair Witch Project* talismans in front of them. The door opens and in walks Euripides. He has on a tool belt, a ball cap that says *CAT*, and is holding a tray with two icy beverages on it)

Euripides:
Gentlemen, these are on the house. **(Handing off the drinks.)** And I am here to fix the fan.

Waldorf Voltaire:
Wonderful!

Statler Swift:
Thank you so much. Double duty, tonight?

Euripides:
Indeed. You know theater: if anything can go wrong, it will during performance.

(All laugh)

Statler Swift:
We were just remarking at the timeliness of the sudden heat wave and the desert scene.

Euripides:
Oh, yes. A thousand apologies. The temperature on stage is ungodly.

Waldorf Voltaire:
I bet.

Euripides:
(Holding up a finger) The smutch of the greasepaint and the spice of the crowd!

(All laugh)

Waldorf Voltaire:
Euripides?

Euripides:
Yes. **(Working on the fan)**

Waldorf Voltaire:
Are you from Lemnos?

Euripides:
No. Salamis. I know where you're headed. Yes, I've been to Lemnos and the desert. I've wandered through it on several occasions.

Statler Swift:
Really? A desert in Europe?

Euripides:
The only one. It is, stunning. Stark. Beautiful. Quiet. Foreboding. There is no place on Earth like deserts.

Statler Swift:
And Waldorf, you've been to a desert?

Waldorf Voltaire:
Algeria. I visited Camus there, years ago. He called me up, so-to-speak.

Statler Swift:
And?

Waldorf Voltaire:
Everything our friend here has said. 'The mournful kingdom of sand', I believe is how the quote goes.

Euripides:
'In the desert the only god is a well'.

Statler Swift:
I'm in, 'What makes the desert beautiful is that somewhere it hides a well'.

Waldorf Voltaire:
'Wisdom from the desert'.

Euripides:
'Inhuman solitude made of sand and God'.

Statler Swift:
'The desert is the theater of the human struggle of searching for God'.

Waldorf Voltaire:
'Nobody takes from the desert anything but aridity and monsters'.

Euripides:
'It is the dwelling place of our demons'.

Statler Swift:
'They make a desert, and call it peace'.

Waldorf Voltaire:
Good one.

Statler Swift:
Though, let us not forget the Prince of Peace, 'Christ shared our experience; he suffered as we suffer, he died as we shall die, and for forty days he underwent the struggle between good and evil'.

(Euripides smacks the side of the fan on the last word-evil-and the fan kicks on)

Waldorf Voltaire:
Well done. And this, **(holding up the beverage)** is divine. Thank you so much.

Euripides:
(Touching his cap and exiting the box) Gentlemen.

(The lights fade on the box as Statler and Waldorf turn towards center stage)

(The lights come up on the narrator's stage. Boss Tweed, Nessie, and Private Centaur stand next to the Kurt Cobain Tree. The wailing of shades and the thunder of their feet is deafening. Private Centaur is rapidly shooting his crossbow toward off-stage, stage left. Nessie is feeding him bolts)

Kurt Cobain Tree:
(Branches pointing toward stage right) Him go that a way.

Boss Tweed:
That fucker!

(The lights fade on the narrator's box)

(The lights come up center stage. We are inside an enormous building of valves, tanks, pipes of all sizes, electrical boxes, conduit,

switches, and boards. Broken glass and plastic, industrial litter, drums and storage vats, all our partially covered with sand, even the uniform gray has been nearly sand-blasted off of the concrete walls. Everything, however, has a dim, luminescent, green glow. The chipped and peeling remnants of a huge sign on the cinder blocks reads: 1st line-large, CHERNOB; 2nd line beneath-smaller, Reactor No. 4. In the center of the stage, toward the front, is a desk and chair, three chairs beside it, a coffee table with three glasses of glowing-green water, and off toward stage right is another chair hidden from the view of the host and guests by a tattered curtain. There is a sign above and behind the desk and three chairs: *The Dumping Game!*)

(The Donald comes stumbling in from stage left. Sweat-soaked and with burn holes all over his suit, he is a mess. He heads straight for the table and downs one of the glowing-green glasses of water. Then, takes a gander at his surroundings)

The Donald:
Man alive, this was impressive. What was this? **(Looking at the table and desk)** And this? How's this fit in?

(Just then, entering from stage right, is your classic Hollywood gameshow host, cheesy suit and all, except this fella has seen some better days. His skin is glowing green, large parts of it are liquifying and falling off, his comb-over can barely comb over, and he is missing digits, ear lobes, etc. Still, he has that smile. As he enters, gameshow music enters right along with him, literally, as a small moving platform replete with Casio and Casio player glides onto stage behind him. He, likewise, has seen better days)

Chuck Bob Woolabarker:
(To the audience) Heeeeyyyy, guys and dolls! You know what time it is? The most exciting thirty minutes in television! Come on you crazy diamonds!

(He is out front working the actual audience and pointing back at the sign) Its time for, for, for-

The Audience Itself:
The! Dumping! Game!!!!!!

Chuck Bob Woolabarker:
That's right. The Dumping Game. And today, it's Celebrity Dumping Game, because we've got America's future President, Donald Trumpet!

(The crowd, in theory, goes wild, as Mr. Chuck Bob Woolabarker pumps them up and walks over to The Donald)

Chuck Bob Woolabarker:
Holy Hell! Are we excited to have you here. Been a longtime fan. Thank you so much for taking time from your busy schedule to be Contestant Number Three.

The Donald:
A, no problem.

Chuck Bob Woolabarker:
So, what brings you to Hell?

The Donald:
Well, I was on my way to a campaign stop, when these three liberal senators accosted me-

Chuck Bob Woolabarker:
That's so interesting! Thank you so much! Now, if you'll just park yourself in the seat closest to the desk, I'll introduce your two fellow contestants.

(Chuck Bob Woolabarker motions The Donald over to his chair, and then walks toward stage right)

Chuck Bob Woolabarker:
Contestant Number One is also a billionaire. He owns lots of property just like Mr. Trumpet, except all the holes on his golf courses are really, really big. You know why? **(To audience, hand beside ear)**

The Audience Itself:
Why!

Chuck Bob Wollabarker:
That's because they're strip mines! Contestant Number One owns swaths of Appalachia, employs thousands, sells the coal to his electric company, and then super charges all of us because there's no where else to get power! Let's hear it for Contestant Number One!

(From stage right enters a squat, fat man in an old suit. He isn't so much glowing green as covered in soot. He coughs persistently, puffs of black powder emitting from his mouth. He is obviously quite sick, possessing a pallor that would make a zombie jealous. Chuck Bob Woolabarker greets him with an elbow-grabbing, double-pump hand shake, the audience reacts, and our host walks him over to his chair)

Chuck Bob Woolabarker:
Contestant Number One meet Contestant Number Three! As if an introduction is even needed.

Contestant Number One:
Pleased to meet you Mr. Trumpet. **(Cough, cough. Sputum-filled handshake which The Donald wipes on Chuck Bob Woolabarker's suit coat)** Those of us in the energy sector are expecting big things from you.

The Donald:
You know, West Virginia might just be the prettiest state in the union.

Contestant Number One:
God! Don't say that word.

Chuck Bob Woolabarker:
And now! **(Walking up to the audience, and then over toward stage right)** Contestant Number Two! This gentleman hails from a land down under! He owns so many newspapers and television stations that the truth doesn't even matter anymore! Instead of raising his game, he's lowered the entire playing field, let's hear it for Contestant Number Two! **(The audience reacts. The Donald nods his approval, and Chuck Bob Woolabarker greets and seats the information mogul. Contestant Number Two is wearing a slick white suit, a Crocodile Dundee hat, crocodile-skin boots, and a confident gait. Things would be looking pretty good for Contestant Number Two, except he's in more Circles of Hell than Jeffrey Dahmer, and he's told so many lies that he has a dozen different facial tics and twitches)** Pretty sure the two of you know each other! **(Contestant Number Two shakes hands with The Donald)**

Contestant Number Two:
Donald. Always a pleasure. I trust my American Story Station is squarely behind you.

The Donald:
Like cars on a train. Truly appreciated. When'd you get down here?

Contestant Number Two:
Took me by surprise. Turns out, the cheap dye for the ink I was buying all those years, thickened with asbestos.

The Donald:
Noooo.

Contestant Number Two:
Swear. My sons are lining up the lawyers, passing the cash, and just waiting for the class-action.

The Donald:
I am so sorry.

Contestant Number Two:
Win some, well, you know.

Chuck Bob Woolabarker:
Alright you two love birds, and now folks, **(walking back out to the front of the stage and working the audience)** that moment you've all been waiting for, its time to introduce our darling Dumpette!

(Cheesy music that sounds like a cross between every bad game show theme and *The Stripper* erupts from the Casio player. Chuck Bob Woolabarker sashays over toward stage right as Iblee enters from stage right. Iblee stops, spins up into Maggie, and stands uneasily in front of her chair behind the curtain. Chuck Bob Woolabarker takes her hand and gives her a kiss on both cheeks)

Chuck Bob Woolabarker:
Whattaya say, guys! Dreamy or what? One of these fellas is in for a hot time in the old Circle tonight! **(Turning to Maggie/Iblee)** Thank you so much for playing The Dumping Game.

Maggie/Iblee:
(Squeak)

Chuck Bob Woolabarker:
So, here's how it works. You have a question for each of the three contestants, they answer the question, and you pick which one is the biggest slime ball. Sound like fun?

Maggie/Iblee:
(Happy squeal)

Chuck Bob Woolabarker:
Alrighty, then. Let's get started. Studio audience? I said, studio audience!

The Audience Itself:
What Chuck Bob!

Chuck Bob Woolabarker:
Its up to you to help our lovely Dumpette pick out the biggest slime ball. So groan, cheer, scream, catcall, puke, throw things, heh, heh, heh, anything goes and do you know why?

The Audience Itself:
Why Chuck Bob!

Chuck Bob Woolabarker:
Cuz we're in Hell and you're watching The Dumping Game! **(Turning to Maggie/Iblee)** Have a seat Toots.

(The Casio Player revives the Dumpette Theme, Maggie/Iblee throws a wink to the audience, circles her chair and sits, Chuck Bob crosses to his chair, and the contestants dance awkwardly in their chairs)

Chuck Bob Woolabarker:
(Taking a beat to smile as the music ceases) Darlin', its time to hit Contestant Number One. **(Chuck Bob cues the Casio Player who hits a button releasing a syncopated drumroll)**

Maggie/Iblee:
Contestant Number One, **(reading from a card)** your mining empire produces tons of heavy metal-laced waste water, filled with such wonders as mercury, arsenic, cadmium, and other fun stuff. Your coal burning plants belch **(fingers to lips and a squeak)** nearly two hundred million tons of carbon dioxide, and produce another quarter-million tons of toxic waste. Each power plant you own will, in its lifetime, create 9.6 million tons of waste. So, Contestant Number One, **(takes a beat, looks at the audience)** how're you gonna dump it!

(Thoughtful Casio music from a disinterested Casio Player)

Chuck Bob Woolabarker:
Well, Contestant Number One, the world is waiting.

(Thoughtful music stops)

Contestant Number One:
Three words: Money, money, and money. Every elected official from the PTA to the United State Senate, every EPA line monkey in every cubicle from ground zero to the gilded halls of D.C., and every potential citation-writing bureaucrat will be in my pocket. And those I can't bribe, or those holier-than-thou do-gooders, I'll intimidate, extort, and silence.

Maggie/Iblee:
But Contestant Number One, what about the actual filth itself?

Contestant Number One:
That's even easier. There are virtually no laws to holding **(fingers held up making quotations)** coal ash, and even fewer in regards to extraction, so, we run the stuff through placebo-like buildings that we say are filtering it, hold it in ponds we say are holding it, and just let it run off into the ground or any convenient waterway. I mean, the country needs energy, and only a fool would drink tap water. **(All three contestants chuckle)**

Maggie/Iblee:
That's pretty slimy, Contestant Number One, but let's see how you stack up against the other two. **(Casio drumroll and a splash)** Contestant Number Two, you're an internationally-known media mogul who's extensive holdings influence everyone on the planet. You've created a global entertainment/information monopoly in which you own the production, the distribution, and the transmission of your programming. Now, investigators have revealed how you've tilted elections, toppled governments, ruined lives, smashed careers, and twisted the truth to further your own interests. In fact, that phone-tapping scandal is going to look like small peanuts once the actual truth comes out. So, Contestant Number Two, **(pause and a smile to the audience)** how're you gonna dump it!

Contestant Number Two:
Plausible denial. That, and the simple fact that I own nearly all the channels of information. In the last three decades I have created a collective consciousness without consciousness. **(Everyone on stage except Contestant Number Two is space-faced as they have no idea what he is talking about)** I have completely reprogrammed the truth. I have manipulated, squeezed, and spun what actually happens into a gooey non-reality. Then, ran this nebulous substance through the candy-like filter of flashy entertainment to such a point, that these minions we call consumers would die without it. In other words, they are addicts, I'm their dealer, and they'll believe whatever I tell them no matter who touts the truth.

(There is a pregnant pause as everyone on stage tries to digest this, interrupted only by the Casio Player doodling "To Anacreon in Heaven")

Maggie/Iblee:
And in the language of Hell?

Contestant Number Two:
Business is war. War is hell. The first casualty of war is the truth.

The Donald:
Fucking right.

(Everyone applauds something they can understand)

Chuck Bob Woolabarker:
Thank you so much! Contestant Number One, Contestant Number Two, you people are slimy. Dumpette, sarcastic Casio Player, its time for Contestant Number Three! **(Slap on The Donald's back, Casio drum roll & splash, oohs and aahs)**

Maggie/Iblee:
Contestant Number Three, we've been meeting each other every year on the same day, in the same hotel room for over a decade, only now, you're in the public eye, and I'm an inconvenience, so, how're you gonna dump me!

The Donald:
Well, I'm not. I'm going to have my cake and-Hey! Wait a minute! How the hell did you get here? What the fuck is this?

Chuck Bob Woolabarker:
Easy there, big fella.

The Donald:
This is bullshit! **(Standing up)** First off, **(pointing at himself)** I never asked to play this game, **(pointing at Chuck Bob)** you don't exist, **(throws arms in the air)** this isn't Hollywood, and **(crossing the stage and ripping down the curtain)**, you're not Maggie!

(Maggie/Iblee squeals and dissolves into nothingness. The audience gasps)

The Audience Itself:
(Gasp!)

The Donald:
(Turning back toward Chuck Bob and the boys) And another thing!

(The stage begins to shake violently. The deafening sound of souls wailing fills off-stage, stage left. A pack of large, black dogs tears across the stage from left to right. Nessie gallops to a stop by the chairs, Boss Tweed on Private Centaur right behind him. Dozens of wicker-shades hop, hobble, and crawl across the stage from left to right. Two angry-shades scream onto stage from stage left, only to be shot by Nessie and Private Centaur)

Boss Tweed:
(Pointing at The Donald) Strumpet! You fucking idiot! I am going to lash you to the underside of this centaur!

Chuck Bob Woolabarker:
Hey, stop making sense.

(More angry-shades burst onto stage, some get hit with arrows, others get through and begin wreaking havoc on the set, on the contestants)

Nessie:
Time to go!

(Nessie canters over to The Donald, who jumps on)

(The stage is beginning to fill with angry-shades. They are swarming over the set, burying the contestants)

Chuck Bob Woolabarker:
(Holding hands up) Please, dear fans, my ego.

(The two centaurs rear-up, angry-shades pulling at them, and exit rapidly stage right. The entire stage is filled with angry-shades, tearing, ripping, devouring)

(Lights fade center stage, the sounds of the feeding frenzy fading a long minute after the lights)

(The lights come up on the narrator's stage. The backdrop is a narrow hallway of faded-gray cinderblocks. Pipes, tubing and conduit run along the ceiling. The light from the right is dim and dark blue. The light from the left has that greenish glow. We hear, everso-softly, a waterfall coming from the far right. We hear echoes of wails, of shouting, of unknown violent noises in the distance from stage left. Then, after moments, the sound of hooves and footsteps. The Donald enters from the back, stage left, Boss Tweed right behind him)

The Donald:
Where's this lead?

Boss Tweed:
In the short term? I don't know.

The Donald:
And the long term?

Boss Tweed:
Down.

The Donald:
There had to be someone smarter than you to be my guide.

Boss Tweed:
If we were smart Strumpet, we wouldn't be down here.

The Donald:
How much more of this?

(Nessie and Private Centaur quietly step in)

Private Centaur:
I think we've given them the slip.

Nessie:
For now. They're combing through all these tunnels.

The Donald:
What do we do now?

Nessie:
Follow this to the cliff.

The Donald:
Whaaaat?

Boss Tweed:
And then?

Nessie:
That's as far as we go. I've heard there's a path behind the falls. I've heard there's a door, and stairs, but I've never met anyone who's been down this far.

The Donald:
(To Boss Tweed) Okay Mr. Guide, now what?

Boss Tweed:
(As the wailing and violent noises intensify) Down we go.

(All four slowly thread their way across the narrator's stage and onto the main stage. The lights come up in deep, dark blues and grays. Mist fills the air on the right side of the stage. Just past center stage, there is an outcropping of black rock, and then the top of a sheer cliff. The sound of rushing and falling water is quite loud. They cross the stage and stand at the edge of the precipice. The sounds of the angry-shades slowly grows louder from stage left)

The Donald:
(Examining the cliff's edge) Are you kidding me? Really? **(Looking back at the tunnel)** Man, does this suck! **(Throwing his hands up)** There's no way down! There's no way back! What the fuck do we do now?

(Nessie and Private Centaur turn and face the way they've come, weapons at the ready)

Nessie:
We'll hold them off as long as we can.

The Donald:
(Looking at Boss Tweed) Well?

Boss Tweed:
Maybe we can reason with them?

The Donald:
What?! For real? You've never been to one of my rallies.

Boss Tweed:
(Stepping away from them. Tapping his brow) A cord.

The Donald:
A what?

Boss Tweed:
A cord. Like a rope. There's something to do with a cord.

The Donald:
(Pulling out his cell phone) Well let me just call the Acme Cord company.

(Several wraiths fly out of the tunnel's entrance. Nessie and Private Centaur shoot them down. The wailing, the noises, the sound of angry feet is growing so loud they have to shout)

Boss Tweed:
(Pacing back and forth at the very edge of the cliff) He pulled out a cord, and then, he, he, and then he, he did something with the cord...

(More angry-shades. More shooting. More freaking out by The Donald)

The Donald:
Tweed! Hurry the fuck up! I'm fricking freaking out!

Boss Tweed:
He. The cord. Dropped? No. Dabbled? No. Dunked? No. The cord. Doffed. Dipped. Discarded. Hmmmm, no, no, and no. Wait. Wait...

(Shades. Shooting. Mayhem. Whining)

The Donald:
(Pointing his cell phone at Boss Tweed) You got us into this mess! And now you can't get us out! (Banging his head with his hands. Pacing toward the front of the stage) What a way to die. On the edge

of a bottomless pit with this dick and two asses. **(Nessie looks over)** No offense.

Nessie:
None taken.

The Donald:
(Wheels back toward Boss Tweed) I demand you think of something!

Boss Tweed:
Eureka!

(Just then The Donald's cell phone rings. Its ring tone is 'Hail To The Chief'. Everyone on stage who is not of the angry-shade variety stares as it continues to ring)

Nessie:
Well?

The Donald:
Well, what?

Nessie:
Are you going to answer it?

The Donald:
This is impossible. **(Still ringing)** What kind of a device is this?

Boss Tweed:
Dangle! We let it **(draws the word out)** dangle.

The Donald:
You scare me.

Boss Tweed:
Answer your tether.

The Donald:
(With trepidation, answering his phone) Hello? **(Pauses)** Yes, this is.
(He covers the mouthpiece) I swear, these folks have towers everywhere.
(Resumes speaking) With whom am I speaking? Really? We're doing great.
Well, not really. We're all about to die. Well, me and the horse-guys, Tweed's
already dead, but then you knew that. Right, right. How'd you know? Sure,
sure. Yes? Yes! We do need a cord!

Boss Tweed:
Who is that?

The Donald:
(Covering mouthpiece) Randy. The truck guy. Remember him? **(Tweed
does an 'oh yeah' fist pull with his right arm)** Where? Okay, okay.
(Walking over by the tunnel entrance) I'm standing there, now. The
right side. Four, no, two, no three paces. **(He moves forward and backward and forward)** Notch in the rock. **(Reaches up)** Got it. Put my what
where? **(Follows direction)** Okay, I've got my right hand in. I've got my
right hand out. I've got my right hand in, and I'm shaking it all about. **(On
the left side of the tunnel entrance, an opening suddenly appears.
A bright, white light emanates from within. A shelf-like piece
of black stone slides out with a perfectly coiled gold rope. The
Donald crosses over to it, picks up one end and shows it to Boss
Tweed)** Yes! Yes! Wow! Thank you so much! You saved our skins. I owe you
one. If you're ever in The City, go to the Tower. I'll show you New York like
nobody's business. Right, right. Alright. Gotta go, now. I know. Yes, thanks.
Okay, getting a bit dicey here. Right. I understand. And, of course. That one
time in truck-driving school. I think we're losing service. No, no, must be
on my end. **(He hangs up, slips the phone back inside his suit coat.
Looks at Boss Tweed)** He just happened to be thinking of us.

Boss Tweed:
How cool is that?

The Donald:
So, here's the rope, er, cord. What now? **(Handing the cord to Boss Tweed)**

Boss Tweed:
We just pull this end over to the cliff. **(Looking closely at the cord)** Hey! It says Acme.

(Many angry shades are coming through the tunnel. Nessie and Private Centaur are being driven back toward the cliff's edge)

The Donald:
Whenever you're ready.

Boss Tweed:
Then we dangle the unattached end over the cliff. **(He does so)**

The Donald:
You mean we climb down that thing? Over this thing? **(Looking over cliff's edge)**

Boss Tweed:
No. I mean, I don't think so. Let's see what happens.

(They stand there. Shades rushing in. Shades getting shot. Nessie and Private Centaur being driven further back toward the edge of the cliff. Nothing happens with the cord)

The Donald:
Maybe if you wiggled it.

Boss Tweed:
(Tugging up and down with the cord) Here fishy, fishy.

The Donald:
We are just completely fucked.

(At that moment, from up out of the misty, inky blue depths, there is the sound of enormous wings. There is the sound of humming, of whistling, of singing)

The Donald:
Why am I not surprised by this.

(The tips of two giant, leathery wings pierce the gloom and come into view as they flap downward)

Boss Tweed:
(Fists in the air) Fish on!

(Rising above the mist, and the stage for that matter, is Geryon. Wavy blonde hair, a long face with a proud nose, a cleft centered on a pronounced chin, and bright, blue eyes, this all sits atop a strong neck attached to the top half of a lion, the hind of a lizard, and ends in a scorpion's tail. He hovers before them with effortless strokes of powerful, bat-like wings. A perfect-teeth, radiant smile shines in the gloom below his red campaign hat, he slowly raises a lion's paw and points his index finger to the roof of the cavern)

Geryon:
(Singing) Here I come to save the day!

Boss Tweed:
You the one that answers the cord?

Geryon:
I am. Are you Nell?

Boss Tweed:
(Utterly perplexed. Looks around and behind him) Huh? Who?

The Donald:
No, he isn't Nell. But we know where Nell might be.

Geryon:
Then climb on my back and we shall save dear, Nell!

(The Donald and Boss Tweed clamber onto the broad lion's back of Geryon. Nessie turns and looks up to the two of them)

Nessie:
Good luck, gents. Bossman, once things settle back down, you're welcome in Circle Seven anytime.

Boss Tweed:
Thanks, bro.

Nessie:
Mr. Trumpet, sir, with all due respect, I truly hope you get a clue, cuz as you can see, our jobs keep us busy enough.

The Donald:
Thanks for getting us here, horseman.

(Nessie and Private Centaur quickly press themselves against the wall by where the golden cord came from. They light cigarettes as angry-shades begin to pour out of the tunnel. Like general admission concert goers trying to get prime spots in too small an area for too many tickets sold, they push, jostle, and stampede each other right off the cliff. Some try to hold onto Geryon's legs and tail, but with little effort he shakes them off)

Geryon:
Great Scott! Where to?

Boss Tweed:
Circle Eight.

Geryon:
Home sweet home. Hi-Yo silver, and away!

(Geryon banks to his right, tucks legs and then begins a descent away from the cascading stream of angry-shades pouring over the cliff. Boss Tweed has a clump of mane in one hand, while the other is lifted above his head as if he were in a rodeo. The Donald sits behind him, arms wrapped around Boss Tweed's waist, head tucked into his back. The lights fade on center stage and Circle Seven with the screams and wails of the damned, the sound of the waterfall, and the twin, red ends of the centaur's cigarettes)

(The lights come up on the box. Statler Swift and Waldorf Voltaire are pressed to the railing, hands gripping the rail, eyes still staring at center stage. There is a long moment as the sounds of the last scene fade)

Statler Swift:
Well.

Waldorf Voltaire:
Indeed.

Statler Swift:
Perhaps we judged too swiftly.

Waldorf Voltaire:
We may have.

Statler Swift:
It is a riddle.

Waldorf Voltaire:
To say the least.

Statler Swift:
What once seemed a farce has gained a tremendous amount of weight.

Waldorf Voltaire:
So many things in life are so. A riddle at first glance becomes a symphony when we simply let the thing be what it is.

Statler Swift:
A riddle wrapped in a mystery inside an enigma.

Waldorf Voltaire:
Ah, dear friend, you are so very close.

Statler Swift:
How so?

Waldorf Voltaire:
The riddle solves itself when we simply let *it* be what *it* is. The nature of the thing becomes apparent over time, *if,* we let it be itself.

Statler Swift:
Cheers to you, Mr. Voltaire, for enlightening me once again. Then, if you would be so kind, apply this philosophy to this play.

Waldorf Voltaire:
You quoted thus: A riddle wrapped in a mystery inside an enigma. This would be apt for this suddenly larger-than-life piece of theater we are witnessing. However, allow me this: a tragedy wrapped in a comedy inside a fiction.

Statler Swift:
You never cease to amaze. A tragedy wrapped in a comedy inside a fiction. **(Pause)** Vision is the art of seeing things invisible and there you are! **(Pause)** Your key could very well unlock doors of understanding, doors of acceptance, doors of respect, doors of unity. On and on. **(Pause)** Let things simply be what they are. A tragedy wrapped in a comedy inside a fiction.

Waldorf Voltaire:
If this was real life, then, oh dear God.

Statler Swift:
Dear God what? What it is it, Waldorf?

Waldorf Voltaire:
If this play was real life, then-

Statler Swift:
Then all might be lost.

Waldorf Voltaire:
Hope, faith and charity, Mr. Swift. We had better hope the leaders of the world understand that these are on a plane above all else.

(There is a long pause. From behind the stage, softly, yet distinctly audible, are the sounds of Hell)

Statler Swift:
I'm not holding my breath.

(The lights fade on the box. The sounds of Hell continue. A lone spotlight comes up on the narrator's stage and on Euripides, seated on a barstool. He waits a moment or two, letting the sounds of Hell swirl about the theater)

Eurpides:
A tragedy wrapped in a comedy inside a fiction. Perhaps, I underestimated the old gents in the box. It seems that when the vessels that would be Mr. Swift and Mr. Voltaire were dipped into the logos, a large portion of wisdom was included.

Seeing the invisible. Understanding the essence of a thing. These days, it is difficult to discern the true nature of things. There is so much information, so much hype, so much concern over how the message is delivered, as opposed to what the message really is. The more distracted you become, the less truth you will find. Though, ultimately, most of what you are bombarded with is no different than the medicine show on the edge of town. And as those peddlers of phony cures would quite often have to escape by the skin-of-their-teeth, so our protagonists have managed to slip the mob.

Now, they descend. To Circle Eight. Malicious Fraud. Where those that deceived their fellow man occupy some of Hell's most nefarious nooks, and suffer some of Hell's most hideous punishments. All the deviousness in the world, cannot hide deceivers from that which places them here. A scorpion is a scorpion is a scorpion, even in the finest of finery. And as they made love to this employment of deception, as so many have spoken daggers disguised as roses, and as the devil may assume a pleasing shape, the play's the thing! And to it, we return.

(The lights quickly fade to black on Euripides and the narrator's stage)

(The lights come up center stage. The Donald and Boss Tweed are astride Geryon. The wind is quite literally in their hair as Geryon lazily descends from Circle Seven to Circle Eight. Great spires and cliffs, broad shoulders of mountains, and steep slopes glide past them in the narrow confines of the canyon they are flying through. The Donald is barely seeing any of this, as his face is pressed into Boss Tweed's back. Boss Tweed is loving every thrilling second, while Geryon is smiling and gliding effortlessly, singing the word 'Nell' over and over)

Boss Tweed:
This is fucking awesome!

The Donald:
This is fucking terrifying.

Boss Tweed:
Where's your pluck, man? We're flying, for Chrissakes!

The Donald:
I fly everyday.

Boss Tweed:
Yeah, I bet you have feathers.

The Donald:
Why's that?

Boss Tweed:
Cuz you're such a chickenshit! **(Busts out laughing)**

The Donald:
Fuck you. Aahhhhh!

(Just then, Geryon banks hard right and increases his descent to the point its almost a dive)

256

Geryon:
By the White Wolf! Is that Nell? On the edge of that cliff? Sweet Christmas!
(Yelling) Nell! Be brave! Hold fast!

Boss Tweed:
Who the fuck is Nell?

(Geryon pulls up suddenly and lands on an aerie, beneath the box. Twin spotlights quickly light up Eagle and Owl who are standing there in an embrace)

Eagle:
Do you mind.

Geryon:
You're not Nell.

Owl:
No shit.

Eagle:
Who the fuck is Nell?

Boss Tweed:
Sorry, girls.

The Donald:
Just passing through.

Eagle:
Not that asshole again.

Owl:
Shouldn't you be meeting pappy, by now.

The Donald:
Shouldn't you be checking for lice.

Eagle:
Bite me, fanboy.

Geryon:
Nell?

Owl:
(To The Donald) Human?

The Donald:
More insults?

Owl:
No, advice. **(She points a wing and a finger at The Donald)** The more you die, the greater chance you have to live. **(The Donald looks away reflective)**

Geryon:
No Nell?

Owl:
I'm afraid not.

Geryon:
Then its hip, hip, hip and away I go!

(Geryon turns around smartly and jumps from the cliff)

Eagle:
How rude.

(The twin spots on Eagle and Owl go out)

(Geryon, The Donald, and Boss Tweed resume their descent, banking hard right and gliding in slow circles ever downward. A light begins to grow brighter beneath them)

The Donald:
(Looking up and over Boss Tweed's shoulder) Holy shit! What is that!

Boss Tweed:
Circle Eight, my friend. In all its perfunctory grandeur.

(The lights dim center stage as Geryon, with The Donald and Boss Tweed astride, exits stage right)

(The lights come up on the narrator's stage. The cornerstone of an enormous building takes up all but a few feet of the stage. The stone is towering, the top of it not even visible. Etched into the stone: Orbis ab malicious fraus. Est. Aeternum. In Deo autem non habeat fiduciam. In front of the wording, the black dust of Hell begins to coalesce into Iblee)

Iblee:
(Acting secretly and looking furtively in both directions) Donny does not like Iblee. Without like, no time alone. No time alone, no switch. (Moves to stage left of the narrator's stage) Must make him trust. But how? Hmmm. Circle Eight. Boring Circle Eight. Temple of fraud. Temple of liars. So many people. So many souls. Files and files and files and aisles and aisles and aisles. Files and aisles and secretary smiles and deceit and wiles and fraud and guile and Donny will be here for a very long while. Hmmmm. Ten ditchy departments. Ten thousand bossy, big bosses. One million boring bosses. One million zillion drones. Buzz buzz buzz. Boss boss boss. So big a place. So many shades. How does one lost soul find its way to where they will

suffer forever and a day? **(A very large Iblee-smile beneath a glowing Iblee eye)** Oh, dear Donny, I am the pea beneath the shell.

(The black dust of Hell begins to swirl all over the narrator's stage as if a helicopter was landing. Iblee looks up and quickly dissolves. From the left lands Geryon. Boss Tweed and The Donald clamber off his back)

Geryon:
Lenin's Ghost! We're here! But I see no Nell. Only this infernal dust.

The Donald:
This is Circle Eight?

Boss Tweed:
Yup.

The Donald:
It looks like one giant building.

Boss Tweed:
Yup.

Geryon:
(Pointing at The Donald) Ragamuffin, you said you knew where Nell is.

The Donald:
I lied. I'm sorry. We needed a ride.

Geryon:
(His face glowers over, and his scorpion's tail rises up above his head, pointed at The Donald) In brightest day…in blackest night, no evil shall escape my sight!

Boss Tweed:

(Stepping out of the way) Dammit, Strumpet! Keep lying. There's a billion shades in here! One of em's gotta be named Nell!

The Donald:

I don't know what came over me. Aaa, Mr. Do Right, may I call you Dudley?

Boss Tweed:

Who the fuck is Dudley? He's Geryon.

Geryon:

Let those who worship evil's might, beware my power!

The Donald:

I said I was sorry.

Geryon:

(The tip of his tail is twitching, centering in on The Donald for a strike) Don't make me angry. You wouldn't like me when I'm angry.

Boss Tweed:

(Making more distance between Geryon and The Donald) By the Hoary Hosts of Hoggoth!

The Donald:

(The tip of the tail dips down toward The Donald's chest. The Donald is pressed against the stone. A bead of venom drops from the tip of the tail to the ground and sizzles) Holy Shit Bossman!

Geryon:

I am the law! **(The tail, venom dripping, rises up to its highest point)**

Boss Tweed:
(Scrambling away) Oh my stars and garters!

The Donald:
Maybe Nell's with Horse!

Geryon:
(Relaxes. His tail settles back to the ground) You are right. Maybe Nell is with Horse.

Boss Tweed:
Who the fuck is Horse?

The Donald:
(Looking up from under his armpit) You should go look for Horse.

Geryon:
Yes, I shall. I shall go and look for Horse.

The Donald:
Thanks for the ride, friend.

Boss Tweed:
(Stepping back beside The Donald) Yeah, thanks for the lift.

Geryon:
By the Goddess! What a strange day!

The Donald:
You can say that again.

Geryon:
(Leaning in toward The Donald, eyes narrowing) What a strange, strange time. **(He taps The Donald's chest with a finger on each word)** With great powers comes great responsibility.

The Donald:
(Gulping) Yes, sir. I get it.

Geryon:
You will. Heh, heh, heh. **(Standing up to full height, chin jutting out and away, a clenched fist held close to his chest)** Truth, Justice and-

The Donald:
(Stepping forward and pumping a fist into the air) And the American Way!

Geryon:
Don't mock me.

The Donald:
I used to watch it in my onesie.

Boss Tweed:
(Head in one hand. Sighing) Why can't I take you anywhere.

Geryon:
(Crouching to fly off) Up, up, and away! **(He jumps up and flies straight away across the audience and up into the control booth)**

Boss Tweed:
(Looking at The Donald as The Donald stares in the direction of a parting Geryon) Dodged another one, dickhead.

The Donald:
(Turning toward center stage) So, now what tortures lie in store? I mean, we're at Circle Eight, what's left?

Boss Tweed:
The brass tacks, you bollocks. And the bottom line. **(This stops The Donald in his tracks)**

The Donald:
(Sheepishly) My bottom line?

Boss Tweed:
That's why you're here before you're here. That's why we met. And that's why you've got to have *sooo* much fun! **(He makes a grand introductory motion toward centerstage)** I give you, Circle Eight!

(The lights, dim, uniform, and industrial, come up on the left side of center stage on the entranceway to Circle Eight. It is made of the same stone and in the same Stalin-esque architecture as its cornerstone. A long steep set of concrete stairs leads up to the entrance. The large, utilitarian door is flanked by two giant, corroded, copper arms holding lamps. Above the door it reads: Circle of Malicious Deceit. The C, the M, and the D are in much larger font. At the bottom of the steps are several dock monkey-like CMD employees sweeping the dust into piles and scooping the piles into an ancient, dented and stained rolling trashcan. Three watch while one works. Boss Tweed nudges the Donald, and they cross to the steps leading to the doorway)

The Donald:
Well, this looks familiar. Am I getting a license plate?

Boss Tweed:
Yeah, for your fat ass. Come on.

(They trudge up the steps halfway)

Boss Tweed:
This place is immense. Like one building the size of Russia.

The Donald:
And you know where we're going?

Boss Tweed:
Oh hell no.

The Donald:
Then?

Boss Tweed:
There's maps and lines on the floor and directories and CMD employees by the wads.

The Donald:
And I'm in here? I mean, I'm going to end up here?

Boss Tweed:
Brother, you and I got this place covered. We've been bamboozling folks since the day mom dropped us!

The Donald:
This is bullshit.

Boss Tweed:
Strumpet! **(He wheels around and gets right in The Donald's face)** There are ten types of fraud in here and you are in every one of them. You think I'm playing around? You think I asked for this assignment? You know what I get for doing this? Nothing! Not a fucking thing! I'm doing this cuz the big guy asked me to do this through Saint Dymphna. I'm doing this cuz

I didn't have the chance you have, to repent and act like a normal human be-ing. I'm doing this so that maybe! Just maybe! One stain on my soul can fade away. Do you get it? Huh? **(He turns, takes a step)** This is a big place, man, and you've got a lot of work to do in here, and I've got a lot of suffering left to do before hopefully, something wonderful happens sometime in the distant future. So pick 'em up and put 'em down! **(He takes a couple more steps)**

The Donald:
I just wondered how we're going to find our way around.

Boss Tweed:
I already told you, I'm not sure. We'll just wing it like we've been doing. Fuck! We made it this far, didn't we?

The Donald:
(Stepping up beside Boss Tweed and throwing an arm around his shoulder) It is kind of amazing. I mean, we've been through some shit. **(Boss Tweed relaxes. The two start chuckling)** I mean, if you could have seen your face when that bloody foot landed.

Boss Tweed:
(Laughing) My face?. How 'bout yours when the *whole* Minotaur showed up!

The Donald:
Holy shit! I thought we were goners.

Boss Tweed:
How 'bout that last ride?

The Donald:
Oh fuck that! Never again. Riding on the back of Dudley Do Right with paws and a stinger.

Boss Tweed:
(Howling) I'm not even sure what that means but its funny as fuck.

The Donald:
Or the boat ride in!

Boss Tweed:
(Knee slapping, guffawing) You barfed up meals you haven't even eaten yet!

The Donald:
Bossman, we really need to walk through that door and get lost.

Boss Tweed:
Lost? **(Wiping tears from his eyes)**

The Donald:
That seems to be when we're at our best.

Boss Tweed:
Well, that shouldn't be a problem. I know that if you walk for days straight back from the entrance, there's this giant atrium that has a full-sized replica of a palace from topside. Or maybe it was built here, but not on Earth. Not sure. Its impressive.

The Donald:
Really? The entire building?

Boss Tweed:
This place is big, buddy. Big.

(They resume walking up the steps)

The Donald:
At the risk of being redundant-

Boss Tweed:
Oh that's in here as well.

(The Donald stops)

The Donald:
Redundancy?

Boss Tweed:
Yeah, the Department of Redundancy Department. **(He starts laughing)**

The Donald:
(Pause) Cut it out.

Boss Tweed:
I shit you not.

The Donald:
This is going to take forever.

Boss Tweed:
Yup. Take a number. You know the drill. **(The Donald takes a weary step. Boss Tweed pauses in thought, a finger to his lips)** You know, come to think of it, for really hard-luck cases, you can get a case worker.

The Donald:
(Turning to Boss Tweed) Fucking A.

Boss Tweed:
Fuck an O.

The Donald:
That could save us tons of time!

Boss Tweed:
Depends.

The Donald:
On what?

Boss Tweed:
On how good the case worker is.

The Donald:
Come on. I got a good feeling about this. Its not so much them telling us how much we bullshitted, as us bullshitting them to get through their whole stupid bureaucracy.

Boss Tweed:
Aaa, yeah. Okay, pal. We'll see how this goes. **(At the top, in front of the door)** After you.

The Donald:
(Opening the door to the CMD) No, no. After you. You're the guide.

Boss Tweed:
(His eyes narrow as he enters the CMD) I'm watching you. Know that.

The Donald:
I know. I do know that. And I respect that.

Boss Tweed:
(As the door closes behind them and the lights fade) You're so full of shit.

(The lights dim on the left side of center stage and come up on the right side of center stage. They are standing just inside the entrance, at the top of a set of stairs. Before them is a giant directory, lit up, with geometric shapes for departments, lots of wording, and many lines of different colors connecting all of it in a convoluted mess. At the bottom of the steps is a red plastic 'take-a-number' machine with a sign saying as much. Next to this is a host stand and a female CMD employee flipping through a magazine and idly turning her fire-engine red hair. Beside this is a bench filled with various shades staring at the numbered pieces of paper in their hands, and doing the institutional wait. The bench is so long it runs clear off of stage right. In the background, *The Girl From Ipanema* plays endlessly and in muted muzak. The Donald and Boss Tweed step up to the directory, arching their necks to try and figure it out)

The Donald:
Ay carumba.

Boss Tweed:
I told you.

The Donald:
This is insane. It goes on forever.

Boss Tweed:
I tried to tell you.

The Donald:
It doesn't make any sense.

Boss Tweed:
The department of redundancy department.

The Donald:
I don't have time for this.

Boss Tweed:
How 'bout a valium.

The Donald:
I'm in the middle of a Presidential campaign.

Boss Tweed:
You're in the middle of Hell, pal.

The Donald:
There might not be much difference.

Boss Tweed:
(Motioning down the steps) We're down here. Let's get this going. See if we can get you a caseworker.

The Donald:
(Starting down the stairs) Yeah, try and expedite this bullshit.

Boss Tweed:
You realize, I'm doing my best.

The Donald:
I know, I know. Its just, well, it feels like I've been down here forever, and time is slipping away, and now I'm even further behind in the polls, and I need some time to think up some sneaky moves or I'm going to lose this thing.

Boss Tweed:
(As they reach the bottom of the steps) I think you should move 'being President' more toward the bottom of your 'to do' list.

The Donald:
Whatever. **(To the CMD girl beside the host stand)** Table for two. Hopefully water view and away from the kitchen. **(No response)** Just a joke. We're in a hurry, and I'm still alive, maybe you've heard of me, and we really need to get to the front of this line. **(No response)** My friend here is Boss Tweed, and Saint Dymphna has tasked him to guide me through Hell, so we're kind of VIPs, and there was supposed to be someone waiting here to escort us through Circle Eight. **(No response)** Ma'am. Lady. Hello. **(He passes his hand between her eyes and the magazine)** Earth to lady.

CMD Girl:
(She looks up) Lady to Earth. **(She points at the sign. Then returns to her magazine)**

Boss Tweed:
Its a wonder how you ever got married. **(Stepping in front of The Donald, he reaches into his coat pocket, pulls out a candy bar, and sets it down on the magazine)** Hi. Sorry to bug you, but my impatient friend here is in need of a caseworker, and though he is rather uncouth, he does have a point in that we were expected, and its been a really bad day and we were hoping that you would please help us out.

CMD Girl:
(Big smile. Candy bar in hand) Well of course I can, sugar. Do you know which department your friend is expected for orientation?

Boss Tweed:
All of them.

(Her eyes get big. All heads turn to look at The Donald. The Donald looks down, looks at his nails)

CMD Girl:
I'm sorry, did you say 'all of them'?

Boss Tweed:
Yes. He's in all of them.

CMD Girl:
(She leans over to get a better look at The Donald. Leans back) Well hasn't he been a busy boy. This is rather extreme. Hmmm.

Boss Tweed:
(Pulling out another candy bar) Its been a really, really long day. Maybe you know someone.

CMD Girl:
Well, yes, and no. I mean, there've been a few cases like this, but. Wow. All ten departments. I mean, you're supposed to live out all your lies. In real time. Over and over. Plus the other punishments and…Was he in other Circles as well?

Boss Tweed:
Yes.

(She leans forward to look at The Donald again. All the shades are staring, watching this like a tennis match. She looks over to Boss Tweed)

CMD Girl:
Dare I ask?

Boss Tweed:
All.

CMD Girl:
(Leans in to Boss Tweed) Evil little fucker.

Boss Tweed:
You have no idea what I've been through. Any ideas?

CMD Girl:
Hmmm, no not really. Wait! Yes. I do! Oh my, yes! Oh boy! I can't believe I get to pull it!

Boss Tweed:
Pull what?

CMD Girl:
The Liar Lever. Well, I mean, **(Chuckle, chuckle)** we're all liars down here, but for really extreme cases, we get to pull *The Liar Lever*.

Boss Tweed:
Pull away.

(Several brightly colored lights come up beneath the box. There is a large, red handle jutting out from the floor beneath a sign in red that reads: Tellers of Truly Tall Tales. There is an overhang above the sign and over the handle giving it the appearance of a booth. The CMD Girl springs giddily and prances over to it)

CMD Girl:
Oh my God! This is so exciting! Never. Never thought I'd get to pull this.

(The Donald is creeping back up the steps)

CMD Girl:
Hey! Where's he going? I have to pull The Liar Lever first.

Boss Tweed:
Strumpet! You get your lyin' ass back down here. Those were the last two sweets I snuck from Randy's truck and they're not going to waste. **(The Donald turns)** Come on.

CMD Girl:
Come on down little fella.

All Shades Waiting:
Come on.

The Donald:
(Reluctantly. Groaning) Ooohhh. I don't want to hear how I suck anymore.

CMD Girl:
We do!

Boss Tweed:
Come on, Strumpet. There's a good boy. Face the music. Sooner we get you a caseworker, the sooner we can get you outta here.

The Donald:
(Still groaning) Alright. **(He crosses from the bottom step to beside The Liar Lever)**

CMD Girl:
Yay! Okay, this is what we do. I think. **(She goes to touch the lever, but can't bring herself to grab it. Everyone is looking at her. She looks over to Boss Tweed. Giggles)** Kinda scared.

Boss Tweed:
Is there a manual or-

CMD Girl:
Right! No. Yes. Hmmm. Think. Think. Oh! Yeah! Right here. **(Beneath the sign is a set of plastic-coated documents hanging from the wall by a thin chain. CMD Girl steps up to them and picks them up. She**

reads, flips, reads, turns, reads, all the while humming *The Girl From Ipanema*, **face twisting with concentration and consternation)** Okay! I get it! Duh, shoulda known. You. **(She points at The Donald)** You step over here, next to The Liar Lever, on this spot with the red 'X'. **(The Donald eye rolls his way over and stands on the 'X')** You. **(She points at Boss Tweed)** You'll have to step back. **(The Donald starts and looks at her)** Just in case. Now. **(She sets her feet apart, gets a good sturdy stance, and grabs The Liar Lever with both hands in a kind of wrestler's crouch)** Alright. **(She stands back up)** You. **(Pointing at The Donald)** You're not all the way on the 'X'. **(The Donald makes a big show of getting squarely on the 'X')** Okay. **(Resumes the crouch, hands on the lever. Then stands back up)** You. **(Pointing at Boss Tweed. Her hands go up and she crinkles her nose)** Maybe back a little further. **(The Donald quickly looks at her. She looks at him slightly exasperated)** Just in case. Okay. **(Resumes the crouch)** Here goes nothin'!

(She makes a big production of pulling a very difficult to pull Liar Lever. She stands up, fingers wriggling beside her face, eyes searching above her for some sort of something. At first, nothing. Then, a low rumble. Then, the sound of an old-time fire alarm, briefly. She steps away from The Donald. So does Boss Tweed. Then, multi-colored disco lights appear only on The Donald, accompanied by red, green, and blue swirling spots, confetti, glitter, and streamers, and the way-too-loud chorus from Lorde's *Royals*)

CMD Girl:
(Clapping and jumping) We have a winner!

(The shades jump up and down applauding and shouting. Boss Tweed smiles and shakes a happy fist in the air, and The Donald places his face in one hand. At the top of the steps, the door opens with a swirl of confetti and streamers, then closes. The glittery

party favors swirl into a cloud and become, oh-so-briefly, Iblee. There is a loud bang and a puff of pinkish-blue smoke causing all on stage to look up at the top of the steps. From out of the smoke steps a shortish, trim guy in an all white leisure suit, gold chains, chest hair, shades, slicked-back, black hair, and a gold toothpick, which in great flourish, he removes from the corner of his mouth)

Sugar Coated Sam/Iblee:
You rang.

CMD Girl:
There's your caseworker! Hi, Sam!

(The little celebratory dance party continues as Sugar Coated Sam slinks down the steps, past Boss Tweed and The Donald, and up to the CMD Girl. He takes her hand, gives it a smooch, and with one finger turns her blushing face toward him)

Sugar Coated Sam/Iblee:
Tiffany, the pleasure is all mine.

CMD Girl:
(Pulling her hand away to waggle a finger at him and sing) He's a smooth operator.

Sugar Coated Sam/Iblee:
Who loves ya. (Looking around, at Boss Tweed, The Donald, the Lever) So, someone here needs some special, sugar-coated success, huh? Which lucky fellow is it? (Stepping up to and placing an arm around Boss Tweed) This big, bullshitter here?

Boss Tweed:
(Showing Sugar Coated Sam a fist) Don't you fucking touch me.

Sugar Coated Sam/Iblee:
Heeeyyy, bit hostile. You sure you're in the right Circle?

CMD Girl:
Not him, silly.

Sugar Coated Sam/Iblee:
(Walking over to the bench of shades) Can't be any of these sorry-assed bunch of losers. **(Plucks a number out of one shade's hand, looks at it, throws it over his shoulder)** These folks barely even sinned.

CMD Girl:
You goofus. **(She points at the "X" on the floor)** Hello.

Sugar Coated Sam/Iblee:
(Walking over to The Donald. Hands on hips. Makes a production of bending over and looking at the "X". Slowly rises to look at The Donald. In a very low, overly dramatic voice) If evil had a face.

CMD Girl:
That's your guy.

Sugar Coated Sam/Iblee:
I'll say! So fella, what brings ya to Circle Eight? Truth get a bit twisty?

The Donald:
(Looking past Sugar Coated Sam to CMD Girl) Can you pull that thing again?

Sugar Coated Sam/Iblee:
(Chuckling) We got a wise guy! **(Backslap)** You and me, pal. You stick with me and we'll get you all straightened out. No one, I mean no one, knows Circle Eight like I do. **(Points at the directory)** Upside down, folded in

half, hands tied behind my back, blindfolded, and with a mouth full of micro-dots, I can lead through this nightmare of bureaucratic butt-juice faster than Slick Willie at a sorority sleepover. You **(backslap)** are in good hands.

The Donald:
(Removing himself from Sugar Coated Sam and walking over to CMD Girl) Are you for real?

CMD Girl:
What? Its just Sam.

(The Donald looks over to Boss Tweed, holds up his hands and shakes his head)

Boss Tweed:
(Quickly crosses to stand on the other side of CMD Girl opposite The Donald) Tiffany, is there any way we could possibly get a different case worker?

CMD Girl:
Do you have any more chocolate?

Boss Tweed:
Ummm, no.

CMD Girl:
Boo hoo. He's yours. Sam, give 'em the plan.

Sugar Coated Sam/Iblee:
Okay tosser, follow me. **(He turns toward stage right)**

CMD Girl:
Good luck, guys!

(The Donald and Boss Tweed reluctantly start toward stage right)

Sugar Coated Sam/Iblee
Whoa, hold on there ginormous. I'm *his* **(arm around The Donald)** case-worker. By the looks of it, you've been floating around down here longer than Madonnas's virginity.

Boss Tweed:
I'm his guide, twinkles.

The Donald:
That's my guide.

CMD Girl:
They came in together.

Sugar Coated Sam/Iblee:
I don't know, this is *way* off the norm.

The Donald:
You're talking about 'off the norm'. **(Looks at Boss Tweed and they share a laugh)**

Sugar Coated Sam/Iblee:
Hey, what's that supposed to mean?

CMD Girl:
Yeah, what's that supposed to mean?

The Donald:
(The Donald steps right up to Sugar Coated Sam/Iblee and CMD Girl. Each phrase causes them to tilt backward) I mean, I didn't ask to be down here, I didn't ask for a tour of shitty Circle Eight, and I didn't ask

for disco duck to be my case worker! That's what I mean. And my guide, Mr. Tweed, goes wherever I go! I go to the shitter, he's in the same stall. We gotta fly on the back of some weird cartoon monster, he's riding shotgun. And we gotta sit at desks, or in group, or whatever the fuck happens in Circle Eight, he's right beside me. That! Is what I mean.

Sugar Coated Sam/Iblee and CMD Girl:
(They look at each other) Well.

Sugar Coated Sam/Iblee:
(Relaxing) Well, live and learn, die and burn. Okay, son, I guess you two are joined at the hip, Mr. Trumpet, Mr. Tweed, follow me. **(He starts once more to exit stage right)**

The Donald:
How do you know my name?

Sugar Coated Sam/Iblee:
(Looks back over his shoulder as the three of them exit stage right) Got a *whole* file on you. Big as a library. Needed *Cliff's Notes*. Right this way.

CMD Girl:
Good luck! Happy recovery! **(She returns to her host stand and her magazine as the shades on the bench return to waiting,** *The Girl From Ipanema* **briefly comes back up and then fades just after the lights go out on the entrance to Circle Eight)**

(The lights come up on the narrator's stage where we see a lobby with three sets of elevator doors. There is a small bench off to one side, a couple sad-looking fake plants, and a 'no smoking' sign. *You've Got A Friend,* **muzak-style, is playing in the background. From stage left, a woman in a soviet-brown pants suit enters and pushes the button for the middle elevator. The doors to the**

elevator on the right open and two CMD dock monkey guys with a rolling trashcan get out as the middle door opens. They say a catcall or two, she tells them to piss off, and enters the middle elevator as they exit stage left. There is a pause, then, the left elevator door opens. Karl Marx, John Locke, and Ayn Rand exit the elevator in deep conversation. They head toward stage left to exit. Sugar Coated Sam/Iblee, The Donald, and Boss Tweed enter stage left, The Donald plowing into Karl Marx as he isn't watching where he's going)

Karl Marx:
Hey buddy, watch where you're going.

The Donald:
(Paying no mind) Whatever.

(The three stand slightly facing the elevators)

The Donald:
Is this the first department?

Sugar Coated Sam/Iblee:
What? These are elevators.

Boss Tweed:
(Eyes lighting up, pointing at the bank of elevators) Love these things!

The Donald:
I know they're elevators. What happens next?

Boss Tweed:
I get to push the button!

Sugar Coated Sam/Iblee:
Department One.

Boss Tweed:
Here goes! **(Pushes all three buttons, visibly excited)**

The Donald:
Which is?

Sugar Coated Sam/Iblee:
Panderers and seducers.

The Donald:
I've never pandered to no one!

Boss Tweed:
Aaaa.

Sugar Coated Sam/Iblee:
Seduced?

The Donald:
(Angry) What's this place called?!

Boss Tweed:
The Circle of Malicious Deceit

The Donald:
Which is?

Sugar Coated Sam/Iblee:
Fraud.

The Donald:
Ten departments?

Boss Tweed:
You betcha.

The Donald:
(With resignation) This is going to take forever.

Sugar Coated Sam/Iblee:
No, no, Donny. You've got me, Sugar Coated Sam. I've got you fast tracked.

The Donald:
Fast tracked?

Sugar Coated Sam/Iblee:
(Has one hand slide across the other) Faaaaassst tracked.

(The Donald and Boss Tweed arch their eyebrows at this)

Sugar Coated Sam/Iblee:
No middle-level managers. Only department heads or movers and shakers.

(The Donald and Boss Tweed look at each other nodding)

Sugar Coated Sam/Iblee:
Quick as silver. Flash, flash, flash. A little bit of this department, a little bit of that department. Here you are in this one, there you are in that one. Boom, boom, boom.

The Donald:
Fast tracked?

Sugar Coated Sam/Iblee:
Greased like pigs.

(The elevator on the right opens, they step in and turn back to the audience, The Donald on his right, the others on their left)

The Donald:
Why do I have a bad feeling about this?

Sugar Coated Sam/Iblee:
Noooo. Is a-okay!

(They pause. The Donald looks over at Boss Tweed and Sugar Coated Sam/Iblee)

The Donald:
Going up?

(Boss Tweed and Sugar Coated Sam/Iblee burst out in laughter)

Sugar Coated Sam/Iblee:
There is no up, silly.

Boss Tweed:
Wow. What a moron.

(The doors close and the lights fade on the narrator's stage, *You've Got A Friend* fading just behind the lights)

(The lights come up center stage. There is one long line of people waiting, beginning just onstage from stage left. It runs from the front to the back, along the back, and then back to the front,

exiting stage right. **There are brightly-colored ropes keeping the shades in line, signs saying you must be over thirteen inches tall to ride this ride, and Demon Clowns who whip at the shades to keep them from cutting the line. The line moves fairly fast considering its in Hell. The lights come back up on the narrator's stage. The plants are switched and the 'No smoking' sign is replaced with 'Smoke 'em if you've got 'em'. The elevator door opens and The Donald, Boss Tweed, and Sugar Coated Sam/Iblee exit the elevator and enter center stage from the narrator's stage, getting right in line. Two of the shades in the middle of the line along the back are actually them, Panderer Tweed and Seducer Donald.** *The Baby Elephant Walk* **muzak-ly bounces along from somewhere)**

The Donald:
I thought we were fast tracked?

Boss Tweed:
Hey! Look! Its us. **(Pointing)**

The Donald:
(Searching) Holy shit! What are we doing here?

Sugar Coated Sam/Iblee:
Living the dream.

Boss Tweed:
(To himself across stage) Hey, me! Tweed! What gives? Why you here?

Panderer Tweed:
(Noticing himself) Hey brother! How's it hangin'? Say, you got any money? You got money, I got a plan. Tammany times ten! We will rule the boroughs! Whataya say? Huh? You and me kid! Just like old times. Hey! Lookie who I ran into! You think we was fast tricks? Trumpster, turn the fuck around.

(Seducer Donald turns to face The Donald. The line keeps moving forward. Demon Clowns keep whipping them)

Seducer Donald:
Boys, you should listen to Mr. Tweed, here. Do you like money?

(Boss Tweed is grinning wildly and nodding. The Donald appears skeptical. Sugar Coated Sam/Iblee is looking on smiling)

Boss Tweed:
Fuck yes!

Seducer Donald:
Do you like power?

Boss Tweed:
One goes with the other.

Seducer Donald:
Then you should listen to me. I can give you what you want, I can give you what you need. Freedom is just a sexy word for carjacking. Donald?

The Donald:
What?

Seducer Donald:
You want to be President?

Boss Tweed:
That's why we're here! Hey, Strumpet, listen to this guy!

Seducer Donald:
(Ducks under the line. A Demon Clown approaches, whip ready to come down. Seducer Donald pulls the Demon Clown close, sensually,

and whispers in its ear. **Hands the clown something in a drug pass. The Demon Clown looks both ways, ducks under the line and exits stage left. Seducer Donald sidles over to The Donald)** Friend, somewhere in the front of your brain are some silly things your mother once said to you.

The Donald:
(Confused. Angry. Scared) What about my mother?

Seducer Donald:
You know: do the right thing, look both ways, chew with your mouth closed, watch out for the jungle fever. You know.

The Donald:
What's this got to do with me being President?

Seducer Donald:
Everything. You want the office. You need me. You let me, you know, that little voice that sits on the top of your spine, the one that gives you the tingles, the one that opens all those delicious doors, the one that curls your toes, you let me guide you. You know why?

(The line moves steadily toward stage right. New shades get in line from stage left, others exit stage right. The Demon Clowns patrol, whipping for the least infraction. Boss Tweed and Sugar Coated Sam/Iblee are rapt by the conversation. Panderer Tweed is as well, from his spot in the line)

The Donald:
(Hesitates) Why?

Seducer Donald:
Because everyone wants what you got. Because everyone wants the same thing. Because sitting on top of every single motherfucker's spine is that same little voice. Do you see?

The Donald:
And so?

Seducer Donald:
You sell them you, and you sell them them, and you sell them us. And while their toes are curling, while the deliciousness is making them wet, you close the deal. You sell them an America where all the seven deadlies are on sale twenty-four seven, but they believe they're listening to their mothers. They believe they're doing the right thing. Inside the hollow righteousness, is a center of hot, white sin.

The Donald:
(Quite taken aback. Pushes Seducer Donald away from him) You need to get the fuck out of my head.

Seducer Donald:
(Turning to get back in line by Panderer Tweed who is close to exiting stage right) Too late. **(Grinning wildly, taps his temple)** Think on it. Dream on it. **(Taps the back of his head)** I'll be right in here. Just call my name. I'll come running. **(He ducks under the line and exits stage right with Panderer Tweed)**

Boss Tweed:
(Trying to shake himself from the spell of Seducer Donald) Man, if words were bark juice. Cat's got me spinning.

Sugar Coated Sam/Iblee:
Words of wisdom, Donny.

The Donald:
Stop calling me Donny.

Sugar Coated Sam/Iblee:
Just saying.

The Donald:
Where's this go? **(He pulls the cough syrup out, checks how much is left, unscrews the cap and drinks, passes it to Boss Tweed)** We getting on some ride or something?

Sugar Coated Sam/Iblee:
Not too much more line. Maybe a mile or so.

The Donald:
Hot Jesus, this sucks. I hate lines. I hate waiting. What'd they do, release the I-Phone Ten down here? This is stupid.

Boss Tweed:
Untwist your panties.

The Donald:
(Getting in Boss Tweed's face) I. Have. Shit. To. Do.

Boss Tweed:
Line's moving pretty good, today. Relax.

Sugar Coated Sam/Iblee:
Circle Eight is all about wait.

The Donald:
I gotta take a leak.

Boss Tweed:
Talk to a man about a dog, huh?

The Donald:
What're you on?

Sugar Coated Sam/Iblee:
(Grinning. Over-acting taking a pee) Whiiiiiizzzzzzzzzz.

Boss Tweed:
You know, bleed the lizard. Ease the monster. Tap the keg.

Sugar Coated Sam/Iblee:
Whiiiiiiizzzzzzzzz.

Boss Tweed:
Write your name in the snow. Get rid of some ballast. Water Ship out-

The Donald:
Alright, already! Where's the men's room?

Boss Tweed:
In Hell? Really? Skip to the loo in Hell.

Sugar Coated Sam/Iblee:
(Skipping in place) Whiiiiiizzzzzzzz to the looooooooo.

The Donald:
(Looking to his right, to beneath the box) There's one there! I thought you people knew where we are. I'll be right back.

Boss Tweed:
(To Sugar Coated Sam/Iblee) I don't remember seeing that before.

Sugar Coated Sam/Iblee:
Me either. New architects.

(The Donald crosses to a door set up between the front corner of stage right and beneath the box. As he opens the door, three spots

light up a bank of three urinals facing the audience beneath the box. The side of the door that had been facing toward back stage has a sign that says 'Uni-Shade'. He enters and shuts the door behind him. From somewhere overhead, *Raindrops Keep Falling On My Head* syncopates in muzak-ness. There is already a shade standing at the corner urinal. It is Flatterer Donald. Quite visible under the middle urinal is a raised floor drain with a fourth spot accenting it. The Donald, oblivious of himself standing at the corner urinal, walks over to the first urinal and gets ready to pee)

The Donald:
Oh man, this is going to feel good.

Flatterer Donald:
You're just peeing, right?

The Donald:
I beg your problem? **(Recognizing himself as Flatterer Donald looks up and over at him)** Hey! What am I doing in here?

Flatterer Donald:
Shaking hands with the devil. How 'bout you?

The Donald:
'parently I'm talking to a man about a dog, whatever that means. Why am I in here?

Flatterer Donald:
This is department two, pal. D2, Circle Eight-Flattery.

The Donald:
Flattery? I'm no flatterer.

Flatterer Donald:
Are you kidding me? You're the best. You could charm the habit off a nun. You could sell oil to a Saudi Prince. You could close a deal with Beelzebub and leave him scratching his head in the middle of the crossroads.

The Donald:
I *can* close a deal.

Flatterer Donald:
Like nobody's business. Hell, you could show a fella a piece of property through the front door, while his wife left through the back door.

(The floor drain beneath the middle urinal starts to spit a brown substance)

The Donald:
Been there, done that.

Flatterer Donald:
Like that golf course in Scotland. The fella with the house. The way you snookered him. Had him thinking he was going to get paid. **(The Donald smiles and chuckles)** Slick. Or, that piano guy. How many pianos did he tune? Two, three hundred. For free! **(The Donald stops smiling)** Oh, I know, **(reaches over and taps The Donald's shoulder)** this campaign. The people backing you. Whataya think about them?

The Donald:
My greatest act, yet.

Flatterer Donald:
Man alive! You're good at this!

(The floor drain is now bubbling shit. The Donald is crinkling up his nose)

The Donald:
Years. Years of grooming just the right kind of people. Years of watching the country slide into the cess pool so I could be the hero to lead them out.

Flatterer Donald:
Only you. Only you could have done this.

(The floor drain is now spraying shit. The Donald is looking around)

The Donald:
Oh, I wasn't alone. I mean, I was but I wasn't. I have to credit parts of of me like you.

Flatterer Donald:
At your service, my liege.

The Donald:
The whole secret to closing the deal, well, its like that one old saying: the ability to tell someone to go to Hell, and have them look forward to the trip.

Flatterer Donald:
Bingo!

(The floor drain is pumping out excrement in the same way a concrete hose pumps out liquid concrete. The Donald takes a look at Flatterer Donald's backside)

The Donald:
Do you smell something?

Flatterer Donald:
Not really. Smells like it always smells in here. Why?

The Donald:
Well, it stinks like shit.

Flatterer Donald:
That's flattery, son. Bullshit. Liquid vaseline. You close that deal by lubing them up with a thick application of what they want to hear. Just like your campaign.

The Donald:
Its been like taking candy from a baby. I mean, for thirty years they've been programmed to hate progress. To hate people who think, who're educated. Its so easy.

Flatterer Donald:
But you stroked them. **(Flatterer Donald makes pelvic thrusts)** You're closing this deal as we speak.

(The floor drain is now gushing fecal material. It is splattering everywhere. The Donald is looking down and tapping his shoes against the middle urinal)

The Donald:
Closing? The Presidency?

Flatterer Donald:
Buddy, you are so fucking good at selling yourself and this warped version of the American Dream, that it is only a matter of time.

The Donald:
I'm winning?

Flatterer Donald:
Winning? This is like Slippery Rock playing Alabama. That bitch doesn't stand a chance.

(The poop stops coming out. There is a low, unearthly rumble from below the floor drain. There are strange, quite concerning plumbing sounds coming from the drain and the urinals. The Donald is looking around with urgency. Flatterer Donald is too busy stroking The Donald)

Flatterer Donald:
My friend, you're like Mr. Haney from that one old show *Green Acres*. Except, you're Mr. Haney on 'roids. You're that fella in the medicine wagon, except the wagon is your personal jet. Town after town, state after state, this is the biggest snow job turned land slide in the history of the *U*-nited States of America.

The Donald:
Think?

Flatterer Donald:
Think? Think about this: you have convinced an entire segment of American society that they are disenfranchised, that they don't count, and that you're the only hope they have. And, after they elect you, and you hand the country over to you know who, you'll walk away from them as fast as you walked away from that one lady you boinked in room two three seven.

(The low rumble becomes deafening. Ceases. Belches. The lights dip as if there is a drain on the power and only come back halfway. The Donald is looking around quite terrified)

The Donald:
Is this normal?

Flatterer Donald:

Is it normal for one man to steal an entire nation? Fuck no. But it happens all the time. You'll see. You'll see the company you're about to keep. All I can say is, you are the cat's ass. You are slick as shit. You're going to take a giant steaming dump on Lady Liberty and come out smelling like a rose-

(The floor drain and the urinals explode kaka. It is hosing both Donalds. It is spraying all over them, against the closed door to the bathroom. Everywhere. The two of them are drenched in it. After several long, stinky moments, it stops)

The Donald:

(Wiping poop from his eyes, his face. Holding his arms out akimbo) What in the royal fuck was that?

Flatterer Donald:

(Zipping up. Backing away from the urinal. Clapping The Donald on the back) Well, that's it for me. This is a wrap. Congratz on the election, keep up the sweet talk, and don't forget to lube 'em up before you plow it home. **(Turns and exits leaving the door open and The Donald standing there dripping)**

(After a beat, Boss Tweed and Sugar Coated Sam/Iblee peek into the bathroom from either side of the doorway)

Boss Tweed:

You okay in there, Strumpet?

The Donald:

Does it look like I'm okay? Does it look remotely, like I'm okay?

Sugar Coated Sam/Iblee:

Nope.

(They gingerly walk in and stand some feet away from The Donald, looking around)

Sugar Coated Sam/Iblee:
Well, that's flattery for you.

Boss Tweed:
Strumpet?

The Donald:
What?

Boss Tweed:
You're the shit!

The Donald:
Fuck you. What do we do about this, huh? **(Looks at Sugar Coated Sam/ Iblee)** Caseworker? Time to work the case.

Sugar Coated Sam/Iblee:
Next department. Clean you right up. Very happy.

The Donald:
Happy?

Sugar Coated Sam/Iblee:
Yes, happy I can't smell. **(He and Boss Tweed burst out laughing. The lights dim on the men's room as they turn to exit)**

(The lights go up on the actual box, where Statler Swift and Waldorf Voltaire are sitting in yellow foul weather gear with clothes pins on their noses)

Statler Swift:
Reminds me ob when we were at Niagara.

Waldorf Voltaire:
Maid ob the Shits.

Statler Swift:
Hope there isn't a whirlpool.

Waldorf Voltaire:
Dis should look like his honeymoon perwiod.

Statler Swift:
I wonder how dare going to clean him?

Waldorf Voltaire:
Maybe dat orange stpuff will come off.

Statler Swift:
Dyou wouldn't tink he'd mind.

Waldorf Voltaire:
Why is dat?

Statler Swift:
Its his natuwal enbwirement.

(The lights fade on the box as they come up on the narrator's stage. There is a large stone font that is bubbling with a liquid that changes color, the glow emanating up from the font. The font is so large an entire human could easily fit in it. Behind it are two large demons, so large they could easily pick up said human and

dunk them in said font. In fact, that's their job. They are dressed as torturers, replete with black leather smocks, high collared brown shirts, thick, black leather belts, and gray-green rubber pants. Despite this, they have perfect Princetons, prescription, rimless eye glasses, silk neck ties-one yellow and one red, buttons on their smocks that read 'I "heart" Orders', and stickers that read, 'Hello, My Name is Charles' and 'Hello, My Name is David'. There are a pair of legs sticking out of the font, kicking this way and that. Behind this, from an ancient speaker on the upper wall behind them, *Yesterday* churns in muzak foreverness)

Charles:
(In an upper-class accent) Christ on crutches, David, this king making is arduous.

David:
(Same accent, slightly higher pitched) Good God, Charlie, you're telling me. I haven't had a proper b.m. in weeks.

Charles:
What do you think our next move should be?

David:
Throw money. It does buy everything, after all.

Charles:
(Leaning in close) And everyone. **(They share a chuckle)** What about this chap?

David:
Good heavens, forgot all about him. What did he do again?

Charles:
David, its Budd. You remember, Mr. Dwyer.

David:

Oh yes. Classic Americana. There's thousands of these born every minute. Should we pull him out?

Charles:

Yes, he's expected back in the forest. Grab a leg, would you.

David:

Right-O!

(The two demons pull up a rotund, balding man in a dark suit with a striped tie. The back of his head is clearly missing, and he scrambles for breath and flails about as they hold him high over the font. They give him a good shake, and then toss him off-stage, stage left, with an audibly loud 'thump and roll')

David:

Why do they have to be so icky?

Charles:

The plebeian horde.

(Sugar Coated Sam/Iblee, The Donald, and Boss Tweed enter from stage left, looking over their shoulders. The two demons look over and hold their noses)

Charles:

My God, man, what is that smell?

David:

Smells like someone had an unhappy visit to Department Number Two.

Charles:

Mr. Tweed, how wonderful to see you. I didn't see your name on the docket?

Boss Tweed:
(Who had been looking away) And you won't find it, either.

David:
Then to what do we owe the pleasure?

Boss Tweed:
(Pointing at The Donald) Been asked to take the Strumpet here, all over Hell.

(The two demons lean in and look at The Donald, fingers holding noses)

Charles:
Merciful Lord, its Donald.

David:
It is! Oh, this makes up for an otherwise dull and dreary day.

Charles:
Donald, why in God's name are you here? We gave you a shit-ton of work to do.

The Donald:
I'd be happy to explain if you could help clean me up.

Sugar Coated Sam/Iblee:
Hey boys! Gonna need a hand with this one.

David:
Sam, how goes the casework?

Sugar Coated Sam/Iblee:
Oh, you know, easy come not so easy go. This fella, whoo whee.

(The two demons pull on long rubber gloves the same shade as their pants)

Charles:
Not a problem, Sam, not a problem at all. David, grab an ankle.

David:
With pleasure, Charles.

(The Donald's eyes get real big as the two demons grab ankles and lift, letting gravity flip The Donald upside-down. They hold him above the bubbling font as he struggles)

Charles:
Now, Donald, you wouldn't use the office of President of The United States to further enrich your companies, would you?

(Before there is an answer The Donald is submerged into the font. The liquid bubbles violently. They pull him up)

David:
Now, Donald, you wouldn't use your influence as President of The United States to influence other nations into smoothing things over for your corporations, would you?

(Another dunk into the font, the hue of the liquid changes as it gurgles up and over the sides. They lift him up once more)

Charles:
Now Donald, you wouldn't use the vast apparatus of America's judicial, law enforcement, and military to avenge those whom you believe have wronged you, would you?

(Bloop. Boil. Bubble. Lift. Look at each other, shrug, bloop, boil and bubble)

Charles:
(A bell sounds) Okay, that's enough for now.

David:
Thank God, I'm starving.

(The two demons lift The Donald up and out of the font, set him down, right-side up, and pull off gloves and smocks)

Sugar Coated Sam/Iblee:
What? That's it? It was just getting fun.

Charles:
We're on break.

David:
Twenty minutes every two hours.

The Donald:
This is a union shop? You guys?

Charles:
Don't tell anyone, but the hours were brutal.

David:
Barely had time to influence.

Charles:
Now, thanks to Local Demons and Torturers, Number Two One Three, we have a life.

Sugar Coated Sam/Iblee:
(Looking at The Donald) You feel better, there, Donny?

The Donald:
(Soaking wet and shaking) Not really.

Sugar Coated Sam/Iblee:
Thanks, boys! Onward and downward!

Charles:
Anytime, Sam.

David:
You *know* who to give our best to.

Sugar Coated Sam/Iblee:
Sure thing. Come on, guys, this way.

(Sugar Coated Sam/Iblee leads The Donald and Boss Tweed across the narrator's stage. He and The Donald exit onto the left side of a dark center stage)

Charles:
(Just before Boss Tweed steps onto the left side of center stage) And Mr. Tweed? **(Boss Tweed stops, shoulders hunched up)** We'll be seeing you in a few short weeks.

(Boss Tweed exits as the lights fade out on the narrator's stage)

(Several spots light up the extreme left side of center stage. There is a large desk facing the audience. On it are several glass pots of different shades with steam rising from them, a Jacob's ladder, a skull, and a different bat stretched out on a different rack in

a different position. Behind the desk, head facing backwards, is Nostradamus. He is shuffling manilla files even though he can't see what it is he is shuffling. In the background is a muzak version of *Witchy Woman*. Sugar Coated Sam/Iblee leads The Donald and Boss Tweed up to his desk)

Sugar Coated Sam/Iblee:
Hey, Noster, we're here for our appointment.

Nostradamus:
What? Who? What time is it?

Sugar Coated Sam/Iblee:
We're over here. It's Sam. I got that one guy here, you know, the one from those quatrains.

Nostradamus:
Oh yes, one Mr. Trumpet. I've got a file here somewhere, aha! Here it is. **(He pulls out a jam-packed file that has bones, rune blocks, and feathers falling out of it)** Now then. What seems to be the trouble.

Sugar Coated Sam/Iblee:
You tell us, that's why we're here.

Nostradamaus:
So, **(looking at The Donald)** presumably you're going to be President of The United States of America.

The Donald:
(They've all gathered around his desk, Boss Tweed examining the bat) There's no presumption about it, I will be President. The guy in the shitter said as much.

Nostradamus:
Right. The guy in the shitter. Well, lets sort of take a snapshot of where you've been, where you're headed, and where we can place you once you come back forever.

(Nostradamus stands up, head still facing the other way, opens up the file and pulls out a *Crown Royal* bag. He clears off a spot on his desk, shakes the bag, turns it over, and empties a pile of bones)

Nostradamus:
(He looks each of them square in the face, lastly The Donald. Looks down. Waves his hands over the scattered bones. The Donald, Boss Tweed, and Sugar Coated Sam/Iblee lean in mesmerized) Now, talk to me. **(Hand swishes)** 'The Bear and The Eagle will join together'. **(Pause)** Fading. Dammit. Hang on. **(Reaches into a drawer, pulls out a handful of rune blocks. He places them in the Crown Royal bag, puts the bones back in, shakes and empties the bag)** Alright, **(waving hands)** talk to me. **(Finger wiggles)** 'The Bear and The Eagle, conjoined together'. **(Pause)** Nope. Not it. **(Sigh)** Alright. Hang on. **(Reaches into a different drawer and pulls out a fist full of feathers. Into the bag. Add the bones and runes. Shakes the bag. Empties the bag)** Whoa!

The Donald:
What is it!

Nostradamus:
(Super intent on the stuff on the desk) 'My mommy and your mommy were hanging up clothes! My mommy punched your mommy', nope, way off. **(He scatters them around)** 'He', yes, yes, 'He wouldn't say his prayers, so I grabbed him by a leg', nope.

Sugar Coated Sam/Iblee:
I like this game!

Nostradamus:
(Scatter and a push of the bones, runes, feathers) Ho, ho, ho, oh yeah.
Coming in like a freight train.

The Donald:
Talk to me!

Nostradamus:
'Donny, dear Donny, how does your country grow!' **(He stops. Looks up
at the three of them)** What's a cock sliver?

The Donald:
This is going nowhere.

Sugar Coated Sam/Iblee:
To market, to market!

The Donald:
(To Sugar Coated Sam/Iblee) Wait a minute! I know you!

Nostradamus:
Got it! Hang on. **(Puts everything back into the bag. Holds up a finger. Reaches into another drawer and pulls out the skull of a rat.
Places it in the bag. Shakes bag. Opens. Reaches inside his coat and
pulls out a small bag of glitter. Dumps it in the bag with a dramatic flourish. Shakes the bag. Looks at The Donald as he empties
the bag. He waves his hands over the stuff as if trying to pull the
aroma up to the back of his head)** Okay, buster, this is it. 'The Bear
and The Eagle will waltz together, under blood red skies in early December.
Moo shu Dragon all guys in the pan, the arrows will fly as will the cans. The

Star grows distant the heat ebbs away, as it did back in my day. All legions are missing not even a man, could put Humpty Dumpty back together' What the! **(Sighs)** Sorry, it faded out.

The Donald:
That's it? Humpty Dumpty? Bears? Eagles? Dragons?

Nostradamus:
Hey, that's what it said, pal!

The Donald:
For fuck's sake. This is useless.

Nostradamus:
You try looking at this shit with your head backwards in a front ways world!

Boss Tweed:
Hey, sorry Noster. He gets a little testy.

The Donald:
What's next? 'One potato, two potato' Let's go! Next department. This one's stupid.

Nostradamus:
Screw you pal!

The Donald:
Oh, yeah!

(The Donald lunges over the desk. Nostradamus lunges as well, and the two end up in a mutual headlock, bones, runes, feathers, and glitter flying. Boss Tweed separates them. They dust themselves off)

Nostradamus:
Thanks, Sam. What a treat. And its Monday!

The Donald:
To think I wasted four hours listening to Leonard Nimoy go on and on over your stupid quad trains.

Sugar Coated Sam/Iblee:
Sorry, Noster. Is there anything else, any other way. Please.

Nostradamus:
(He turns around and takes a long cold look at The Donald) Yes. There is. **(He turns around, opens the top drawer of his desk and pulls out a ouija board)** There is, this. **(He sits down. Motions for The Donald to sit down opposite. He pulls out the planchette)** This is an original. Elijah Bond. 1890.

The Donald:
(Clearly interested. The others crowd in) So, these are real, huh?

Nostradamus:
Oh, yeah.

Boss Tweed:
How'd you get it?

Nostradamus:
(Looks one way, then the other. Leans closer) E-Bay.

The Donald:
What?

Nostradamus:
Fucking love E-Bay. **(Points at the stretched out bat)** Bat stretchers? Four pages! Amazing. Anyhoo. Place your fingers on the planchette and close your eyes. **(The Donald does this)** Now simply let go. Empty your mind.

Boss Tweed:
This shouldn't take-

The Donald:
Fuck you.

Sugar Coated Sam/Iblee:
Shhh. This is the best part.

Nostradamus:
Everyone! Close your eyes. Let go.

(Nostradamus slowly waves his hands above the board. He begins some sort of chant that sounds like humming the alphabet. The Donald's hands begin to move around the board on the planchette. Boss Tweed starts to sway and Sugar Coated Sam/Iblee uncoils in a poof of glitter and cloud, becoming Iblee)

Nostradamus:
Its coming. Its coming. Oh, boy. Oh my God. Oh God. Oh God oh God oh God. Here it comes. Here it comes! Here! It! Comes! Wow!

(Iblee coalesces back into Sugar Coated Sam. Boss Tweed starts and stands up straight. The Donald bounces out of his chair, and Nostradamus half rises out of his)

The Donald:
What is it! What is it!

Nostradamus:
(Motioning for The Donald to come closer. He does and there is a beat) You're penis is going to fall off.

The Donald:
(Lunging across the desk and the donnybrook restarting) Fuck you, you fuck-witted non-seeing charlatan!

(Sugar Coated Sam/Iblee is busting a gut. Boss Tweed is as well, but is pulling The Donald away from strangling Nostradamus. Nostradamus is dying of laughter)

Nostradamus:
Thanks, Sam. **(Boss Tweed has successfully removed The Donald and is tugging him toward center stage)** What a great morning. You people kill me. Stop back anytime.

Sugar Coated Sam/Iblee:
Have a good one, Noster. Thanks for the laughs!

(The spots fade on Nostradamus and his desk as several come up beside it at center stage proper. Sugar Coated Sam/Iblee follows The Donald and Boss Tweed through a door that opens on the rim of a pool. The pool runs from the front of the stage to the back, from center to stage right, with enough room for entities to walk between the stage's edge and the rim of the pool. There is a raised lifeguard chair, a sign that reads 'Surface at Your Own Risk', coils of ropes attached to grappling hooks, gaffing poles with wicked-sharp points and barbs, and a large plastic container of white goo that says; Light Block-SPF 443,556. Standing

beside the rim of the pool is a demon-lifeguard. He is about three times the size of the largest human ever, has glistening red skin, is ridiculously buff despite a collection of warts, bumps, and other surface protrusions, has horns twisting out of bleached blonde hair, and is wearing only ear buds, *Billabong* swim shorts, and wraparound *Ray-Bans*. His head bobs slowly to the beat, as the three walk up to him)

The Donald:
Excuse me. **(No response. Clears throat. Still no response)** I said, excuse me. **(Nothing)** Young man! Hello! **(Turns to face Boss Tweed and Sugar Coated Sam/Iblee)** This fella couldn't save Pamela Anderson from a one-armed drummer.

(Sugar Coated Sam/Iblee walks over and taps the demon on the hip. The demon turns, perturbed, then smiles)

Malacoda:
(Pulling an ear bud out and beaming a perfect smile. From the ear bud we hear a small, tinny version of Surfer Girl) Little dude! What's the word! **(Places a giant fist by Sugar Coated Sam/Iblee's ear. Sugar Coated Sam/Iblee gives it a fist bump)**

Sugar Coated Sam/Iblee:
Not much, brah. You?

Malacoda:
Just punch'n the clock 'till I can punch some waves. **(Looks over to Boss Tweed)** Hey, brah, shouldn't you be **(hikes a thumb over his shoulder in the direction of the pool)**.

Boss Tweed:
Not today, I'm on a mission.

Malacoda:
Rad. Cool. **(Looks at The Donald)** What about the skeg?

Sugar Coated Sam/Iblee:
These guys are with me. The pork chop there is my latest and greatest. That's why we're here, need some anglin'.

Malacoda:
Bitchin', dude. Whatever you need, brah.

The Donald:
What we need is to clear through here as fast as possible.

Malacoda:
Well, dork, that just isn't as possible as it was some two thousand years ago. See, the bridge's been out since the big quake.

The Donald:
(To Sam) Sam! What now? Where's the head honcho, here?

Malacoda:
Brah, you're startin' to send me on a double spinner.

Sugar Coated Sam/Iblee:
This is the head honcho.

The Donald:
Who? **(Pointing at Malacoda)** Biff? We are right and truly fucked.

(Another Surfer-Demon enters from stage right with Corrupt Donald in front of him, being held up, off the ground, by both arms. Corrupt Donald is covered in black pitch and has a grappling hook sticking out of the side of his head)

Barbariccia:
Brah, caught this little fucker trying to make a break for it. Says he has an appointment with you and Sam. Hey! Sam! How's the surf, brah.

Sugar Coated Sam/Iblee:
Nothin' but blue skies and pipes. You?

Barbariccia:
Totally tube, brah. Well, it was, then this kook showed up. Hey, wait a minute. **(Looking at The Donald)** Aren't you him?

Malacoda:
This is so fucked up. Who is this cat and why are there two of him?

Sugar Coated Sam/Iblee:
I can explain. He **(two hands on The Donald)** is my case. And he **(two hands not quite on Corrupt Donald)** is a fax smiley of **(two hands back on The Donald)** him.

Malacoda:
This is still so fucked up.

Boss Tweed:
(Holding a hand up) Lemme explain. I was minding my own business, suffering all over Hell, when Saint Dymphna appears to me, somewhere between Circle Five and Circle Six, and says to me, 'There's this severely challenged individual back in your hometown, and you need to show him all of Hell, so he doesn't blow the entire world into smithereens'. Then, after attempting to do this, after much trial and tribulation, Sam here, becomes his caseworker so we can get through Circle Eight as quickly as possible.

Barbariccia:
That is so fucked up.

Malacoda:
So, like, what do you need from us?

Sugar Coated Sam/Iblee:
Easy peezee! You boys show him **(two hands on The Donald)** what happens in Department 5, Circle Eight, using him **(two hands near Corrupt Donald)** as an example.

Malacoda:
Got it. Bar, toss that geek back in the drink.

(Barbariccia tosses Corrupt Donald back into the pool where he disappears from view, screams of pain ensuing. The Donald rushes to the edge of the pool to see where he went)

The Donald:
What the hell?! What'd you just do to me?

Malacoda:
Dude, what is your big, hairy deal?

The Donald:
I thought you rescued people!

(Blank looks on all faces but an infuriated The Donald)

The Donald:
You **(two hands motioning toward Malacoda)** pull souls **(two hands motioning toward the pool)** from drowning.

(Looks of why is this crazy person invading our space)

The Donald:
You're lifeguards!

Malacoda:
Dude, **(eye roll)** don't think I don't know what you're talking about. I've been to Cali. Venice Beach, brah.

Barbariccia:
Fit right in.

Malacoda:
(Fist bump with Barbariccia) Walked the boulevard.

Barbariccia:
Even *we* got hit on.

Malacoda:
Remember that little bar.

Barbariccia:
Drinking with Lemmy.

Malacoda:
Brah, it was raining Jack and Cokes.

Barbariccia:
For sure.

The Donald:
Hello! I'm drowning in there. **(Two hands pointing to the pool)**

Sugar Coated Sam/Iblee:
That's the point. Face in the muck.

Boss Tweed:
Just like the sticky fingers we had on Earth.

Malacoda:
Just like all the black secrets and the hidden agendas and the grafting.

Sugar Coated Sam/Iblee:
And the banzai schemes.

Barbariccia:
Yeah, lil brah, close enough for Circle Eight.

The Donald:
(Slaps Malacoda on the back of his thigh) I demand you pull me from that!

Malacoda:
(Incredulous. Looks over at Barbariccia who is just shaking his head real slow) Dweeb, I'll do you one better.

(Malacoda grabs The Donald by his back collar and tosses him over the lip of the pool and into the pitch. Horrifying screams pierce the air)

Malacoda:
As I was trying to say, **(to Sugar Coated Sam/Iblee)** the bridge is out. So, you gotta take the bombora.

Barbariccia:
Its okay, lil brah, we marked it.

Malacoda:
Yeah, like go the normal way, along the edge of the pool-

(The screaming abates slightly as The Donald and Corrupt Donald are pushing themselves out of the pool)

Malacoda:
Brah, a little help.

Barbariccia:
(Pushing both back into the pool with one hand on each forehead)
Back to the bone yard, boys.

Sugar Coated Sam/Iblee:
So, you marked the path?

Malacoda:
Right. You'll see. Bar?

Barbariccia:
Brah?

Malacoda:
Time to get beached.

Barbariccia:
Like, you so read my mind.

Malacoda:
(To Sugar Coated Sam/Iblee) We're out, lil dude. Time to snack. Go easy.

Sugar Coated Sam/Iblee:
(Fist bumps with Mal and Bar) What about them? **(Two hands pointing at the pool)**

Malacoda and Barbariccia:
(Together and both flipping double birds) Fuck 'em.

(Malacoda and Barbariccia exit stage left, heads doing a quick tilt up to Boss Tweed)

Boss Tweed:
(Tilts head up at the two Surfer-Demons and walks over to Sugar Coated Sam/Iblee) So, what about the Strumpet?

Sugar Coated Sam/Iblee:
Grab that hook thingie.

(Boss Tweed grabs the grappling hook)

Sugar Coated Sam/Iblee:
Throw it at him. (Pointing at the pool)

(Boss Tweed awkwardly twirls and releases the grappling hook in the direction of The Donald, the rope running through his hands)

The Donald:
(From the back part of center stage) Ouch! Goddamnit! What the fuck's the matter with you!

Sugar Coated Sam/Iblee:
Nice shot!

Boss Tweed:
I've been waiting to do that since I met the bastard. Now what?

Sugar Coated Sam/Iblee:
(Walking toward stage right, where little tiki-god lights twinkle on and away marking a path) Pull him this way.

Boss Tweed:
My pleasure. Hey, Strumpet! Hold tight, brah. Heh heh heh.

(The two exit in a slow saunter stage right, singing quite off key, *Surfer Girl*. Boss Tweed pulls and sometimes yanks the rope, screams and cursing coming from The Donald, unseen somewhere in the pool. After they exit stage right, all lights fade except the tiki-god lights, which stay on until their rendition of *Surfer Girl* fades as well)

(From the darkness we hear the beginning of *A Whiter Shade of Pale* played in perfect muzak-ese, from stage left. The lights come up on the narrator's stage. There is a pulpit, opulent in white marble with a brass lamp and a gold microphone. A banner hangs from a brass stand behind the pulpit, on it is depicted a dove flying with the dollar sign in its beak. A tall, thin man in a white, designer suit is polishing the pulpit and humming to the muzak. He is in his late-fifties, quite well groomed, and gushingly happy)

The Right Reverend Z:
(Humming and singing to the music with a Southern accent, but with these words) Hmmm, Citation. Or a Lear. Hmmm, hmmm, a Gulfstream, or Hawker, or maybe Challenger or a Legacy. Hmm hmm hmm, polish polish clean clean. Jesus is my co-pilot. God is my Sovereign, I am a Falcon, my church is Glo-*bal*. La la la la. Hmm hmm-

(The Donald enters the narrator's stage. He is covered in pitch, and has a grappling hook sticking out of his shoulder. It is trailing a short length of rope that is frayed on the end, and drags behind him a few feet. Sugar Coated Sam/Iblee enters trying to step on the rope end. Boss Tweed can be heard bellowing behind them, off-stage)

Boss Tweed:
Holy shit, Sam, stop that crazy fucker!

The Donald:
You sons of bitches! What the hell are you doing to me?

Sugar Coated Sam/Iblee:
Donny. Donny. Hold up, man. Hold up. Donny.

The Donald:
I thought Circle Eight was boring? I thought we were fast tracked? I'm getting the tar knocked out of me!

The Right Reverend Z:
(Throwing himself in front of his polished marble pulpit) Unseemly sinners! Back away from my cockpit! Unclean! Foul! Demons from the pit! Why do you trespass on my runway! Why do you bring your filth to this temple of aeronautic holiness!

The Donald:
(Taken aback for about one beat) Fuck you.

Boss Tweed:
Strumpet! Goddammit! Hold up! **(Boss Tweed enters the narrator's stage)**

The Right Reverend Z:
Please! I implore you! Little ears and inside voices! And, and stay away from God's Seat.

The Donald:
Who are you? I know you. I've seen you somewhere.

The Right Reverend Z:
I am the Right Reverend Z. Founder of The Church of Eternal Prosperity. Creator of the Soaring Dove Evangelical Ministry, the largest spiritual organization in the history of the world. A movement that has spread to over one hundred and sixty nations across God's Green Acres. A way of life that has touched more than one hundred million of God's Children. A message that has flown across the planet by every type of media created by man and inspired by God, from bullhorns to bugles, from Facebook to flyers, by voice, by prayer, and by donation. I am the Right Reverend Z, and this! **(He spreads his arms out over the expanse of the theater)** This! Is my temple!

The Donald:
You're dead.

The Right Reverend Z:
I am not.

The Donald:
Then why are you in Hell?

The Right Reverend Z:
Hell, is for sinners.

Sugar Coated Sam/Iblee:
Donny. Psst. Donny. Over here.

The Donald:
Where do you think you are?

The Right Reverend Z:
This is God's Special Chapel. And we are waiting to be called.

Sugar Coated Sam/Iblee:
Yoo hoo. Donny. Psst.

The Donald:
I know you're dead. Billy Graham gave your eulogy. You were practically laid in State. Three days of coverage.

The Right Reverend Z:
That, was my ascent. My, climb, if you will.

The Donald:
Bullshit. You were poisoned. Your wife. An affair. That porn star from Slovenia. What happened in Vegas didn't stay in Vegas.

Sugar Coated Sam/Iblee:
(A very loud whisper) Donny! Psst. Now.

Boss Tweed:
Strumpet. **(Pointing at Sugar Coated Sam/Iblee)** Hello. Listen.

The Right Reverend Z:
My filthy friend, what once possessed me as a mortal, can no longer touch me here in God's Special Chapel. I did not die. I was not poisoned.

The Donald:
Then how did you get here?

The Right Reverend Z:
I mis-swallowed some pound cake that my loving and understanding wife had made for me. While I was choking, the tower cleared me for take-off, and now I am here, preaching to my flock as I did on Earth, on television, on the internet, on radio, on short wave. The means does not matter, it is the message of Eternal Prosperity that resonates like a Rolls Royce engine at the very moment we all go wheels-up.

The Donald:
You're insane.

(The Right Reverend Z returns to polishing his pulpit)

Sugar Coated Sam/Iblee:
Donny! **(Tugging on The Donald's sleeve and then wiping the tar on Boss Tweed who is looking around dumbstruck)**

The Donald:
(To Sugar Coated Sam/Iblee) What is it!

Sugar Coated Sam/Iblee:
He's crazy.

The Donald:
Do you think?

Sugar Coated Sam/Iblee:
No. Crazy, crazy. Like batshit. Like we need to leave crazy.

The Donald:
Well, what about this. **(Gesturing to himself)** How do I get all this shit off of me? How do I get this shit *out* of me?

The Right Reverend Z:
You poor children of disgustingness, I must ask you to refrain from cursing in God's Special Chapel. One must have pure thoughts, be surrounded by pure light, be ever in the presence of purist purity, so as to allow the opportunity to take-off when God asks us for that one last flight.

The Donald:
(To Sugar Coated Sam/Iblee) How the fuck do we get out of here.

The Right Reverend Z:
My mama, saintly woman, Southern Belle, Daughter of The Revolution and Grand Daughter of a survivor of The War for Independence of Dearest Dixie, she once washed my mouth out with soap for saying a bad word and by golly, I swear upon Robert E. Lee, I will do the same to you.

The Donald:
(To Sugar Coated Sam/Iblee) What's the lesson here, huh? Where are we? What department is this?

Sugar Coated Sam/Iblee:
Hypocrisy.

The Donald:
I do what I say. I say what I mean. I do what I want. Anything else, is just, well, oversight.

Boss Tweed:
So what are you saying?

The Right Reverend Z:
My good fellow, what this tar-heeled, impudent gentleman is saying, is that in his life he has never been guilty of the sin of hypocrisy.

Boss Tweed:
(Beat) Bullshit. He's hypocrisy's poster child.

The Donald:
My ass.

The Right Reverend Z:
(Melodiously) Language.

The Donald:
How've I been a hypocrite?

Boss Tweed:
You lied to the people.

The Donald:
You're full of shit. How so?

The Right Reverend Z:
My vulgar and sticky-fingered friend, you told the hard-working men and women of the South, of Appalachia, and of the often misguided Upper Midwest, that you were their champion. That you, and only you, could deliver them to a place where they once more mattered. A place where their values and diligence would be appreciated and rewarded.

The Donald:
So how does that make me a hypocrite?

(Boss Tweed sighs and looks toward the ceiling. Sugar Coated Sam/Iblee looks down. The Right Reverend Z stares at The Donald for a moment)

The Right Reverend Z:
My pitch-smeared, sewer-mouthed fellow citizen, when you were down over ten points in the polls, with whom did you have meetings.

The Donald:
Its a free country.

The Right Reverend Z:
It was.

The Donald:
I'll keep my promises!

Sugar Coated Sam/Iblee:
Yes. You will. And soon.

(The four figures on stage look in opposite directions. From all points around the theater, we hear the sounds of Hell rising, then fading)

The Donald:
(To Sugar Coated Sam/Iblee) How do we get out of here? **(To The Right Reverend Z)** Where's the exit in God's Special Chapel?

The Right Reverend Z:
(Pointing all the way across stage) There. **(An 'EXIT' sign illuminates, stage right, above the actual exit to the stage)** But you'll have to get through that.

(The lights come up quickly on center stage. There is a host of shades, all in heavy, ornate cloaks, moving swiftly in all directions. They thunder into one another in great collisions. They moan, scream, wail, and curse at each other in an endless game of human pinball)

The Donald:
What the hell is that?

Boss Tweed and Sugar Coated Sam/Iblee:
(Together) Circle Eight. Department Six.

The Donald:
Its like Arena Football. How'm I supposed to get across?

The Right Reverend Z:
(Holding up a cloak) With this! I bet it fits like a glove. (Turns it around so the back shows to the audience. 'Strumpet' is written in sequins)

Boss Tweed:
(Gushing) It even has your name on it!

The Donald:
This is such bullshit.

Sugar Coated Sam/Iblee:
Only way. Put on the cloak. Cross the field.

Boss Tweed:
Do it for Johnny!

The Right Reverend Z:
For the Gipper.

The Donald:
For fuck's sake.

(The Donald steps closer and puts an arm around Sugar Coated Sam/Iblee)

The Donald:
Really?

Sugar Coated Sam/Iblee:
Would I steer you wrong?

(The Donald sticks out an arm and The Right Reverend Z puts the cloak on him. The cloak, lined in lead, is so heavy that The Donald crashes to the floor)

The Donald:
Are you fucking kidding me?! What the fuck is in this thing?

Sugar Coated Sam/Iblee:
Lead.

The Donald:
Why?

The Right Reverend Z:
The weight of hypocrisy.

The Donald:
Tweed? You in this department?

Boss Tweed:
No. I told people I was stealing from them right to their face. No cloak for me. But, if I do say so, you cut a pretty nice figure in yours.

The Donald:
(Struggling to his feet) No way. Too heavy. I'll take my chances without it.

Sugar Coated Sam/Iblee:
No. Squish.

Boss Tweed:
Hell no! We didn't come this far for you to get pulverized. You've still got places to go and shades to see!

The Right Reverend Z:
You must wear the cloak. You must cross the pitch. But Mr. Tweed, yankee that he is, can coach you from the sideline.

Boss Tweed:
Hear that, Strumpet! Now get out there and hit somebody!

(The Donald ponderously makes his way onto the left side of center stage. He looks over his shoulder. Boss Tweed gives him two thumbs-up. And he's off, Boss Tweed coaching, Sugar Coated Sam/ Iblee and The Right Reverend Z watching and cheering. A muzak version of *Yea, Alabama* **warbles on)**

Boss Tweed:
At a boy, Strumpet! Move to your left. **(The Donald gets smashed into violently)** The other left. Now, dodge to your right! **(The Donald gets crushed violently)** Sorry. My bad. Snake over to the left! **(Bash!)** Now, cut to the right! Quickly! **(Crash!)** Ouch. That might leave a mark. Over! **(Boom!)** Further! **(Sock!)** Now hold it! **(Biff!)** Wait for it! **(Bang!)** Hang on! **(Pow!)** There! Right there! There's your hole!

(A hole opens up in the chaos. The Donald, teetering one way and then the other, makes a break. He's just about to the 'EXIT' sign when an enormous cloaked-shade comes out of nowhere and lays The Donald flat out on his back. The sound of *Yea, Alabama* **sputters off, and there is a moment of silence. The giant cloaked-shade looking down on him does a dab, then he and the rest of the shades exit stage right. The lights on the narrator's stage fade to black as The Right Reverend Z, Boss Tweed, and Sugar Coated Sam/Iblee cross the empty field to stand over The Donald)**

The Right Reverend Z:
(Staring down at The Donald) Brother, that was epic. **(Pointing at Boss Tweed)** That man was like Bear Bryant, and you were just like Forest Gump!

Boss Tweed:
(Who has been dying of laughter since the last collision) Strumpet.
Wow. All I can say is, wow. What a blast! Strumpet?

The Right Reverend Z:
Mr. Trumpet? Mr. Trumpet?

Sugar Coated Sam/Iblee:
(Poking The Donald with a finger) Hey, Donny? You okay?

The Right Reverend Z:
He's not moving.

Boss Tweed:
(Taking a knee beside The Donald) Strumpet!

The Right Reverend Z:
Is he breathing?

Sugar Coated Sam/Iblee:
(Quietly) The more you die.

The Right Reverend Z:
(Turning to sugar Coated Sam/Iblee in astonishment) The greater
chance you have to live.

Boss Tweed:
(Slapping The Donald's face) Strumpet! Strumpet! **(Boss Tweed
stands, looks toward stage left. Loud and in the actor's own voice)**
Do we have an understudy?

**(The lights instantly go out on center stage. The lights come up on
the box and Statler Swift and Waldorf Voltaire)**

Statler Swift:
Good God!

Waldorf Voltaire:
What if they can't finish?

Statler Swift:
They'd better finish! We've been here forever.

Waldorf Voltaire:
This could be like *Jesus Christ Superstar*, or *My Fair Lady*, or *The Pajama Game*.

Statler Swift:
More like *The Dance of Death*.

Waldorf Voltaire:
Well played. We scored Anthony Hopkins on that one.

Statler Swift:
Yes, but lost Laurence Olivier.

Waldorf Voltaire:
But, what if there is no understudy? What if they can't finish. What if this was the one and only time this play could have been performed?

Statler Swift:
Indeed. And what if the manuscript never surfaces again?

(The lights come up on the narrator's stage. Euripides is standing beside the pulpit)

Euripides:
Then its up to the gods.

Statler Swift:
Rubbish. Men before gods.

Waldorf Voltaire:
We created them with our holy brains.

Statler Swift:
Now we follow them like puppy dogs.

Euripides:
Perhaps fate or destiny would be a better choice of words.

Statler Swift:
Destiny is tripe.

Waldorf Voltaire:
Then what legacy will this play leave?

Statler Swift:
Legacy is for people who are afraid to die. Be here now.

Euripides:
Gentlemen, these are dangerous days.

Statler Swift:
Perhaps the American Experiment has reached its fourth and final turn.

Waldorf Voltaire:
Perhaps a new generation will lead?

Statler Swift:
Millennials?

Euripides:
Just what *is* so funny about peace, love, and understanding?

Waldorf Voltaire:
Maybe Gandhi was right?

Euripides:
Maybe Christ was right?

Statler Swift:
Maybe this is just part of the script.

Waldorf Voltaire:
Oh bravo, he wrote us into the script.

Statler Swift:
How? This moment? Impossible.

Waldorf Voltaire:
What if its all just happening and whatever we do means absolutely nothing?

Statler Swift:
We need more port.

Euripides:
At the end of the day, gentlemen, I'm fairly certain we will be graded on how we treated those around us.

Waldorf Voltaire:
Good acts.

Euripides:
And the best act is coming.

Statler Swift:
The show continues?

Euripides:
How could it not.

Waldorf Voltaire:
But, what about the lead?

Euripides:
Yes, the lead. The lead, the cast, the crew. Yourselves and myself. And our audience. **(Looks out to the audience)** Our stalwart and enduring audience. We must press on. The game is afoot. What comedy has brightened, and fiction enlivened, tragedy harkens, to darken our door. We'll see how the sky catches fire. We'll see how she feeds the flames with her implacable hate. Through fingers splayed across fearful faces, we watch together, what is left to transpire, in this the womb that gives birth to all our fears.

And so, **(a nod to the box)** my good gentlemen, **(a nod to the crowd)** and to our audience, a noggin, a dram, or a shot, a glass, a mug, or a yard, a skin, a flagon, or a methuselah, fortify yourselves for the final act.

(The lights fade to black on the narrator's stage as well as the box. House lights slowly come up. Intermezzo III)

Midtro III

There is that feeling of watching an accident. Slow motion. Exaggerated dimensions. The impending collision of metal, plastic, glass, and flesh, as sure as releasing the breath you are holding. That moment, held forever in your memory as it is held before your eyes, is fixed. Inside that moment, there is one split second in which the certainty of the impact may not be a foregone conclusion. As if hope, like a god, can stop the reality.

There is that feeling of watching a horror film. The edges of the screen washed-out, the score slightly warbled, the sets dark and confusing, we are transfixed. We are the prey before the snake. The pupils of its eyes hypnotize, pulsing like the music at a rave. On the edge of our seat, we wish we hadn't given ourselves over so easily. If only we had held onto just a little disbelief, then maybe, just maybe, the girl escapes unscathed. The voyeurism of the experience makes our scalp tingle, our hands sweat. We know all too well what is about to happen.

There is that feeling of crushing inevitability. Like when you have done something horrible, and are simply waiting for the shoe to drop. No turning back. It simply isn't possible. Your mind racing with what you should or shouldn't have done. Each moment an eternity, the sound of the clock is a time bomb.

Temples pounding, sweat seeping out like guilt. Waiting for the knock. The call. The exposure.

There is all of this now. Here. In America. The surreal scene of everyday life like an unending acid trip. A nation walking through the holidays like actors checking their blocking. The looks on people's faces screaming to please make everything normal. As if the election that just transpired was a nightmare, and we're simply waiting for the alarm to go off.

In our shared memory, in our duality, in that collective consciousness that sits like a Stygian pool deep beneath the surface of our waking brain, we have been both the throat and the boot, we have been the victim and the guard, we have been hunted and done the hunting. Because of this, we know that the accident will be violent, we know what will happen to the girl lost in the dark woods, and we know that the terrible thing we did lies in far too shallow of a grave.

Lacrimae mundi. The tears of the world. Collected. Dried. Heated in a silver spoon and shot into the veins of a nation built on top of the blood and bones of one hundred million human beings. We all know what's going to happen.

Don't we.

Act IV

"The house lights dim, leaving the theater in darkness for several long moments. A film, projected onto a screen at center stage, flickers on. It is in black and white. There are numbers counting down from ten, the film itself can be seen running through the projector. It flashes bright and dark and bright: three, two, one. Between grainy black and white footage of Hillary Clinton and Donald Trump debating and speaking, the two candidates pressing the flesh, and the director of the F.B.I. making an announcement, there are clips from D.W. Griffith's 1915 film, *The Birth of A Nation*: Clansmen on horses, Clansmen marching, civil war battles, generals signing documents, and Clansmen lynching. Interspersed between footage of Hillary Clinton and Donald Trump on television and in memes, people voting and protesting, are clips from the 1915 film showing parades with the American flag, the Confederate Army marching, and the Clan riding out. The soundtrack to this montage, played over the house speakers and in random timing, are quotes from cinema:

"Do you like scary movies?"
"Did you know I'm utterly insane."

"A boy's best friend is his mother."
"I see dead people."

A shootout between black men running in the streets and Clansmen riding them down. Protesters confronted at Clinton and Trump campaign rallies by police, security, supporters.

"Whatever you do, don't fall asleep."
"They're coming to get you, Barbara."
"Happy Fourth of July, Julie."

Black men in ropes. A Confederate general leads from the front as battle rages. Scenes of violent reconstruction and legislatures in heated argument. Donald Trump looms behind Hillary Clinton at a debate. Donald Trump acts like a disabled reporter. Donald Trump orating and gesticulating, cut with footage of Mussolini.

"Its all for you, Damien."
"They're all going to laugh at you."
"Hi, I'm Chucky, wanna play?"

Balloons fall on the 2016 Republican Convention. Abraham Lincoln is assassinated.

"Sometimes dead is better."
"The power of Christ compels you."

Balloons fall on the 2016 Republican Convention. Abraham Lincoln is assassinated.

"I'm your number one fan."
"Here's Johnny!"

Balloons fall on the 2016 Republican Convention. Abraham Lincoln is assassinated.

"Be afraid. Be very afraid."
"Help me. Help me."

Balloons fall on the 2016 Republican Convention. Abraham Lincoln is assassinated.

"Death has come to your little town, sheriff."
"Do you like scary movies?"
"Death has come to your little town, sheriff."
"Did you know I'm utterly insane."
"Death has come to your little town, sheriff."
"It rubs the lotion on its skin."
"Death has come to your little town, sheriff."
"I took a souvenir."

There is a pause. The last image freezes. Lincoln leaning forward in the box.

"Death has come to your little town, sheriff."

The film trails off leaving only light being projected onto the screen. In front of this, rising up from the black dust of Hell, is Iblee)

Iblee:
I want to play a game.

(The light from the projector goes out. The theater is plunged into darkness. Lights come up on the narrator's stage. Boss Tweed enters from left with a very wobbly and incoherent The Donald)

Boss Tweed:
Jesus Christ, Strumpet, I'm sorry. I never saw that big fella.

The Donald:
(Teetering and tottering) I do not live in my own reality!

Boss Tweed:
Man, what a collision!

The Donald:
It could also be someone sitting on their bed that weighs four hundred pounds, okay?

Boss Tweed:
Are you sure you're alright. I mean, you're acting kinda funny.

The Donald:
(Rubbing his head. Looking around bewildered) That line's getting a little bit old, I must say.

Boss Tweed:
(Leaning in and looking at The Donald's forehead) That's more than a goose egg.

The Donald:
If she wins, I will absolutely support her.

Boss Tweed:
I think you might be concussed.

The Donald:
Death has come to your little town, sheriff.

(Sugar Coated Sam/Iblee enters from the darkness of center stage)

Sugar Coated Sam/Iblee:
We're going to play a game!

The Donald:
(Snapping to and pointing at Sugar Coated Sam/Iblee) I thought I was crazy!

Sugar Coated Sam/Iblee:
Come on guys! Department Seven! The pit! You're going to love it!

Boss Tweed:
No we're not. I hate the pit.

The Donald:
(Shaking his head. Shaking his body. Shaking himself loose) What's the pit? What's this department about?

(Boss Tweed looks away and down. Sugar Coated Sam/Iblee walks up to The Donald and pulls him close with a lapel)

Sugar Coated Sam/Iblee:
(Drawing out the word in a hushed tone) Thievery.

The Donald:
Yippee skippee.

(The three of them walk to the edge of the narrator's stage, just before center stage. Boss Tweed and The Donald stop. Sugar Coated Sam/Iblee turns back to them)

Sugar Coated Sam/Iblee:
Come on, guys. The pit. Department Seven. Game time.

Boss Tweed:
You sure seem anxious.

The Donald:
I got a bad feeling about this.

Boss Tweed:
Yeah, me too.

Sugar Coated Sam/Iblee:
What are you talking about? We're almost out of here. **(Walks up to Boss Tweed)** Bossman? You've been wallowing around in there for over one hundred years. **(Walks up to and then behind The Donald)** Donny? They haves a special place just for you. Come on. Plus, you've got no choice. Sugar Coated Sam leads the way!

(Sugar Coated Sam/Iblee pushes the two of them from the edge of the narrator's stage and onto the left side of center stage. Low blue and green lights come up revealing the front edge of the pit. To the audience it looks like a tank. It covers most of center stage, leaving enough room to walk in front of it. Its walls are of ancient, black, slimy rock. There are no real corners to it and its symmetry is wholly unnatural. Lights accent it from above and below. The sound of water in a large vessel in an enclosed room with a low ceiling, reverberates. There are several uneven steps leading onto its front from the stage left side. It is to these that Sugar Coated Sam/Iblee pushes The Donald and Boss Tweed)

The Donald:
There's that goddamn smell again.

Boss Tweed:
Sorry, Strumpet.

The Donald:
(He is starting to retch) What's in that thing?

Boss Tweed:
A whole lot of Hell, Strumpet. A whole lot of Hell.

(The three of them are now up on the front edge of the pit, center stage. Three spots light each one of them. There is some spacing between them, The Donald on the right, Boss Tweed on the left, and Sugar Coated Sam/Iblee in the middle)

Boss Tweed:
Where is he?

Sugar Coated Sam/Iblee:
I don't know.

The Donald:
Who? Minos? Why's it have to smell like the reptile house?

(At that moment, two large hands come up, out of the pit and grab its lip. Cacus, the Department Head, lifts his enormous self up onto the edge. He is over twelve feet tall, kind of scaly and hairy, and looks like he has been pumping iron and taking steroids for centuries. His thinning hair is tied back in a man bun, one large diamond stud glistens from his right ear lobe, a thick gold chain with a sagittarius pendant is nestled in overly abundant chest hair, and he is wearing a pink, *Ralph Lauren* loin cloth. Despite his size, despite the enormity of his extremities, he moves with feline grace as he saunters over to Sugar Coated Sam/Iblee)

Cacus:
Sam the man, so good to see you. How's tricks?

Sugar Coated Sam/Iblee:
Well, boyfriend, tricks are starting to pop.

Cacus:
Shut up.

Sugar Coated Sam/Iblee:
Swear. Take a peek at these two.

Cacus:
Well, **(placing a gigantic arm around Boss Tweed)** I've known this beauty for a good many days. Bossman, feel like a swim?

Boss Tweed:
Not today, Cacus, I'm on the Lord's business.

Cacus:
(Removing his arm very quickly) Ewwww. **(To Sugar Coated Sam/ Iblee)** What's up with that?

Sugar Coated Sam/Iblee:
You didn't get the memo?

Cacus:
Down here? Get real. **(Looks over at The Donald)** Got something to do with this sugar biscuit?

Sugar Coated Sam/Iblee:
You so smart. **(Cacus sashays over to The Donald)** Careful, **(low voice)** he's alive.

Cacus:

(Shrinking away) Double ewwww. **(To Sugar Coated Sam/Iblee)** What's the story, morning glory?

Sugar Coated Sam/Iblee:

(Sighing) Too long to tell. He **(pointing at Boss Tweed)** knows the whole chalupa. As far as me? This fella **(pointing at The Donald)** had The Liar Lever pulled on him, their business down here is super important, and so every Department Head has to jump up and do the big Satan Salute so this guy **(points at Boss Tweed)**, can get this guy **(points at The Donald)**, down to the big guy **(points downward)**, so this guy **(points at himself)**, can find an empty barstool by unhappy hour.

Cacus:

Yowsers. What's my role?

Sugar Coated Sam/Iblee:

I need you to whistle up the Kraken.

Cacus:

Why wake up that grumpy fucker?

Sugar Coated Sam/Iblee:

Tentacles. **(Cacus knits some abundantly hairy eyebrows)** This way I don't have to slug all over the pit trying to find the future shades of Sugar Biscuit. The Kraken can just reach out and snarf them.

Cacus:

Future shades? **(Sugar Coated Sam/Iblee motions for Cacus to lean down close. Whispers in Cacus' ear. Cacus' eyes get real big. He looks over to The Donald while Sugar Coated Sam/Iblee continues to whisper. Cacus shakes his head, makes some clucking sounds. Stands up and addresses The Donald)** What a bad little biscuit you are.

We're going to have some nice long swims together. **(Turning to Sugar Coated Sam/Iblee)** Okay, Sammy, here ya go. **(Cacus turns to face the pit, places two fingers in each corner of his mouth and lets go the loudest whistle ever)**

(The lights above, around, in, and below the pit, shift. There is the sound of splashing, of something titanic moving through liquid. Then, stillness. Then, chittering)

Cacus:
He's all yours, Sammy. Enjoy. I'm out. Mani pedi and a perm. Big hair is back and I don't want to miss out. Lock up, would ya? Can't have these slimy suckers crawling all over Hell. Ciao.

(Cacus exits stage right, slapping The Donald on the ass on the way out)

(The sounds in the pit get louder, more agitated. Some thick, black water splashes up and over the side)

The Donald:
What the hell is this, Sam!

Sugar Coated Sam/Iblee:
Is real fun game.

Boss Tweed:
No, its not.

The Donald:
Talk to me, Bossman.

Boss Tweed:

This is the pit. In the pit is every thief ever. In the pit is every reptile ever. They bite and tear at each other. One becomes the other. The other becomes the one. Only, after being bitten so many times, after changing into each other so many times, you don't know what any of them are.

(A tentacle breaks the surface of the pit and lunges up into the air. It sways back and forth. There is an unearthly, chittering roar, and a second tentacle comes up)

The Donald:

What the fuck is this! Sam!!!!

Boss Tweed:

Sam! Why'd you call the Kraken?

Sugar Coated Sam/Iblee:

Because I'm not Sam.

(The Donald and Boss Tweed both quickly look at Sugar Coated Sam/Iblee)

Sugar Coated Sam/Iblee:

(The surface of Sugar Coated Sam/Iblee begins to melt off of him)
Because I'm sooooo sick of living in Hell.

(The Donald and Boss Tweed shrink back in disgust screaming)

Sugar Coated Sam/Iblee:

Because I want to live! **(Sugar Coated Sam/Iblee begins to unwind throwing-off Sam's outer shell in fleshy, gooeyness)** Because I want to go topside! (Sugar Coated Sam/Iblee stops unwinding and is now Iblee, swirling in unending chaos, one eye lit up, the body of the entity seeming to heave with panting breaths. It points a swirling appendage at The Donald) And I'm going as you!

(The two tentacles suddenly wrap around The Donald and Boss Tweed, lifting them up and pulling them into the pit. Iblee begins to turn, but in a quick second is snarfed up by a third tentacle and likewise dragged behind the edge of the pit and into the drink)

(There is a brief moment of stillness, water sloshing around making the blues and greens of the lights swim over the walls. Then, a tentacle places something on the edge. It is the head of The Donald with the body of Boss Tweed. Another tentacle places the head of Maggie/Iblee with the body of The Donald. The first tentacle disappears back over the side taking The Donald/Tweed with it. A third tentatcle sets Sugar Coated Sam with cuttlefish legs beside Maggie/The Donald)

Maggie/The Donald:
(Squeak)

(These two tentacles disappear back over the side, as a third tentacle sets The Donald's head with a snake's body, tiny little T-Rex arms, and T-Rex legs)

The Donald T-Rex:
(Sounding like Peter Lorre and rubbing tiny T-Rex hands together) Heh, heh, heh, heh.

(A tentacle sets a full Maggie/Iblee beside The Donald T-Rex)

Maggie/Iblee:
Hey, big boy.

(Back over the side with these two, as a third tentacle sets a thing with Cacus' head on Boss Tweed's body)

Cacus/Tweed
Not funny!

(That tentacle sweeps back into the pit as another sets Boss Tweed's head on Cacus' body onto the edge, cotton balls between fingers and toes)

Tweed/Cacus:
(Looking down at his buff, ripped body, and then back up at the audience) Give me ninety days and you'll look like- **(pulled back over the side)**

(One tentacle splashes up from the depths and places a thing with the head of The Donald and the body of a swirling Iblee)

The Donald/Iblee:
Noooooooo- **(back over the side)**

(The head of Iblee on the body of The Donald)

Iblee/The Donald:
Yesssssssss- **(back over the side)**

(The head of Boss Tweed, the body of a gila monster, and Cacus's head at the end of the tail)

Tweed/Gila/Cacus:
Noooooooooo- **(yank and splash)**

(Two tentacles rise high up out of the pit and together set a thing on the edge. It is an amalgamation of The Donald and Iblee. Their bodies are entwined, swirling back and forth, each entity struggling for dominance. Tissue, bone, and fluid transfused with the black matter of Hell. Beneath the violent sound of this event, we can hear The Donald scream. Within each of his cells is Iblee. Inside every nano particle that makes up The Donald is Iblee, vying for control)

The Donald:
You can't have me!

Iblee:
I am you!

The Donald:
Stop hurting me!

Iblee:
You must have pain!

The Donald:
Why!!!

Iblee:
To know you're alive!

The Donald:
Get the hell out of me you slimy, fucked up monster!

(They are pulled over the side as a tentacle sets a whole Boss Tweed on the edge)

Boss Tweed:

(Screaming. Then looking at himself and stopping. Quite satisfied)
Well, that's more like it. **(Back over the side)**

**(The Donald is placed on the edge, except The Donald's face is one
giant swirling eye. The Donald is struggling to breathe. His chest
heaves. From out of a hole below the eye comes a terrified scream
of pain and anguish. This thing is pulled from the edge as Maggie's
body with The Donald's head attached is set down)**

The Donald/Maggie:

(Looks down) Hmmmm. **(One hand goes to a breast while the other
goes toward the nether regions. The Donald/Maggie is then suddenly pulled back over the side)**

**(Boss Tweed is set back on the edge. Looks at himself. Nods. Gets
into a boxer's crouch. Throws a couple jabs. A tentacle comes up
from the pit. It lunges for Boss Tweed. He socks it once. Twice. Then
a combo. The tentacle shrinks back and Boss Tweed jumps down
from the edge onto center stage. Two tentacles raise The Donald
and Iblee, conjoined, violently struggling against each other, up
out of, and above the pit. They are punching, kicking, gnashing,
biting, pushing, pulling, falling, tumbling, being caught, being
submerged, being swept across the pit from one side to the other,
until they are each set beside each other on the edge. The tentacles
slip beneath the surface. Iblee lunges for The Donald, who, bottle
of cough syrup in hand, splashes Iblee in the face. Smoke rises.
Sizzling is heard. Blue light arcs from all over Iblee's face. Iblee
recoils and jumps into the pit. Boss Tweed pulls The Donald down
from the edge onto center stage. The Donald starts to turn toward
stage right)**

Boss Tweed:
No! That's what it would expect. I know another way. Through the atrium. We're getting the fuck out of this bureaucratic mess!

(They turn toward stage left, where The Donald collapses just before the narrator's stage)

The Donald:
I can't. I'm done. Hell wins.

Boss Tweed:
Come on, man. Down this way. **(Head motions toward the back of the stage)**

The Donald:
That swamp sucks.

Boss Tweed:
(As he grabs The Donald from under each arm and drags him toward the back of the stage) Tell me about it.

The Donald:
(As they exit stage left, very back) Maybe if they drained it.

(Maggie/Iblee comes up out of the pit and stands on the edge, dead center stage, sobbing. Looks left. Looks right. Jumps down)

Maggie/Iblee:
Is this what it is to be human? **(Sob)** So much pain. So much rejection. I was in you. I could feel your pain. I could feel your feelings. Think your thoughts. Who hurt you so much that you are you? **(Sob, sob)** I felt hate. And anger. And jealousy. And, and. **(Iblee turns toward stage right. Moves slowly**

to exit) Something else. So deep. So buried. I shrank from it. It hurt me. What is it? **(Stops before exiting stage right)** Why am I not good enough? **(Exits stage right)**

(The lights fade to black on the pit. From the house speakers, low but distinct, is a muzak version of Bad Moon Rising**)**

(The lights come up on the narrator's stage and Euripides. He is holding a copy of the script and shaking his head)

Euripides:
You know, you'd think two people could just follow the script. Go from point 'A' to point 'B' in Hell. Learn what they can along the way, realize they were both narcissistic assholes in their lives. And then make the corrections necessary for the rest of humanity to live and see another day. But nooooo, not these two fuck sticks. Now we have no idea where in the hell in Hell they are. Time is running out, in Hell, and more importantly on Earth, where the rhetoric is bitterly divisive, the sabers are rattling, and the doors to the silos are open. I tell ya, its enough to make a man move to an island and live in a cave.

(Euripides exits via center stage, left side to the back, as Boss Tweed drags The Donald onto the narrator's stage)

The Donald:
I feel so dirty.

Boss Tweed:
Hang in there, Strumpet. I think I bought us some time.

The Donald:
It touched me in places I've never been touched.

Boss Tweed:
Be honest.

The Donald:
Where are we?

Boss Tweed:
Service hall. These things criss cross all over Circle Eight.

The Donald:
How do you know about these?

Boss Tweed:
That fucking Cacus and his pit. Its like the pool at camp, right. I mean, its not candy bars those kids are dropping in the deep end.

The Donald:
So, you skipped pool.

Boss Tweed:
Fuck yes I skipped pool. Every chance I could. This way. **(Heads toward the back)** Nope. This way. **(Heads toward center stage)** Can you make it now, or do I have to drag your ass all over hell and gone.

The Donald:
I can make it. **(Takes a moment. Places a hand on Boss Tweed's shoulder)** Thanks.

Boss Tweed:
Yeah, no problem. Don't get me wrong, you're still an asshole, but you're my kind of asshole.

(They cross from the narrator's stage to center stage. Two dim lights spot them on the left side of center stage. There is a white,

steel door with black, stenciled lettering saying 'Department Eight: Radiodrome'. Beside the door is a large window. Inside the window, we can see a radio announcer's panel, microphone, chair with a very large suit coat over it, an 'On Air' light lit up, and a very hefty, husky, overweight, many-chinned, radioman leaning forward in the chair, mouth close to the mike. A pair of headphones, half-on and half-off, are on his head. He turns as The Donald and Boss Tweed cross in front of the window, waves at them to stop. Says something into the mike as he stands, opens the door and enters the service hall)

Fat Radio Host:
Donald? Did you die?

The Donald:
No, no. Just being shown Hell. What about you? Are you dead?

Fat Radio Host:
I come and go. Technically, I've been dead for years. Overdose. But, the Devil and I came to an agreement, Mr. Goebbels needed some tips, and I was still under contract, so.

The Donald:
Great, great. So this is Department Eight?

Boss Tweed:
Yeah. Well, its the back of Department Eight.

The Donald:
I'm sorry, this is Boss Tweed.

Fat Radio Host:
The one and only? Mr. Tweed, I feel as if I already know you. Are you sure you weren't reincarnated as Bill Clinton. **(Chuckles from him and The Donald)**

The Donald:
(To Boss Tweed) What's Department Eight about?

Boss Tweed and Fat Radio Host:
(In unison, Fat Radio Host looking away) Fraudulent advisors.

Fat Radio Host:
(There's a pregnant pause) Hey! Great seeing you. Can't wait to see your Cabinet. (Turns toward the window and door) Gotta finish that show.

The Donald:
Keep up the good work.

Fat Radio Host:
(Wheels around real quick) Thirty years of convincing the majority they're being discriminated against. Who else could do that?!

The Donald:
(Matter-of-factly) Long live the new flesh!

Fat Radio Host:
(Over his shoulder) You betcha.

(Fat Radio Host re-enters the door and takes his place in the chair behind the mike. The lights inside the room fade to black, The Donald and Boss Tweed walk past it, turn toward the audience, and cross to the front of the stage. There, another blank, white door stands all by itself)

The Donald:
Now where.

Boss Tweed:
Through there.

(They open the door and center stage fills with the eerie glow of an atrium in the middle of a giant building in the middle of Hell. Indiscernible, distant marching band music can be heard)

The Donald:
What the hell is this!

Boss Tweed:
This is the atrium I was telling you about.

The Donald:
Its the size of Queens!

Boss Tweed:
Take another two steps and look to your left.

(The Donald takes two steps and looks toward the back of the stage. Lights rise on an enormous building in the distance. It is wedding cake-tiered, opulent in gray and white concrete, is of Stalin-esque design, and has scaffolding around a giant figure on the very top. As they stare at the Palace of The Soviets, an enormous tarp is pulled away from the statue atop the cupola that sits on the building's dome. The figure is The Donald)

The Donald:
(Stepping toward the building, dumbstruck) I, I don't get it. Is that me?

Boss Tweed:
I don't get it, either. But, that is most definitely you. I wonder, if-

The Donald:
If what?

Boss Tweed:
If we're too late.

The Donald:
How? I'm here. What could have happened? How could I do anything? This doesn't seem like an honor.

Boss Tweed:
Oh no. Its not. This is Hell. This is Circle Eight. One more Circle to go, and then-

The Donald:
Then what?

Boss Tweed:
Then you're on your own.

The Donald:
(Turning sharply at that) Whaaaat?

Boss Tweed:
I'm not cleared any farther than Circle Nine. Not to the lake. Not even to the path that leads to the lake. If there even is a lake? Or Old Scratch himself? Not a clue.

The Donald:
Then what happens to me?

Boss Tweed:
You'll have to find that out for yourself. But I'll tell you this: they wouldn't have replaced the statue of Stalin, with one of you, unless something really fucking horrible happened.

(They stare for a minute longer. In the distance the marching band plays *Hail To The Chief*)

Boss Tweed:
(Turning toward stage right) Come on. I don't know what that thing was you were possessed with, but I bet its right behind us.

(As The Donald turns, and the two take a step, spots light up a quartet of young men. They are all blonde with blue eyes, in brown uniforms with black belts, black gloves, and have arm bands on their left upper arms. The insignia on the arm band is the number eight, with a smaller number nine as an exponent. The only incongruous things at odds with their martial unity are the brown and blue barbershop quartet hats they're wearing, and the disfiguring wounds that they bear: a sword slash across the forehead, a hacked-off arm, a thrust and turn into the lower abdomen, and Department Nine Minion #4 is carrying his severed head. Upon seeing The Donald, they rush over and introduce themselves)

Department Nine Minion #1:
Mr. Trumpet! Mr. Trumpet! Is that really you?

Department Nine Minion#2:
Of course it is.

Department Nine Minion #3:
What great fortune.

Department Nine Minion #4:
This is easily the best day ever.

(They mob around The Donald. Boss Tweed stands away, arms crossed)

Department Nine Minion #1:
Sir, this is a great honor.

Department Nine Minion #2:
To think, The Donald himself. Here?

Department Nine Minion #3:
We've been following you for years.

Department Nine Minion #4:
We throw quotes from your books all the time.

Department Nine Minion #1:
Dammit! I wish we had a pen and paper.

Department Nine Minion #2:
Oh, for sure.

Department Nine Minion #3:
On the skin. Autograph on the skin.

Department Nine Minion #4:
(Holding out a wrist and pulling up his sleeve) Sign here, Mr. Trumpet.

(The other three do the same as Department Nine Minion #3 produces a black indelible ink marker. The Donald signs all four left wrists)

Department Nine Minion #1:
I am so getting this tattooed!

Department Nine Minion #2:
Oh, for sure.

Department Nine Minion #3:
Meeting *The Man* on the same day as the unveiling.

Department Nine Minion #4:
This is just so surreal.

The Donald:
So, who are you guys?

Department Nine Minion #1:
We're from Department Nine.

Department Nine Minion #2:
Sowers of Discord.

The Donald:
Really. So, what do you do?

Department Nine Minion #3:
We're part of the new wave.

Department Nine Minion #4:
Youth movement.

Department Nine Minion #1:
New ideas. New methods.

Department Nine Minion #2:
We helped you out a lot.

The Donald:
How's that?

Department Nine Minion #3:
Fake news.

Department Nine Minion #4:
Syndicated news feeds.

Department Nine Minion #1:
News based on rhetoric instead of facts.

Department Nine Minion #2:
Fudged facts. Lies. Distortions.

The Donald:
Well, thank you so much! Where would I be without you guys?

All Department Nine Minions at Once:
At the bottom of the polls!

(There is much laughter)

The Donald:
So, you enterprising young lads came out to see the statue unveiled?

Department Nine Minion #3:
Well, yes and no.

Department Nine Minion #4:
What #3 is trying to say is, well, we've been taking our second whistle break, the long break, out here anyway.

Department Nine Minion #1:
See, we've been rehearsing a tune for the Circle Eight Statue Unveiling Celebration Gala.

Department Nine Minion #2:
(Looking at each of the other guys) You don't think Mr. Trumpet would want to hear it?

The Other Three Department Nine Minions At Once:
Nooooo.

The Donald:
I very much would like to hear it.

Department Nine Minion #3:
Well, golly, alright.

Department Nine Minion #4:
Guys?

(The four Department Nine Minions line up in front of The Donald. One of them pulls out a kazoo, blows it, and they all adjust their voices to the key, making a more or less, perfect chord. They take a beat, and bust out this song with Minion #1 the lead, Minion #2 the tenor, Minion #3 the baritone, and Minion #4 the bass)

All Four Minions:
(One after the other, rising from bass to tenor and holding) Hello!

All Four Minions:
Hello ma Donny, Hello ma honey, Hello ma C. Bag Pal, Send me a gift by wire

Three Minions **(Tenor, Baritone and Bass)**
Pleeaaasseeeee!

Lead Minion:
(While they harmonize) Donny my heart's on fire

All Four Minions:
If you refuse us, Donny you'll lose us, Then you'll be quite alone

Bass Minion:
Oh buddy

The Other Three Minions:
Listen!

All Four Minions:
Why tweet when you can phone!

All Four Minions:
(One after the other, descending from tenor to bass) Hello!

All Four Minions:
(The quartet goes to their knees with jazzy hands) Please send us, **(holding each syllable for four beats)** some Rus, sian oil!!!!!!!!

Bass Minion:
And then you'll be our goil.

(The song stops. The quartet holds their pose. Boss Tweed walks over. Crickets resume being crickets, and a lone tumbleweed tumbles across the plaza)

The Donald:
That was great guys. Really great. Greatest ever. Thank you so much.

Boss Tweed:
We gotta go, pal. Come on. This way. **(Grabs The Donald by the arm and pulls him stage right)**

(The lights fade to black on the atrium, the plaza, and our starry-eyed Department Nine Minions, still kneeling with jazzy hands, as Boss Tweed pulls The Donald to extreme stage right, where one spot lights up a small area)

Boss Tweed:
You gotta stop wasting so much time.

The Donald:
Me? I'm not doing anything! How am I supposed to know what the hell is going on? You're the guide!

Boss Tweed:
Right, right, I know, I know, you never wanted to do this; you got an empire to run; you're going to be President, blah, blah, blah. Whatever. I got one job to do and that's get you down to the bottom of the bottomless pool. So, you need to wise up and listen to me. Ya hear?

(Before The Donald can answer, there is a commotion across stage)

Imposter Donald:
(Entering as the commotion, a spot picking him up) See here! See here! I say!

(Imposter Donald is dressed as a poor imitation of Abraham Lincoln, fully kitted-out with black suit, black bow tie, black stove pipe hat, and a fake beard. He charges across the plaza to

The Donald. He has a full head of steam and is not in a very good mood. He rolls up both sleeves on the way, cocks back and lays The Donald out with one to the chops. Boss Tweed is startled at first, then steps out of the way smiling)

The Donald:
(From the ground) What the hell, Abe? Where'd you come from? I'm a republican, too, you know.

Imposter Donald:
I'm not Abe Lincoln, you Jack Wagon! Now get on your feet cuz that first one felt pretty good!

The Donald:
What'd I do? Who are you?

Imposter Donald:
(Leaning over The Donald like a drill sergeant) I'm you, dumbass! I'm a fake! A phony! I'm the worst fucking thing that ever came down the pipe! Now get up! Get on your feet!

Boss Tweed:
He's from Department Ten. He's got something you need to hear. And stand up like a man.

The Donald:
Fuck both of you. This Circle is bullshit. All that's happened is me getting the shit knocked out of me.

Boss Tweed:
Welcome to Hell!

Imposter Donald:

You listen to me! You think you got what it takes to be President? Think again! You're the worst. All of Department Ten, all of Circle Eight, hell! All of Hell! Rolled into one spoon-fed, cushy, mama's boy. You've been coddled your whole life. I know twelve-year old girls who are tougher than you! **(Imposter Donald is quite literally fuming. Punching the air. Kicking the air. Raising fists to heaven)** Why in hell, God, did you let this no good, lyin', counterfei- tin', political alchemist sit in the oval office. **(He stops. Looks down. Then points a finger at the ceiling)** Do you have some sort of death wish for all of us, or what? Are you a comedian? Is this supposed to be funny? Are we all supposed to die laughing? **(He turns as The Donald starts to get up. The Donald see Imposter Donald right over him and goes back to the ground looking a lot like a turtle)** Get on your feet! Turn around! Look at me or I'll turn you into Claude Lemieux and I'll be Darren McCarty! **(The Donald turns and looks at himself from the ground)** The whole world knows what you are. They're laughing at us! By the time your four years are up, the country will be in shambles, the world will be starving to death, and there'll be wars on every continent! By the time you leave office, the dollar will no longer be the standard, there'll be runaway inflation, and soup lines will have returned to every corner. If. **(Spittle a-flying, eyes closed, fists clenched)** If! We survive your one and only term, this country will implode from the hatred you breed, from the lies you have fostered, and the discord you encourage. You NEVER dreamed you'd become President. And now! With Satan's Monkey at your side, you will assassinate the United States of America! You will tear down the one noble bastion of political progress this ape-like spe- cies ever thought up! You will keel-haul liberty, justice, and freedom in the largest money-grab in the history of the world!

(There is silence. The Donald is staring at the ground, but is obvi- ously ticked-off at being called out. He slowly rises and walks over to Imposter Donald)

The Donald:
I just want to make America great again.

Imposter Donald:
(Slowly shaking his head) You. Just. Don't. Get. It. **(Turns to walk back the way he had entered. Takes a couple steps. Looks over his shoulder)** It already is.

(From the back of the house, below the control booth, there is a loud 'bang' and a puff of purple, glittery smoke. A lone spot picks up Maggie/Iblee. She is wearing a short black leather skirt, and is quite literally dressed-to-kill. She walks from the back, up a main aisle, to the narrator's stage, where she mounts, turns and stares across the stage. Lights have gone up all over the stage, show-ing us the Palace of The Soviets, the plaza, and the quartet, still kneeling with jazzy hands. Maggie/Iblee slowly struts across the stage. She kicks the tumble weed and it starts on fire. The quartet stands making wolf whistles and cat calls. She eviscerates them into a black and red, gooey sludge with a look. Imposter Donald tries to get out of the way, she touches him with one finger and he implodes. Boss Tweed and The Donald, while everyone has been looking the other way, have exited stage right)

Maggie/Iblee:
(She is shaking angry. She inhales slowly and deeply through pursed lips and all the lights in the place slowly fade to black. One bright spot explodes on her) Where are you! You little shit. Show your-self! **(There is silence. She shrieks and columns of flame streak up beside her)** You were the shot I had to get out of here! The one chance to see what life was all about! The one time I thought I could know physical love. Or any love! **(Silence. Shriek. Flame. Thunder-like rumbling)** Donald Trumpet!

(The lights go up on the box. Statler and Waldorf are holding each other and shaking with fear. Behind them are The Donald and Boss Tweed who are likewise holding each other and shaking with fear)

Maggie/Iblee:
(Notices them. Points a finger at the box. Hisses) You! (Hands go to her side. A shriek of frustration, vehemence, and Hell-like fury. More flames. More thunder. Flickering lights. She points at The Donald) How could you!

(Statler turns to grab The Donald while Waldorf clutches at his chest above his heart)

Statler Swift:
Here! Take him! He's all yours! You can have him! (Notices Waldorf grabbing his heart. Calls out) Oh my God! Is there a doctor in the house?!

Waldorf Voltaire:
No! I'm not covered.

(All the lights flicker and dip dramatically. There is a deep, low rumble that is different from the 'Maggie-thunder'. All the actors sway on their feet or in their seats. The statue of The Donald tumbles off the cupola and crashes to the ground)

The Donald:
What was that?

(It happens again. Rocks, earth, fire, and brimstone crash around Maggie/Iblee and all over the stage. The lights go out and emergency lighting slowly comes on. In the darkness, Maggie/Iblee has exited. The deep, low rumble happens again and more debris and dust fall on the stage. **The Donald and Boss Tweed are now below the box. Dim spots and emergency lighting reveal them)**

The Donald:
What is that?

Boss Tweed:
(Shaking his head) I don't know. Let's get out of here. Come on, this way!

(They exit stage right as a single spot lights the narrator's stage. Euripides stands amid the swirling dust, rocks, and debris about him)

Euripides:
And so it begins. By the gods. By God. By our very natures. By Nature, herself. O Dionysus! We feel you near, stirring like molten lava under the ravaged Earth, flowing from the wounds of your trees in tears of sap, screaming with the rage of your hunted beasts! O Lord! Come down from Olympus and stifle the murderer's insolent fury! This man must learn how much it costs to scorn God. We thought we were of Apollo, but we spring from Bacchus. Our very hands will rip ourselves apart. The blood we drink is our own. The flesh we eat comes from our loins. The gods of this new world are empty and plastic. God himself has shrugged, and our greed will drown us. **(He pauses. Low rumbles echo around the stage)** Talk sense to a fool, and he calls you foolish. Preach to the choir, and all you'll ever hear is your own voice. He who believes, needs no explanation. Only now, the question isn't what *is* the explanation, but is there anyone left for the explaining. **(Pause)** Like Babel, so all temples of men must fall.

(Euripides exits stage left. The lights fade on the narrator's stage. Low rumbles. Dust. Emergency lighting. Then, even all of this fades to black)

(The lights come up on the box. There is an EMT standing over Waldorf. Statler is close at hand, arms crossed and very worried)

Statler Swift:
Is he going to live?

EMT:
Oh yeah.

Statler Swift:
He's going to be okay?

EMT:
(Giving Waldorf a couple big white tablets) He's going to be just fine.

Statler Swift:
What was it? Was it his heart?

EMT:
Acid reflux.

Statler Swift:
What?

EMT:
Too much bacon and too much wine.

Statler Swift:
(More angry than concerned) You pig. I told you to take it easy. What the hell? **(To the EMT)** What now?

EMT:
The antacid should do the trick. But your friend here needs to take a little more notice to what he's eating and drinking. **(Closes up his EMT box and makes to go. Takes a step or two to exit)** You know, you guys aren't getting any younger. **(Exits)**

Statler Swift:
We can only hope to live all the days of our lives.

(The lights fade on the box)

(Emergency lighting comes up on the narrator's stage. There is the distant sound of a klaxon going on and off from off-stage, stage left. Dust hangs in the air. A yellow light mounted on a black, rock wall fades on and off. We hear a distant wind blowing from stage right. There is frost on the ancient rocks that litter the stage. Boss Tweed enters, leading The Donald)

The Donald:
Holy shit! Its cold.

Boss Tweed:
Just wait.

The Donald:
I thought Hell was hot?

Boss Tweed:
Keep your voice down. I don't want that thing finding us. **(He stops and grabs The Donald by the collar)** You idiot. What the hell were you thinking? Huh? We're on a mission. We have a job to do. And what do you do? Who *is* that tart?

The Donald:
I don't know. When I met her it wasn't a her. It was this weird, spacey cloud of something.

Boss Tweed:
Oh yeah, when I meet a weird, spacey cloud of something the first thing I do is make friends with it. **(He cuffs The Donald on the back of the head. Looks at him, and then cuffs him again)**

The Donald:
He said he could get me out of here. What do you want from me?

Boss Tweed:
Always thinking of yourself.

The Donald:
So, here we are.

Boss Tweed:
Yeah. Here we are. Let me get my bearings.

The Donald:
Circle Nine.

Boss Tweed:
Right. Circle Nine. There's a path, sort of. Hmmm. **(Walks over to the right side of the narrator's stage)** Somewhere. Near. Here.

(Spots suddenly light up a Giant right in front of Boss Tweed. The Giant is Nimrod. Nimrod is a solid fifteen feet tall and is imbedded in ice from the hips down. He is wearing a short, gold crown, a false beard made of several shades of gold, long golden earrings, gold arm and wrist bands, and has a spear of bronze that is a trident on one end and sharp-tipped on the other. He is bent at the waist, staring face to face with Boss Tweed. Ice drips from all parts of him as he is encased in ice for eternity. This naturally makes him more than a little pissed off)

Nimrod:
(Yelling very loud) BOOGABOOGABAHROEROOOOBOOGA-BEDDAGRAAAPPPAA BOOGGGA AABEIDDAPAADAPOOPADIGGA!!!!

Boss Tweed:
(Having just landed from jumping clean out of his skin)
Aaaaahhhhhhh!!!!!

Nimrod:
BADDABAYBOODABAH?

Boss Tweed and The Donald:
(Once more clutching each other and quite rooted to the spot)
Aaaaaaahhhhh!!!

Nimrod:
Baddabayboodabah?

The Donald:
Baddabayboodabah?

Nimrod:
Baddabayboodabah.

The Donald:
(Unclutching Boss Tweed and stepping forward) Deeeshrahnomokafah.

Nimrod:
Deeeshrahnomokafah?

The Donald:
Tak.

Nimrod:
Deeshrahnomokafah antophodeeshloppto?

The Donald:
Si.

Nimrod:
Antophodeeshloppto ankarrospee?

The Donald:
Oui.

Nimrod:
Ankarrospee doophisnokah?

The Donald:
Ndiyo.

Nimrod:
Doophisnokah Impnotuureegnaspah?

The Donald:
Ie.

Nimrod:
(Scratches fake gold beard. Eyes narrow) Zimrohdouer? Zimrohdauer?

The Donald:
Zim. Just, Zim.

Nimrod:
Ahhh, Zim. Opaynohee. **(Throws a thumb over his shoulder)**

The Donald:
Kiitos. **(To Boss Tweed)** Follow me.

Boss Tweed:
(Incredulous) How'd you know what he was saying?

The Donald:
I've worked with Congress.

(They pass past Nimrod downstage)

Nimrod:
Take it easy.

(The spots go out on Nimrod and the narrator's stage as The Donald and Boss Tweed cross onto the main stage. A lone spot picks them up as they stop. It is deathly quiet. A wind rises from stage right, sweeps through the stage, and causes them to shiver)

The Donald:
I *am* going home after this, right?

Boss Tweed:
Well.

The Donald:
What do you mean, 'well'?

Boss Tweed:
We've been down here a long time, man.

The Donald:
And that's my fault?

Boss Tweed:
Well.

The Donald:
What do you mean, 'well'?

Boss Tweed:
You keep wandering off. And this is your life. These are your sins. You committed them.

The Donald:
So has everyone we've met down here. And I'm not dead, yet. I have time to atone.

Boss Tweed:
I understand that. And that's why we're down here. But, its more complicated than that.

The Donald:
How?

Boss Tweed:
We've been down here a long, long time. And, it seems like shit's changed topside. It seems as if you may be President. It seems like all that could happen has happened.

The Donald:
Like what?

Boss Tweed:
Like everything that Saint Dymphna was warning you about.

The Donald:
I don't get it. Can we finish this so I can go home?

Boss Tweed:
(He pauses giving The Donald a very hard look. A warbled, haunting calliope slowly grows in volume over the wind) Yeah, pal. I'll take you home. This way.

(Boss Tweed turns and steps out of the spot, as does The Donald. Green, red, blue and yellow lights slowly come up revealing empty fair grounds. Papers, wrappers, and tattered streamers tumble across the partially frozen ground from the stiff, cold breeze. The empty shells of games and food booths sit tilted and forlorn. A lone pole leans hackneyed with forgotten ribbons and torn posters hanging and splattered on its peeling wood. As they cross to center stage, the lights rise to halfway, and the lamenting, calliope music becomes discernible: *When You and I Were Young, Maggie*)

The Donald:
This is fucking weird.

Boss Tweed:
Spooky, huh?

The Donald:
I hate clowns.

Boss Tweed:
No mirrors where you come from?

The Donald:
Fuck you.

Boss Tweed:
Hey, you got any of that green bark juice left?

The Donald:
Good call. Let me check. **(The Donald reaches into his coat, pulls out the bottle)** Yup. Last swigs. **(He unscrews the cap, tosses it over his shoulder, and hands Boss Tweed the bottle)**

Boss Tweed:
A toast, sir.

The Donald:
Not to my health, I hope.

Boss Tweed:
No. To your soul. And to your friendship. Its been, different. (**He drains half of what's left, hands the bottle back**)

The Donald:
Thanks, I think. (**He kills the rest of the bottle and tosses it over his shoulder**)

(**While this is taking place, a carnival barker pokes his head out from the curtain at stage right. His face is grotesque, reddish, and pock-marked. His teeth are yellowed, broken fangs. A tarnished gold ring hangs from his nostril and connects by chains to a ring in his lip, and one in his right ear lobe. A weathered, slimy black top hat sits atop a head covered with long, stringy black hair, ribbons of unknown color twisted into the locks. His eyes are as blue as ice; the pupils dilated and fixed. He is wearing a mottled wine-red vest, a black shirt with one million tiny eyeballs like pol-kadots, black gravedigger's pants, dark purple suspenders and tie, and boots that are covered in muddy earth. Attached to his belt are a whip and a wine skin. He is long and lean, several feet taller than The Donald and Boss Tweed. He winks to the audience, then enters and crosses to center stage, whistling the calliope tune in a mocking way**)

Antaeus:
Gentlemen! Welcome! (**To the audience**) Welcome one and all! Welcome to the House of Horrors! Welcome to the Museum of Frozen Freaks! Welcome

to Humanity's Penultimate Side Show! See the most hideous of all mortality! Witness the butchery and betrayal! The torture chambers! The killing fields! The camps! Man's inhumanity to man. All of it! Frozen for eternity! Imbedded in ice caves on the surface of exotic Lake Cocytus! And you, lucky you, have seats waiting in a car that you have slowly reserved all your miserable lives. I give you the experience of a lifetime, yours for an eternity, yours forever. Memories etched in your mind's eye like rime on a window, and all it costs is your soul. Step right up, gentlemen, step right up, your chariot awaits!

(From stage right an amusement ride car slowly crosses up to them. It is a bench seat for two sitting in the mouth of a snake woman. It is green, red and yellow, and in black, in a swoosh, it says 'Echinda'. Antaeus casually reaches out and stops the car with one hand before it runs into them)

The Donald:
(Startled and scared) Hey! Hey! Hey! Now where did you come from?

Antaeus:
Well, that's an interesting question. Do you mean originally? Of late? Or just this very moment?

(The Donald has moved behind Boss Tweed)

The Donald:
Who are you?

Antaeus:
I am Antaeus. I'm the barker. And I am your host.

The Donald:
To what?

Antaeus:

To what? You should know. Circle Nine. Come now, you must know where you are. You've come this far. You've travelled this long. You've lived your entire life just for this moment. So, welcome.

(The Donald and Boss Tweed are inching backward, shaking, terrified. From stage left in the very back, an enormous and hideous giant of sea green scales comes up from behind them. They turn and scream as they bump into him)

Antaeus:

Gentlemen, 'tis not folly that brought you hither, but intent. Cold-blooded intent. Step right up! Relax. You were born for this. How's about a drink?

Boss Tweed:

Yes, please.

(Antaeus removes the wine skin. Unscrews the cap. Proffers it to Boss Tweed, who squeezes some into his mouth. He takes a step back, drops the wine skin, eyes bugging out, his hands going to his throat. Antaeus grabs the wine skin out of thin air. The Donald has some squeezed into his mouth before he can see Boss Tweed's reaction)

The Donald:

(Spitting, gagging, and holding his throat) What the hell is that shit!

Antaeus:

No likey? Don't normally give out trade secrets but, **(looks both ways, leans in)** a decoction of blood steeped with amanita muscaria, bufo alvarius, wormwood, peyote, a pinch of indica, and I really can't get too far away from good ole corn squeezin's. **(Stands back up)** What's not to love.

The Donald:
Any of it!

Antaeus:
(Slapping The Donald on the back causing him to gag even more)
Come on, sport! You should be excited! This is it! The culmination of a life-time! **(He spins the car around so it is facing the audience. Slaps the back of the car. A forked-tongue that is the lap bar falls out allowing them to be seated. The Donald and Boss Tweed start inching away)** Typhus! My dear, old friend, would you please show these two, timid sinners to their seats.

(Typhus picks both The Donald and Boss Tweed up by the backs of their collars. Takes one giant step over to the car and sets them down. They do not move. Typhus pulls out a can of *Monster* Energy Drink. Slams it. Crushes the can between two fingers into the size of a dime. They get on board the car)

Antaeus:
Gentlemen, before we embark, a few things to make our insurance company happy. **(He presses the same spot on the back of the car and the forked-tongue lap bar rises and locks)** Do not at any time try to leave the car. Please keep your hands and feet inside the car at all times. Do not touch the ice, approach the ice, or have any contact with the ice at any time. Do not feed the animals or attempt to make contact. Do not make faces at the flying monkeys. **(He produces a wicker basket that is covered in dried blood)** If you still happen to have any crucifixes, rosaries, prayer beads, prayer cards, sacred amulets, religious totems, statues, icons, or New York City Subway Passes, this would be a wonderful time to deposit said items into the basket.

(The Donald and Boss Tweed look at each other. Then look at Antaeus)

Antaeus:
Gentlemen?

Boss Tweed:
(Reaching into his pocket and pulling out a medal on a leather cord) Aw, c'mon! My Aunt gave it to me at my Christening. **(He drops it in the basket)**

Antaeus:
How sweet. **(To The Donald)** And you, sir.

The Donald:
(Looks from Antaeus to Boss Tweed and then back to Antaeus) Well, there is this. **(Pulls out the *Cliffs Notes* copy of The U.S. Constitution)**

Antaeus:
Hmmm. **(Turning the book over. Flipping through the pages)** This is a first. **(Pause)** Not applicable. You can keep your icky book. **(To Typhus)** Old chum, you are the engine. **(Typhus spins the car around so it is facing stage right and stands behind it, arms extended, ready to push. Antaeus takes a beat and crosses to center stage)** Ladies and Gentlemen, each day and every hour, through the grim task of living, frustration, exhaustion, misery and poverty, lust, greed and jealousy, pride and contempt, they badger, bugger, and bind you, taunt you, tease you, and tempt you. Everyone fails. Some, repent and rise. Rise to Purgatorio. Still fewer, rise to Paradiso. Most, fall. Fall into these Circles. Fall, because of your very natures. Fall, from the needs to sustain your very lives. The oh, so mortal coil. The fuel to power you. The need to reproduce. My friends, the carbon that makes up your shell is simply food for worms. *But your souls.* Your silly, sugary, slippery, sensuous souls, they are much more than that. And each day and every hour, by willful corruption, there is betrayal. Souls betray souls. Betrayal of family. Betrayal of country. Betrayal of guests. And betrayal of lords. And to here, in your lack of repentance, you fall to Circle Nine. To the

Lake. To him. **(Turns his head to look up)** Masters of Oblivion, crank up the calliope! **(The calliope music grows louder)** Open the chasm! **(Twin giant black rocks part in front of the car at extreme stage right)** And! **(Turns and nods to Typhus who begins pushing the car toward the opening. Antaeus raises his arms spinning toward the opening)** Send in the clowns!

(A wicked blue-white light emanates from the opening. The Donald and Boss Tweed sit up in their seats. As they near the opening, they begin screaming in terror. Typhus pushes the car through, exiting stage right. And Antaeus, cavorting with the audience, slowly dances over to the opening, a lascivious wink and grin as he exits. The calliope continues until just past the lights fading to black)

(The theater is still and dark. We begin to hear the crystalizing sounds of an ice cave. The low wind gusting. The lamentations of the frozen souls echoes and rings just above the wind. After several long moments, a bluish light just barely rises from stage left, and we hear the voice of Antaeus, the fear-wrought whispers of The Donald and Boss Tweed, and the creaking of the car. All of these sounds echo slightly)

The Donald:
(Just off-stage. Whispering) This is the worst. Its freezing. Where's that wind coming from? Fuck, I hate tight places.

Antaeus:
(Just off-stage) We'll keep that in mind.

Boss Tweed:
(Just off-stage) I hate this place.

The Donald:

(Just off-stage) You're here?

Antaeus:

(Just off-stage, after a pause) Oh come now, Mr. Tweed, regale your new friend on Anternora. **(There is a loud crash. A soul screams in pain. The sound of ice falling)** Typhus, my man, do watch out for the souls. No, no. The left-side front. I think its wedged in his mouth. **(Creaking of the car. Squeaking of the wheel. Shrieking of the soul. Fearful muttering of The Donald and Boss Tweed)** You'll have to back up some, and then veer to the right. That's it. **(Another crash. A different soul cries in pain)** Oh, bollocks! **(Entering stage left backwards)** Souls here, souls there, souls everywhere! Careful! Mustn't hurt the damned. **(A most wicked laugh)** You're almost there, almost back on track, young Typhus. Put your back into it. Ouch! Right up the chin and over the noggin. Kind of like splitting a coconut. Right this way!

(The car creaks onto stage, The Donald peering out one side and Boss Tweed the other. Typhus pushes it until it is in full view then stops, bends over, and places his hands on knees)

The Donald:

(Loudly. Pleading) How much further! How much more! I can't take this! I want to go home!

Antaeus:

Shhhhh. This is a fragile place. Millions of millenniums of ice building. It seems solid, but? And find your backbone, Mr. President. First Round of Circle Nine. Kind of like the front nine of a long weekend at your golf club. You're going to have to reach into the bottom of your bag and find that last dose of Soul Viagra.

(There is a gut-wrenching wail of pain. A spot lights up an ice wall. Caina Donald is frozen standing up, his suit-covered body distorted through the ice. His head and neck are above the ice)

The Donald:
That's me! Why am I here? What bullshit is this?

Antaeus:
(Walking over to Caina Donald) This is you. This is you in Caina.

The Donald:
Why? I've never betrayed anyone!

Antaeus:
(Hugely wicked laugh. Ice and snow fall all over, there is the sound of distant ice sloughing and crashing. Antaeus quickly stops his laugh and looks over his shoulder) My not-so-good man, let me do my job. **(Clears his throat. Typhus rolls his eyes, sits, opens a can of *Monster*)** Caina. Betrayal of family. How heinous. How evil. Your very kin. Sold out.

The Donald:
Bullshit!

Antaeus:
(Chipping away at the ice in front of Caina Donald's chest with a long, yellowish fingernail) This tie pin, what is that symbol?

The Donald:
Its the American flag.

Antaeus:
Next round. Back nine, so-to-speak. Who gave it to you?

The Donald:
My daughter.

Antaeus:
How sweet. Too bad, and all.

The Donald:
What do you mean, 'too bad'. What've you done with my daughter?

Antaeus:
Not I. You.

The Donald:
Bullshit!

Antaeus:
Father daughter relationships. So many dynamics. So many ties. What was her name? Ivey?

The Donald:
Don't you dare speak her name!

(Caina Donald awakens with a scream of pain and terror. Antaeus steps away grinning)

Caina Donald:
Iv?! Is that you? Where are you? Where am I? Are you okay? **(He starts weeping)** I am so sorry. So very sorry.

(The Donald can't take anymore. He squeezes past the forked-tongue lap bar and confronts Antaeus who looks at him, his feet)

The Donald:
What the fuck is this bullshit! I demand to see my daughter and know she's okay!

Antaeus:
Excuse me? Excuse you. **(Pointing)** Do not leave the car. Do not touch the ice.

The Donald:
Rules are meant to be broken!

Antaeus:
So are spirits. Go talk to yourself.

The Donald:
Where's Iv!? Where's my daughter!?

Antaeus:
Ask yourself.

(Antaeus turns to the audience, smiles, and walks over to Typhus. Boss Tweed stares dejectedly at the middle distance. The Donald stands for a second, then crosses to face himself frozen in the ice of Round One, Circle Nine, Hell)

The Donald:
Why am I here?

Caina Donald:
(Turns to face himself. Screams in pain and woe) You fucker. How could you do this to us? To me? To your wife? Your children? To Iv? Iv!!!

The Donald:
What are you talking about? I'm not dead yet. This is a masquerade. A fiction. An example.

Caina Donald:
Look in your eyes. Look.

(The Donald takes a long look, leaning close into his own face. He turns quickly away, a hand covering his mouth)

Caina Donald:
An unspoken vow. From father to child. From husband to wife. From patriarch to family. To protect. To provide. To pass on the most holy name, the revered reputation, the sacred history of tribe, hearth, home, of integrity, valor, and honor.

The Donald:
(Quietly) I did all of that. **(Takes a step toward the car and Antaeus)** I did all of that.

Antaeus:
(Turning, crossing behind the car and past The Donald. He points to heads in the ice beside Caina Donald. Spots light the faces as he says the names) Maybe you should ask Mordred. Or Barsi. Or Borden. **(Turning to The Donald)** You know, you are the company you keep.

The Donald:
(Crossing to the front of stage left) What did I do?

Caina Donald:
If there is anything left, our name will be a plague.

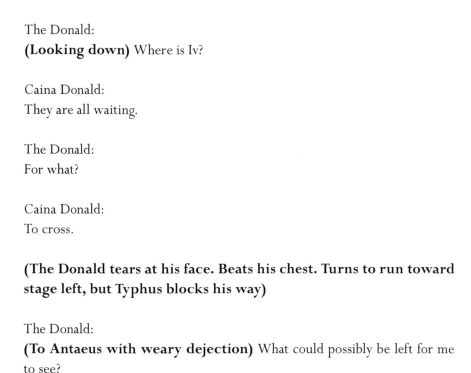

The Donald:
(Looking down) Where is Iv?

Caina Donald:
They are all waiting.

The Donald:
For what?

Caina Donald:
To cross.

(The Donald tears at his face. Beats his chest. Turns to run toward stage left, but Typhus blocks his way)

The Donald:
(To Antaeus with weary dejection) What could possibly be left for me to see?

Antaeus:
(With icy maliciousness) Get in the car.

(The Donald returns to his seat beside a completely deflated Boss Tweed. The spots go out on Caina and its souls. A set of red, white, and blue lights come up on the right side of the stage, revealing more of the ice cave, and sinners who are buried up past their chins. There is a hole in the ice toward the back of the stage. It is big enough to fit a very large man. Antaeus, a fang-filled grin leading the way, walks in front of the car to stage right. The sounds of Hell, of the wailing, of the ice, of the cave, of the echoes, grows louder)

Antaeus:

Auntie Nora! That's what I call this Round. **(Turns quickly to face the car)** Like that one relative who did such-and-such and brought down the whole fam. You know, there's one in every clan. Auntie Nora. Except the clan in this case is community. Community. Commonwealth. Country! To betray one's own nation. To sell out, to the highest bidder, your very own people!

The Donald:

(Trying to stand in the car. Fighting with the lap bar) More bullshit! These are lies! Lies! You might as well have a press card around your twisted fucking neck!

Antaeus:

(Crossing quickly to get in The Donald's face. He grabs The Donald by his tie and pulls him up and out of the car, slamming him to the ice) Who do you think you are? Where do you think you are? For pages we've shown you why you're here. And still, like one thousand Thomas' rolled into one, you doubt. Look! **(With one hand he viciously turns The Donald's head to where he points with the other hand)** There! **(Red, white, and blue spots light up Antenora Donald encased in ice up to his mouth. Single spots again light up soul's faces as they are called)** Beside Benedict Arnold. Next to the Rosenbergs. Slumming it with Aldrich Ames. Slapping hips with Tokyo Rose and Doña Marina. Look! **(He lifts The Donald up and in one giant step brings him face to face with Antenora Donald)** Have a word with yourself. I have a little business down this way.

(Antaeus stands, turns toward the car, dusts himself off of ice flakes, and crosses to the car. The Donald stands also. Reaches out with tentative fingers, and touches the cheek of Antenora Donald)

The Donald:
(Weeping) We didn't make it great, did we?

Antenora Donald:
To faithfully execute the Office of President of the United States. To preserve, protect, and defend the Constitution.

The Donald:
We didn't make it great, did we?

Antenora Donald:
Three hundred and twenty-four million, six hundred and sixty-six thousand, three hundred and twelve souls entrusted you.

The Donald:
What in God's name happened?

Antenora Donald:
As Commander-in-Chief, you vowed to defend the Constitution, and thereby each of those persons, from all enemies, foreign and domestic.

The Donald:
What happened?

Antenora Donald:
You failed.

(The Donald half-rises and crosses to the front of stage right)

The Donald:
How did I fail?

Antenora Donald:
You failed to protect them.

The Donald:
From the Chinese?

Antenora Donald:
From yourself.

(The Donald turns toward the car, but falls to his knees. Boss Tweed is being led out of the car by Antaeus. His head is down. He goes with great tiredness, and miserable acceptance)

The Donald:
(Looking up) Bossman! What are you doing? You're my guide! You're my only friend! Where are you going?

Boss Tweed:
(Walking to the hole in the ice) This is it, Strumpet. End of the line. What's a soul to do? We lived for the moment, but forgot about eternity. **(He has reached the hole. The Donald is staggering over to him)** Time to say good-bye, pal.

The Donald:
No! No! This can't be happening. This isn't supposed to end this way. I thought you were going to get a reprieve, or soul points, or an upgrade.

Boss Tweed:
(Holding out a hand to stop The Donald) Sin is not to be pitied. And the more we die, the greater chance we have to live.

The Donald:
What does that mean?

Boss Tweed:
(Pauses) Give an old friend a hug, would ya?

(The two embrace, ice falling from their eyes, freezing to their cheeks. After a long moment, Boss Tweed breaks the hug, turns, and steps into his hole)

Boss Tweed:
C'est la mort.

(And at that, Boss Tweed is encased in ice. The spots go out on the ice, on the stage right portion of the ice cave, on everything but The Donald, Antaeus, the car, and Typhus)

Antaeus:
(Gesturing toward the car) Table for one?

(The Donald turns toward stage right, staggers a step or two. Antaeus motions to Typhus with a head movement to follow. Typhus pushes the empty car, Antaeus is just ahead of it. A spot lights up a figure beneath the box, encased in ice and all alone. It is Adolf Hitler. The Donald stops in his tracks, as does Antaeus, Typhus, and the car)

Adolf Hitler:
(To The Donald) Pssst.

The Donald:
(Looking around. Points at himself) Who? Me?

Adolf Hitler:
Brilliant.

The Donald:
What?

Adolf Hitler:
Ingenius.

The Donald:
What are you talking about?

Adolf Hitler:
I didn't have half the freedoms to contend with. You? Incredible.

The Donald:
(Very uncomfortable talking with Adolf Hitler) What is this about?

Adolf Hitler:
Your coup. Your consolidation of power. How you stripped the civil liberties away from a nation of over three hundred million. And they, **(starts to chuckle, rolls eyes)** they just rolled over like drunken cows.

(The Donald turns again toward stage left, but this time Antaeus is standing there, a broad smile on his face)

Adolf Hitler:
You need to write a book.

The Donald:
I've already written books.

Adolf Hitler:
No. A new one.

The Donald:
A new one?

Adolf Hitler:
I have a title in mind. **(He motions The Donald to come closer, which is rather difficult for someone encased in ice up to their chin. The Donald looks over his shoulder, Antaeus raises his eyebrows. The Donald leans in to Adolf Hitler)** Mein Coif. **(Everyone but The**

Donald erupts in laughter, including Typhus. Snow and ice fall. The laughter and its echoes die away)

The Donald:
You were a bad person.

Adolf Hitler:
But I can't hold a candle to you.

(Antaeus, Typhus, and Hitler break out in more laughter. Echoes resound around the cavern. Snow, ice, and icy stalactites fall. The Donald turns and exits stage right in humiliation and shame. The lights fade to black. The laughter, the echoes, and the mini-avalanches continue in the eternal darkness until the lights come up on the narrator's stage and Euripides. He is casually feeding flying monkeys from a *Crackerjack* box)

Euripides:
Lovecraft once said: the most merciful thing in the world is the inability of the human mind to correlate all of its components. Somewhere, nestled on top of the brain stem, is an abyss of fear. And it is this, that moves us to the shadows. It is the very raw, burning, emotional drives from this tiny, yet infinite sac that propels us to commit the most heinous of crimes. Maybe, in between developing drugs to increase an already over-the-top sex drive, they'll come up with a pill, or a procedure, to render this sac sterile. (He hands the box off to the outstretched hands of a flying monkey and walks to the very front of the narrator's stage) Poe: Deep into that darkness peering, long I stood there, wondering, fearing, doubting, dreaming dreams no mortal ever dared to dream before. And so, those that have immersed themselves in the inky oil of this sac, who have dared to tread where angels fear to tread, who, from their cells in asylums call out to gods we never knew existed, have sign-posted a future our natures are guiding us towards. Words have no power to

impress the mind without the exquisite horror of their reality. **(Euripides turns to exit, looks back to the audience)** That's Poe, as well.

(Euripides exits, petting a flying monkey on his way out)

(The lights come up on the box. Waldorf Voltaire is feeding popcorn to a flying monkey that is sitting on the railing)

Statler Swift:
Well, good sir, here we are.

Waldorf Voltaire:
Indeed. Not much left.

Statler Swift:
This has become much more than the trifle we thought it would be.

Waldorf Voltaire:
Indeed, again. I wonder if the author anticipated all of this?

Statler Swift:
Hard to say. He seems a wily rascal.

Waldorf Voltaire:
Indeed a thrice. Given the political mood of this nation, he's either very brave or very foolish.

Statler Swift:
'Tis a fine line between those. I wonder how this will be received?

Waldorf Voltaire:
It is hard to free fools from the chains they revere.

Statler Swift:
(Nodding) There's none so blind as they that won't see.

Waldorf Voltaire:
(Shaking his head) Men argue, and nature acts.

Statler Swift:
Ah, my dear friend, I never wonder to see men wicked, but I often wonder to see them ashamed.

Waldorf Voltaire:
I hope and trust there is a world waiting for us once we leave the theater.

Statler Swift:
A bevy of stouts will be needed to digest this one.

Waldorf Voltaire:
To say the least. Great thinkers and great drinkers!

Statler Swift:
'Tis a fine line between those.

Waldorf Voltaire:
I wonder if that's how this play received its inspiration?

Statler Swift:
Don't they all.

(The lights begin to fade on the box)

Statler Swift:
(Proffering his hand) Sir?

Waldorf Voltaire:
(Shaking hands) Yes, my friend.

Statler Swift:
(As the lights fade to black on the box) I'll see you on the other side.

Waldorf Voltaire:
Indeed!

(Deep blue lights come up lowly on the stage. It is the ice cavern, only more so. Darker, more frozen, thicker ice, souls lay flat in icy tombs. Their faces tilted up, frozen tears cut trails down their cheeks. All over the stage, on the ice, hanging from the curtains and lights, are flying monkeys. They are casually going about their business: picking at the ice, grooming each other, looking for food. The Donald is already on stage, toward the left, frozen to the spot, wide-eyed with fear, standing in front of a bank of ice. A flying monkey perched on the bank, pulls at his tie. From just off-stage we hear Antaeus)

Antaeus:
I think the little bugger went through here. **(Enters stage left)** Ah yes! Here he is now. Typhus, hurry up. **(To The Donald)** I say, sir, one shouldn't go wandering around Hell, one never knows what one might find. I see you've made a friend. **(Looking around)** I see your friend has brought his friends. Damn the luck. **(Turning as Typhus enters stage left with the car)** Now, Typhus. Ignore them. **(Typhus has stopped dead in his tracks, wide-eyed with fear)** Fuck's sake. **(Turns to The Donald)** I see you've met yourself, there in the ice. Ptolomaea. That is the name of this round. This was really your first resting spot in Circle Nine, here in Round Three. **(Leans in toward The Donald)** Betrayal of guests.

The Donald:
(Turns his head at this. Angrily) I have always been the consummate host!

(The flying monkeys begin to chitter)

Antateus:
(To Typhus) Its okay, Typhus. **(To The Donald)** Strumpet? Isn't that what the doomed Mr. Tweed called you? How apt. You see here, Strumpet, as President, you are the nation's host. When you throw a party, not everyone who attends has an invitation, but you are still the host. You still have to make them feel welcome. You still have to feed, water, clothe, give care. All of the great societies had iron-clad rules on how to treat guests. Even in Afghanistan, there is the code of life. Melmastia. Nanawatai. These are the first two principles. Hospitality and protection. You did none of this. In your own vernacular, you are the worst host ever. By the standards of your enemies, you are a savage. A heathen. An uncivilized rube.

The Donald:
We're at war!

(The flying monkeys begin to chitter loudly. A nervousness goes through the troop)

Antaeus:
Typhus, stay with me. **(Typhus begins to nervously bob from foot to foot. To The Donald)** No, Strumpet. You are not at war. Congress never declared it.

The Donald:
There are Resolutions! **(Louder flying monkey chitters and screeches)**

Antaeus:
Ha! What a great word to authorize lethal force. Maybe you can have a *Congressional Come Together* to purge the world of those you don't like. Or, a *Presidential Kumbaya* to get rid of those you feel threatened by. **(A brief, sharp laugh cut off by flying monkeys screeching)**

The Donald:
I shouldn't be in here. I shouldn't be any place in this stupid, fucked-up fantasy!

Antaeus:
(Leans in and whispers) But you are. Every single Circle. Every single corner. You are here. Forever. Get fucking used to it. You earned it. What did Uncle Adolf say to you about a candle? **(He turns toward the car)** Typhus, let's go. I'm weary of this worm and we're about to get crushed with shades. **(Typhus stands stock still)** Come on, lad. Where's your courage. Your pride. They're just flying monkeys. You're Typhus. The world trembled with your rage.

(Typhus stands still. The Donald is wiping freezing tears away from his cheeks and chipping frozen tears away from Ptolomaea Donald's cheeks)

Antaeus:
Typhus? Who's a big giant? Come on. Who's a big giant? You are. That's who. Typhus? They're just little, old monkeys. We talked about this. Remember? You said you'd be just fine. You said they didn't bother you anymore.

(While this is going on, The Donald is beginning to slam his fists into Ptolomaea Donald. Blood splatters the ice from The Donald's now mangled hands)

The Donald:
I want to wake up! I want this to end! I want out of here! **(He slaps the flying monkey off the ice bank)**

(Pandemonium. Flying monkeys are flying all over the stage. The screeching is deafening. Typhus has abandoned the car, turned tail and fled, exiting stage left. Antaeus turns toward The Donald, toward Typhus, back toward The Donald, and finally gives up and exits behind Typhus. The Donald is flailing his arms to ward off flying monkeys. He staggers and careens across the stage. A cyclone of snow and ice rises up from the floor of the ice cave beside the stage right exit. It forms into Iblee, a swirling tornado of frozen particles some nine feet in height, its one eye glowing red. The flying monkeys leave the stage on foot and by wing. The screeching instantly dies away, leaving only diminishing echoes, an empty, eerie stillness, and the sound of ice hardening. The Donald stops, looks cautiously about, and then over to Iblee, who is staring at him)

Iblee:
Dearest Donny, we meet again.

(The Donald stammers, dumbstruck)

Iblee:
Can't you say hello. (Nothing) I had so hoped to use you to go topside. To see the world. To feel grass and water, see the sky, see stars, to eat and drink and chat and laugh. To fall in love. (Beat) You say to all of us down here, that you never asked for this. But you did. Each and every day, step by step, sin by sin, you made your way here. But me? I was born here. And I'm fairly certain that the grass is greener where you come from.

The Donald:
Are you the devil.

Iblee:
(Laughter. Laughter by something that has never laughed nor heard laughter nor would know what makes laughter, or how to

laugh or why to laugh. Laughter that sounds confused. Laughter that sounds absurd, awkward, and out of place. Laughter that echoes throughout frozen, unforgiving Hell. Laughter that is anguish, that is weeping) Pappy Sátan? Pappy Aleppy? No. I am not him.

The Donald:
Then, who are you.

Iblee:
(Leans down, the one red eye is inches from The Donald's blue eyes) I am all of you. (Iblee crosses past The Donald toward stage left. Dissolves into a cloud of ice and snow. Maggie walks out of the cloud as it dissipates. Turns, and steps up to The Donald)

Maggie/Iblee:
(Whispers into The Donald's ear) There is a new opening. A stairway to Earth. Something has happened to cause a rift. The show is about to begin, thanks to you. (Kisses The Donald on the cheek) I knew you'd get me up there, somehow. (Crosses to exit stage left. Over her shoulder) Do you like fireworks? I've never seen them. (Stops. Turns toward The Donald) Tell Pappy not to wait up, a girl's got to do what a girl's got to do. (Turns and exits stage left)

(As Maggie/Iblee exits, Antaeus enters looking back at a departing Maggie. Crosses over to The Donald) You keep some unusual company down here, sir.

The Donald:
When does this end?

Antaeus:
Well, that's a thorny question, now isn't it? I mean, in what context? You must mean for yourself. And, even that's convoluted. Your journey to the

bottom of the bottomless pit is nearly over: one more Round, and then himself. But your existence here has only just begun. Now, when does it *all* end? When does the *end of days* happen? **(Pause. They look at each other)** How the fuck do I know. **(Pauses)** Now then, right this way. **(Antaeus motions with his arm toward the small stage beneath the box)** Mind your step. This part of Hell is a bit cramped, and more than a little rundown.

(The blue lights of Round Three dim on center stage, as deep, deep blue lights come up beneath the box. Completely encased in an ice wall are two souls. They are twisted into painfully, uncomfortable positions. Though distorted by the ice, it is obviously Judecca Donald and another rotund man, also in a suit coat, sans tie. Their wide, washed-out, blue eyes stare into frozen eternity)

The Donald:
(Going quickly up to the ice wall) Steve. Me. Why?

Antaeus:
Judecca. Named for the greatest betrayer of all time, Judas Iscariot.

The Donald:
Who'd we betray?

Antaeus:
He betrayed you.

The Donald:
Impossible.

Antaeus:
He used you like a blunt instrument. He played you like a piano. He had his own plans.

The Donald:
We talked about all of that. I asked him if he was crazy.

Antaeus:
And whom did he compare himself to?

The Donald:
(Quietly and with clear understanding) Rasputin.

Antaeus:
Might be a sign.

The Donald:
(Hesitates. Reaches up with his right hand and touches the ice in front of himself encased in ice) Who did I betray?

(Antaeus draws close to the ice wall. Looks long and hard at Judecca Donald)

Antaeus:
Yourself.

The Donald:
I, I don't follow.

Antaeus:
Precisely. **(They look from Judecca Donald to each other)** The very Light of God fuels each and every Soul. In this, we are each obliged to be faithful and true to one's self, as we are to the Creator. You failed in this at a level that is unprecedented. In failing at this, every single sin, your placement in every corner of Hell, was assured.

The Donald:
What did I do?

Antaeus:

(Steps back, hand up) I'm just an old carny. In fact, my existence here has always been in question. But, one gets used to doing the devil's work. The answer to your question, Mr. President, is waiting for you right around the corner. **(He motions with his hand, and The Donald looks at him for a very long time. The Donald takes a step toward exiting stage right, turns and looks at Antaeus)** It seems, you'd like some advice, before turning this last corner.

The Donald:

Yes, please.

Antaeus:

(A hand goes to his chin. He looks up and over the audience. Turns back to The Donald) For each of us, each soul, the more we die, the greater chance we have to live. Suffering and death are only one part of The Wheel. Unfortunately for you, the part of the world you come from seems to only dwell on the dark. This little light of mine is buried beneath planets of guilt, an eon of shame, and endless dogma. But, all of that is moot, as you soon shall see. Now, **(motions again toward stage right)** lest you be any later than you already are.

(The Donald exits stage right. Antaeus slowly turns and crosses to exit stage left. The lights fade to black beneath the box, one spot on Judecca Donald fading several beats later)

(The theater is wrapped in darkness. A cold wind rises. There is the feeling of a very large space, of wind sweeping across the surface of something very still, and very cold. The crispness can be heard in the air. The stinging bite, the slap of frozen air so cold it is audible. Beneath this, sonically low, is something immense. Abyssal. Barely discernible movements of a leviathan that rumbles at frequencies so deep they are felt rather than heard.

And then, footsteps on snowy ice. And The Donald's voice. And then, oh so dimly, following The Donald from stage left, a feeble, blue glow)

The Donald:
(Voice breaking. Panting for breath) I don't see why I have to do this alone. I can't even see where I'm going. Its so cold. I can't feel anything. My fingers. My nose. My ears. My bones! I can't even feel my bones.

(He pads slowly across the surface of a frozen lake. At center stage we see the dim outline of stacked ice. It is to this that he crosses)

The Donald:
(Center stage. Standing in a half-ring of ice that has been pushed up from below. Looking around) Well, I'm here. I've been all the way through Hell. Now what?

(A glow from beneath the ice. The movement of something dark. It is gigantic, the size of the lake itself. The Donald leaps in horror. Tries to climb the stacked ice. The light from below shines on hundreds of reflective surfaces. The Donald sees his own face in all of these. He is literally surrounded by images of himself)

The Donald:
Wh, wh, what is this? What kind of Hell is this?

(The theater shakes as the entity beneath the ice shifts. The glow from below becomes brighter. Above the stage, from the left and the right, an endless succession of muffled explosions. Particles of snow, ice and rock begin to fall)

The Donald:
What's going on? Who's here? Satan? The Devil? Pappy whatever the fuck?

(Stage left. Halfway back. The ice breaks open in a deafening roar like a submarine surfacing. It is a mouth of blackish, brown, and gray scales. Filaments of unknown substance hang from cancerous lips. Inside its maw, forever being ground, is Judas Iscariot. The mouth is the end of an appendage that looks like a lamprey. The mass of this limb, with the weight of the ice, causes it to shake, sway, dip. The Donald falls into a ball)

(Silence. The wind is still. The Donald looks up from the ice. Stands)

The Donald:
(In exasperated anguish) What have I done?

(Next to The Donald, a large hole opens in the ice. Slush, ice, and thick, black water boil up through it. The thing beneath the ice shifts. The stage shakes. The Donald rocks back and forth. A series of eyes, as large as tires, dozens, flicker past the hole. Then just one. It stares at The Donald. The Donald falls again to his knees and vomits blood, bile. He dry heaves. A black, squid-like beak comes up through the hole)

The Donald:
(Scooting away. Spitting. Wiping his mouth with his tie) Who, who are you? What is this? I want to wake up! I want to go home! Too much! Too much! Too much!

Satan:
(Discordant harmony. Many frequencies and pitches. Working in bandwidths that are not known. It vibrates. It rumbles. It is piercing. It speaks in ten thousand languages at the same time. It is the sound of pure insanity) You know who I am.

The Donald:
(Covering his ears. Shouting) Why am I here? What did I do?

Satan:
You have wiped the Earth bare.

The Donald:
Not true! Not true! I wouldn't do that!

Satan:
Look into my eye.

(The beak leaves, the last eye returns, rolls over. The Donald leans closer. On his face, the reds, oranges, and yellows of mushroom clouds are reflected. He shudders. Wails. Smashes his head with his hands. Smashes it on the ice. He curls into a ball and pushes himself away from the eye. The beak comes back up through the hole)

The Donald:
I am so sorry.

Satan:
Too late.

The Donald:
What's next?

Satan:
Oblivion.

The Donald:
What is that?

Satan:
It is this.

(From stage right, another mouth crashes up through the ice. This one is empty. The teeth, not bone, not stone, unknown, have carvings in them that are the same as the inscription above The Gate To Hell. The mouth, open and sucking, rests on the ice to The Donald's right)

The Donald:
No. No! I'll go stand by Bossman. I'll stand by Steve. I'm already everywhere here! This is so fucked-up! No! Noooooooo!

(Thick, reddish-black cords erupt from the empty mouth and wrap around The Donald. They pull him screaming into the mouth. He tries to turn, to escape. The mouth closes. The Donald, kneeling, hands on teeth like the bars to a cell, wails with every last ounce of his soul. Wails in a voice that is picked up by billions of shades all over Hell. The beak disappears. The mouths sink below the ice. The lights fade to black. And the sounds of Hell swirl around a dark theater for agonizing minutes)

(A light rises out of the gloom on a side stage, stage-left, illuminating a figure. The light comes up just enough to reveal a man dressed in a dark toga, grape and oak leaves in his wild, unkempt hair. He tilts his head as the light reaches its highest point)

Euripides:
Well, what did you expect? The Donald to go running across the stage like Ebenezer Scrooge or Jimmy Stewart? Merry Christmas! Merry Christmas everyone! Merry Christmas! Did you expect him and Boss Tweed to move to Minnesota and fall in love with Ann-Margret? Did you think that he wakes up alone screaming, passed out on a sofa somewhere on the second floor of the

Whitehouse, an empty bottle of green cough medicine on the floor next to an outstretched hand? No. He is who he is. This **(motions all around the theater)** is but a tragedy wrapped in a comedy inside a fiction. This is theater. *You. You* are real. *You* live. *You* breathe. *You* make the difference. All the darkness of the void cannot extinguish the light of even one soul. Three hundred million souls? Seven billion souls? We hold these truths to be self-evident, that all men are created equal, that they are endowed by their Creator with certain inalienable rights, that among these are life, liberty and the pursuit of happiness. Now, my good friends, those are words worth fighting for.

(The lights fade to black on Euripides and the narrator's stage)

(There is a pregnant pause. From beneath the box, we hear the sound of a banjo. A lone spot rises on Abusive Donald. He is sitting on top of the ice wall that houses Judecca Donald and Steve. He is wearing bib overalls and nothing else. He is playing the opening riffs from *Dueling Banjos***)**

Abusive Donald:
(Nodding in time with the music. A shit-eatin' grin across his mug)
Uh-huh. Fuck yeah. You knew I could play this. You was thinkin' it the whole time.

(From the narrator's stage, sitting atop his pulpit, Right Reverend Z answers Abusive Donald's banjo with a banjo of his own. They go straight into *Dueling Banjos***. Entering in time, cheshire cat-grinning and waving, replete in whatever misery that particular Circle of Hell has chosen for them, fanning out from stage right to stage left, are the following: Limbo Donald, Lustful Donald, Gluttonous Donald, Young Donald, War Shade, Bully Donald, Commander-in-Chief Donald, Corporate Raider Donald, Seducer Donald, Flatterer Donald, Corrupt Donald, Imposter Donald, Caina Donald, Antenora Donald, and Ptolomaea Donald. Once**

they have spanned the front of the stage from right to left, they square up and face the audience, clapping and trying to stay in time with the music. As *Dueling Banjos* comes to a close, the Piper-pipes shouldered and playing a tin whistle, and the Children's Choir enter from stage left and fill the back of center stage on risers. The Casio Player, and Randy, also on Casio, enter stage right and left respectively, and flank the Choir. Then, the lead-in music to *This Land Is Your Land,* by Woody Guthrie, starts up with all musicians taking part. After one full verse has been done instrumentally, all of The Donalds sing with these lyrics:)

This land was your land, now its my land
I stole it fair and square, and that's a fact, man;
From the piles of rubble to Ground Zero
This land was made for me and me

(A jump to the left by all the Donalds)

As I pondered, the road that took me
From humble millions, to the Presidency;

(A step to the right by all the Donalds)

I thought of all the people, like grapes I trampled
This land was made for me and me

(Hands on their hips by all the Donalds)

Saw the four horsemen, from that lonely stable
And I released them, when I was able;

(Knees in tight by all the Donalds)

I watched them break seals, while I made deals
This land was made for me and me

(Pelvic thrusts by all the Donalds)

This is a tragedy, Inside a comedy
Wrapped in a fiction, It's just fantasy;
If you want your children to be happy
You must rip this land from me and me

(The music stops. All eyes on stage swing to the small stage beneath the box. Several spots light up Boss Tweed, who is encased in ice from the waist down. He strikes a pose, and Boss Tweed, in beautiful a cappella baritone, sings this:)

O Canada! our home and native land!
True patriot-love in all thy sons command.
With glowing hearts we see thee rise,
The True North strong and free!
And stand on guard, O Canada
We stand on guard for thee

O Canada, glorious and free!
O Canada, we stand on guard, we stand on guard for thee.
O Canada, we stand on guard for thee!

(He holds this last note until *This Land Is Your Land* is picked back up by the musicians. His spots fade to black, and with a little help, exits stage right)

(Saint Dymphna flies in from stage left while the music continues. Behind her, driving all of the Donalds off stage, stage right,

are Antaeus, Typhus, Cacus, CMD Girl, Geryon, Owl, Eagle, Crow, Robin, Nessie, Private Centaur, Medusa, Megaera, Alecto, Tisiphone, Greeter Dwayne, Phlegya, and Walter Cronkite. They sing the next three verses looking a lot like a Pentecostal Choir with the music following suit)

As I went walking, I saw a sign there
Free cheese and groceries, could be had there;
But I was still hungry, for something yearning
We must make this land for liberty

Hiding in shadows, I saw my people,
Starving and lonely, I seen my people;
Up the man that died there, Up the man that tried there
We must resist to set us free

(The Donald and Maggie enter from stage right, cross to center, and sing along)

Nobody living, can ever stop me
As I go walking that freedom highway;
Nobody living can ever make me turn back
This land was made for you and me.

(As the ensemble repeats this last verse, the lights go up on the box, where Statler Swift, Waldorf Voltaire, and Euripides toss lilies onto the stage, glasses in hands held up in toast)

Statler Swift, Waldorf Voltaire, Euripides:
Bravo! Bravo! Bravo!

(The Ensemble repeats the last verse a third time)

(The music is now only instrumental, the characters exit slowly stage left. As they depart the stage, lights dim and go out. The Donald and Maggie exit stage right. The Choir exits stage left, humming the melody, Randy and his Casio exit behind them. The Casio Player exits stage right leaving only the piper. The melody ends. There is silence. The theater is dark except one spot on the piper. The piper, who this entire time had been playing a tin whistle, picks up his pipes. He hits one note to set key, then plays *The American National Anthem*. When the last note rings out, the lone spot fades to black)

Outro

To all of those from whom I shamelessly liberated inspiration and lines: thank-you. I blame the muses. More than in any project that I have endeavored, they roared. At times, I felt more like the pen than the author.

This book was started in September, 2016. It was completed just before the ides of March, 2017. In that time, America has changed dramatically. This wasn't, 'just another election'. This was a point in the history of a nation where the values we profess at the pew, where the standards of civility with which we hold the rest of the world accountable, where the very words written in the Constitution, were duly set aside for baser interests.

Once upon a time, a wise old man taught me this: the road to Hell is absolutely paved with good intentions, but the walls of Hell are lined with flowers. Molière: It is not only for what we do that we are held responsible, but also for what we do not do. Without active participation from the grassroots up, and sensible oversight from the Federal Government down, the door to the chicken coop is wide open, and the fledgling democratic republic is vulnerable. In a nation defined by the Darwinian concepts of rugged individualism and frontier mentality, it would be naive and foolish to trust in the better angels of our natures.

Now, we can sit back and wait for someone like Saint Dymphna to swoop down from above. Or, we can be Saint Dymphna. We can be her every single day, seventy times a day. We can be the change we want to see in the world. We can be the smile that lights someone's darkness. We can be the hand that holds the head up off the pavement. We can be the defiant fist thrust into the sky. We can be the spirit that will be not broken, and we can be the strength that unconsciously gives other people the strength to shine.

All the darkness of the void cannot extinguish the light of even one soul.

Peace.

-Liam Sean

Made in the USA
Lexington, KY
26 July 2017